FAB

A Novel

Kieran Batts Morrow

•

Tiffany Anderson

•

Adrienne Carter

•

Tracy Richelle High

DOUBLEDAY

New York   London   Toronto   Sydney   Auckland

E

PUBLISHED BY DOUBLEDAY
a division of Random House, Inc.

DOUBLEDAY and the portrayal of an anchor with a dolphin are
registered trademarks of Random House, Inc.

Book design by Ellen Cipriano

Library of Congress Cataloging-in-Publication Data

Fab : a novel / Kieran Batts Morrow . . . [et al.].—1st ed.
p. cm.
ISBN 0-385-51348-8
1. Young women—Fiction. 2. Female friendship—Fiction.
3. New York (N.Y.)—Fiction. 4. Los Angeles (Calif.)—Fiction.
I. Morrow, Kieran Batts.

PS3600.A1F33 2005
813'.6—dc22
2004063468

PRINTED IN THE UNITED STATES OF AMERICA

August 2005

First Edition

1 3 5 7 9 10 8 6 4 2

To our parents,
who told us that the world is
ours for the taking

· 1 ·

Bianca

The Glamorous Life

Two weeks ago, somewhere between Tucson, Arizona, and the California border, I freaked the fuck out. I was on the I-10 West in my '93 Volkswagen Cabriolet, which was crammed full of my worldly possessions, when my decision to quit my job as a fashion publicist in New York to take a job as a TV publicist in L.A. suddenly struck me as absolutely insane. I was leaving behind a secure, if annoying, job, my three best friends in the world, and a series of connections from maître d's to makeup artists who'd made it easy to be fabulous on a relatively low budget. Now I was headed to what was practically a foreign country where I didn't know anyone and nobody knew me, and I was starting to wonder if I'd made a Poor Decision; something up there with marrying Bobby Brown or backing *Gigli*.

Yes, when I first decided to do it, it made perfect sense. I'm twenty-eight years old and my career in fashion had definitely hit a wall of sorts, that wall being my sanity. Everyone in my senior class at Harvard was green with envy because we were all convinced that I was going to be lunching with Karl and Donatella before jetting off to Paris on the Concorde for the spring shows. Please. Baby-sitting neurotic second-tier designers and delivering unmarked packages to glassy-eyed models are not exactly the best use of an Ivy League education. So, when I met the American Television Network's (yes, ATN, but they're working on becoming a real network instead of a haven for *Comicview* rejects) senior vice president of publicity at an after-party for the VH-1/Vogue Fashion Awards, I used my considerable powers of persuasion to convince him to offer me a job as a junior publicist. (Minds out of the gutter, please; I'm talking about the gift of gab, which I've got in spades.)

In any case, after narrowly avoiding crashing the Cabriolet into a cactus, I pulled myself together and made it here in one piece. And now that I'm here, I'm feeling great about my decision, because it was definitely the right thing to do, and almost everything is better out here. I have my own business cards that say "Bianca King, Junior Publicist" (in New York I had to use my boss's card and write my name on the back—*tres ghettoir, non?*) and I'm actually getting paid a decent wage (not Dolce & Gabbana good, but definitely Banana Republic good). I'm making more than what I made in New York both on paper and in cost of living, which will hopefully make up for my temporary lack of hook-ups. The job is very fast-paced, but it's exciting and I feel that what I'm doing is actually important. I'm in charge of coordinating details like talent travel, tracking stories about ATN in the press, and even writing those episode descriptions you read in *TV Guide*—it's like being published every week! Plus, the hours aren't crazy, so I'll still have time to work on my screenplay (everyone in L.A. has a screenplay—it's the law). Mine's about dating in the year 2040 when women have to BUY their men at a special store. Writing is very therapeutic for me, so why not get paid for working out my issues? As for L.A. itself, I am so home! Being a Southern girl, I never really felt at home in New York in the middle of all the noise, the rudeness, the public transportation, and, frankly, the urine. I'm really more of a riding-in-my-convertible-on-my-way-to-the-mall-on-a-sunny-afternoon-with-no-urine-involved kind of girl, so this is the perfect place for me. Also, the cost of housing in Manhattan? Absurd. There, what I'm now paying for a spacious one bedroom with hardwood floors, a patio, and enough closet space to make Imelda happy would get you your very own cardboard box under the 59th Street Bridge. With two roommates. Also, in NYC, there's no such thing as a gated apartment complex with a pool and a gym; the only thing standing between you and the insane addict rapists is an under-paid, unarmed doorman. So I don't miss New York one bit.

Except for one thing. Well, three things. Three people, rather. I miss Carolyn, Roxanne, and Taylor terribly—I've known them for almost ten years now, we're practically sisters, and I'm not sure what I'm going to do without them. Sure, they're still just a phone call away, but it's not the same. No more hungover Sunday brunches, no more emergency group shopping sessions, no more Urban Prankstering (*Girls Behaving Badly*, you are the rankest of the rank amateurs). I'm supposed to go out with whom? I'm getting to know a couple of women out here, but it's clear they aren't going to be adequate replacements. Rachel's sort of sassy, but I can already see her jealousy issues, and Selma's sweet but utterly sass-free. Neither one of those is a good thing when you're hanging out, trying to meet men.

And, oh, God, the L.A. men. Well, that's another thing that's not good. I don't know if I'm getting older or the men are getting dumber or what, but it's ALL WRONG. I've been here for *two whole weeks* and I don't have ONE sparkly bauble to show for it, I had to pay for my own din-ner at Katana last night, and I haven't even made any boys cry yet! It's def-initely time for a new game plan, so I'm going to entertain the advances of *all* the men who approach me, given that they are attractive. This is a big step for me, but clearly I need a sponsor. I only go first class, and some-body (other than me) needs to bankroll all of it; from the wardrobe ex-penses to the fact that the Cabriolet simply will not do (I have an appointment at Beverly Hills BMW tomorrow—in L.A. you don't actually have to have any money to purchase a luxury automobile, thank God, but you do have to have an appointment).

In any case, I'm finally abandoning my long-standing rule of only dating men who wear a tie to work. It's just that I absolutely cannot date another Hi-my-name-is-Bradley-and-every-Saturday-morning-I-play-golf-with-every-other-uptight-Hugo-Boss-wearing-ex-Jack-and-Jill-loser-you've-ever-dated-and-would-you-like-to-ride-in-my-Porsche-Boxster-before-a-round-of-unimaginative-sex-during-which-you-will-not-even-come-close-to-having-an-orgasm, especially because those are the ones who see my light skin and light eyes and feel compelled to ask me what I'm "mixed with," which is a no-no. In New York, and especially back home in Houston, it was like dating the same guy over and over again. So, no more playing "Who do you know that I know?" before I will agree to a date. Now my M.O. is whoever's cute. And employed. With no police record. With a car. And doesn't live with his mother. And doesn't punctuate all of his sentences with "Na-I-mean?" So, any cute, literate, gainfully employed man who has his own car, has never been in prison, and resides at least ten miles from his mother is fair game. (I can't change overnight, okay.)

As these grandiose and partially true statements fall effortlessly from my lips, I feel at peace. Did I mention that it's seventy degrees here? In January! I'm home!

Carolyn

Analyze This

"And how did you feel about that?" Dr. Guisewite says after I have finished telling her that last Thursday I set a new world record for being stood up—four ditches in three weeks—and got so drunk that I woke up in my bathtub wearing nothing but a Yankees cap and a pair of vomit-soaked stiletto heels.

"Seriously? Like I'd just won 'American Idol' and the Rose Bowl and been elected prom queen and gotten the key to the city, all at the same time," I say tartly. "I felt grand. Of course I was pissed about the shoes; they were Jimmy Choos and they were new."

"You're using sarcasm as deflector shield," Dr. Guisewite says gently. "This isn't about the shoes. It's about what triggered this drinking episode, being stood up, which caused you a lot of pain, didn't it?" I glare at her. I am in a really bad mood this evening. She sighs and changes tack.

"Let's go back to why you haven't gone out with your friends for the past three weekends," she says. It is my turn to sigh.

"Because they're all gorgeous tiny little size sixes or smaller and I am really tired of being the big fat troll among the pixies—"

"Carolyn, again, you are not fat," Dr. Guisewite interrupts. "You are nearly six feet tall and you vacillate between a fourteen and a sixteen. That isn't fat, not by any stretch of the imagination."

"When men see me standing next to my friends," I continue, ignoring her, "they wonder what's wrong with me that I don't look like that, and that's only on the rare occasions when they aren't too blinded by my friends' beauty to notice me at all. They're running around the party in super-tight low-rise jeans and sexy halter tops and I'm plodding behind them in whatever smock halfway fit, looking like I'm trying not to look for hors d'oeuvres. The short story is, I love *hanging* out with them, but I hate *going* out with them because it's just a major self-esteem bulldozing every time. It's got nothing to do with them personally, because they're very supportive and always tell me I look beautiful and there's nothing wrong with me, but—"

"But it doesn't matter if they say it, or if I say it, or if anyone says it, because you don't believe it, so you can't believe that anyone believes it," says Dr. Guisewite. At last count, she has said this 4,581 times over the past six years.

"I just really wish I looked like them," I say softly.

"I still want to talk about why exactly you believe that you are unattractive."

"Dr. Guisewite, my dress size has doubled—*doubled*, mind you—since my college graduation. At the rate I'm going they'll have to readjust gravity to accommodate me by the time I'm forty. I don't know how you expect me to feel," I snap.

"Do you consider dress size the only measure of your attractiveness?"

"The rest of the country does, so it doesn't really matter what I think, does it?"

"It matters to me. And it should matter to you."

"What I think is that I'm pretty gross."

"Carolyn, as I've mentioned before, the average American woman wears a size twelve."

"We just discussed the fact that I am *not* a size twelve," I say, and clam up, refusing to add that I wish I were because I can afford designer clothes, but very few designers consider women larger than a size twelve worthy of their effort and attention. Instead, I stockpile designer shoes; I do not have fat feet.

"Aside from your negative body image, are you able to recognize that you have many very attractive qualities?"

"I guess," I say sullenly.

"And you do recognize that others find you attractive? Such as Gil Merriweather?"

I have to smile in spite of myself. That would be the infamous Gil "He Got Skills" Merriweather, product of Yale and the Kennedy School of Government, currently Deloitte Touche's go-to young blood in the area of environmental consulting. Gil, who spent all of Monday night talking to me despite the Coping With Being Thin and Pretty support group clustered at the other end of the bar, then asked for my number at the end of the night. And then, crazier and crazier, Gil, who actually called just yesterday.

"I guess. I mean, I don't know. We're supposed to be going out on Friday," I say, stifling the urge to cross my fingers. Dr. Guisewite nods.

"Do you have any expectations for this date, Carolyn?"

Right. I expect Gil to open the door and I expect his eyes to light up when he sees how incredible I look. I expect to be coy and witty and erudite and bewitching and maddeningly aloof and desirable all at once, and I expect Gil to fall in love with me over the course of the evening and then beg me to let him take me to bed, where I expect no less than four mind-blowing orgasms. I expect a fabulous and intimate summer in the Hamptons, followed by an emerald-cut grade D solitaire, an announcement in the *Times,* numerous fittings at Vera Wang, a wedding at Westminster Abbey performed by the pope, reception entertainment by Beyoncé and Aerosmith, and transportation on Air Force One to a honeymoon on a private island named after me.

"Oh, you know. Nothing too insane. I'd just like to have a nice time, see where it goes, take it easy, not rush things." I shrug.

The good doctor nods and makes a note on her pad, and I suspect that she is not fooled, but she moves on to another topic anyway. I sometimes feel bad for her; having me as her last appointment on Wednesday evenings is probably a bit exhausting sometimes.

Dr. Guisewite is saying something about the effect of my rotten self-image on my social interactions when I tune back in. I nod, although I have no idea what she said. She looks at the clock.

"I'll see you next week," she says. I hand her a check for $175 and let myself out.

Today is the light-year anniversary of my nervous breakdown. I lean against the wall of the elevator and actually permit myself to think about those very bad times, which is something I almost never do. I was an extremely high-strung child, particularly from an academic viewpoint. In part, this is because academe has always been taken very seriously in my family: My parents met at Harvard while my mother was getting her Ph.D. in history and my father was completing his master's degree in architecture at the GSD; my father's father had a Ph.D. in Classics from Yale, my mother's father got his M.D. from Penn, and on it goes. So there was always external pressure to do extremely well in school, but it paled in comparison to the amount of pressure I put on myself; from the third grade on, any grade below an A- drove me to ecstasies of self-flagellation. As one might imagine, the problem intensified when I reached Harvard, a place considered by many to be home to the best of the best; I, Carolyn Ware Phillips, was hell-bent on being the best of the best of the best.

Right up until the breakdown, my concentration was Economics, and I hated every single second of it. I had chosen it because it was hard-core, and I was not interested in being the best of the best of the best in some pussy concentration like English, and English was obviously a pussy concentration because I loved it, loved it just as much as I hated Econ and was really good at it, whereas I was really struggling with Econ.

And because I was losing control over my academic situation, I decided that I would, at the very least, master my own physical being and take off the "Freshman Ten," most of which had come from pizza binges with Bianca that took place when we told everyone we were going to work out. Suffice it to say that "dabbling" in anorexia is like "dabbling" in crack, so by second semester sophomore year, I was a wild-eyed skeleton who slept no more than two hours a night and spent most of her waking hours in a deserted corner of the fifth-floor stacks in Widener Library. I started losing my hair in late March, and shortly thereafter, Roxanne, who was my suitemate in Eliot House and therefore the most acutely aware of how bad things had gotten, corralled Bianca and Taylor for a late-night pow-wow and suggested that it was time to call my parents. The three of them were gracious enough to understand that my furious response to their "interference" was nothing more than the ravings of a lunatic, and when I returned from my "time off" the following September with a more rational attitude and a more normal body weight, we picked up exactly where we had left off before I started to deteriorate. We never discussed it, but how could I be anything but grateful for the kind of friends who would make a call like that and do the right thing instead of not getting involved, which would have been the easy thing?

When I returned to school, my Econ textbooks went floating down the Charles River on a small but brightly burning pyre and I changed my concentration to English and took some classes in the Visual and Environmental Studies (i.e., "Art") Department. Twice a week I crossed the river to see a psychologist in Chestnut Hill, twice a month I went to see a psychiatrist in the Back Bay, until the middle of senior year, when it was decided that medication was no longer required. When I graduated, my psychologist recommended Dr. Guisewite, and we have been working together for a little more than six years now. Needless to say, I keep her busy, because after having acknowledged that food was not my enemy, I took that conclusion one step further and began to treat it as my very bestest friend, and the result is that I am now attempting to tackle an entirely different universe of body image and self-esteem issues.

I walk across the lobby and out the door. The rain has stopped, and the wind that has taken its place is almost mild, reminding me that spring will be here before we know it. I do not feel like going home, so I wander north and west, craning my neck to see the sky above the tops of the midtown skyscrapers. It is nine o'clock at night but the windows are ablaze with lights, and I wonder how many of the lights are in the offices of junior lawyers like Taylor, for whom yet another night of drudgery is probably just getting under way downtown.

Eventually I find myself on Fifth Avenue across from FAO Schwarz and I stop and gaze into the windows of Bergdorf Goodman. It is a fashionista's dream: There are flirty dresses of gauze and chiffon; sleeveless, strapless silk blouson tops that stay in place courtesy of God and gravity; sheer cotton peasant blouses paired with battered hip-slung jeans and thick belts of butter-soft distressed leather; Indian-print silk peasant dresses; pale cashmere cap-sleeve sweaters with matching cardigans and slender capri pants; evening gowns with no back and not much front to speak of. I imagine myself lounging on a couch at the hot new club, Groove, in a midriff-baring peasant top and low-rider jeans as some dark swain hands me a martini and perches on the arm of the couch; being coy and dazzling at a cocktail party in a little pink dress with perky slingbacks; being a seductive vamp at a gala fund-raiser in a sleek ivory silk satin gown as business magnates and celebrities alike nudge one another and ask "Who is that? Who is that?"

Suddenly I catch sight of my reflection in the store window. The buttons on my coat are straining across my stomach and my Vuitton *sac plat* may be wide, but I can still see at least four inches of hip on each side of it. My face is as round as the moon skimming the tops of the buildings and even my fingers are pudgy.

"The fat girl, that's who that is," I say softly to myself as the daydream fizzles. I turn my back on the glittering parade of mannequins and start walking toward the subway.

· 3 ·

Taylor

Out, Satan, Out

I want you to know one thing about me, just one: You're going to hate me. Why? Because I've been fortunate. I've always been lucky in love. Well, after the fact, anyway. You see, every man who has left me before *I* could have the honor of ending the relationship—always under the mistaken impression that life would be better without me—has come crawling back when he realized the truth. I say "lucky" because she who laughs last laughs hardest. Although this time around, I don't think I'm going to be laughing at all.

After two years, it seems I'm single, once again. I think I liked breaking up better when I was younger, when there really weren't a lot of complicated issues. The problem is, once you get into your late—really late—twenties, the complicated issues are the only ones left.

My two-year relationship with Vincent came to a screeching halt when he woke me up a few hours ago. Like a man, I love early-morning sex. There is truly no better way to start the day. Some favor breakfast, but I like a good hard romp followed by a strong cup of coffee. There would be no such luck today. I realized something was wrong as I turned around to face him. He was staring at me with a look that was somewhere between early-morning desire and pain, as if he were trying to burn my image into his memory. You know that faraway stare men get; the "I did something/ I'm about to do something/I'm about to really piss you off, but I can't help myself" look? That one.

Instantly, I knew the relationship was over. I wanted to scream. Something I also like to do in the morning, but from an orgasm, not from this. Not. Again. I couldn't believe it was happening again. The point at which every single one of my relationships unfailingly arrives, sometimes sooner, sometimes later. Inevitably and invariably, a man will do something to fuck a relationship up.

You know when your heart just drops? When you know everything that is going to be said and you don't have the energy to complete the scene? What was there to say? Why bother saying anything at all? I'm long past the age where I would consider attempting to talk my way out of a break-up. The only problem was, I'd poured so much of my time, love, and energy into Vincent. While I hadn't exactly set a schedule for marriage, it seemed like a foregone conclusion that we would one day tie the knot. I didn't want to rush into anything, but we got along so well that I didn't foresee any serious problems. We had the same personality, likes, and dislikes. But here he was, telling me that it wasn't going to work. As I've always said, if a man doesn't want to be with you, no matter how badly you want to be with him, practice the art of letting go. And normally, I wouldn't mind doing that, but this time I hadn't even had a clue that this was coming. I guess I was asleep at the wheel while he was quietly losing his mind.

To confirm this fact, Vincent told me that he couldn't continue our relationship, or any relationship for that matter, until he was able to wrap his head around the idea that he would be getting married someday. I fucking hate New York men. These bastards just want to run in the damn streets until their dicks are all worn out, then, at age forty-five, they want to get married, after they've fucked their way through the entire city. By that time my ovaries will be fully encrusted with cobwebs, and I won't be able to have any children at all.

To hear Vincent tell it, I'm the person he wants to spend the rest of his life with. He just can't deal with the fact that he has to start thinking this seriously about his life. Isn't there some point in time when a man becomes mature enough to accept that he has to grow the hell up? I simply can't believe this bastard. He turned thirty-two two weeks ago. What kind of bullshit nonsense is this? I just knew that once Vincent escaped his twenties, I could relax and feel secure in the knowledge that I'd finally be able to ride off into the sunset. I finally thought I had found a man who could deal with me and my many quirks, someone who was interested in sharing something that had real substance. I never thought that there might be a day when he'd just go away for no valid reason.

Vincent is biracial, but right now I think he's bipolar, just like his dumb-ass father, who also had no desire to stick around. Ah, the sins of the father. Vincent's father left his mother—and Vincent—long before Vincent was born. Anybody could see that Vincent was a product of a mother who, at one point in time, believed and lived the civil rights movement, but after Vincent's father left them, his mother finally did what her family had been suggesting all along and found a "nice Jewish boy" to marry. And so that very evening, I, a nice Roman Catholic girl, and Vincent Schwartz, a biracial Jewish man, were supposed to partake in his mother's birthday celebration at the family home.

Perhaps his mother's final, albeit reluctant acceptance of me made him think marriage was the only thing left for us. It's funny that Vincent decided to use the "I'm not ready for this" excuse because I'm not one to talk about marriage much. In fact, I haven't firmly decided whether it's the best thing for a woman, any woman, to do. Right now I'm vibing on the whole Goldie Hawn/Kurt Russell thing. I don't feel any special pressure to make my relationship into a contract, although as a lawyer, it's pretty ironic that I feel that way. I do know one basic equation, though: marriage equals prenuptial agreement. Only a fool ends up penniless for love. But at the rate things are going, I won't have to worry about that.

Thank heavens Vincent had moved into my place. At least I didn't have to worry about divvying up furniture, or how I was going to pay all of my bills. I paid these bills before he came, and I'll pay these motherfuckers now that his ass is moving out. My father always taught me not to be financially dependent on any man, and I'm glad I learned that lesson well. Although I'll miss the $2,500 Vincent contributed to the household every month, one monkey won't stop this show.

I stared blankly at the ceiling for a moment after Vincent finished his little I-love-you-more-than-anyone-I've-ever-known,-but-somehow-I've-found-a-way-to-fuck-this-up-so-you'll-hate-me-yet-I-have-to-be-true-to-myself-and-my-feelings speech. I wanted to ask him why he thought his mother didn't have an abortion, knowing that she'd be giving birth to Satan, but I decided to take the higher road: "You mixed up, fucked up bastard! You are *DEFINITELY* fucking with the wrong bitch today!" Yelling always made me feel better.

I truly hate the end of a relationship. What should you do? Or say? Or not do and not say? Or scream about? I was too shocked to cry or to think my way through this thing. Rather than clawing his eyes out, I decided to do what I do best. I reverted into business mode. Time to take a shower. Time to go to work. I said the only thing that made sense to me at the time, "Move your stuff out while I'm at work and leave your key on the fish tank." I left out what he already knew—that it was the one we bought to celebrate our moving in together. That damn feng shui specialist told me it would be the perfect addition to our bedroom because its chi would preserve the life in our relationship. Fuck her, too.

I dragged myself out of the bed, made it into the shower, and nearly dissolved in tears. When Vincent came in to ask that inevitable stupid question men ask right after they've done the most fucked up thing imaginable, "Are you all right?" I told him, "Hell no!" The companion line of "I hate to see you cry" made me see red. No, this bastard didn't. What was the next step? Torture? Instantaneous death? Better to go with the quick version. I pried the plastic safety (ha!) cover off my Lady Bic and tried to slit his throat. He bolted for the front door, yelling over his shoulder that he'd pick up his things later in the day after I'd left.

I ran after him, shouting: "You know what, Vincent, when you shut your beady little eyes tonight, sleep easy knowing this one thing for certain: You'll pay for this. And I'll get you when you least expect it, because, motherfucker, I WILL have the last laugh." My next-door neighbor came out into the hall. We can't stand one another; mainly because she was always in my damn business, and I was always (impolitely) telling her to stay out of my way. Rather than greet her with a fake "good morning," I asked her what the fuck she was looking at and slammed my apartment door.

That was two hours ago. And I'm still staring into the bathroom mirror, Chanel suit neatly buttoned (I only own one and it's reserved for days when I absolutely, positively have to look my best), trying to muster the energy to put on my shoes, dig my mink out of the closet, put on a game face, and head off to work. Fuck this sad shit, where's my bravado? I don't need to sit here bemoaning the fate of a relationship that obviously wasn't worth shit. I've got a lot to look forward to. I'm a pretty fucking decent person. I've been blessed with above-average intelligence. I'm pretty fucking good-looking (fuck yeah!), and I'm generally not mean to anyone until they start barking up this wrong motherfucking tree. Despite my foul mouth (one foible, what can I say), I'm a good fucking person.

Shit, I exercise five times a week; I get my hair, hands, and toes done weekly; I have a standing monthly appointment at one of the trendiest spas in the city, where my aesthetician makes my face glow and my masseuse drains my lymph nodes, wraps me in seaweed, and massages me until I'm like putty; I have a great job at a top law firm; I've had a wonderful education, thanks to the hard work and dedication of my parents, and I'm spiritually grounded (except for that cursing, but hey, I'm a work in progress). I keep it real. I don't take shit—especially because my mother said don't ever take anything that people are giving away for free. So fuck this sorry sad-sack moping shit, it's off to work. Time to kick some ass and get my mind right. Getting pissy is a much better emotion (for me) than pathos, since I tend to be more productive when spitting venom.

· 4 ·

Roxanne

Scratchin' and Survivin'

I must be cursed. Someone has put a root on me, because try as I might to get to this fucking audition on time, the Heavens are conspiring against me. I cannot be late, tardiness being my number one pet peeve. I was on the number 2 train from 135th Street; it stalled at 96th Street. There was no downtown service of any kind at 96th Street, so I had to walk the three longest blocks on earth—Broadway to Central Park West—to get the C train, which of course stopped providing local service at 72nd Street, forcing me to take the M10 bus down to 42nd Street to give me a fighting chance at being punctual. I usually give myself an hour to get to all of my appointments, hoping to have at least fifteen minutes to decompress, but the public transportation gods were not smiling on me today. This is why rich people take cabs—you can never predict what lovely surprises the MTA has waiting for you. But I am at 330 West 40th Street on time, actually with six minutes to spare, thank God. I breathe deeply three times so I seem less maniacal and hit the elevator button. It arrives quickly, and I get on and press the "door closed" button before anyone else can get on to give myself a few precious seconds of solitude. I select the twelfth floor and reach in my carefully packed but still overflowing all-purpose black bag and rummage past my yoga clothes and mat, train reading, comb and brush, makeup bag, water bottle, Altoids, monthly planner and journal, to retrieve my sexy stiletto-heeled black boots, and quickly slip off my tennis shoes and replace them with the boots before I reach twelve. As the elevator doors open, I make a mad dash to the ladies' room at the end of the hall, which thankfully, unlike those in most New York City office buildings, doesn't require a key. I refresh my lipstick, powder my shiny nose, and do a quick hair fluff, while going over my lines in my head. Inhale. Exhale. Inhale. Exhale. Okay, I'm ready.

I coolly open the door to suite 1215, shaking off the last fifty-four minutes of subway and bus hell, and enter the tiny waiting room, where four pairs of very judgmental eyes examine every inch of my body, my hair, my clothes. I quickly scan the room, filled with movie posters that this office has cast, in a search for (1) familiar and friendly faces and (2) the most strategically located empty seat. To my immediate left is a "glamorous" model type, about five feet ten, wearing Marc Jacobs and a ridiculously long, brown weave. I think she's been the face of a few beauty product campaigns. She keeps twirling "her" hair as if to say "I'm so bored. Why am I forced to wait with these commoners?"—or rather, that's what she would say if the word *commoners* was part of her severely limited vocabulary. To my right is the "ethnic" model type: tall, lean, very dark-skinned with short, spiky dreads—very Benetton. Right in front of me is a real, live Pop Singer, dressed head to toe in Versace, flawless hair and makeup. And then, there's me: five feet four, thin, pretty (but in a very accessible way), dressed in my souped up H&M, off the rack, on-sale fashions, which consist of a kimono top and low-riding, hip-hugger jeans that together cost no more than forty dollars. I just look like a regular, cute Black girl next to these women, whose weekly hair and makeup appointments alone probably cost more than my monthly rent. Great.

Hello, my name is Roxanne, and I am a struggling actor.

This situation is by no means unfamiliar. Every audition is different, but there are standard signs as to whether I have a chance in hell of booking something or not. When I walk into the model/celebrity-filled rooms I might as well go home, because chances are they're not looking for a girl like me. I feel most comfortable when I enter the waiting room with the

Usual Suspects—other recent Yale, NYU, and Juilliard MFA program grads—Black girls who are pretty but also care a great deal about technique because they bothered to spend three to four years and about $75,000 to learn the craft of acting. *Real* actors. This is not one of those situations. This is the Slash Call: the model/actor, the singer/actor, the dancer/actor, the acting-as-a-last-resort-to-pimp-my-fame-as-much-as-possible-even-though-I-have-no-talent call. I do not like these auditions, but I always hope that my talent will triumph and someone will notice me. I know not to take anything personally in these situations. The director generally has no idea what he wants and will sacrifice talent for a "name," a "face," or "product placement." That's just the way the business works, and after three years of acting professionally, I am beginning to tire of it. But I'm not ready to give up just yet. That's the sick part that keeps me going: I cherish the hope that one day, the perfect part will meld with the synchronous perfect opportunity and Kismet! it will launch my career into the stratosphere. The chances of that happening are slim, but if I wanted a sure thing, I would have gone to law school.

However, I'm at an interesting point in my career. I've booked plenty of regional theater, a little off-Broadway, gotten some great *New York Times* reviews, had guest spots on several TV shows, but I'm still struggling to make ends meet. The question remains: At what point do you break on through to the other side of fame and fortune, and at what point do you just break? I have this conversation with myself more frequently these days, and usually every few months, my PMS-fueled depression urges me to quit the business altogether. They say it takes ten years to build a career, but do I have that much patience? Can I keep subjecting myself to rejection after rejection, with the hope that one day in the next seven years I'll get the payoff? But aye, here's the rub: I love acting more than anything else in the world. It is the one thing that makes me truly feel alive.

But right now, fuck personal fulfillment, I have to focus on nailing this audition. I spent two hours yesterday working with Susan, a drama school classmate, on this part. It's a very big role in an independent film (the female love interest) from last year's darling director-writer team from

Sundance. This would be a very good break for me. So I will focus. The casting assistant comes out, "Roxanne, you're next." I enter the room and the assistant introduces me.

"This is Roxanne Newman."

"Hello. Nice to see you all," I say brightly.

"Roxanne, this is the casting director, Lisa Hastings." I shake her hand. "This is the writer, Christopher Higgins; and this is the director, Scotty Randall." Christopher extends his hand and I shake it, but Scotty looks at me like I'm insane. He is one of those moody types.

"So, Roxanne," Scotty says. I can already tell he's a real asshole/slimeball with his bleached blond, spiky, aggressively hip hair styled with way too much product. "We see that you went to Harvard and the Yale School of Drama."

"Yes, I did."

"We want you to forget about all that. Camilla is a regular, uneducated, down on her luck girl, and . . . well . . . let's just read the scene." I do my thing. They whisper among themselves. I can tell they are impressed.

"Wow, you're really good," Christopher says.

"Thanks."

"No, seriously, you're the best person we've seen," Scotty volunteers.

"Thank you." That makes me feel happy.

"And we just want you to know that we've changed Camilla from a waitress to a stripper, and the scene that was in a restaurant now takes place in a strip club, where our hero falls in love and takes her away," Scotty adds.

"She's a stripper?" I say weakly, the happiness escaping my body like air from a rapidly deflating bike tire.

"We feel that her being a stripper is more hard-core, more true to life, more new millennium," Christopher says.

"Yeah. Besides, she's too hot to wait tables. Guys know that chicks that hot can make more money stripping, so we figured we needed to speak to our audience more truthfully," Scotty adds.

"Really?" I am dumbfounded.

"How do you feel about nudity?" Lisa, the casting director, asks.

"In private I think it's great, but on film, I think it really has to be earned," I tell them.

"Yeah, but since we've changed Camilla to a stripper, she's definitely gonna have to get naked," Scotty replies.

I'm searching for another solution. "Uh, not necessarily. Jane Fonda played a call girl in *Klute* and we never saw her naked."

"Yeah, but that was the seventies. Kids like seeing tits nowadays," Scotty informs me.

"Right," I say, feeling totally defeated but trying to sound chipper.

"Well, thanks for coming in. We think you're really great. You're definitely on our short list, but we have to take the nudity thing into consideration," Christopher says as he stands up to shake my hand again.

I hesitate for a moment before saying, "Well, it was nice meeting you," and exit the room, keeping my confident façade intact, fighting the inevitable anger and disappointment. I almost turn back and say, "Yes, I'll show my tits, my ass, anything, just make me a star," but I'm sorry. This early in my career I can't be the Desperate Naked Girl. Especially the Desperate *Black* Naked Girl. I just can't. Although this movie would be a great opportunity, I don't want my first major role to be ass up in the air. I change back into my tennis shoes, rush to the elevator, and prepare to take the train to my favorite class at Yoga Zone. It will help me make sense of all this and release the frantic anxiety I keep feeling. Two hours rehearsing yesterday, two hours getting ready today, a terrible hour-long commute and costume consideration for a measly five minutes in the room, only to probably lose the part to the Pop Star or model who will show her tits. What a terrible fucking business when having standards is a liability. Fuck yoga, I need to get laid. An orgasm will clear my head much quicker than standing in tree pose. But I don't feel like talking to anyone right now, particularly a man. Alrighty then, an extended masturbation session with the BOB (Battery Operated Boyfriend) is in order. Or maybe I should call my agent, Maureen, to scream about this. Why didn't she tell me these changes had been made? I am so upset, but I refuse to cry. I will not let these fuckers defeat me, but it's too late for a pep talk, because I feel the tears steadily streaming down my face. I put my huge, black Jackie O sun-

glasses on so no one can see me crying. I must look like a complete fucking moron. I hate being this vulnerable in public, but these daily assaults
are taking a toll.

● ● ●

Although the business frequently depresses me, Carolyn, Taylor, and
Bianca have kept my spirits up and my insanity to a minimum here in the
Big Apple. No matter how many times I get rejected for a part or how
shitty the men in my life are acting, my girls provide constant support.
Because my parents are in San Francisco, the girls have become my urban
family, the sisters I never had. And even though Bianca's now holding it
down on the West Coast, we try to talk or e-mail every day, and I hang out
as much as possible with Carolyn and Taylor, whose hectic work schedules
preclude too much fun in the streets. Men and money may come and go,
but good girlfriends are forever.

· 5 ·

Carolyn

Papadum and a Postmortem

"Start talking, Carolyn," Taylor says, thrusting a bag at me as she and Roxanne burst through the door of my apartment. "It was your seventh date with Gil last night, you took a personal day from work today, and it doesn't take Encyclopedia Brown to solve that one. Here's your jhinga masala; get to spilling the beans."

Roxanne pulls a bottle of vodka out of her tote, which is larger than she is and is, as always, overflowing with changes of clothes and hair products. She kicks off her shoes, marches over to the cabinets above the sink, pulls down three highball glasses, and starts pouring as she chants, "WhathappenedwithGilwhathappenedwithGilwhathappenedwithGil—"

"You shut up, missy," Taylor says, turning to Roxanne, then turning back to me. "The only person who needs to be talking right now is Carolyn, and the only thing she needs to be talking about is whether Gil Merriweather put it on her last night." Roxanne plucks her lamb vindaloo from the bag and marches over to the chaise longue, where she sits down and looks at me expectantly.

"You're *glowing*," she says. "Gil must have torn you *up*."

I grin.

"I knew it, I knew it," Taylor says triumphantly, raising her glass. "I *knew* that's why you didn't go in to work. Speaking of work, you need to yoke up your damn secretary because she's taking that Ghetto Queen Supreme shit to the extreme; how is she going to let your line ring sixty-eleven billion times and then when she finally bothers to answer I can *hear* her eyes rolling? Ghetto ass! I hate it because there are too many women who came up in the worst parts of the worst ghettos all over the country who handle themselves in a professional manner and then you've got Shauntequia pulling all kinds of okeydoke shit and acting like she doesn't know any better just because she's from the projects. That makes me so fucking mad when—"

"Boom!" Roxanne interrupts. "That was the sound of your soapbox collapsing. Although I admit it'd be nice if she answered the phone by saying 'Miss Phillips's line, Shauntequia speaking, how may I help you?' instead of 'Halloa?!,' like I interrupted her in the middle of getting her fuck on or like she's got Hillary Rodham Clinton on the other line. But there's fucking to talk about, so sit your happy Black asses down and Carolyn, get a move on."

"Don't get me started on the top graduate of Lil' Kim's Academy of Deportment an' Shit, please," I say, tossing forks across the room to Roxanne and Taylor and joining Taylor on one of the big velvet floor pillows scattered across a mishmash of kilim rugs. "If we have to talk about work, let's talk about the fact that Getty himself told me on Monday that they're giving me my very own intern, who is supposed to be a cross between a personal assistant and a trainee; I'm pretty psyched."

"Do you think you're slick or something? She must think she's slick," Taylor says as Roxanne commands, "Don't try to distract us with tales of your chillingly ghetto secretary and your new intern; inquiring minds want to know whether last night was The Night the Drawers Came Off? Did Gil ravish you? Did Bank Street echo with the sounds of your impassioned moans of ecstasy? Did his rigid manhood penetrate to the core of your being? Did he go south of the border and ring your Taco Bell? Did you wear the Thong-Thuh-Thong-Thong-Thong?"

"*Did* he, and *did* I," I say, flushing at the memory. "But the thong didn't last long, and I'll never wear it again, because he tore it off me. With his *teeth.*" I get up, go back through the small book-lined alcove that leads to my bedroom, and return with a torn scrap of nylon that I hold above my head like a heavyweight hefting the championship belt.

"Holy shit," Taylor says in awe, and then she and Roxanne burst into spontaneous applause.

"He's a fucking savage. He's a slavering, merciless beast, a veritable G-spot gladiator. Fifty bucks down the toilet, worth every penny," I say proudly.

Roxanne and Taylor hoot and applaud again.

"You got the D! You got the D!" Roxanne yells, spraying fragments of lamb all over the vintage Moët et Chandon posters on the wall. "Sorry," she adds, dabbing at them with her napkin.

I fan my face as I remember how gently and skillfully Gil cupped and cradled my breasts as he made lazy circles around my nipples with his tongue.

"Fuck flashback!" Taylor crows, reaching in her Louis tote for a cigarette. "Look at her, she's all dewy-eyed!"

"You're damn skippy," I reply breathlessly, reaching for the chutney. "No smoking," Roxanne and I add in unison. Taylor rolls her eyes but puts the cigarette away.

"You guys are worse than Bloomberg," she complains.

"Fuck off," Roxanne replies. "It stinks and I've got an audition tomorrow and I'm not trying to show up smelling like the devil's asshole."

"Break a leg," I say.

"*I'll* break her leg," Taylor offers. "So Carolyn finally got some. It's about damn time."

"So what's the deal?" Roxanne says, suddenly serious. I lead them into the bedroom and show them the glass vase of calla lilies by the bedside.

"Wow," Roxanne breathes. "Already?"

"Read the card," I say, handing it over.

" 'Carolyn: This is the least I can do to let you know how I feel about last night. Do you know how pretty you are when you first wake up? Gil.' "

"Damn," Taylor says. "This is looking more than a little serious."

"He's smart, funny, spontaneous, and sexy," I say, practically hugging myself. "We talked about *Mama Day* and *The Moor's Last Sigh* last night for three hours—"

"Oh, God, now you two can start a book club," Roxanne says.

"—and he did one of his two senior theses on French pulp fiction—"

There is a brief silence. Taylor and Roxanne exchange glances.

"Personally, that doesn't get me too wet," Taylor says, "but clearly it ices your cake, and that's the whole point, I guess."

It does indeed ice my cake. But there is more.

"—and he's cooking me dinner on Friday," I crow triumphantly.

"Oh, my God, he sounds like the real thing!" Roxanne says, almost in a whisper.

"That's what *I'm* talking about," Taylor replies, grinning. "I'm glad he recognizes how incredible you are. Finally, a man who knows how to act right!"

· 6 ·

Roxanne

Bombay Sapphire

Since I'm between gigs, instead of spending another Wednesday afternoon in front of the TV switching back and forth between *Oprah* and *Divorce Court*, lamenting my lack of a fulfilling career, the lack of any men worth mentioning, and the major lack of cable, I force myself to hop on the train and go to my favorite Barnes & Noble at Union Square. When the sunlight hits those huge windows and there are floors upon floors of books to read, I always manage to find some tiny kernels of inspiration, run into someone I know at random (a wonderful coincidence very specific to New York City), or scrape together my change to buy a peppermint tea, sit at a cafe table, and indulge my diverse literary palate. B & N is great because you can sit and read as long as you want and there's no "Are you going to buy that or not?," so I can see all the hot new novels, self-help books, and magazines that I'm too broke to have subscriptions for.

Today I'm feeling rich, so I buy a tea *and* a chocolate chip cookie, then snag the last table. I rock. I savor the chocolaty goodness of the cookie, knowing that I can't have any more sweets for the rest of the week. I start reading my favorite Lucille Clifton poem from her *Book of Light* collection, dramatically bemoaning my fate as a poor, struggling artistic Black woman, when a male voice interrupts my thoughts.

"It's pretty crowded in here today, huh? Is this seat taken?" he inquires. I am pissed because I was hoping to spend this afternoon in surrounded solitude, not having any energy to deal with some dumb jackass.

"Well, actually, uh . . ." I say looking up into the most beautiful brown eyes with the longest, prettiest lashes I have seen on a man in my life. Oh shit. I'm glad that I put on my faux Juicy Couture sweat suit and sassy pink Pumas instead of the terrible Salvation-Army-meets-homeless-lady ensemble I've been rocking for three days straight.

"Oh, if you'd like, I can sit somewhere else," he offers.

"No, you seem pretty harmless," I tease. He is very cute. His teeth are perfectly straight and white. Yum.

"That's what everyone thinks when they first meet me," he chuckles.

"Well, I haven't met you, so I'm not sure," I spit back. Flirting is one of my favorite hobbies.

"I'm Ram," he says, extending his large hand my way.

"Ram, like the animal with the big-ass horns?" I ask, shaking his hand quite firmly. Nice grip.

"Exactly, but the A is a little longer and more rounded. Your lips should be opened wide when you say it, like you're eating a thick banana," he smirks. Ooh, I like this one already. He seems a little dirty, and I like 'em filthy.

"Okay, Raaam Baanaaanaa," I say, lengthening and rounding my A's, opening my lips wide enough for him to know that I'm just as much trouble as he is. He takes it in stride.

"Let me see what you're reading," he says, as he flips through my choices and sits down with confidence. "Uh huh, *Book of Light*, *The Best of Peanuts*, *Mad Magazine*, *Architectural Digest*, *Condé Nast Traveler*, *Loose Woman* by Sandra Cisneros. Interesting mélange. Are you?"

"Am I what?"

"Are you a Loose Woman?"

"Well, it depends on your definition. If you're coming from a traditional patriarchal perspective, you'd probably say yes. But if you're looking from an open-minded, nonsexist, nonjudgmental perspective, then no," I respond.

Ram pauses and his eyes narrow. "Okay, let me guess. You're either a postmodernist, Ivy League Comp Lit Ph.D. or a Seven Sisters nouveau Feminist?"

"Aren't you smugly sure of yourself? How about this: Sit here and read the book, and once you finish it, you can take me to dinner and judge for yourself. Meanwhile, as to your good self: cocky neo-Bollywood Anglophile?"

"Pretty perceptive. I produce documentary films. I'm interested in merging the literary with the authentic. You know what? Forget reading the book, let's have dinner now. I am intrigued," Ram suggests.

"But it's only five o'clock."

"Great! We have at least six hours to become acquainted before the kitchen closes at my favorite restaurant. I hope you like Indian." He is flirting quite heavily. I am smitten already.

"Food or men?"

"Both."

"I love Indian food, but I've never had an Indian man," I confess.

"Well, I guess I'll be your first. Shall we? Wait, do you have a boyfriend, fiancé, or husband?"

"Actually, I just sent my latest conquest packing."

"Why?"

"He was an actor. Too much competition for the spotlight."

"An actress! I should have known."

"I prefer to be called an actor. It's more P.C. Let's eat. I'm famished." I leave my stack of solace on the table, and Ram and I head for the escalators. Who needs Snoopy when you've got a real live man on your arm?

• • •

Conference call, topic being my sudden and mysterious disappearance.

"So where have *you* been all night and all day, Little R?" Carolyn inquires with that tone that lets me know I've been caught.

"Yeah, bitch, your cell has been turned off and has gone straight to voice mail. I hope some trouble got into you," Taylor stresses. I can hear her lighting up a cigarette.

"I met a really great guy, and we spent the last twenty-four hours together," I state confidently.

"Really?" Bianca asks, quite skeptically. They know I'm up to something.

"He's Indian, his name is Ram, and he's so fucking smart and gorgeous and seems to be crazy about me," I offer.

Bianca starts singing Prince's "International Lover."

"Does he have a big dick?" Taylor asks, getting straight to the point.

"What kind of girl do you think I am?" I ask innocently.

"A really, horny, nasty one," Taylor adds. I'm glad that she is just as crass as I am. Sometimes I think we have serious mental problems and possible sex addictions.

"No, we just kissed, and we kept our pants on," I reveal.

"So when are you going to fuck him?" Taylor demands.

"Can you hoes just slow your roll? I actually think I might like him as a person, not just as a piece of meat," I confess.

"Here *you* go again," Carolyn says, followed by a collective silence. I am positive this time will be different.

"Well, be careful, because we know you have a tendency to fall in love in five seconds," Bianca warns. It's sad, but true.

"That's why I'm not going to fuck him yet. Don't want to confuse good fucking with genuine feelings," I say. They know me too well.

"He's not an actor, is he? You *cannot* date another actor," Carolyn states.

"Documentary film producer," I reply.

"That still means he's broke, doesn't it?" Bianca asks. Leave it to Bianca to get straight to the money.

"I don't think he's rich, but he seems to enjoy life. Look, I'm just gonna go with the flow and take it slow," I say.

"And remember to blow," Taylor adds.

Laughing, I say, "You are the most hateful bitches I know."

"And we love you, too," they sing in unison.

• 7 •

Bianca

The Beautiful Ones

Can I just say that the overall standard of beauty in this town is completely ridiculous? The thing about Los Angeles is that every person who was voted Most Beautiful their senior year of high school has moved here (those voted Most Likely to Succeed moved to New York). The ratio of attractive people to unattractive people is dangerously skewed to the attractive side. It makes life for normal people very difficult. But, luckily, I'm cute. Especially today, because I've got on my fabulous new Marc Jacobs jacket (yes, it was a splurge, and I shouldn't have, but life is short and that's what credit cards are for). But I digress.

This overabundance of Beautiful People can be a man-catching nightmare. Not only are all these creatures gorgeous, but they're also thin and tan. Even worse, many are actors. Let me explain what happens when you live in the land of the Beautiful People. First, let's talk about the men. Again.

There are fine men everywhere in L.A. The guy who pumps your gas is fine so you end up paying extra for full service so you can see him bend over in your side-view mirror. The guy in the shoe department at Nordstrom's is fine so you end up buying *another* pair of black Charles David sandals (like you needed more black sandals). Let's not forget the bartenders; you've never seen so many women rush to buy their own drinks. This all gets to be rather expensive. Not to mention the fact that fine men have piss-poor attitudes. They do not cooperate because they do not have to. Nobody needs that kind of frustration on a daily basis. Especially me.

I was at an Industry Party at the Sunset Room recently and was introduced to a Television Actor whose show I had never seen, but was about to start watching religiously. Over six feet, beautiful brown skin, eight percent body fat, *and* he was wearing a suit. I almost passed out. Now, normally I would never date an actor, but I was merely trying to adhere to my new rule of giving every cute guy a chance. The sacrifices I make! Anyway, we got to talking and it turns out he's smart, ambitious, and has the kind of smile that makes you want to cook him dinner—*every* night. We were starting to hit it off, he'd even thrown a couple of compliments my way, and miracle of miracles: I was there with Angela, one of my coworkers, and when our champagne glasses were empty, he bought us BOTH a refill. I was in love. That's when SHE came along: Pseudo-Celebrity Bitch.

Pseudo-Celebrity Bitch (a.k.a. PCB) is either a supporting cast member on a bad TV show or a model/video dancer. Either way, she's useless. She serves no purpose but to remind me why "sleeping your way to the middle" is NOT a career option. So when she interrupts my conversation with my future husband, I'm a little salty. The problem is that Pseudo-Celebrity Bitch is every man's dream come true. Why would a man put up with me and my opinions when he can have Pseudo-Celebrity Bitch, who is just as cute, puts up with all kinds of bullshit, plus has the added cachet of being one of the original Vivrant Things? Me and my silly Harvard degree couldn't possibly compete with that, right?

Wrong. You see, the joke's on her. First of all, Pseudo-Celebrity Bitch isn't very smart. She is so caught up in short-term notoriety that she ends up making Very Poor Decisions. Although posing for *Playboy* will get you a lot of dates in your twenties, no man wants to marry someone all of his friends (and half of America) has seen naked. When a man gets older and decides to settle down, his priorities will shift dramatically in my favor. Eventually, his monosyllabic girlfriends will seem out of place among his friends' wives, who are more interested in politics than prostitution. He will then seek out a partner who is an articulate and well-respected member of society (me) as opposed to someone who used to bounce on Jay-Z's lap for a living (PCB).

In addition, her earning potential is extremely limited. Sooner or later, her enormous ass will start to sag, but her fake boobs will remain oddly perched on her chest, making her both freakish-looking and sad. A career based on your looks lasts about as long as it takes them to produce your "E! True Hollywood Story." A successful woman with her own career (and her own stock portfolio) becomes the obvious choice.

This is all very satisfying in a long-term sort of way, but at this exact moment I needed a distraction to get rid of this particular PCB. Back in New York, this wouldn't have been necessary, my girls would have swooped down on her like vultures, pretending to be fans, and clamored for her autograph while Television Actor and I escaped into another room. But out here I was on my own, and immediate action was required, because she was about to start whispering sweet nothings (like there was anything else in her head) into my future husband's ear. I scanned the party, desperately searching for bait. At last, my eyes rested on Dexter Conway. Thank God! I caught his eye, and he started to make his way over to greet me. Dexter is a running back for the Oakland Raiders whom I dated for about two seconds when we were both living in New York and he was playing for the Jets. Dexter is twenty-nine, rich, and unbelievably fine. Unfortunately, Dexter also has the attention span of a two-year-old. When I realized that he couldn't even commit to what to have for dinner on a given night, I had to cut him from the roster. We've remained friends though, and his particular brand of eye candy was just what the doctor ordered.

"Hey, Dex, how are you?" I said as I gave him a friendly peck on the cheek.

"Much improved, now that I've seen you," Dex replied, his voice oozing sex. Why do guys do that? You can tell a man four thousand times in ten different languages that they aren't getting any, and they still give it the old college try. Maybe they just like the sport of it. Dexter is, after all, a trained athlete.

"Aren't you sweet," I replied a little too nicely. Normally, I would have delivered a scathing reply to that garbage and Dex looked a little thrown off by the fact that he didn't get a severe tongue lashing. Playing on Dex's confusion, I moved in for the kill. "Dex, have you met . . . I'm sorry, I didn't catch your name," I said innocently to Pseudo-Celebrity Bitch.

"It's Candi," she replied.

"Of course it is. Dex, meet Candi."

As Dexter extended his hand to Candi, I saw her eyes light up with recognition. Five minutes later, Dexter escorted the lovely Candi to the bar for a drink so that his lies would sound a bit more convincing, throwing a wink over his shoulder as he walked away.

How do you get rid of a piranha? Dangle a bigger fish at it. Now that the Television Actor could more clearly focus on how well I was able to keep my balance while wearing three-and-a-half-inch Manolo Blahnik heels, even after my third glass of Moët, things were starting to look up.

"So Bianca, can I take you out sometime?" he asked.

I pretended to think it over as I imagined him without that suit on.

"Sure," I replied as I handed him my card. As I was leaving the party I saw Candi climbing into the passenger seat of Dex's Escalade. Poor thing, she never stood a chance. Everyone knows that class trumps ass every time.

From: baubles4bianca@yahoo.com
To: carolyn.phillips@gettyassoc.com; twilliams@mwdc.com;
          TheRealRoxanne@hotmail.com
Subject: I've gone Hollywood

Are you ready for this? I've managed to secure two passes to the premiere of the new Black Wedding Movie! I'm talking limos, paparazzi, and movie stars. My biggest concern is of course: whom do I take? It's tomorrow, so I'm operating under the assumption that none of you have time to fly here. So, here are my three choices:

1. Kevin. You remember him. We dated junior year and I ran into him at a party last week. He's still fine as hell, but after a ten-minute conversation, I realized why we're just friends now. Anyway, he's a good arm ornament, connected (TV agent at Ultimate Talent

Management), and always has an appropriate outfit on. He knows lots of people and can introduce me to someone who might want to buy my screenplay! However, I don't want people thinking we're "together" (i.e., "fucking").

2. Rachel. She's a junior executive at AABN (the African-American Broadcast Network) and she's pretty cool. We've hung out a few times, but I sense she takes a couple of nips from her flask of Hater-Ade every now and then. We're not going to be best friends, but she's a good Running Buddy. Besides, if I invite her to high-profile events, then she'll feel compelled to invite me when she gets tickets to stuff.

3. Selma. She's my next-door neighbor and she teaches seventh-grade English. She's real cool, but she's not really into the Hollywood scene. However, she's trustworthy, fun, and not a Hater. But I think she might get a bit overwhelmed at functions like this. Please advise.

From: twilliams@mwdc.com
To: baubles4bianca@yahoo.com
Cc: carolyn.phillips@gettyassoc.com;
          TheRealRoxanne@hotmail.com
Subject: Re: I've gone Hollywood

I won't even mention, or maybe I will, the fact that you listed Kevin in slot number one—unintentional or not, your subconscious is speaking volumes. The other two choices are really nonchoices. Re: Rachel, she'll only get tickets for AABN events, and you can do that your damn self. Let's only spend time with women who are going to love us for the fascinating ladies of distinction we are; Hater-Ade-sipping beeyotches need not apply. Re: poor Selma (are women named Selma ever any fun?), I'm sure you'd like to show her a taste of the good life, and I do understand that even we have feelings, but save your sympathy for kids you can tutor on Saturdays. Let grown folks who aren't getting beaten, pimped, or going hungry handle their own business. Sure, she'd be the obvious foil to the "I am the finest thing in here" posture you carry so well, but you don't need to bother with that because the truth shall set us all free and you can't hate on that. Get your mack on with Kevin, a man who evidently has enough sense to know that if he's not going to come correct, he doesn't need to block the path for those more suitable. Aren't you glad you're my girl? Advice like this would've cost a good paying client nearly two hundred bucks.

From: The RealRoxanne@hotmail.com
To: baubles4bianca@yahoo.com
Cc: carolyn.phillips@gettyassoc.com; twilliams@mwdc.com
Subject: Re: I've gone Hollywood

Always take the boy. He'll pay for things, keep unwanted suitors at bay, and you might even get a little Pok-e-mon. Also, AABN events? Seriously, Bianca! You're about to be in violation of the Scraping the Bottom of the Barrel for Shit to Do Act of 1993.

From: carolyn.phillips@gettyassoc.com
To: baubles4bianca@yahoo.com
Cc: TheRealRoxanne@hotmail.com; twilliams@mwdc.com
Subject: Re: I've gone Hollywood

Um, why are you considering taking a Hater anywhere other than outside in the back? So she can get you event tickets? So what? She works for AABN, so the most she'll be able to hook you up with is passes to next year's Coonspade Awards at the El Segundo Econolodge, co-hosted by Stoney Jackson and Marilyn McCoo. Selma's likely to make you both look like bumpkins by passing out when some back number like Arsenio Hall walks by, so I'd take her to something where she can ooh and aah, but where you aren't really on the spot in a business sense. Take Kevin.

Also, your pictures from the Golden Globes are incredible! Am I mistaken, or were you wearing the same Giuseppe Zanotti sandals that Jennifer Aniston had on in *Glamour* last month? Which poor pussy-whipped suitor ponied up the $475 for those, you naughty thing?

Carolyn

You Are a Liar Over There, You Are a Liar Everywhere

Six hours ago I strutted out the door en route to my fifteenth date with Gil, equipped with newly waxed legs and bikini and terrific hair, looking rather incredible if I do say so myself in a fabulous black Donna Karan number from Salon Z (the plus-size store) at Saks Fifth Avenue that I had bought months ago and kept in its original plastic to be unwrapped for a special occasion. Three hours ago, I was spread-eagled on Gil's California king, his head buried between my thighs, getting off on the gesture just as much as what he was actually accomplishing down there.

Two and a half hours ago I was nestled in his arms, feeling for the first time in a very long time that everything in my life is going according to plan. Things are going very well at work: I was promoted to creative project manager last week after my asshole boss signed his own pink slip by green-lighting a spot for a foot-long hot dog that featured a series of grinning, mustard-mouthed little girls and is best described as being somewhere along the lines of *Debbie Does Dallas* meets Megan's Law; the driver who stinks of onions and stale sweat and grumbles to himself in some guttural language every time I ask him to do so much as change lanes is being reassigned; I have lost some weight because I am spending time with men other than the Keebler Elves, and, most of all, I have realized that I am falling in love with Gil.

I slip out of bed and walk down the hall to the bathroom. When I come out, I see that we have left the lamp in the living room on, and I go to turn it off. I walk past the coffee table, piled high with back issues of the *Wall Street Journal* and *The New Yorker,* and stop to admire the bookshelves, crammed to bursting with everything from Nietzsche to James Patterson to *Bloom County.* This is a far cry from my last remotely serious relationship, which was with a man whose shelves contained row upon row of X-box cartridges with names like Rocko Hardy's Basketball Motocross Fantasia VII and a DVD collection that was equal parts kung fu and porn and who firmly believed that Toni Morrison was the 1999–2000 wide receiver for the Miami Dolphins. I feel extremely fortunate to have found a Man Who Reads; the breed seems to be dying out.

I turn off the light, make my way back to the bedroom, and slip back under the covers. Gil rolls over and pulls me closer.

"Bring that incredible body back over here, woman," he murmurs sleepily. "And you better get some sleep because I'm going to wear you out again in the morning."

That is one of the things that I appreciate the most about being with Gil. In my other relationships, I and some member of the opposite sex who had no business being in one another's company outside of the bedroom would suffer through hours of unbearable "quality time" activities because we felt that three courses of fork-dropping and stilted small talk or two hours spent yawning behind a *Playbill* lent legitimacy to the wild uninhibited rutting that was the real purpose of the entire evening. With Gil, however, while the sex is world class, it is not the primary purpose of or the driving force behind our relationship. It is merely part of something much broader and complex. This is the first time that I have experienced this kind of relationship, and I silently promise myself that if for some reason things fall apart with Gil, I will never go back to "the old way."

But the thought of things falling apart with Gil seems alien and ridiculous now, as I lie in the crook of his arm and breathe in his cologne. Those dark, pointless days are far behind me, and I finally permit myself the luxury of admitting that after eleven long, nasty years in the dating arena, I have finally met my Knight in Shining Armani, and I cannot stop smiling into the darkened room.

Twenty minutes afterward I am awakened from a dreamy half-doze by the click of Gil's answering machine as it begins to record a message.

"Sweetheart," says a woman's voice, confident and intimate with a slight Southern drawl, "I talked to Momma and Daddy, and they've invited us down. I said fine because it'll give us all a chance to sit down and talk about the wedding plans—"

Gil lunges for the phone but it is far too late. He barks something into the handset while I lie there, feeling as if someone has just dropped a boulder on my chest. When I do eventually sit up, Gil, still muttering into the telephone, tries to push me back down but I smack his arm away and swing my legs over the edge of the bed. I can hear her voice on the other end, alternately protesting and apologizing. I start looking around the floor for the delicate bra and panty set I had purchased in a happy daze during lunch, little dreaming that I would be hunting for it under these circumstances. Finally I locate it, then stuff my stockings and garter belt into my bag and struggle into my dress, hearing a seam rip and not caring. Gil bangs the phone onto the cradle and turns to me.

"Don't go, Carolyn," he says. His eyes are hot and his voice is pleading, but I cannot look at him or listen to this. Trying not to cry, I shove my foot roughly into one of my shoes and stalk unevenly around the bedroom in search of the other one. He sees it on the floor and darts for it.

"Carolyn, please, just hear me out," he says, holding the shoe hostage just out of my reach and trying to grab my hand with his other hand. "I don't want you to go. I want—"

"Give me my shoe," I say in a strained voice, "you lying, cheating son of a bitch."

"Carolyn, don't, please! I care so much for you, you can't understand—" he protests, still holding the shoe above his head. "I've never met anyone like you, anyone so smart or so funny. I can't talk to her about the things you and I talk about. She doesn't understa—" Before he can get any further, I knee him in the crotch as hard as I can. His eyes bulge and he gurgles in the back of his throat. When he doubles over, I grab my shoe from him, jam it onto my foot, and storm out of the bedroom, grabbing my coat from the back of the sofa en route to the front door. Forty-five minutes later I am lying amid a sea of empty Styrofoam takeout containers from the Waverly Diner and waiting to cry.

• 9 •

Taylor

MWDC

Thankfully, work gives me a reason to get up every day. And after this breakup, I surely need a distraction. Unlike most people, I wasn't filled with dread by the sight of the granite flight of stairs leading into my office building. I had the right corporate attitude: *pay me.* Cha-motherfucking-ching. I'd spent many a night working at Mills, Waters, Dennis and Cois (MWDC), or Motherfucker, We Don't Care, as I semi-affectionately called it. Every time someone asked me when I was going to leave the firm for good, I told them I didn't know. And I really didn't. I watched people drudge through the eight or nine years it took to become partner and feel like worthless jerks if they didn't make it, and I knew that would never be me. All it takes is the right corporate attitude: cut my check. With all deliberate speed.

Working this hard, at this level, meant it was only about one thing: the *dinero.* I was most certainly professional. But I always had this dreadful feeling that one day, someone—a client, partner, senior associate—was going to push my ass to the motherfucking edge and force me to curse them the fuck out like a chickenhead on a Newark street corner. I'd had my "almost to the edge" moments before; fortunately, so far, things have remained pretty cool. But inevitably, someone will push this Black woman to the limit, and they will invariably draw back a fucking nub.

Today I was only running into work to pick up my briefcase so that I could run straight to court to argue a motion. Now, I must admit, I'm just a junior attorney at my firm, so I shouldn't even be anywhere near the courthouse. When clients are paying MWDC the money they pay, they want the most senior attorneys to handle all the courtroom action. Fortunately for me, both the senior associate and partner on my biggest case like me well enough. Or more realistically, they know I'll bust my ass to do whatever it takes to make sure I'm fully prepared for any curveball opposing counsel might serve up. Or, even more realistically, they were all so swamped with other cases that I was the only one on the team left to do it. With my reputation for working well into the wee hours of the morning to make sure that every last detail was in place, they knew I wouldn't let them down. Which is probably why they didn't bother to re-arrange their schedules.

Most people don't know what lawyers do all day (and night) in those big New York skyscrapers. When you see the lights on at one A.M. in office buildings around town, let me tell you, it's some corporate lawyer pounding away at court papers for filing, memoranda for clients, and var-ious official documents for submission to the numerous government enti-ties that regulate big business. I decided to come to the most prestigious firm in town because big business pays big dollars. But being at the most prestigious firm in town means that I have to work myself into the ground to give clients the perfection they feel they've paid for. And honestly, I can't blame them; at the rates MWDC's clients are paying, I'm surprised they don't make the firm guarantee them absolute victory. But I don't care, because I'm finally a lawyer. I'm not in law school *preparing* to be one; I *am* one. And after many years of hard work, I've climbed out of the junior ranks and made it into the junior field. Now, I have to work harder than ever to make certain I keep my eye on the prize: partnership. And if I obtain a favorable outcome on this motion, I'll be one small step closer to the big leagues.

• • •

When I arrived in court, my face damn near frozen from the icy wind outside, I saw that Sandy Callum, opposing counsel, was already sitting at the counsel table. I sat down across from her and pulled out ten manila file folders—everything I would need to make certain that Sandy didn't stand a chance. We both stared ahead blankly. The judge didn't show for another forty-five minutes. Whoever said justice was swift had never appeared in New York State Supreme Court. I decided to count my blessings though, because Family Court was even worse: three-hour waits and bad attitudes were routine.

"What case is this and who represents whom?" the judge bellowed when he finally showed up. Judge Judy would be scared of this fool.

"Your honor, Sandy Callum, counsel for plaintiff in the matter of *York v. Intertec Corporation.*" This pissant shareholder derivative lawsuit is, truth to tell, the least of Intertec's problems. The Securities and Exchange Commission is all over them for the same reason this plaintiff is, and if you didn't know, permit me to tell you: the SEC is the monkey that *can* stop your show.

"Your honor, Taylor Williams, counsel for defendant Intertec."

"What's going on?" he grumbled. Like most State Supreme judges, he hadn't bothered to read the documents I'd spent all night cranking out.

"Your honor, Ms. Callum has issued yet another subpoena to Intertec in the hopes that she will be able to find one shred of evidence to support her case. She won't." Although lawyers always make long speeches on TV when they were in front of a jury, judges don't want to hear all of that bullshit. They want a quick and dirty introduction into the case and the reason why you should win.

"Discovery closed in this case two months ago. If she needed anything else from Intertec, she had plenty of time to ask for it. I know I don't need to remind you that we've been arguing about document discovery from the inception of this case."

"No, you don't." The judge scowled. So far, so good. He wasn't happy at all—and Sandy and her client would pay.

"Your honor, I do admit that discovery has closed, but it's quite essential to my case that—" The good judge cut her off.

"Discovery's closed, defendant's motion is granted. Good-bye. And don't bother this court with such nonsense again." The judge stormed off to his chambers without a second glance back. His clerk scurried off behind him.

Thank Goddess! I looked at Sandy and smiled the "win-some, lose-some" smile.

"Taylor, my client's ready to talk settlement."

"I don't know whether the phrase 'that bastard will not get a dime out of Intertec unless he comes in with a shotgun' meant the same thing to you that it did to me, but I'll talk to the client again to see whether they're interested."

I knew Intertec wouldn't settle, but the attorney code of ethics requires settlement offers to be disclosed to clients. I was too junior to engage in a full-blown settlement discussion, but I figured I'd come back to the senior associate and the partner with my winning news and maybe with a start on the path of getting this case over with.

"What's the ballpark?" I asked nonchalantly.

"Nothing less than a million."

Was this bitch on crack? I furrowed my eyebrows.

"Well, seven-fifty," she amended.

I knew what she meant, but I had to try. "Seven hundred fifty thousand or seven hundred and fifty dollars?"

"Come on."

"Is that your final offer?"

"What do you think they'll take?" she asked, confusing my youth with inexperience.

I wanted to say "A hammer to the head of your client" just to see the look on her face, but instead I said "If that's your final offer, I'll tell them and get back to you."

"No lower."

"That's still a mighty long way from zero."

• • •

The cab sailed back to work in record time. I was on a true high. A win on the motion and a settlement offer. Now that wasn't bad for the beginning of the morning. But then I saw them. Couples everywhere. I was reminded of Vincent and so I tried to steel up my nerves, silently praying that I would make it off the elevator and into my office so I could have a nervous breakdown in peace. As the tears welled up in my eyes, I willed them not to fall until my door was locked behind me. Before I could turn the bolt, though, my secretary stopped me and gave me a package. It was from Him. I put the package down on my mahogany desk and booted up my computer. It had better be his pro-rated portion of the rent. Well, I guess there was one positive thing I could say for him—he wasn't a complete bastard. As Windows started to whirr, I picked up the package. Too heavy for a check. Unless it had a lot of zeroes on the end of it. Okay, this isn't joke time. I opened the package and nearly passed out. A fucking "parting" gift. Is this some idea of a sick joke? When I looked in for a closer inspection, I thought I would really scream. Inside was the Mikimoto pearl necklace I'd been eyeing. The black ones. I can't even call him Satan now. But he's definitely Satan's son. I can't stand being on a fucking emotional seesaw, but having Uranus as a ruling planet will do that to you. I wanted to bang the shit to pieces with a hammer, but I decided that I wasn't quite that angry. My heart was broken; that was enough destruction for now.

• • •

From: twilliams@mwdc.com
To: carolyn.phillips@gettyassoc.com;
          baubles4bianca@yahoo.com;
          TheRealRoxanne@hotmail.com
Subject: Vincent is Satan's son.

Like Dan Rather, I've got breaking news. Newsflash One: I won in court, and the partner is amped that I got opposing counsel down from a $1M settlement figure! I tell you, hard work has its rewards. Newsflash Two: Vincent sent me those fucking Mikimoto black pearls I've had my eye on. Although the bastard said I'm the person he wants to spend the rest of his life with, he also said he just can't deal with the fact that he has to start thinking this seriously about his life. What he needs to start thinking seriously about is what I might do with this knife that he stabbed in my back—I don't go for the cowardice move, I'll get that fool right in his neck.

From: baubles4bianca@yahoo.com
To: twilliams@mwdc.com
CC: carolyn.phillips@gettyassoc.com;
               TheRealRoxanne@hotmail.com
Subject: RE: Vincent is Satan's Son.

Forgive me for not spending more time congratulating you on your win, Taylor, but what is going on here? Are the planets not aligned or some shit? I'm so tired of waiting for these fools to "realize" that it doesn't get ANY better than this! They leave you to wander out into the dating world, deluding themselves into thinking that they're going to find ANOTHER beautiful, intelligent, witty, clever, sophisticated, captivating woman who can cook AND fuck. You're only young once, and I'll be damned if I'll waste my best years waiting on trifling men to get with the program.

From: carolyn.phillips@gettyassoc.com
To: twilliams@mwdc.com
CC: baubles4bianca@yahoo.com;
               TheRealRoxanne@hotmail.com
Subject: RE: Vincent is Satan's Son.

1. Of course you won; you're the best lawyer in the city.
2. As for The Asshole, don't bother to hack him to pieces because you'll get disbarred, so try to keep it together and give me a call if you get a second.

From: TheRealRoxanne@hotmail.com
To: twilliams@mwdc.com
CC: baubles4bianca@yahoo.com;
               carolyn.phillips@gettyassoc.com
RE: Exorcism indeed

Taylor, we're going club-hopping to celebrate your win as soon as you get a chance to leave work at a decent hour. As for Jackal Boy, poof, be gone! The best way to get over old dick is to get new dick. So let's go to Mellow, where we can celebrate your victory and find you someone to help you exorcise your demons.

I have a little bit of good news of my own, ladies: I just found out right this second that I got a national Overnight Express commercial, which means that my one day of work could result in as much as $50,000. I'll be playing "a dancing hip-hop fly girl" for these two rappers who want to use Overnight Express for their shipping needs. What the fuck these thugs might be shipping and where they're shipping it to, only God knows, but whatever.

From: baubles4bianca@yahoo.com
To: twilliams@mwdc.com
CC: carolyn.phillips@gettyassoc.com;
          TheRealRoxanne@hotmail.com
Subject: RE: Congratulations!

Get that money so we can sip (nondomestic) champagne on the deck of that yacht you'll be buying.

From   twilliams@mwdc.com
To: carolyn.phillips@gettyassoc.com;
          baubles4bianca@yahoo.com;
          TheRealRoxanne@hotmail.com
Subject: RE: Congratulations!

Shake whatcha mama gave ya. It's about damn time people recognized that you are a star.

From: carolyn.phillips@gettyassoc.com
To: twilliams@mwdc.com
CC: baubles4bianca@yahoo.com;
          TheRealRoxanne@hotmail.com
Subject: RE: Congratulations!

Bianca has some fresh-ass New Jack Swing B-Girl gear that she can donate to your total look.

From: baubles4bianca@yahoo.com
To: twilliams@mwdc.com
CC: carolyn.phillips@gettyassoc.com;
    TheRealRoxanne@hotmail.com
Subject: RE: Congratulations!

I see that the activator from someone's 1989 Wave Nouveau "body perm" has finally seeped into her brain and caused permanent damage.

• 10 •

Roxanne

Hip-Hop Mama

Well, I'm hoping this Overnight Express shoot will be fun, but the spandex chartreuse tube dress the costume designer pulls from her extensive wardrobe selection is a huge red flag. For some reason, we both think it will be a great idea to cut it in half and make it a tube top and miniskirt. Apparently girlfriend got a little scissor happy while I was in the next room, because now the top is so short that it doesn't cover the bottom of my breasts and the "skirt" has to be pulled down to my pubic bone so that my ass won't hang out. I'm lucky I got waxed a few days ago, or this would be an even "hairier" situation. I am about to lose my cool as the inept costumer tries to avoid a fight by saying, "Well, you've definitely got the figure to wear that."

"Uh, my tits are hanging out of the bottom and you can see my ass crack. I'm not wearing this! Everyone I know will see me on national TV looking like a hooker!" I protest. My demons are showing.

Lil' Z, one of the other actors, sees the possible drama and swoops in with a rap, "Yo shorty, you don't look like no ho. You look mad good to me fo' sho."

D-Strong, his partner in idiocy, comes over and chimes in with, "That's my word. I would make you my queen / our life would be a dream / you can't understand the beauty in front of me."

Lil' Z continues, "Hey pretty lady with the thugged-out smile / I haven't seen your fine ass in a little while / why don't you slide your phat ass to my Escalade / and we'll be makin' thug love like lemonade."

"Guns, hoes, cash, that's what I'm about / ain't a motherfucker around that will make me shout / I'll bust my gat in yo neck while you scream fo' more / can't no nigga kill a bitch like D-Strong hard-core."

"Yo, that's tight, man," Lil' Z says as he daps D-Strong up and they wander off into their ignorant world, rendering me speechless. Is this a commercial shoot or Freestyle Friday on *106 and Park?* Wannabe rappers are so tiresome.

The free impromptu concert having ended, the costumer's frantic assistant attacks me with a black strapless bra and says, "If you put this on, it will stretch the fabric, guaranteeing that your breasts are fully covered, and if you put these belly chains on, you won't notice the back cleavage."

Then they weigh me down with cheap-ass gold-plated jewelry from the Fat Boys Era. Yeah, the rope-a-dope twisted gold chain with the huge scorpion pendant will class this right on up. And the dukey fresh bamboo gold earrings will complete my look as Round the Way Girl of the Year, 1986. Where is my union representative? I try to avoid Tweedledum and Tweedledummer and their merry rap brigade, but they keep hovering like vultures. I need them to stop spitting game at me.

Thankfully we are ready to start shooting, but D-Strong and Lil' Z, the rappers/actors/losers who are supposed to be the centerpiece of this commercial, freeze once the cameras start rolling. All their witty repartee, free stylin', and blazin' lyrics go on hiatus at the word *action*. So we have a frustrated director, trying to encourage these b-boys to keep it gangsta, keep it flowing, while D-Strong and Lil' Z turn into insecure, sniveling bitches. Earlier, while they were in hot pursuit of my ass, D-Strong told me that he was "in this rap game and acting game, trying to keep his head up, pimp this shit, and keep it light." But now he's telling the director that he just feels "very pressured to live up to a certain image that is a lot harder and more violent than he really is, and he's more of a P.M. Dawn Righteous Brother." So much for keeping it real. With visions of steak dinners and unlimited cab rides dancing in my head, I step off the giant speaker I am dancing on and desperately try to salvage the nightmare.

"I can rap a little, if you want me to freestyle with him over the beat," I offer. I've gone from Downtown Julie Brown's crackhead stand-in to Scorpion Queen hottie lyricist in about five seconds flat and realize, far too late, that I shouldn't have said anything. Sometimes it's better to keep your mouth closed and just shake your ass, because I'm now Lil' Kimming it up about Overnight Express.

"All you homies and homegirls out there in the cut, call Overnight Express to SHIP IT UP! Holla! Go Ove Ex, Go Ove Ex, GO! Send them packages, get them dollaz!"

The director stares at me blankly, as if he can't believe what just happened. A beat passes. He finally opens his mouth. "Cut! Um, uh, thank you so much for your hard work, but I think we're going to break for the day."

I optimistically ask, "When is this going to air?"

"Never," the director says with conviction.

So I have no future as an MC, I won't be getting any residual checks, and I hope against hope that this footage won't turn up on an episode of *Before They Were Stars*.

· 11 ·

Carolyn

Assistance Meets Resistance

"You got a Carter Holden out here," says Shauntequia.

"Who's that?" I say shortly. "What does he want?" The name sounds vaguely familiar, but I cannot place him.

"I ain't ax him," she says. "What you want me to do?" Shauntequia has become even more stank since HR told her that she will be relocated to the reception desk downstairs, where she will no longer be able to read *Black Celebrity Hair* magazine and make personal long-distance phone calls. Exasperated, I look up at the wall clock, then down at my watch, as if they will say something other than that I have seven minutes until my next meeting. It does not matter; seven minutes is nowhere near enough time to deal with the work I should have been doing all morning instead of having yet another furious two-hour emergency self-esteem maintenance conference call with the usual suspects, who, as good girlfriends must, continue to insist that the now long-defunct Gil—whom I saw at a bar last night with The Fiancée in tow, and who pretended not to recognize me—is an absurdly pompous asshole who did not deserve to lick my boot under any circumstances and is quite frankly not only nowhere near as cute as any of us originally thought but also probably a closet serial killer, while I am perfect and beautiful, a veritable martyr-angel in Jimmy Choo stilettos who could not possibly get any thinner without vanishing into thin air.

Now I have six minutes.

"I'll see him, thanks," I say. Shauntequia rolls her eyes and slams the door behind her. I flip her the bird energetically and inadvertently knock a pile of papers off my desk. As I duck down to pick them up, I hear my office door open.

"Yes, Mr. Holden, what can I do for you?" I say from under the desk.

"I'm Carter Holden," he says unnecessarily, "and I'm—Ms. Phillips, are you—well, in any case, I'm your new in—"

I straighten up from behind the desk and he stops in mid-sentence.

"What is it?" I say sharply, although I already know what it is. This is the I'd Thought You Were White hesitation and mental readjustment, a phenomenon you will frequently observe if you have an ethnically neutral name and sound like Brooke Shields on the phone but look like Kim Fields in person.

"Nothing," he says at length. "I was just saying that I'm your new intern." He grins disarmingly. I look him over briefly. Six feet and change. Rugby player's build. A last name for a first name, wavy dirty blond hair, Dudley Do-Right jaw, a bred-in-the-bone Brooks Brothers disaster. He is the brooding young elephant hunter in a Ralph Lauren ad, one of F. Scott Fitzgerald's Princeton cronies, and every Rich Popular Guy from every John Hughes movie rolled into one, and I have a twenty-dollar bill that says that there is either a III or IV after that name that he neglected to mention. In short, we have us here a gen-yoo-wine result of the Old Boys Network "favor for a friend" routine, and I have apparently been assigned to babysit this spoiled young slacker, with his smarmy, patronizing smile, until he gets tired of this artsy-fartsy stuff and buggers off to his father's brokerage house or law firm, which is where he should have gone in the first place. Until this moment, today was merely a bad day; it is now officially awful, so bad that I am permitted to have something unhealthy for lunch rather than the sashimi I was originally scheduled to consume.

"It's very nice to meet you," I lie, removing a dust bunny from my shoulder and shaking his hand at the same time. I see him trying not to look at the snowdrifts of papers all over the floor, one of which, I now see, is a memo to me about the fact that my intern's name is Carter Holden and he will be arriving at noon today. Now I understand why there there has been a steady stream of guys from Maintenance in and out of the small office next door to mine for the last couple of days.

"I just moved offices," I say, which is not exactly a complete and total lie, "so I'm still a little disorganized."

He shrugs and nods politely.

"So, I'm really sorry, Carter, but I have a meeting upstairs in about two seconds, so I have to get going." I pick up the portfolio and walk him to my door.

"Is there anything I can do to help out?" he says.

"No, thanks," I say. "Shauntequia, would you mind showing Carter around the office?"

"I go to lunch in three minutes," Shauntequia says sullenly, and crosses her arms defiantly. I am torn between letting it go and setting aside my home training in order to cuss her the righteous fuck out regardless of the audience when the audience interrupts.

"Looks like I got you at a bad time," he says. "Tell you what, the office isn't that huge, so I'll just show myself around and you can show me the rest as we go?"

"Thanks, that sounds perfect," I say, confining myself to glaring at Shauntequia and racing off toward the internal stairs.

As it happens, Jackson, the head of our division and the person to whom all team leaders, myself included, report, turns out to be in a far worse mood than he was this morning when I saw him banging on the coffee machine and swearing, and although he routinely tears us new ones on a regular basis, I was already behind the emotional eight ball, so two o'clock finds me in the last stall of the deserted basement-level ladies' room with my head buried in my hands. I am so tired of Jackson's temper, so tired of being lonely, so tired of being big, so tired of putting my best foot forward to try to engage men who simply have no interest in what I have to offer, so tired of going for months without sex, so tired of trying to cheer myself up with new shoes, so tired of all of it. I am twenty-eight years old and I feel like I look sixty-eight, and I am absolutely, completely miserable. I keep thinking about last night, when I saw Gil's fiancée, a perfect size four in a killer St. John by Marie Gray suit, laughing up at him and putting her arms around him, then turned away and saw my own reflection through a haze of tears in the mirror behind the bar. And suddenly it seems to me that I understand Gil's behavior, though I cannot excuse it; what is a summa cum laude from Harvard and a razor-sharp wit compared to delicate wrists and a waist he can fit his hands around?

• • •

The phone rings. Carter, who has been here for approximately ten days and turns out to have fairly decent drafting skills, is off somewhere making copies, so I put on the headset and pick up.

"I'd just like to ask the cosmos this one question," Taylor says testily. "What exactly did it mean by giving your ungrateful, ignorant ass a rich Brendan Fraser doppelgänger to fetch your coffee while my secretary, who is very sweet, looks like Tito Jackson, mustache included? You don't even know what to *do* with him."

"Why, it's the Pointer Sisters," I say, unwrapping a Gordita. "And they're so excited that they just can't hide it." I am ignored because they have an agenda.

"He better *not* be fine," Roxanne says. "That's too unfair, unless he's a total fucking idiot, which would be a little fair, although still not really."

"No, the man is fine," Taylor says. "I stopped by her office last week and I can confirm that he is guaranteed Grade-A dirty blond white-boy meat."

"And no, he's not a total fucking idiot," Bianca chimes in. "Not that it takes a nuclear physicist to answer a phone, but he's already memorized my number, and while I will miss being referred to as 'Who?!,' I believe that I can get used to being greeted with 'Good afternoon, Bianca.' " There is a clattering sound and a splash.

"Shit, hold on," Bianca says. "I was so overcome by the notion of a hot man with some sense that I knocked over my latte." There is a clattering sound as she puts the phone down, followed by a muffled sponging sound. I straighten the row of colored pencils on my desk as if that will somehow compensate for the piles of copy, stencils, and discards from the drawing board that have created a makeshift carpet on the hardwood floor.

"Taylor's right, she *wouldn't* know what to do with him," Bianca continues, "and I almost don't know why we're wasting our breath on that topic, because I can't possibly be the only one who's noticed that ever since that Nigerian diplomat's son from the Business School—what was his name? Oingoboingo?—gave her a taste of the motherland senior year, Miss Mandinga hasn't given the time of day to anything that isn't chocolate and built like a racehorse, locks and posh British accent optional but preferred."

"His name was Dennis Adebayo, you ridiculous twat, and you are both disgusting and hideously politically incorrect," I say, getting hot and bothered by the mere memory. Six feet five inches, body by Equinox, economics degree by Oxford, locks to his shoulders, fluent in five languages. Including Cunnilingus. "But I'll let you off the hook for taking his name in vain because you have pointed out Reason #2 why I will not be sniffing around this boy, which is that he's not my type, period, end of story. You know who he is? He's Arthur Holcombe, that dickhead who wrote that asshole editorial in *The Crimson* junior year about the 'absurdity' of affirmative action and how admissions should be based on merit alone. I know I'm not the only one who remembers that."

"Oh, yeah, because Artie Holcombe's bitch ass got his summer job in the American embassy in Paris on 'merit' and *certainly* not because his daddy gave thirty-eleven jillion dollars to the presidential campaign," Roxanne snarks.

"Carter hasn't done anything yet to suggest that he's another Artie Holcombe, so you're just being a jackass, and an unfair one, too," Taylor presses. "And what, pray tell, was Reason #1?"

"Reason #1 is don't shit where you eat. He works under me; are you out of your collective fucking minds? And even though I don't need any reasons other than those two, you know he's got supermodel heiresses falling out of his ass anyhow, so what would be the point?"

"Ah," Taylor says triumphantly, "now why do I think that's the *real* reason?"

"Please shut up," I say wearily. I need food. I think a Chalupa. No, two Chalupas.

"I'll take that as an acknowledgment of the fact that I'm right," Taylor says, lighting a cigarette. "I'll let you off the hook now because I know you're still pissed off about the whole Gil thing, but don't forget that there's something to be said for keeping a fine-ass man under your desk; now that Vincent's gone, I'm taking applications for a new Keeper of the Royal Twat, word is bond."

"Well, as much as I really hate to agree with Carolyn when she's making excuses for not getting ass, she may have a point about being careful about handling her business interoffice," Roxanne says. "It's different for you over there in The Sweatshop because you've got a thousand anonymous people in there and you can close your door and keep your business out of the street, but she can't do that; her office looks like something out of a movie but the design isn't very good for someone who wants to have sex in private."

This is very true. The open floor plan is supposed to foster creativity but actually just fosters everyone getting in everyone else's business. I have an actual office with four walls (one glass) and a door that closes, so people may not be able to hear me on the phone, but they would certainly have an unobstructed view of me getting my swerve on on top of my desk. And because I have minimalist Danish Modern office furniture, the section of my desk that faces my door is essentially four steel pillars and a teak plank, so under the desk would not be any better.

"Not that anyone's listening to me, because my opinion on this topic doesn't matter, but all of this absurdity is completely beside the point because I'm quitting the dating game and I don't care if I never have sex again," I say sulkily. The girls splutter in disbelief. Roxanne bursts out laughing and tells me to move away from the window before I catch a thunderbolt in the teeth.

"You're kidding who, do you think?" Bianca is saying.

"God, you are so full of shit," Taylor says. "I'm hanging up on you now, I'm so disgusted." And she does.

• 12 •

Bianca

The Red Carpet

The general consensus was that I should ask Kevin to escort me to the premiere screening and party for the latest Black Wedding Movie, and that's precisely what I did. It was the real deal and ALL of Black Hollywood was in attendance. I must say that a Black movie premiere is quite a unique phenomenon in Hollywood. It is a rare event full of spectacle and fraught with drama.

First of all, let me just say how painful it is to walk down the red carpet and have NOBODY take your picture. I was tempted to just start posing and FORCE them to take my picture, but the only thing worse than having no one take your picture is having no one PRINT your picture. And my outfit was begging to be memorialized in celluloid: I looked absolutely darling in a gauzy BCBG Indian-inspired creation and the Zanotti sandals Carolyn had exclaimed over. (I sure wish some pussy-whipped suitor HAD paid for those—I had to delay some bill payments to cover that particular expense. But it's all in the name of fabulousness.)

The next thing you need to know about Black movie premieres is GET THERE EARLY. For us, that means get there ON TIME. The problem is, they always give out more passes than there are seats. Unless you were IN the movie, you cannot arrive late. If you do, you're going to end up either not getting in or sitting in the "overflow" section (kind of like getting to church late). Once you're inside, there is a lengthy mingling session. Seats are being saved, publicists are scrambling to seat VIPs, and stars are graciously greeting friends and fans. I don't understand that part. This is the time to sit your ass down. All the same people will be at the after-party. You can see them later.

There are two unique things about seeing a movie at its premiere: (1) The excessive clapping and cheering, which leads to (2) the inability to actually enjoy/hear the movie. Naturally, many of the people in the audience are going to be the friends and family of the stars, but clapping over the entire credits and cheering every time your Baby Boo comes on screen is a little much. Hello, I'm trying to watch the (free) movie.

When the movie is over, remember: Don't dawdle. Go directly to the after-party. Do not pass go. Do not collect $200. Do not gawk at horrible outfits. (Okay, that last part is just for me.) While everyone else is loitering outside the theater trying to catch a glimpse of Shemar Moore, you should be at the party securing the ever-important TABLE. Again, unless you are IN the movie (or your name is Halle Berry) there is no table for you. There is nothing worse than trying to look cute while you eat a plate of chicken standing up.

This particular party was a lot of fun (i.e., as soon as I walked in there was a waiter with a tray of champagne). After that, I was good for the rest of the night. There was a great D.J. and everyone was actually dancing. There was less Hollywood standoffishness than usual. People were mingling and having a good time (i.e., it was open bar).

As far as attire, there were the requisite "Hollywood" outfits: super-mini-miniskirts that you can't possibly wear panties under, paper-thin camisole tops that you can't possibly wear a bra under, and, of course, sunglasses at night (I STILL don't get that one). I also spotted quite a few ladies dressed in white. Did I mention that it took place in February? Since I'm fairly certain they didn't move Easter to January, there were several people in violation of the Fashion Faux Pas Act of 1991.

And finally, yes, there were a lot of celebrities present, but only one I cared about: Bishop Don Magic Juan, everyone's favorite pimp. Some of you may remember him from the HBO documentary *Pimps Up, Hoes Down*. Others closer to me know him from my constant at-home screenings of the aforementioned special. Deviating from his usual signature color—green—Bishop was wearing a (no doubt custom-made) black-and-gold-checkered ensemble with matching shoes and pillbox hat. I was also relieved to see he had his signature jeweled goblet (yes, he brings his own cup to parties—one simply cannot drink from the glasses of commoners). I must say he lends a certain class to any affair, spitting game left and right. Keep spreading the word, Bishop (he's a SAVED pimp).

In other exciting sightings, the Television Actor was also in attendance at this star-studded event. We had been trading phone calls but hadn't been able to actually go out yet, because he had been in Philadelphia for two weeks filming a movie. I wasn't aware that he was even back in town. Hmm, time to call in the reinforcements. I scanned the room for Kevin and finally spotted him in a corner with his tongue in some Pseudo-Celebrity Bitch's ear. Great. He's useless, as usual. The Television Actor hadn't spotted me yet, but when he did, I was determined to be otherwise engaged. All of a sudden behind me I heard, "It's Bianca, right?"

I turned around and found myself face-to-face with the cutest thing I had seen since my last trip to Christian Dior (yesterday, and I hadn't intended to buy anything, but the road to hell is paved with good intentions). How could I have forgotten meeting THIS man? Hmm, a little on the thuggish-ruggish side (velour sweat suit and T-Mobile Sidekick), but he didn't sound like too much of a mush-mouth.

"I'm Franklin. We met at the VIBE party a couple of weeks ago," he continued.

"Oh, right. You're Rachel's friend."

Now I remembered! I had pushed him from my memory for a couple of reasons. For one, when Rachel introduced us, I got the distinct impression that she wasn't trying to have us make a love connection. Apparently, Rachel and Franklin went out a couple of times, but it didn't work out. So, instead of throwing him back into the dating pool, she was keeping him on her Injured Reserve List. I swear, she's such a Hater sometimes. Anyway, the second reason he was eliminated from competition was that I had trouble verifying his source of income.

"So, are you here alone?" he asked.

The Television Actor was turning my way. I guess Franklin would have to do.

"I came with a friend, but he seems to have found someone less opinionated to talk to," I joked, giving him my full attention. He laughed just as I caught the Television Actor's eye. I gave the Television Actor a friendly, yet cool smile and turned back to Franklin.

"So, did you enjoy the movie?" I asked.

"Yeah, it was good, but I've seen it a bunch of times before. I produced a couple of songs on the soundtrack."

"Oh, so you're a music producer?"

I could see the Television Actor across the room out of the corner of my eye, trying to decide whether or not to come over. He must have decided not to, because I saw him head toward the bathroom before I lost sight of him.

"Yeah, I guess you could say that."

Hmm, that sounded a little shady. But no matter.

"We should get together for a drink or dinner sometime," Franklin said.

I wasn't sold on Franklin, but he DID serve his purpose of making the Television Actor jealous. I guess it couldn't hurt to go out with him once.

"Sure, here's my card. Give me a call."

We parted and I searched the room for Kevin, but he was nowhere to be found. Good thing I was smart enough to drive my own car. I was on my way out the door when I felt someone catch my arm.

"I know you weren't going to leave without saying hello," the Television Actor said, trying to sound cool, but merely sounding pressed.

"Well, actually I was. Did you enjoy the movie?" I asked.

"I missed the screening. I came straight to the party from the airport."

So you say.

"When are we going to hang out, Bianca?" he continued.

"That's up to you," I said in my most mysterious voice as I continued out the door. "You have the number." Let's see if he's as smart as he is pretty.

• 13 •

Taylor

Back in the Saddle,
with a Dominatrix's Whip

Partying at Mellow was a good idea. I'd had an easy day at work—which meant leaving at nine p.m. instead of midnight—and I was able to hook up with Roxanne and Carolyn.

As soon as I stepped inside, I liked the scene, because I love any place with throngs of handsome men milling around. I strolled into the club, and saw Carolyn at the center of the bar. Luckily, she had a VIP booth for us. The perfect seat for Roxanne's exhibitionist ass—dead center, right in front of the dance floor, although it was still far too early for that. And that was also Carolyn's gift to me, I suppose. She must've gotten here pretty early to grab (and pay for) this prime piece of club real estate. And if Carolyn gets anywhere on time, much less early, you've got to thank your very lucky stars.

As I crossed the empty dance floor, I turned to check out the opposite side of the bar and nearly died. It wasn't Roxanne with this week's boy toy. It wasn't Vincent. It was Michael, the soon-to-be doctor that I had just broken up with when I met Vincent. I was a first-year at MWDC and Michael was still a senior in college. Maybe you think I should be embarrassed for "robbing the cradle," but if you think I give a damn, you've got the wrong woman. He was too fine to leave to the other shameless women of the world, especially since I saw him first, and he was so good in bed—once we made it there—that being a brazen hussy had been fruitful.

Since the breakup, we hadn't spoken much, but it was apparent that time had been good to Michael. And hopefully, tonight he'd be good to me. He was just the treat I needed. A hard day of work deserves a nice hard man at home, right? Oh sure, call me callous, or shallow, or even un-real. But sex is a basic human right, and I had learned a long time ago that men never stop doing what feels good in order to mourn the loss of you. I was still sad about Vincent, but I could save that for later when I wanted to reminisce about all that used to be, not now, when I was young, hot, single, and beautiful in New York City.

I nearly busted my ass run-walking over to Carolyn to tell her that the booty gods had indeed rained on me tonight and boy did I owe her a drink and some thanks. Turns out, she and Roxanne had already seen Michael and had ordered several drinks for us so I'd have something waiting for me when I arrived. Now that is friendship. Setting up the ass and making sure I had a drink as soon as I hit the door. I should get dumped more often. Damn straight. Enough with all of these foolish committed relation-ships. On to enjoying myself. I could mourn in the morning and moan at night. Fuck these tired, pitiful boys masquerading as men. The jackasses of the city are about to suffer, immeasurably. Hide your hearts and your wal-lets, fools, and just wait till you get wind of this bitch.

Michael glided into our booth and snapped me out of my visit to hatred's heartland. Knowing that I needed a bit of privacy to reconnect with Michael, the girls left under the pretense of getting yet another round of drinks. Michael gave me a high-voltage smile. It was so disarm-ing that I suddenly couldn't remember why things hadn't worked out in the first place.

"Taylor, you look fabulous, as always. What a fool I must have been to let you go."

"You always know what to say," I laughed. "And your timing is im-peccable, because it just so happens that I am currently single." His eyes lit up.

Carolyn's and Roxanne's timing was also perfect, because they appeared with a round of champagne for everyone. "To us being single and fantastic!" they crowed.

We all went through our ups and downs, with our relationships being no exception. And when one of us ended a relationship or got dumped, we took that opportunity to celebrate the fact that we had a new beginning ahead of us.

"Damn straight," I yelled over the now blasting music. Like a gentleman, Michael excused himself to buy more drinks.

"I can't believe that bastard Vincent," I hissed.

"Honey, we know you're still hurting," Carolyn empathized.

"It's all good, though—nothing like some new dick!" Roxanne exclaimed.

"Michael's coming, so stop daydreaming about long-lost loves when you've got just-found dick only ten feet away," Carolyn whispered, elbowing me.

"Damn, you're right."

"Guess what I got in the mail today?" Roxanne asked, looking quite pleased with herself.

"Don't tell me, the world's biggest dildo?" Carolyn questioned.

"I know you two haven't been home from work yet today, but I got the mailing for the Harvard/Yale game. It's the fiftieth anniversary of the official birth of the Ivy League, so they're planning a blowout Jubilee with ten thousand different events, and I think we *have* to go—not just to see our friends and because the streets will be running with liquor, but because you know that all the seriously connected alums will show for this." Roxanne knew that if the appeal of partying didn't work, the chance to schmooze with the Old Boys—and Girls—Network would make me book the quickest flight to Boston that I could find.

"So that's a very done deal and we'll be there," I said.

"Speak for yourself," Carolyn replied, less than enthused.

"I wonder if John Alden's going to drag his carcass back from Nairobi for this?" I asked.

As Roxanne said, "If he finds out that you're going to be there, you know he will," she shot me a look that said, "So you'd better not call him just to 'catch up on old times.' "

John and I met when he was a first-year at Harvard Med School and I was a freshman. We were together for seven years. And if I saw him again for an entire weekend, who knows what could happen.

Michael returned to the booth and winked at me. I eyed the front of his pants and imagined Vincent fucking some cheap slut with the tried-and-true techniques that I had taught him. I nearly choked as I thought about how some other bitch would profit from all my hard work. I had to get out of there, had to even up the game. I sent Michael out to fetch a cab.

"I think I'm going to leave now, it's been a hard day, and I need . . ."

"Something to bring some closure to your opening?" Carolyn interrupted with a smirk.

"I'm starting to feel unappreciated here, so I'll be . . ."

". . . making your exit so you can get entered," Roxanne finished sarcastically.

"Am I that . . ."

"Obvious? Why, oh my goodness, yes," Carolyn said.

"Do you think he knows?" I asked.

"Uh, *yes*," Roxanne replied.

"Good. Then I won't have to waste my time with a bunch of bullshit small talk when we get home because we both understand that it's on."

• • •

As I poured two glasses of champagne from a 1984 bottle of Cristal that Vincent and I had been saving for a special occasion, I thought wickedly that our breakup was special enough to celebrate. That and the fact that I'd get a chance to have some new dick after two years with the same man. I was toasting to a new me.

I headed for the bedroom, but Michael called me from the bathroom. I made a detour and nearly lost my breath. He was naked and beautiful and sprawled lazily in a steaming tub full of bubbles. I put the champagne on the toilet tank and stepped into the water, but before I could sit down, he turned me around and bent me over, planting a warm kiss on my ass and running his finger gently between the cheeks. Then he turned me around again and pushed me into a sitting position on the edge of the tub, where he eased my legs open and put his tongue to work on my clit. I poured his glass of champagne between my legs as he moved his hands up to my nipples. He remembered what I liked. And it is for this reason in particular that I know God is a woman—sometimes the Universe sends them back toilet-trained and eager to please.

Roxanne

The Girl and Ipanema

"You're crazy, you know that?" Ram asks.

"Why? I think selling home refinancing is a perfectly legitimate job," I respond.

"It is. But you don't know anything about finance. You don't have a home."

"True. But I'm reading *Mortgages for Dummies*, and it tells me everything I need to know."

"Roxy, I wish I had a million dollars so you could work only when you wanted to," he says, wrapping me in a hug.

"Thank you. Now give me a piggyback ride." I jump on his back and Ram barrels down Central Park West, artfully dodging the brigades of brown nannies, white babies, and lost tourists. He tells me he's my human rickshaw.

I cannot believe how well things are going with him. I mean, he's everything I could want in a man: attentive, creative, supportive, funny. We definitely have sexual chemistry, but we haven't actually had sex yet. This is deviant behavior for me. I wouldn't consider myself a slut, just very sexually liberated. But I'm trying to break the bad patterns I've set in the past. Meet a guy, think he's great, go out on a date with him, get stinking drunk and fuck him. If the sex is good, then we date intensely for several weeks, until his true nature comes out, my romantic visions of eternal love are dampened by the reality of us both being broke and a little crazy, and things fizzle out. If the sex is bad, I don't return any of his calls. We'll see how long I can last in the land of heavy petting.

• • •

Ram's right about the home mortgage job. I am horrible with numbers, my own finances are a sloppy mess, and I know nothing about home owner-ship. I met the guy who owns the business in a bar and he said I could set my own hours and make a lot of money on commission. After I learn everything about mortgage refinancing. Hmm. Maybe this isn't as easy as it sounds. However, after my less than stellar commercial performance, I am desperately in need of cash. But I am sick to death of office temp jobs, in which I pretend to care while bitter pear-shaped women in white Reeboks tell me that if I "make nice" I, too, can become a full-time recep-tionist with my very own cubicle, restroom key, and company password. No thanks.

Being a "working" actor in New York makes it very difficult to main-tain/sustain a steady survival job. You can't work nine-to-five gigs because you need days free to audition. It only works if your hours are flexible, if you can plan your work schedule around your auditions. But why would any boss want to hire someone who might not come in every day? Most nighttime jobs suck because you get home very late, and if you are work-ing at clubs or bars you go home smelling like an ashtray with very little voice left.

If you book a part in a play, you're rehearsing during the day, and you're too tired and consumed to take on additional employment. But many off-Broadway shows pay no more than $400 a week after taxes. How can you live on that in the most expensive city in the country? Unless you're independently wealthy, supremely connected, or marry rich, being a New York actor is a nonstop fucking hustle to make ends meet. Most of us live below the poverty line, unless we're fortunate enough to make big bucks with commercials, which clearly hasn't worked so well for me. I can't commit to a nine-to-five job because that is admitting defeat—I am not an office girl, I am an ACTOR. I've had my fill of standing up through an eight-hour restaurant shift, wearing uncomfortable cute shoes and seating snobbish magazine editors and overweight tourists from Duluth. I seem to have a new survival job every week, and they're all killing me. What stings even more is that Finlay Burrows, my college nemesis, is having a hell of a career. As soon as she graduated, she had a part in an NBC miniseries. She had a development deal at Fox for two years, but she's not any good. Her daddy happens to be a powerful Hollywood producer, so everyone kisses his ass by giving her jobs. She was always competing with me for parts in college, and I almost always beat her. It makes my skin crawl that I'm hustling for a job while she's popping up in the pages of US Weekly.

My phone rings. It's Sebastian, my uncle. "Roxy, baby, how goes it?"

"Not too great, Sebastian. I'm broke again," I inform him.

"There's more to life than money, Roxy," he tells me.

"Not when the light bill's due, student loans have kicked in, and American Express wants to send a collection agency after my ass."

"But how's the art going, man?" Sebastian asks.

"I don't have time to make art, I gotta make rent," I snap.

"But that's what you've been put on this planet to do: change the world through your art." He is so impractical.

"Sebastian, that would be great if I didn't have a million other things to do, like not go crazy," I retort.

"I understand all of that, but you can't forget your destiny, little girl. Why don't you come to Cali? You can learn to surf, and you can just mellow out." A thing to know about my mother's younger brother is that he's the black sheep of the family. He moved to La Jolla, California, long before it was hip and rich. He's a total free spirit, and while I admire his sense of freedom and total lack of concern about what the rest of the world thinks, his advice is not always practical for my life. He owns a surf shop and surfs every day. He's the exact opposite of my overachieving nuclear family, but he genuinely seems happy. Sebastian's always been completely supportive of my artistic endeavors, and I really appreciate that. His hippie dippie "follow your heart" stuff doesn't erase the fact that I still need a job, though, and that I shouldn't be asking my parents for any more money.

Just as I am seriously starting to consider seeking employment in the sex trade, I open my mail and find that I have the opportunity to change not only my fate but also my immediate surroundings. The Yale School of Drama has forwarded me information about the Gray Foundation, which offers travel grants for "artistic enrichment." If I write a proposal, I can get up to five thousand dollars to go someplace that will fuel me creatively. I guess Uncle Sebastian isn't wrong after all. I've been trying to write a one-woman show for the longest, but I'm at a creative dead end, and a trip abroad would be the perfect cure. Brazil is a dream destination for me, and not just because it has the largest Black population of any country outside of Africa—I can study capoeira, Afro-Brazilian dance, the spirituality of Candomblé, and the leisure of the beach. Good for my body, good for my mind, and who knows what inspiration I'll find? Brazil could end up being to me what Tahiti was to Gauguin, and I can't pass up that opportunity. Things are going well with Ram, and while that's a long time to be away from him, I know he'll understand; he's leaving for Somalia next week to get some footage for his latest endeavor; we artists must go wherever the muse sends us.

The application deadline is in six weeks, so I have to get on top of this. This opportunity would be a welcome change from my current New York drudgery. I'll take some language classes, and maybe it'll be so amazing that I'll never come back. Expatriates Rule! Next stop, dancing topless on a Carnival float!

SPRING

• 15 •

Bianca

The Guidelines

Okay, so that whole I'm-just-going-to-date-whoever's-cute thing isn't working out. A while ago I went on a "date" (and by date I mean I drove myself to the appointed location and paid for my own drinks) with Franklin, the "music producer" (and by "music producer" I mean someone who drives an expensive car with temporary license plates and types incessantly on his Sidekick) at a "club" (and by "club" I mean a sweaty, crowded warehouse with no valet parking that is crawling with part-time hookers and full-time date rapists) to see a "concert" (and by "concert" I mean an incoherent thug wearing a Fat Albert sweater flanked by two equally untalented friends on a stage screaming about stacking cheese and checking hoes). I finally reached my limit when a passing chickenhead slopped Alizé Red down the front of my new white on sale Michael Kors capris. (I mean, I got a coupon for ten percent off my next purchase if I use my Neiman's card, which is sort of the same thing.) When he walked me to my car, I thought my luck was changing, but that hope quickly fizzled when he pinned me up against the door and became, shall we say, amorous. Then he had the nerve to turn nasty when it became clear that the only thing he would be hitting that night was the streets—alone. I am a petite woman, but I have a very large can of pepper spray, and a couple of spritzes later, I was in my car—alone—and headed for the 405. Now he has a legitimate reason to wear his sunglasses at night, fucking scumbag.

So, after that disaster, I have reaffirmed what I have always known to be true: It is extremely important to have Guidelines for everything. Especially behavior. Especially male behavior. More specifically, women need Guidelines for *dealing* with male behavior. Forget The Rules. I have found that my Guidelines are much more practical and effective. However, they are not easy. You see, the real problem with men is that there are simply too many women out there just letting them act any kind of way with no consequences. Which is totally unacceptable. We as females need to agree on standards and maintain them. So, in an effort to reclaim some semblance of order in the never-ending parade of "Bianca, will you go out with me?" I have come up with some basics to help women who may find themselves in a similar casting dilemma.

THE GUIDELINES

1. There must be an actual date to properly begin a relationship and set the correct precedent. (If you meet him at his place on the first date, he ain't taking your ass nowhere. Ever.)

2. On this date, he must pay. No exceptions. If he doesn't have a lot of money, he needs to get creative, but I'm not even going to front and reach for my wallet during the initial six-week probationary period (most men who like to act foolish can't hide it for more than six weeks). Also, keep in mind that stingy with the tips = stingy with the gifts.

3. On this date, he needs to pick you up AND drop you off either in a suitable car (West Coast) or via a suitable means of public transportation (East Coast). Some notable exceptions:

   a. This is your first encounter with him and you don't want him to know where you live yet, *or*

   b. You are REALLY attracted to him and if he takes you

home, you might foolishly invite him in and blow the whole deal.

4. He must have an actual first and last name. (Maybe it's just L.A., but lately all the men I meet seem to be named "Poet" or "Michelob" or some other such nonsense.)

5. He needs to have an actual, verifiable job. Entrepreneurs are fine, but no entre-po-niggas. (However, independently wealthy is acceptable.)

6. He must have at least one pair of decent shoes that aren't sneakers. (Or else you're going to spend too much time shopping for him and not enough time picking out sparkly baubles for you.)

7. And finally, ladies, if you're not at least mildly attracted to him right off the bat, it's not going to work. (Life's too short to be wasting time "learning to love" someone who's not cute.)

It looks good on paper, doesn't it? I mean how hard can it be to simply give checks or minuses for these seven categories and make an intelligent decision about a man's suitability? If only it were that simple. I wrote The Guidelines, so trust me, I know the loopholes better than anyone.

• 16 •

Carolyn

The "Rules" Are Off

I am a feminist. I am a liberated, liberal, independent woman. I am adamantly pro-choice. I wrote my congressperson long before September 11 to urge him or her to stamp out the violently misogynist Taliban, and I contribute on a regular basis to funds for the victims of female circumcision. I despise Phyllis Schlafly and Ann Coulter. I am the daughter of one of the foremost women's studies scholars in the country, who has been married happily to my father for the past thirty-three years, and from the time I was in utero my parents have insisted that I, and all other women, can do anything we want, any time, anywhere, and that I can have it all and do it all just by Being Myself.

Myself is therefore somewhat confused as to why I am in the self-help section of Barnes & Noble in a trenchcoat and dark glasses, trying to choose between *How to Make Yourself Irresistible to the Opposite Sex* by Holly Dunwoody-Waterstone or *How to Shop for a Husband* by Betty Kate Hollingsworth. Every so often I cast a furtive glance over my shoulder, as if Angela Davis and Gloria Steinem are going to pop up behind me at any second and publicly revoke my membership in the Society of Women Who Really Should Know Better. However, my Future Old Maids of

America membership is about to be renewed again, and desperate times require desperate measures.

I swear that I do not want to settle down so that I can quit my job and start wearing an apron and a girdle and baking things in round pans while my husband works, manages all the money, pays all the bills, makes all the decisions, and fucks around on me with nubile liberated career women. I do not care to (unless, of course, it is part of a kinky sex game) meet my man at the door when he gets home from work, hand him a drink, give him a peck on the cheek, hand him his slippers, and tell him that the pot roast will be ready in just a sec and ask "How was your day, dear?" In truth, this urge to settle down is tied primarily to the need to have someone meet *me* with a drink after a shitty day, peck me on the cheek, tell me he ordered takeout, and tell me that there is just enough time for a quickie up against the fridge before the delivery guy shows up. I need someone to snuggle up with on rainy weekends, someone to get drunk with at a sidewalk cafe or on the beach on lazy summer Saturdays; someone to have inside jokes with, buy a Christmas tree with, and do absolutely nothing with. And, maybe someday, someone to have kids with. Being a feminist cannot possibly mean that you have to prefer being alone at all times to being with a man sometimes; almost everything, from housework to sex, is more fun with a partner.

Especially sex. Clearly.

I do not *need* a man, but I do *want* one, and although I want one for what I consider the "right" reasons, I still feel like a traitor to the feminist cause for saying so.

In the meantime, I am not sure that the resolution of this dilemma is on these shelves. All of these books seem to suggest some variation on the theme of Bullshit Your Way to the Altar. You must stifle your natural instincts and urges. You must pretend to be interested when you are not and pretend not to be interested when you are. You must drape a dropcloth over those parts of your personality that the prey might find off-putting. In short, you must lure or trick your victim into marrying you, then flip the script on him as soon as you get home from the honeymoon. Somehow I cannot imagine that any marriage resulting from this program would last longer than it takes to write the thank-you notes for the wedding gifts;

even if under normal circumstances he would have liked your true self just as much as or more than he likes the *Rules* You. I cannot see any man not being wary, distrustful, and resentful of a woman who pretended to be someone else for months, even years, for as long as it took to catch the brass (platinum, rather) ring. To ensure longevity, it seems to me that the charade would have to continue until he is too senile or too dead to notice the difference, and what woman wants to subject herself to the strain of maintaining a façade twenty-four hours a day for the rest of her life?

Furthermore, as I flip through another hundred pages, I see that the tricks in these books will not work on educated, affluent Black men because these guidelines, which were obviously written by and for White women to apply to White men, do not allow for the Brother Factor, i.e., the fact that there is one eligible brother for every twelve eligible Black women, so that every time one of us refuses to put up with a Black man's shit, there are eleven eager Desperadoes, as Bianca calls them, standing right behind us who will be more than happy to wallow in it and even go so far as to eat it if they believe that there is an engagement ring somewhere at the bottom of it.

I turn a page and see the chapter heading "Getting to Know Him But *Not* in the Biblical Sense." Here I am told that "If he calls you, do not return his call for a minimum of three days. You must not seem overly available or desperate; men enjoy the thrill of the chase." I sigh and shake my head, realizing that this is going to be like trying to make dinner for myself using one of my mother's "feeds six to eight" recipes. Three days adjusted by the Brother Factor becomes one and a half days, and if he is particularly delicious, it becomes three quarters of one day. If you do not return a Black man's call for three days, you should continue not to return that call for the rest of your life, because two days ago he called someone else and will be wining, dining, and/or bedding her when you are at home with nothing but your vibrator and the satisfaction of having followed The Rules.

I flip some more pages. Seven days between meetings. Pay zero percent of the tab for the first five dates. No more than three minutes on the phone. Wait eighty billion dates until sex. Applying the Brother Factor to this already-numbers-heavy approach is going to involve far too much math, and math was always my weakest subject. I will have to bring a calculator on every date and set alarms on my BlackBerry to let me know when it is okay to call, meet, or sleep with someone.

I am desperate, alone, and unhappy, but I am also lazy.

I leave without buying anything.

I will have a burrito instead.

• 17 •

Taylor

Malaise

Ever since Roxanne had first brought it up, I hadn't been able to stop thinking about the Jubilee. After my initial enthusiastic reaction, I'd started to wonder whether going was such a good idea. I hadn't planned on heading back for any alumni events until I had made my mark in the legal world, and I hadn't yet. Carolyn was busting her ass at Getty, but at least her ads were appearing on buses and billboards all over town. Bianca was always sending us e-mails about her tireless quest to improve ATN's shit-ass reputation, and her efforts were paying off—she was moving into an office on the same floor as the top-level ATN management. Roxanne had actually guest-starred on a couple of TV shows, so she'd been seen on national television and also had residuals to look forward to.

But me, I'm not seeing or feeling any tangible results of the backbreaking work I've been putting in, and I've been feeling out of sorts as a result. Not quit-my-job crazy or anything like that, just wondering whether working day in and day out to earn money for someone else is really the way to go. I never thought there would be a day when I would question my career choice. The problem is, I don't know what else to do. I like being a lawyer, but the hours are getting to me—maybe it's just that I'm not getting any younger and I have nothing to show for it. I mean, believe me, I have possessions to show for it, but what about a husband? Kids? UGH. This *can't* be me. It must be PMS.

I must admit, over the past three months, I've been wondering whether the seniority that I'm gaining at MWDC just means that I now have the ability to see what the world of business law really entails. As I continue to pound out interrogatories, briefs, document requests, direct and cross-examinations for depositions and trials, I'm starting to wonder whether I can, or want to, continue working so hard for a living. I wish I could blame that on PMS, but I don't think that's what this is.

I gazed out the window. The clouds were hanging high in a gorgeous blue sky. Real life was passing me by as I spent yet another evening in my office, and then it hit me: I'm stuck, I'm shackled to this desk with golden handcuffs. I couldn't blame anyone though, because those jokers had been fitted when I was a summer associate, and as my salary got higher and higher, they got tighter and tighter. When I first entered MWDC, I had every intention of working the eight years to trade up to the platinum model the partners wore. Now I realized that they were still just cuffs, and my, how snugly they fit.

I watched the time creep by. I shot a crumpled up paper wad through the basketball hoop stuck onto the backside of my door. I watched my phone lines light up. I saw the e-mail piling up in my inbox. I heard the mail carts sail past my closed door. I picked up a cigarette, then I put it down, remembering that I couldn't smoke in here anymore anyway, but also realizing that a cigarette wasn't going to make any difference. I needed to quit smoking. And I told myself this every day.

I looked over my matching mahogany desk, bookcases, and banker's lamps. My little tokens of appreciation from clients. Life was good. Just not good all the time.

From: twilliams@mwdc.com
To: carolyn.phillips@gettyassoc.com;
           TheRealRoxanne@hotmail.com
Subject: Cancellation

Sorry guys, I am not going to be able to make tonight's dinner. I just got stuck with a new assignment, as usual, which means, once again, no fun for me. I have to defend a client who's going to be deposed by the SEC tomorrow, and I have no idea what the case is about, who the witness is, or what the government might try to question him about, so I have to figure all of that out by 9 A.M. tomorrow, or else I can begin picking up a check at the welfare office instead of at the firm.

From: carolyn.phillips@gettyassoc.com
To: twilliams@mwdc.com; TheRealRoxanne@hotmail.com
Subject: It figures.

Based on my extensive, television-based knowledge of the law, may I suggest the following strategy: Object to everything on the grounds of crapulence and be sure to call for a bill of particulars as well as a bill for your dry cleaning. Hand the stenographer a hundred dollars when you get there and be sure to let the government attorneys know that there's more where that came from. Pop some pills during the deposition and show a lot of skin. Then maybe you'll get fired and you can hang out with us before your fiftieth birthday.

From: TheRealRoxanne@hotmail.com
To: twilliams@mwdc.com; carolyn.phillips@gettyassoc.com
Subject: AGAIN?

Dammit Taylor, when will we ever get to see you? I wanted to see you before I left for my play in Minneapolis. And when will you get some time to get out of the office to meet someone new? Not the boy toys, but someone with some substance? We'll have fun without you, but it won't be the same.

I had been looking forward to a night out with the girls all week. Now I'm just looking to see whether my windows will open so I can take a thirty-story header onto Maiden Lane.

Shit, they don't open; I guess I'm not the first person who tried that.

But even with all my grousing and moaning, I love my job. I like trying to do the impossible, although I bitch and moan the entire time I'm doing it. I never thought of myself as a workaholic, but Roxanne enlightened me one day by patiently explaining, after I told her that I was going to cut back from working seven days a week to six, that I had a serious mental problem. I asked Bianca and Carolyn what they thought and Bianca laughed so hard she couldn't even answer my question. Carolyn sent me an article from the *New York Times* about people who work impossible hours and how they're actually, scientifically, "hardier" people who thrive on stress and perform at their best under circumstances that most people try to avoid. Carolyn's ever the diplomat.

But the sad thing is, if, for some reason, I actually manage to make it home at seven or eight P.M., I look around my apartment and don't quite know what to do with myself. One week into a vacation, and I start getting bored. I start reflexively reaching for my BlackBerry and cell phone, almost willing them to start beeping, buzzing, and ringing.

Although I hate to admit it to myself, what really had me down was not my career at all, which was on solid ground. It was the thought of going to the Jubilee and seeing John. That made me so mad I could scream.

I'm mad. Really mad. And have been for a long time. And not just at John, but at all men for their refusal to be what women expect them to be. What we need them to be. What we know they can be. Mad at men for not living up to the ideals that we, as women, know they can. But, as my Vincent used to say, "You can't get mad at men for being men, we're different from you, and nothing's going to change that." Well, Lady Bic almost changed that when I tried to slit his throat, but I digress.

I'm all for people not understanding how to behave when they're young. You grow, you learn. It just seems that men never learn—even though they can, and they should. I'm angry at men for refusing to be realistic, for refusing to grow up and take care of their responsibilities, for refusing to take on responsibility, period. I'm angry and I'm tired of having to hide it. How come it's not okay to admit that you're mad at men? How come that's such a bad thing?

A woman can be attractive enough to take to bed, but not home to mom. Smart enough to school the kids, but too boring to inspire monogamy.

A great cook, but a lousy lay. Men sample all the goods until they finally find the one who comes as close to their "ideal wife" as possible. No matter that they've created Hell on earth for all of the women they picked up and discarded along the way.

Women, on the other hand, strive to make every date into a relationship and every relationship into their final salvation. Women never take things at face value. We always try to improve, try to work it out, try to wait for a better day—we never accept that perhaps, with some dates and some relationships, a better day is never going to come. Every man is not THE one for you. And that's no one's fault. That's life. Accept it. Have fun while you can and move on when it's time to move on. That's it. That's the answer.

My phone rang and snapped me from my random thoughts. It was David, an ass of a senior associate who liked to work me into the ground.

"Taylor, how's that outline moving along?"

"Just fine," I smiled into the phone before hanging up.

One day I am definitely going to kill that fool, but today, grousing isn't going to get the job done, or pay any of my bills. I couldn't head back to the Jubilee with no job at all to speak of! Back to work.

• 18 •

Roxanne

Mama's Always Onstage

As should be obvious by now, being a struggling/sometimes working actor in New York City involves very little glitz and glamour. Most of us can't support ourselves with our art and you probably won't make it to Broadway, particularly if you're a Black girl who doesn't sing and dance. So I have to make adjustments on my road to fame and fortune.

Much like being a migrant worker, being a theater performer often requires that I travel around the damn country doing plays that a very small percentage of the population sees. We call it Regional Theater. All major U.S. cities have these LORT (League of Resident Theaters) houses that run anything from Shakespeare to the latest Broadway or off-Broadway hit to Tennessee Williams revivals to August Wilson plays. It pays decently and allows you to be onstage with good actors and directors and perform for receptive audiences. Local papers review you, and if it's a prestigious house, *Variety* reviews the show as well. But succeeding regionally will not make you a star; it just looks nice on your résumé and adds some weeks to your health insurance. I wish that we were living in Elizabethan England or the days of Sophocles and Aeschylus, when actors were revered and everyone, from the queen to the chambermaid, attended the performance, when the art and skill of fine theatricality was appreciated and actors commanded a level of respect, unlike here in celebrity-obsessed twenty-first-century America. Actually, what am I talking about? There were no female actors back then, and you can be sure my Black ass would have been out working in the fields or in the dungeons. That's the difficulty with nostalgia about the "days of yore" for Black folks, this is the best we've had it. Because even back when we "were kings and queens," only a few of us were like Hatshepsut and Cleopatra; the rest of us were building fucking pyramids for them and running after their pain-in-the-ass cats. I often wonder why I endure such degradation and poverty, but the truth is, acting fuels me. It's the only thing I'm passionate about, but unfortunately, drama school doesn't prepare you for so many things—like motherfucking reality and the racist, sexist world we inhabit, and, more specifically, the elitist entertainment industry. There are no courses in Career Frustration.

I'm currently in Minneapolis (bringing its Black population to a total of five) at the Guthrie in a wonderful play called *The World Keeps Moving*. It's a change from last spring, when I was Viola in *Twelfth Night* at the Philadelphia Shakespeare Festival, and that's part of what I love about this profession so much: one day you're a Venetian woman who cross-dresses to win the love of a nobleman, the next you're the rebellious granddaughter in an incredible Black family. And this is not your typical "I burned the hog maws and please Lawd don't let my good Black man leave me on the gospel wings of this couch" play. There are no Negro spirituals in it. No one screams about the paucity of Black men. There are no actors from *Good Times*, stand-up comedians, flaming gay hairdresser stereotypes, or stripping midgets. It is not a Coon Show; we are not on the Chitlin Circuit. That being said, problems arise when our production designers and director, none of whom are Black, start trying to interpret what Black culture means to them and to the audience. Most of the Guthrie's season-ticket holders are White, but we still have to maintain authenticity in portraying our heritage on stage.

I shouldn't complain because this schedule has given me plenty of time to do other things. The beauty of regional theater is that you're usually in a city without a lot of distractions, and I'm only spending a month in Minneapolis since we rehearsed in New York. It's nice to be removed from the everyday minutiae of my life in New York. I wake up, work out, go for a walk, do some reading, and so on. It's nice not having bills, creditors, or terrorist threats looming over your head. Doing a play is such a great physical workout that I can eat whatever I want and still lose a few pounds. Acting makes me thin. Another good reason to keep doing it.

I do my vocal warm-ups and go to the theater. Focusing solely on my art is like being a monk. I like that, and it reminds me of why I got into this in the first place. It's all about the work. You can always come back to the work.

I've also been daydreaming about getting a Gray Foundation Grant. My director wrote me a stellar letter of recommendation, and my application was quite strong and thorough. I won't hear for a few months, but I went ahead and bought some language tapes to get me going and to occupy some of my downtime. The more research I do on Brazil, the more excited I am about the possibility of actually going there. What if it really happens? I definitely need a break because as much as I love acting, I'm having serious doubts about this show business thing. Unfortunately, none of my friends from NYC or Ram can come see the play because of their hectic schedules, but an old college buddy and former fellow actor, Juliette, lives in Minneapolis. She and her husband are coming to opening night, and we'll have a chance to catch up.

They are waiting for me in the lobby after the show.

"Roxanne, you were so wonderful!" Juliette exclaims. She gives me a big hug and introduces me to her husband. "This is Sam." Sam gives me an awkward handshake and says he's got to get home and finish some work. They exchange a quick peck and he leaves. Juliette and I head for the bar across the street from the theater.

Juliette catches me up on what's been going on in her life, and we have a good moment of Finlay Burrows bashing.

"I don't understand why Hollywood is going crazy over her. She's so bland," Juliette says.

"It's disgusting, isn't it? If you're blond and have the right daddy, the world is your fucking oyster," I spew.

Before I can get revved up, Juliette puts the brakes on. "Let's not have

Finlay ruin our evening, when you're clearly a million times more talented than she is. It may take a little while for you to get it off the ground, but sweetie, you've got staying power. You've got the 'it' factor."

I'd forgotten how much I like Juliette, and as she imbibes more cocktails, the boring truth about her life oozes out.

"Roxanne," she says, "don't ever get married. It's never as good as they say. I wish I had waited."

"But you and Sam seem so happy," I say, trying to get her back on a positive note.

"I envy you so much," she says, ignoring me and shaking her head. "You're doing what you love and you're so good at it. I always regret taking the safe road. All of those crazy plays we did in college? Best time of my life."

"Juliette, don't romanticize my life just because you're unhappy. I've got struggles just like everyone else."

"But you are your own person, and you don't have to answer to anyone's expectations." She stares moodily into her Amaretto sour.

"I think we should agree to disagree on the fabulousness of our respective lives," I say to break an awkward silence. "I'm sure after a hard day, it's a relief to come home to a man who adores you and puts you first. I hope to have that someday. And it's never too late to start acting again."

Juliette helped put things in perspective. It seems no twenty-something woman is completely happy with where she is in life. And it's usually only when you see yourself through someone else's eyes that you realize how fortunate you are. Maybe this struggling actor thing isn't so bad.

• 19 •

Carolyn

C-Cups and Cereal

Carter squints at a sketch for the new line from Paulina's of Half-Moon Street, the "Sexy Slimmers."

"Is that what women want, a 'come-hither and curvaceously feminine hourglass shape'?" he says curiously, reading the all-caps script beneath the graphic of the half-clad vixen reclining seductively on a chaise.

"Carter, the relevant question regarding that garment, in fact regarding that entire line of lingerie and clothing, is not whether we want it, but whether you do," I say, absentmindedly twirling a can of a new and "improved" sports drink, which apparently contains both clover and ground bull pancreas for energy and sounds filthy. I have to develop "a concept" for it by four P.M. So far, the only idea I have had is never drinking this drink, ever, ever, ever, which may save my life but will not generate any revenue.

"For example," I continue, "consider the thong: It provides neither comfort nor coverage, yet millions of women are stalking around each day with Paulina's 'Silken Strand' line riding straight up their asses because you guys apparently consider that sexy."

"Guilty as charged," Carter says, winking rakishly as he uses a compass to pick up an actual Sexy Slimmer, which is draped across the drafting table. "Is this one of Them?"

"Yep."

"Looks like a polyester sausage casing."

"Feels like one, too."

"You tried it?"

"Yep."

"So did it work?"

I look up at the Slimmer dangling from the point of Carter's compass and pause. The garment "works" by forcing the intestines into the chest cavity, and there needs to be a warning on the package stating that the resulting oxygen deprivation can result in a series of colorful hallucinations on the southbound number 5 train, including visions of Fat Albert and the Junkyard Gang, several Ewoks, and, last but never least, Morris Day and The Time, performing their hit single "Oak Tree."

"In a manner of speaking, yes," I say.

Carter glances doubtfully at the Slimmer and lets it slither back onto the table.

"Sorry, but if I'm undressing a woman and I get down to something that looks like this, I'm dressing her and sending her home," he says, looking over at me.

"This is obviously for those look-but-don't-touch occasions, dummy," I say around a mouthful of colored pencils. How am I supposed to push this combination of Gatorade and hoof-and-mouth? Shit. Shit. Shit.

"There's no such thing, baby, not when Carter Holden the Lovin' Machine's on the job," he says. "Nobody walks out of Carter's Den of Love untouched—nobody."

I choose to ignore his last comment and ask him if he has finished the Captain Sabatini Overproof Rum draft, which he has, and it looks quite good. I make some quick changes to it as Carter shakes his head.

"I still can't get over how in the hell you do that," he says. "You draw five lines and a Spanish fortress comes out of nowhere."

"It's genetic, I guess," I reply. "My dad's an architect. You think I'm good, you should see him. By the way, the breasts on the serving wench are out of control; would you mind bringing her down to a C-cup?"

"Her breasts are perfect," Carter protests, "and I guarantee that those breasts will make me, and a lot of other men all over the world, buy Captain Sabatini Overproof Rum. In bulk."

"First, there's no such thing as a pair of perfect breasts," I say, "and second, she looks like she's smuggling ostrich eggs."

"I beg to differ with you on both counts," he retorts haughtily. "Perfect breasts most certainly do exist in nature; I am a breast man, and I know." He stands back and squints at the sketch, frowning.

"Knockers aside," he says, ignoring my "Ew!" of protest, "something's off with her, proportionally," he says contemplatively. "Maybe it's the waist?"

"Sure, God forbid a woman who's supposed to be attractive doesn't have a wasp waist, right?" I snap before I can stop myself. Carter looks taken aback and I must admit that the amount of venom in my voice was uncalled for.

"No," he says carefully, "what I was getting at is that her waist looks a little low and maybe I should shorten her torso." He looks at me strangely out of the corner of his eye.

"Oh," I say, and step back to take a look at the sketch. He's right.

"Yeah, okay. Why don't you give it a try?"

There is an awkward silence as he selects a gum eraser and a charcoal pencil from the drafting table. I stare fixedly at the oversized vintage aperitif ads on the exposed brick wall.

"And in answer to your question," he says, still not looking at me as he begins to erase the serving wench's midsection, "no, I don't think that a wasp waist is a prerequisite for beauty. Although I might think differently if I were a wasp," he adds, lightening the mood somewhat.

"You sure look like a WASP to me," I say, trying for the laugh.

"Maybe so," he says evenly, "but you're the one with a little bit of a stinger on you." I blush, chastened.

"Sorry I snapped at you," I mutter. He nods.

"No worries. I've gotten worse. Not that I didn't deserve it."

Jesus, did he ever. Things have not always been this easy between Carter and myself; there was a time not too long ago when it seemed that he was intent on putting the "ass" in "assist" and had to be yoked up.

Things came to a head on the day of a key meeting with the Sweety Frooty Froots people. Sweety Frooty Froots is the most disgusting, unhealthy cereal on the planet, and ingestion results in a gastrointestinal holocaust for anyone over the age of thirteen, but America's dear sweet children cannot get enough of the garbage, so this account is one of my largest. Their marketing director harbors some kind of strange grudge against our firm and never misses even the smallest opportunity to take a chunk out of my ass, so when Carter informed me sheepishly fifteen minutes prior to the start of our meeting that he had brought the wrong portfolio, all I could do was stare at him in utter disbelief.

"The last thing I said to you before we left is 'Do you have the SFF portfolio?' And you said yes," I hissed.

He started to make an excuse but I cut him off.

"Not now," I said, holding up my hand. "Shut up and let me think." It was pouring outside, and it had taken us nearly forty minutes to get from Mercer and Prince to the client's midtown office, so returning to the office to get the right portfolio was not an option. So there I was, faced with the choice of looking stupid and unprofessional by presenting an entirely visual concept without any visuals or looking stupid and unprofessional by canceling the meeting right before it was supposed to start. Neither option was particularly attractive.

Shit.

I squeezed my eyes shut so tightly that I saw stars, and shortly a glimmer of an idea came to me.

"Go over there and tell the receptionist that we need an extra ten minutes," I said to Carter. He looked at me quizzically. "Go *now*," I added, shoving him in the shoulder. I reached into the portfolio case and pulled out the storyboard. I flipped it over. The back was brown, but it was clean except for the gray maker's mark in the center. Carter sat back down as I rummaged in my purse for an Artmarker.

"Turn around and lean forward," I said brusquely. Puzzled, he did. I slapped the front of the storyboard against his back (harder than necessary, I am ashamed to admit), looked up at the clock, marked off sixteen boxes freehand, and started drawing. Fifteen minutes later the receptionist beckoned to us.

"Ms. Grady's ready for you, Ms. Phillips."

I snapped the cap back onto the Artmarker and surveyed my hastily re-created work. It could have been worse.

Not much worse, but worse.

I took the board off Carter's back and handed it to him. He looked down at it and then looked at me.

"Let's go," I said shortly. "Showtime."

The first several minutes of the subsequent cab ride back to the office were silent and tense. The marketing director had given us sweet holy hell about the condition of the storyboard and had refused to be pacified by my explanation. She did, however, have to admit that, presentation aside, the idea was good, and she was mollified ever so slightly by my promise to have the real storyboard delivered to her by hand within the hour. There was still, however, a sixty-five percent chance that Jackson would receive a stank phone call from her, and I did not relish the prospect.

Carter turned to me.

"That was really something," he said. "I've never seen anything like it. You drew that freehand, from memory, and it looked as good as the original sto—"

"It looked like absolute shit, Carter," I said sharply, "and you and I need to get something straight right this minute, something we should have gotten straight the very first day."

"Carolyn, I'm really, really sor—"

"Shut up, okay, please?" I said, turning to face him. "This is not just my job, Carter. It is my career. I never wanted to do anything else, and I love what I do, and I take it very seriously. So if you don't feel exactly the same way about it, have your daddy get you a job somewhere else, because you can't work for me and you can't work for Getty. To recap: Get it together or get out. Is that clear?"

He was clearly very angry; there were red blotches on his cheeks and forehead and he was glaring at me.

"*Is that clear?*" I said again, glaring right back at him.

"Yes," he said finally, through clenched teeth, then turned away and looked out the window.

"Fantastic," I said.

The cab proceeded to advance ten feet in as many minutes. I had a throbbing headache and I desperately needed a burrito.

"My father didn't get me this job," Carter said tonelessly. "I applied for it because this is the kind of work I want to do, and I got the job. So don't think I didn't get here fair and square."

"Right," I said tiredly.

"I mean it," he said, turning to me. "My dad offered to set me up at J. Walter Thompson back home, but I said no because I wanted to come to Getty specifically."

"Why Getty instead of an old-school industry giant?" I said.

"Why did you go to Getty instead of Saatchi?"

"I figured it would be easier to get noticed and get somewhere at a smaller shop."

"Exactly," he said. "Plus, I liked the frog," he added.

"The which?" I said, taken aback.

"I always liked the frog," he repeated. "Frooto, the Sweety Frooty Froots Frog. *Your* frog. His hat is cool."

"Yeah, I guess so," I said, thinking of the little red Kangol-style hat, which I based on a sunhat that I treasured when I was eight.

"You ever try the cereal?" I said curiously.

He nodded. "Shitty Farty Farts would be a more accurate name," he said wryly.

I stared at him for a second, and then I began to laugh. Eventually he laughed, too, and when we finally stopped for breath, the silence in the cab was no longer tense.

· 20 ·

Taylor

Film School 101: The Horror Show

When it rains, it pours. Work was, well, work—I'm obviously a miracle worker since I not only managed to successfully defend the witness in front of the government, I even managed to convince them to leave our client out of its investigation! A little bit of sunshine on the work front now meant that I was able to turn my attention to the pitiful fact that I didn't have shit going on the social front.

My renewed "relationship" with Michael was going nowhere fast. I knew that while Michael was fun to have around, he wasn't someone who could ever truly be real relationship material. Playing around with him late at night after I'd left work was convenient for me, but now that I was in the seat of power, it was like I was in the relationship, but was also, at the same time, some omniscient third party who knew exactly how things would eventually end because I was going to make sure they ended that way.

While Michael was great, kind, sweet, and all of that good stuff, he was also far too young for me to consider in a serious fashion. He had five more years of medical school to finish as he was in a combined M.D./Ph.D. program. By the time he graduated from medical school, I'd be a partner at a law firm, maybe even MWDC, and he would be an intern. He'd still need seven more years of training before he could finally call himself a member of the medical profession. Who could wait that long? Why would anyone? I would have been practicing law for fifteen years before he even began his career. It seemed so ridiculous, but I could only look at him for his nighttime potential. In fact, I'm going to end this "relationship" tonight. As any devotee of horror flicks knows, everything that comes back from the dead has serious problems.

I wasn't just dreadfully bored, I was also getting lonely. Maybe it was time to expand my horizons and start dating White men. Why not?

My phone rang. It was my secretary, who wanted to let me know that I had a new voice mail message. I had decided to work from home today, since I felt half-dead from a cold I'd managed to catch a week ago from Carolyn, and I still hadn't shaken it. The senior partner on my largest billing case had kindly suggested that I stay at home to work on the brief (rather than rest!). I had taken the fax machine and printer out of the closet, and used the glass dining room table as a huge desk. I had retrieved my laptop from under my bed, propped it up on the "desk," and voila! I had my own home office. I dialed into the firm's voice mail system.

"Tay. It's John."

I paused the voice mail and put the phone down to catch my breath; my heart was beating a mile a minute and I felt faint. Only one person calls me "Tay." He's coming to the fucking reunion. I know it. Finally I got my shit back together and listened to the rest of the voice mail.

"Sweetheart, it is so good to hear your voice again, even if it's on your voice mail. It's been too long." God, that voice. I remembered how it used to be the first thing I heard in the morning and the last thing I'd hear at night. He went on to say that he was in town from Nairobi for a month, staying at the Mandarin Oriental, and really wanted to get together. Damn, damn, damn.

"So I really hope you'll call me, although I'll understand, but be disappointed, if you don't. Good-bye, sweetheart." John, John, John. I try not to let myself go there very often, because John made me melt. Made me whole. Made me believe in love. Made me believe in karma, star-crossed lovers, all that bullshit. Made my heart break. Made me an adult. It was through my relationship with John that I realized you didn't always get everything you wanted. He wasn't my first love by any stretch of the imagination, but he was my true love, and if things had worked out well, he would've been my last love. But things, as I said, don't always work out.

As much as I ranted about men, John was an incredible man. And everyone else recognized how incredible he was, so much that we were offered too many opportunities to be away from each other and not enough to be together. The girls rarely bring him up, since they know he's the closest thing to a soulmate I've ever met so far, or for that matter, probably ever will. That's why Roxanne gave me that dirty look that night, and that's why she was right. Calling off our impending marriage had been too hard, and I couldn't put myself through that again.

John proposed to me at his graduation from med school, in front of his entire med school class, who burst into frenzied applause and hooting when I accepted. We moved into an apartment on Bennett Street, as John had chosen to do his residency at Mass General to be closer to me. And for a moment, it was perfect. I loved him more than any man I'd ever been with before, and he loved me in that same frenetic, fragile, fantastic way. A love that was not yet hampered by bills, everyday life, or anything resembling reality. And while a part of me knew that it was so good it was almost too good, I was still young enough to convince myself that it was all worth believing in, even if one day the bubble might pop. And so I did believe, because I had never yet experienced that pop. Although I was losing Bianca, Carolyn, and Roxanne to a world beyond college, I was gaining a husband—what more could a woman want?

A happy ending. But, as my luck is my luck, I just got the ending.

The bomb dropped just as I finished my First Circuit clerkship. John and I had moved into our place in D.C. MWDC, my top-choice law firm, had a D.C. branch, and John was participating in a program at Johns Hopkins. We'd decided to start planning the marriage as soon as I finished studying for the New York bar. I had just gotten back from Albany, where I'd taken the New York bar, and I was on the treadmill. John bounded into the apartment at eight P.M. and I hopped off and asked him why he was home so early. Turns out that he'd been nominated for—and gotten—a position as Chief of Residency in Nairobi's Canton Clinic. He was extra thrilled because the clinic had a specialty division for children with facial abnormalities, and they'd promised him that twenty-five percent of his time would be spent in the specialty arm. As for me, there was a teaching position at the local university, and wasn't it just wonderful?

That was our first—and last—real fight. I explained (at the top of my lungs) that he had no fucking right to exclude me from his decision to apply for this position, knowing how deeply it would impact our lives if he won the job. His (flawed) argument was that he hadn't told me that he'd applied for the position because he didn't want to distract me during the bar. I told him in no uncertain terms (punctuated with airborne dishes) that I had no intention of packing off to Africa with him because (1) I had no interest in teaching and never had and (2) jumping off to Africa a month before I was supposed to start at MWDC made me look crazy and irresponsible because they (like I) should have at least been informed that there was something in the works. I also let him know that the alternative—marrying him and then sending him off to Africa alone—wasn't in the cards either. He asked me if I was saying that my career was more important than our relationship, and that's when things got Carrot Top ugly. The long and short of it is, we tried to patch things up but couldn't make a go of it; too many irrevocable things had been said that night, and too many irreconcilable issues had been raised by what he had done. Two months later, John was in Kenya and I was in New York.

At first I think we both believed that when he got back from Kenya, we might try again, but when twelve months became eighteen, then twenty-four, I moved on to Michael, then on to Vincent, thinking that it might do me good to stick to men who lived in Manhattan (needless to say, I was dead wrong). I saw John last year, when he was in the States for a conference, and he was more beautiful than ever, but I was good: I told him about Vincent, and I wouldn't let him steer the conversation toward "us," although he kept trying.

But here is he is again, and I'm scared by what I'm thinking. The smart thing to do is run, run, run screaming, because I'm in a weak place and liable to do something stupid as shit that I'll regret forever. But I miss him, and I'm lonely as fuck. Maybe the Universe is trying to tell me something by having the man I loved to a fault show up at my doorstep right after Vincent left me?

Time to call in the reinforcements and present the issue to the Inter-Galactic Counsel of Girlfriends. They'll know what I should do.

After I had connected the girls, I muttered, "Jackals never die, they multiply. John's back in town. He wants to see me."

"I thought you were sick." Roxanne wasn't going to make this easy for me, that was already apparent.

"So are you going to see him?" Bianca said.

"That's what I'm asking you," I said.

"I say run screaming," Carolyn said shortly. "Not that I need to remind you, but the man applied for a job in *Africa* and never said a word to you about it until after it was a done deal."

"And then the brother expected you to drop all the shit you'd busted your ass for and pop off to the jungle with him," Roxanne hissed.

"Nairobi's not 'the jungle,' " I said.

"Stop trying to sidestep the issue," Roxanne said.

"That happened almost four years ago," Bianca protested. "People change."

"Oh, what*ever*. You believe that if you want," Roxanne retorted. "But aside from the fact that they *don't* change, I don't think that a Recycle of that particular nature is what Taylor needs right now."

"Yes, I totally agree," Carolyn said. "New or none."

"I do have to co-sign on that," Bianca said. "Although I still think people can change."

They had a point. Vincent had hurt me so badly that I'd been prepared to kill him, so does it make sense to let the man who hurt me first and worst back into my life? I'm going to give the Supreme Jackal another opportunity to chew on my heart because I'm wallowing in self-pity and Booty Dementia? Have I lost my fucking mind? Fuck that, and fuck him.

And yet, although I wanted to delete the voice mail, I just couldn't.

• 21 •

Roxanne

Boy, You Turned Me Out

Ram is at my apartment making dinner when I get an unexpected phone call.

"Hello?"

"Roxanne Newman, please."

"This is she," I say, then put my hand over the receiver long enough to say "Just egg whites" just as Ram cracks eggs into a bowl for a spinach quiche. He groans. I know he's thinking about last week, when it was three meals a day of tofu squares, washed down with hot lemon water and celery juice, and the two weeks last month I spent on the Cabbage Soup Diet, which is based on the notion that cabbage soup tastes like shit, so if that's all you can eat, you'll eat nothing at all. I didn't care; I had two auditions that following week and needed to drop a quick five pounds.

"Miss Newman, this is Paul Harper from the Gray Foundation. I called to let you know that you are a Gray Fellowship Finalist."

"Oh my God, that's fantastic!" I mouth to Ram that I'm a finalist. He starts doing a little jig.

"We will be making a decision soon, and I'm not supposed to tell you this, but your proposal is ranked very highly. We will be in touch."

"Well, thank you so much for calling." I hang up.

"Congrats, baby! You're so gonna get it," Ram says assuredly.

"Well, let's not jinx it by talking about it too much." We do a victory dance around the apartment. He's so fucking sexy. I'm really falling for him, and we still haven't had sex yet. I want to, but now he's the one saying we should wait. I guess we're waiting for my pussy to overtake my body and swallow him whole, which could happen at any moment. However, the anticipation is deliciously excruciating.

• • •

I'm now doing an off-off-Broadway show, making about seventy-five cents a week, and for the past three nights I've been out drinking at a local dive bar with actors from the show. We've played darts and challenged each other to tequila shots. I think the guys were all shocked at my ability to knock 'em back and keep going. This is a very un–New York environment, what with the country music, the dartboard, and the cheap drinks. It's very outback, Texas, masculine, and sexy. Tonight, however, Ram is joining us, and I decide that I won't get drunk like I've been every night this week, that I will be the perfect picture of genteel grace and ladylike manners. I plan to keep my legs shut and my filthy comments to myself. But Ram starts buying rounds of shots, and I can't be rude and pass up free drinks.

"Did you know that if I rub certain parts of your foot, it stimulates other parts of your body?" Ram asks me, his hand aggressively rubbing my feet.

"Like my pussy, perhaps? Because she sure is throbbing," I respond. This feels excellent!

Ram says, "Hey, it's body shot time!"

"You have to be kidding me. We're not in college anymore. I'm not doing body shots," I protest.

Several body shots later, Ram and I are involved in heavy petting and my initial apprehension and intended teetotaler status have gone the way of the dinosaur. Ram's friend Victor asks, "When are you guys gonna have sex?"

"We have to get to know each other better," Ram says indignantly.

"We've been sticking our tongues down each other's throats and having phone sex for several months. How long does a horny bitch have to wait?" I protest. Drunk Roxanne is taking over.

We are making out heavily in the back of the bar. He runs his hands through my hair, which I usually don't allow, and starts whispering all kinds of dirty things in my ear about what he wants to do to me. "I just want to tear your clothes off and put my mouth on your breasts so I can caress your nipple oh-so-gently with my tongue. Then I'll take your other nipple between my teeth and bite it—just a little, just enough to hear you moan. Then I'm going to get my tongue in your pussy and make it so wet. I want you to sit on my face and drip all of your juices all over me so I can lick them up. I want to stick my tongue in your sweet ass until you're begging me to stop. Then I'll start eating your pussy again . . . you like being eaten, don't you?"

"Oh, God, yes," I say as he surreptitiously eases his finger inside my jeans and starts stroking my clit with his index finger while he sticks his middle finger inside me. He pulls them out and sucks both fingers.

"You taste so fucking good." Oh, my God, I'm dying.

Another very drunk ten minutes go by, at the conclusion of which I announce to the entire bar, "I'm taking him home to fuck him right now." And with that we take the long train ride back to his place. On the subway, he has his hand down the back of my pants as if everything is normal, his finger riding up and down the crack of my ass.

Ram grabs the back of my neck, like you would a cat, as we walk from the 79th Street station to his gorgeous apartment on Riverside Drive, a gift from his parents a few years ago. We can't keep our hands off each other in the elevator ride up to the seventeenth floor. His tongue is in my ear, my hands are on his dick—which is *so* fucking big, by the way—and I can't keep my mouth off him. He smells delicious. I lick his face.

"Fuck, I can't find my keys," he says, searching his pockets frantically.

"Allow me to help you," as I lower my mouth to his crotch, placing my right hand in his pocket, unzipping him with my left, ready to take him in my mouth, fishing the keys from the recesses of his pants. "Tada, here they are, but I've got to blow you now."

"No, no, no," as he stops me. "I have to taste you first," he says, pushing me inside the apartment, quickly pulling down my pants and lowering me to the ground. "I've been dreaming about this all day. I can't wait to taste your pussy." He forcefully licks my clit as he pushes his fingers in and out of me. I try to move my hands down to his dick, but he tosses them away. "No way. I want to lick you until you're exhausted," he says, pinning my hands above my head and holding them there with a very strong left arm grip. He plunges his tongue in and out of me until I think I will explode and flips me over, just as he promised. "Oh, your ass is so fucking sweet," he moans as he devours it. "Oh, your ass tastes so good. Oh Roxanne, Roxanne, my dick is so hard." After coming four or five times I scramble for his dick, finally taking it all in my mouth, loving the taste, the smell, the feel of it. He's so big that I almost gag several times, but I love giving head. I want to make him come, but he insists that the longer it takes, the better.

We take a break. I go into the kitchen searching for water. As I open the refrigerator, he bends me over again, smacking my ass until it is red. Oh, to be manhandled. I may talk a lot of shit, but at the end of the day, I want to be pawed, groped, and fucked up against a wall. I take some ice cubes out of the freezer, put them in my mouth and suck his dick some more.

"Oh, so you wanna get freaky, huh?" he says and carries me into the bedroom, biting my nipples with each step. He reaches for a condom in his bedside table, slips it on, and looks at me. I am lying on my back, my eyes rolling inside my head, panting.

"I really need you to fuck me right now," I gasp.

"Do you want me inside you?" he asks.

"Yes, right now."

"Are you sure?" he teases again. I grab his hips and shove him inside of me.

"Oh fuck, oh fuck, oh fuck!" I scream.

"Do you like that, Roxanne?"

"Oh, *fuck!*"

"You like it when I fuck you?"

"Oh, God, yes, I love it! Let me on top!" I beg.

I ride him for a while. It is as if a demon has been unleashed inside me.

I haven't been fucked this well in a long, long time, if ever. As I ride him, we are looking directly into each other's eyes with such concentration, such passion. The connection is intense. He then gets behind me, my favorite position, and just fucks me and fucks me and fucks me. Oh fuu-uck! He gets on top of me missionary style, and as I wrap my legs around his neck, he does the most amazing thing. He makes his dick jump. Yes, jump. He starts each stroke slowly, as if he's going to stop and then BAM! Jumping dick! Slow, slow, slow, slow, BAM! Dick jump! He is hitting the highest point in my vaginal canal. As if he jumps any higher my-guts-would-be-pushed-up-in-my-throat-type stroking. I come about seventy billion times, getting wetter and wetter.

"Your pussy is so juicy. You keep making my dick harder and harder." Bam! Bam! Oh fuck! Jump! Jump!

I can barely breathe. He looks me in the eye with that super-focused "I'm going to make you fall in love with me or at least get whipped on my dick so that you can't go anywhere else and will never be able to fuck anyone else without thinking of me" stare. That round ends with about a trillion orgasms. The tequila has been sweated out of my system as he proceeds to eat my pussy again.

He pauses for a moment, looks up at me from between my legs, and asks me, "Well?"

"Amazing," I gasp. And was it. No question: I am definitely in love.

Bianca

The Enforcer

I love Sunday mornings. My Sunday ritual is sleeping in and, when I do wake up, making myself a nice Florentine omelet, and eating it out on the patio. This past Sunday I had just finished my omelet and was settling in on my couch to watch a stalker marathon on the Lifetime Movie Network when my doorbell rang. I was still in my pajamas, so imagine my relief when I realized it was just my neighbor, Selma. She looked terrible, like she'd been crying for hours. I invited her in, made her an omelet, and before I knew it, her whole sad story came tumbling out. Apparently, Marc, Selma's boyfriend of three years, wanted some "space." We all know that's just code for he wants to "fuck other women," but given Selma's present condition, I refrained from pointing that out. What should she do? Act like she was okay with that? Because she most certainly wasn't. Should she kick him to the curb? But that would be like throwing out a pair of Ferragamo loafers because they have a scratch—it's difficult to part with things you've invested so much in.

So I gave her a little pep talk and told her that she should do what she really *wants* to do, even if she thinks others would disagree. I told her, as long as she can still look herself in the mirror, she's made the right decision. Selma nodded through her tears and vowed that she would just wait out Marc's foolishness. Once he realized how much he missed her, he would come back, but Selma would make him sweat a little to make sure he didn't pull this bullshit again. I told her they always come back. It's just a matter of whether you still want him when he does.

Pretty soon, a dry-eyed Selma was pacing my living room like a tiger, ranting and raving about how she was going to make Marc lick her boots before she would even *consider* taking him back. She finally left, looking downright fierce. I was proud of her (and a little scared). Unfortunately, the next morning I spotted Marc leaving Selma's apartment with the jaunty swagger that says "I've got her right where I want her."

Selma's situation is all too common and is really indicative of a much larger problem. To me, the Guidelines are clear, but different women have different ideas of how the Guidelines should be interpreted. You see, there are three basic types of women out there: The Desperadoes, The Exceptioners, and The Enforcers.

Let me start by saying how much I loathe Desperadoes. They are fucking it up for everybody! These pitiful creatures scurry around without an ounce of sass and delude themselves into believing that sacrificing their own desires and needs will land them the man of their dreams. They have no idea that every time they forgive a man for the unforgivable, they are only making it more difficult for the rest of us to elicit any type of cooperation. Selma, unfortunately, is a classic Desperado. I know that on some level, we must have pity on these women. Surely many of them suffered terrible childhood tragedies that have resulted in low self-esteem. However, I am beginning to think that many Desperadoes are just lazy. Or stupid. Or both. They all need to be locked in a room with a therapist to work that shit out. The worst part is, many Desperadoes try to pass for Exceptioners (they couldn't *begin* to pass for Enforcers). Don't let them fool you. If she's got his dry cleaning in her car during the initial six-week probationary period, buy her an (unstylish) T-shirt with a big red "D" on the front and tell her the D stands for "Dazzling." She'll believe you.

We all know an Exceptioner (some of us need not look farther than the mirror). Their ranks are the largest. These are the women who will put up with a lot of nonsense, but they do have their limits. Unfortunately, this ambiguity makes imposing standards upon men very difficult. Either follow the Guidelines or don't. Just don't go around changing your mind every five minutes. Here's a typical example of Exceptioner behavior: After dating Buster #237 for five weeks, The Exceptioner suggests that they meet for dinner at the hot new sushi place. They have a lovely evening, and since she suggested the place, the Buster makes it clear that he expects her to pay. Unacceptable. The Exceptioner will reason in her mind that five weeks is close enough to the six-week probationary cut-off to start going dutch, but I beg to differ. You can't go around following some rules and not others. It confuses them, and Lord knows men are already confused enough as it is.

The Enforcers are what we should all strive to be. They go into a relationship with an open, honest attitude. They give every man a clean slate and don't punish one man for the sins of another. They are smart, educated, successful, and "well put together." They want to be treated like the ladies they were bred to be, but not patronized. The Enforcers demand respect because they know they are "marriage material." They know what they want in a man (a terrible burden, by the way) and they don't settle for less. For example, if a potential suitor were to call up and ask an Enforcer to meet him at his house and then further ask her not to forget to pick up a six-pack on her way during the probationary period, she would laugh at this ridiculous request right before she hung up in his face. She feels no remorse for this—he was clearly in violation of Guideline number ONE (there must be an actual date) and doesn't deserve to spend even one minute in her fascinating company. It's on to the next candidate without a backward glance. Occasionally, an Enforcer may give a candidate a second chance, but this rarity is generally only reserved for multimillionaires (Enforcers like diamonds). Enforcement, though satisfying, can be a lonely life. Their numbers are few and they must constantly fight to keep their ranks strong (defection to the enemy camp of The Exceptioners is common). However, I believe it is The Enforcers who have the best chance at building a solid relationship. An Enforcer compromises, but she does not settle.

I have definitely been enforcing the rules with the Television Actor, but I think I may be doing my job a little too well: I haven't heard from him in days. Unfortunately, the more of a catch a man is, the more *elusive* he is. It's so annoying. Now I am definitely not one of those women who wants a man all up under her all the time. I have a life and a full-time job. I don't have time to worry about where a man is when he's not with me. But lately, I can't seem to pin the Television Actor down on anything. It's always a call at the last minute to see if I want to go to some fabulous party, a restaurant opening, a premiere. Well, no more. I don't care if it's New Year's Eve at Oprah's house and every guest gets a Cartier tank watch and an hour in the sack with the celebrity of their choice; if he doesn't give me proper notice, he gets a no. Period. There ain't shit in this town I can't hustle my way into on my own, and if he weren't so fine, I'd be just about through with him. It's hard work training men. No wonder my mother is so tired; I'm sure it's taken her thirty years to whip my father in shape. Why can't men stop being so slippery and just admit when they like you instead of putting you through all these changes?

Oh hell, my cell phone's ringing. Hmmm. Speak of the devil.

"Hello?" (I always pretend not to know it's him even though I haven't answered my phone without looking at the Caller ID since 1992.)

"Hey, B. What's up?"

"Not too much," I say, trying to sound bored, yet busy.

"What are you doing later?" Here we go again with the last-minute bullshit.

"Later today?" I ask, feigning innocence. I don't care if it's a week in the Loire Valley in my own chateau with a private chef and my own personal grape stomper; I'm saying I'm busy. He needs to learn.

"Yeah, I wanted to see if you want to take a drive down to Geoffrey's in Malibu for lunch?"

OF COURSE I WANT TO GO TO GEOFFREY'S IN MALIBU AND SIP CHAMPAGNE COCKTAILS BY THE OCEAN WITH THE BEAUTIFUL PEOPLE, YOU ASSHOLE!

"Sure," I respond casually. As if the thought of a romantic drive down PCH in his Mercedes convertible and lunch at one of the most fabulous places in L.A. wasn't slightly more exciting than watching infomercials and eating microwave popcorn.

"Cool. I'll pick you up in an hour."

"Okay. Bye."

I know, I know. I was supposed to put my foot down, but he didn't play fair. He backed me into a corner. I had no choice. It's Geoffrey's! In Malibu! If I don't go, then my new Pucci headscarf will go to waste. There is *no* excuse for wasting good fashion, people, and no excuse for not being seen at Geoffrey's on a Saturday in the company of someone who is well on his way to becoming A-List. I've got this under control.

• 23 •

Carolyn

Pouting Flygirl, Hidden Drag Queen

"So tonight's the night you guys finally meet Ram Banana, the latest entry in Roxanne's Cotillion of the Damned?" Bianca says, adding, "I hate that I can't be there. Really."

"Carolyn and I are supposed to be meeting the two of them at Waterfall tonight around eight," Taylor says, and she does not sound any more hopeful than I feel.

"Maybe this one won't be insane, underemployed, or devious," I say cautiously.

"He'll probably be all three," Bianca says brightly. "But pick your poison, ladies: an insane, underemployed, devious straight man, or a fine, intelligent, partnership-track closet case? Because if you're down with the Down Low, I'm sure Thomas is still out there somewhere, looking for a beard—"

I groan at the mere memory. Roxanne has founded many a figurative colony in many a figurative malaria-ridden swamp, but Thomas Oates was quicksand with a Tumi briefcase and perfectly shined shoes, and he was The Worst Ever. Thomas was six feet three inches tall, with liquid brown eyes, full lips, and a Denzel smile—a broad-shouldered, narrow-hipped Adonis, soft-spoken but articulate and polite, well-groomed, and clad in spotless Cerruti. When we were introduced to him, Taylor and I exchanged impressed, somewhat surprised glances, and nodded approvingly. We complimented Roxanne on her good luck and good taste, declared that Thomas was a definite improvement over her previous endeavors—including Panache, the rapper/singer/actor/model/dancer/coke mule, and Tyrone Terrell Whitman Jr., the Republican—and toasted their future. We laughed at Thomas's genuinely funny jokes, he paid for our drinks, and a little pit of something that was not exactly envy began to well up in my stomach because it really did appear that Roxanne had found The One. I was truly happy for her, but I wished that for just a second I could have been in her shoes, sitting next to a handsome, accomplished Black man who called me his and considered himself mine.

At about ten P.M., Thomas's cell phone rang. He said hello, then told the caller to wait and put his hand over the mouthpiece.

"Business, Roxy," he said. "I'm just going to take it outside." Roxanne looked after him affectionately, then went to retrieve her coat from the coat check. Taylor and I followed suit.

"I'm going to head downtown," Thomas said, coming back inside.

"Oh, I'm headed that way, too," I said. "Want to share a cab?" He hesitated for half a second, but Roxanne nodded.

"You guys should share. Taylor and I can share going uptown." She turned her face up to him for a kiss, and he smiled down at her and gave her one. He hailed a cab for them, then one for himself and me, and we headed downtown. He took another call, and I played Brick breaker on my BlackBerry to keep myself occupied.

Just before the intersection of Fifth Avenue and 21st Street, Thomas told the driver to stop. He smiled a good-bye to me, got out, and started walking east. The cab pulled up to the stoplight, which turned green. Out of idle curiosity, I turned around as we pulled off and saw Thomas sprinting back across the street in the opposite direction.

What the hell?

The urge to play Nancy Drew overwhelmed me and I told the driver to stop, then got out and strode rapidly up Fifth until I reached Twenty-first and spotted Thomas making his way to where a long line of men snakes down the street.

He was headed toward Tiger.

It was Wednesday night.

Wednesday night at Tiger was, always has been, and always shall be, Gay Night.

Not wanting to make any premature judgments, I slunk along the street until I found a recessed doorway where I had a good view of the line. Thomas was walking up the length of the line, craning his neck in search of someone, when a handsome Morris Chestnut type leaned out of the line and grabbed his hand. Thomas turned and a look of recognition passed over his face, followed by a wide smile. Followed by a passionate kiss, followed by a long, electric glance.

Shit.

I picked up my cell phone and called Taylor. She did not answer. I left her a frantic voice mail, hesitated, and dialed Roxanne. This was a serious issue, and it was far better if she saw what I had seen with her own eyes and drew her own conclusions. My personal conclusion was that this du-plicitous douche bag was auditioning for the role of "Basil" in the For Real Repertory Theater Company production of *Invisible Life*; there might have been other logical explanations, but I was unable to think of any. Roxanne answered on the fifth ring, and luckily she was still below the Park, so it was not as hard to convince her to meet me at Tiger as it might normally have been, although I did tell her that it was an emergency. When she arrived, looking absolutely bewildered but asking no questions, we joined the line. We ignored the snickers of the assorted men around us, who probably thought we were the world's largest and smallest drag queens. Once inside, we waded through the fake fog to a throbbing techno beat until we made our way downstairs, where I finally spotted Thomas and his friend in a clinch on the dance floor. I tapped Roxanne's shoulder and pointed.

She stood silently, her throat working, her eyes enormous, as the rela-tionship skidded to a screeching halt inside her head. Thomas apparently felt her eyes on him, as he turned and spotted both of us standing woodenly at the edge of the dance floor. Abruptly he stopped dancing. Roxanne stalked up to him, stared squarely into his eyes, then wound up and slapped his face so hard it echoed.

"Bitch," she said in a low, strained voice. He did not move. She turned on her heel and stormed past me. I could see that her eyes were dry. I followed her up the stairs and out of the club, and she did not cry until we got into the cab.

• 24 •

Taylor

Malaise, Part II (The Remix)

So I did it. I called John. We decided to meet for a very late dinner at my place. I thought really hard about cooking myself, but I came back to my senses when I looked at the clock and realized that it was already four P.M. and that just wasn't happening. I managed to sneak out of work at eight P.M., made a last-minute hairdresser's appointment, got a manicure and pedicure in record time, and was home in enough time to make the pre-cooked lobster look like I'd just pulled it out of the pot. Thanks to Balducci's, a woman really could do it all.

I didn't have any expectations that this would work out, or that we would have anything other than a night that was owed to me by the gods. Each moment would be filled with the dread, longing, and excitement that only occur simultaneously when you know your time is short. John and I would never be able to be in the same place, on the same page, at the same time, but we could snatch one night back from our past. And then, after that, we'd both have to move on.

After we called off the engagement, we spoke every day. And then every other day. And then once a week. And then once a month. And then not at all. As the months turned into a year, then into a year and a half, John didn't come back. Neither one of us wanted to say that it was over, so we didn't, but we both understood that it was, although I think we also both secretly hoped that neither of us would really move on and that one day it would all work out, like magic.

I haven't spoken to John in a year. And now he's back, just as if he never left. And while I'd normally rant and scream about how "this is so just like a man to waltz his happy ass right back into a woman's life with no thought for what the fuck she wants," I was too delighted even to hear my own bitching.

When the doorbell rang, no one could have braced me for what John looked like. Amazing. He seemed taller than six feet two. His skin was as dark, even, and smooth as ever, and he had gained muscles where I didn't think anyone could. I must admit, I looked fabulous, too. I was damn sure not going to look one ounce less than stunning.

We ate. We talked. We ate dessert. We talked some more. And then, we had a few drinks. Just as I thought the night was beginning, with no further ado, John left to go back to his hotel room. I stood facing the closed door for five minutes. I couldn't believe it. Did he think I went to all this trouble for that? It was great to see and talk to him and all, but a picture and an e-mail could've solved that problem.

After my shock wore off, I ran to pick up the phone to call the girls, but the doorbell rang again. I knew he couldn't have been so stupid. And when I answered, I saw the huge bouquet of flowers. With a note that asked me to come to the lobby. What nonsense is this? I ran downstairs and saw the hired limo with John standing next to it. So he did have something up his sleeve after all.

"Your mother called to tell me that you and Vincent had finally broken up. I didn't know whether this was the best thing to do, but she said I should try. My flight leaves in a week, and I want you to come with me. I can't promise when I'll leave Nairobi, but I *will* leave, but until then, I want you by my side. I can't move forward unless I give us one more try," he said, taking my hand and smiling. I didn't smile back.

"What do you mean you can't move forward? That sounds to me like you've found someone else, and want to see whether you should move forward with her, or come back to me." I was not pleased.

"I have. But she isn't you. And she won't ever be."

"I'm glad you said it before I did. Should I be flattered because I'm first pick, although off in the wings, the first-runner-up awaits?"

"It's not like that and you know it. At least I had the decency to tell you."

"Next time you think about doing me a favor, cancel the plan."

"Taylor, I didn't mean for it to sound that way."

"But it did."

"So what, you'll pass up on this because I didn't phrase it right? You had Vincent, you can't expect that I didn't do the same."

"You're right. I can't. I can expect to be first, with a first-runner-up on the sideline. I can expect to be second to your career and in return, you can expect to be second to mine. We don't speak for a year, and then you walk back into my life and want to move me to Africa, and you don't seem to understand that I can't go now any more than I could then, and for the same reasons, only now they're even stronger. I want this to work, I always have. But I want this to be right. I don't want either of us to have to make such large sacrifices for the other that we start to resent one another and lose sight of what we were all about in the first place. I don't want one of us to be unhappy to make the other one happy; I don't want this to be a zero sum game. If that happens, we aren't *in* a relationship, we're just trying to stay in one."

"Taylor, the electron is always going to move if you look at it."

"Thank you, Mr. Heisenberg. What I'm saying is that either it wasn't meant to be, or we don't know how to do it yet."

"Don't you want to make me happy, make our families happy?"

"I wish I could."

"So you're saying you won't."

"I'm saying I *can't*."

As the limo pulled away from the curb, I hoped I would never see John again. It was too bittersweet to be right and to lose anyway. It took all of my strength not to run after the car, and all of my will to stay the hell away from the Mandarin Oriental for the rest of that week. I still don't know whether I did the right thing. God, I hate it when old adages are right: be careful what you wish for. But I'd wanted to control the situation, and take the bull by the horns, and I had. Now maybe if I click my heels together three times, I'll get no bull at all.

• 25 •

Bianca

Cut!

Despite the lobster salads and dim sum brunches, the nights spent on the red carpet and in VIP rooms (J Lo asked me what color Chanel Glossimer I was wearing—Unity, of course—in the bathroom at Dolce, which officially makes me a badass), and the geeked feeling I got from seeing my beau on billboards all the time, I've come to terms with the fact that the Television Actor refuses to act right. I know I should have kicked him to the curb ages ago, but dating him was fun—that is, when I actually saw him, or rather, when I actually saw him when he said I'd see him. He was always "on the set" or "going to an audition." The final straw was when he stood me up last night. Again. He didn't show, and when I finally got him on his cell phone, he said taping ran late and he didn't have a chance to call me. I know he's busy, but a phone call takes three seconds, so that's pretty much unacceptable. And, as I said, it was hardly the first time. Normally he'd've been pink-slipped by now, but the thought of cutting off one of the few human ties I have out here in LaLa Land and starting all over solo was just too depressing. There was only one way to find out if the situation called for a more intense training regimen, or if it was time to cut my losses and bounce. I picked up the phone and dialed Carolyn, who conferenced in Taylor and Roxanne.

"Fuck him," Taylor said, sounding rushed. "Nobody has time for that bullshit. Least of all you. How are you going to take over Hollywood if you're waiting around for motherfuckers to get with the program?"

"Tell him to beat it!" said Roxanne.

"But he's really fine," I whined. "You've seen him, you know how good this man looks."

"If he were a Royal who looked like Benjamin Bratt," said Taylor, "and he were disrespecting you, he would still need to get the boot. And he's *not* a Royal, and he *doesn't* look like Benjamin Bratt, but he *is* disrespecting you, so he gets the *hobnailed* boot, period, end of story, bye, stupid motherfucker."

"But, you guys, everything is so perfect, so—"

"Wow, do words mean different things out on the West Coast than they do here in the City? Because *I* would describe the constant blowoffs and last-minute nigger-rigged dates and no-explanation no-shows as 'shitty,' not 'perfect,' " snapped Roxanne.

"I mean the whole package," I said irritably. "The face, the house, the car, the clothes, the—"

"You're right. Let's take inventory," interrupted Carolyn. "He has a Mercedes coupe that must have a sketch transmission because he almost never makes it over to your house when he says he will, and he has a Rolex that's either slow or entirely broken because he never manages to be on time when he's supposed to meet you. So do we cut him slack because he owns sparkly things? No, we don't, because that shit might as well be a Garfield Timex and a Gremlin for all the good it's doing you."

"You're the one always making up all those damn rules," pointed out Roxanne. "You need to try and stick to them."

"I know, I know," I said sadly. "I have to let him go."

"Yes. Famous or not, he's acting the fool, and like any other fool, he gets cut. And please don't bother calling me back until you've cut him," said Taylor, hanging up.

"Listen, I know he's cute and you like all the attention," said Carolyn sympathetically. "But he's got to go. And so do I; I'm late for a meeting. Bye, sweetie."

Then it was just me and Roxanne on the phone.

"I told you not to date an actor," Roxanne said. "Just imagine what it's like dating me!"

Good point.

. . .

Okay, the girls made it quite clear that things weren't meant to be with the Television Actor. But dating him was exciting; I loved the fact that we never had to wait in a line with regular people. But the cons outweighed the pros, and we have officially parted ways. Not that it was a particularly dramatic breakup; I'm not even sure you can call it a breakup. I called him up and told him in no uncertain terms that we could no longer see each other. He said "that's too bad" and then clicked over to take a call from his agent. So that sucked, but it wasn't a total loss: I'm a big believer in learning from my mistakes, and I've reminded myself—in writing—of eight reasons NOT to date an actor:

1. *Constant interruptions from "fans"*: There is nothing worse than trying to have a quiet, romantic dinner with your man and being (rudely) interrupted by a woman named Re-Re with a disposable camera and poor diction. Not only does she want to take a picture with YOUR man (so she can lie to her friends back home in Bugaboo, Mississippi, and say that he was trying to "get with her"), but she will do so WITHOUT EVEN AC-KNOWLEDGING YOUR PRESENCE. Any (Black) actor knows that in order to remain popular, he needs to be nice to his fans. You understand this and, in addition, you realize that, indirectly, Re-Re (and others like her) paid for your dinner at Crustacean. So even though you want to cuss her out and perhaps do her bodily harm, you have to sit there and smile like the lady you are. It's so annoying.

2. *He's obssessed with appearances*: A big part of being a successful actor is taking care to look your best at all times. That's fine (and so is he), but this can get way out of hand. It is very unsexy when a guy asks you, "Do these pants make me look fat?" What's worse, his obsession may spill over onto YOUR looks.

The minute my man tells me I might want to try his new conditioner because my hair's looking a little dull, I'm out of there.

3. *Paparazzi*: When dating an actor, you will have an opportunity to attend lots of high-profile events and have your picture taken on the red carpet. Sounds like a dream come true, right? Well, try being cropped out of a picture when it's printed, or worse, being referred to as "and companion" in the caption. They do, however, use your name (and spell it correctly) in all the unflattering tabloid photos.

4. *His publicist*: Any hot young actor will cool right off once the public knows he's seeing someone seriously. The only women who won't hurt his heartthrob status, it seems, are large-breasted actresses. There is nothing worse than your man attending the MTV Movie Awards with the newest Hollywood "It Girl" while you watch at home with your bitter, divorced cousin Sheila. Then there is the added embarrassment of having your man show up on a Most Eligible Bachelors List while you run around town talking about how "He's going to propose any day." Yeah, right, pumpkin.

5. *Watching him kiss other women on screen*: Need I explain this one? The worst is when he compliments his leading lady. No one wants to hear her man going on about how good some other girl smells. You're pretty sure nothing's going on, but like they say: What happens on location, stays on location.

6. *The constant ego stroking*: Due to the fact that ninety percent of acting involves rejection, actors need more ego stroking than the average man. As you know, normal amounts of ego stroking can be exhausting, so with an actor it's positively coma-inducing. When he goes on ten auditions and ten people say they don't want him, he simply cannot handle a lecture from you about dirty dishes in the sink when he gets home. Because you are a Nice Girl, you start sparing him many of the

tongue-lashings that keep a man in his place. Pretty soon, he's out of control and you're doing the dishes (again).

7. *He thinks it's all about him*: Poor thing. It's actually all about *me*. Without a grasp of this basic concept, there really isn't anywhere for this relationship to go.

8. *Unwillingness to cooperate*: Unfortunately, actors/athletes/musicians have TOO MANY OPTIONS. They are generally unmotivated to cooperate with you because other women are constantly hitting on them. The minute you start to get "out of line," he reminds you that there are a hundred women ready to take your place. Hearing that ridiculous threat every other day gets real old, real quick.

So, take it from me, and stick to "regular guys." They don't have all that extra baggage. I know it seems like there are lots of perks involved in dating an actor, but in the long run, it is much easier (and preferable) to go out there and get some fame of your own. This is Hollywood. Just go around telling everyone how *utterly fascinating* you are. Sooner or later, you'll be like Ivana Trump: famous for being fabulous.

• • •

With the Television Actor long gone—and now connected, according to *US Weekly*, to Candi, the same PCB I tried to cockblock when I first met him—I've decided to make an effort to break out of the tedious Black Hollywood scene and am going to try to meet some new people by attending a Harvard Alumni mixer.

The mixer was being held at the very posh Brentwood home of Frederick Castillo, the president of the Alumni Association's Los Angeles chapter and a semiretired television director. It was a lovely affair and I was hoping to reconnect with some of my old college pals. I arrived at the party and was a little dismayed to discover that the average age of the attendees was sixty, but I smiled politely anyway and made a beeline for the bar. I was waiting patiently in line for my white wine when I noticed a guy my age in line in front of me. He wasn't my usual type. He was wearing some unfortunate glasses and wrinkled cords, but hey, beggars can't be choosers, and since things are not really going as planned out here and I haven't had a conversation with anyone outside work in ages, I introduced myself.

"Hi, I'm Bianca. Are you an alum?"

He turned around and looked startled that I was talking to him.

"Yes," he said extending his hand. "I'm Jordan Matthews. Class of ninety-six." Hmm, don't remember him from school, but dressed like that, he wouldn't have been hard to overlook.

"Bianca King, right? I remember you," he said. "I was in Sociology and Sexuality with you, second semester, junior year." I withdrew my hand and backed away a little bit, wondering if I'd just jump-started a stalking episode, but he laughed.

"Are you surprised?" he said. "That presentation you did on Sexuality and Footwear was pretty unforgettable. If I were a foot fetishist . . . well, let's just say we would have met earlier. And often." I had to laugh at that. I'd demonstrated everything from bound feet to the stacked heels of Louis XIV's court to six-inch bondage stilettos; it had been quite a successful little lecture. And, yes, there had been more hangups than usual on Taylor's and my answering machine that semester; even in college my pedicures were always perfect.

Jordan politely offered to get my drink and we found a bench in the corner to chat. At closer examination, he was really rather cute, sort of a nerdy Adrian Brody type. And really his eyes were a lovely shade of coffee brown. Too bad he hid behind those terrible glasses. As my thoughts drifted toward a makeover, I heard Jordan ask me if I liked jazz.

"Sure," I replied giving him one of my most dazzling smiles. Isn't it funny when people ask you if you like jazz? I mean, it's fine in the background, but it would never occur to me to listen to it on purpose. I always thought it would be sophisticated and worldly of me to acquire an appreciation for it, but I never got around to it. I guess I was too busy listening to old Prince CDs. But before I knew it, Jordan and I had made a date for a jazz concert some of his friends were performing in, and I started to think that I'd done the impossible and met an intellectual man of substance in

L.A.; what else could wrinkled corduroys and jazz mean? As he continued to gaze at me as if he were the luckiest man alive to be chosen by me, I felt at peace. Good men are like a pair of black Jimmy Choo slingbacks marked down seventy percent. Only the most skilled of shoppers has the ability to actually find them and make them hers.

• 26 •

Roxanne

Teach for America

A glance at my increasing stack of unpaid bills and the slim to none chance of booking the lead in a major Hollywood blockbuster in the next three days led me to apply for a substitute-teaching position in the New York City public school system. After all, it is a noble profession, and I can decide whether or not I want to work each morning based on my mood and audition schedule. Yes, the kids need me. The girls especially will benefit from being exposed to a cultured young lady like myself. After paying eighty dollars to get fingerprinted (don't want any child molesters or convicted felons tampering with America's youth) and going through the interview process, I enter this new phase of my life with poise, wisdom, and pride.

My first assignment is to spend a week at Camden Hall, an academically accelerated middle school that opened its doors a few years ago and promotes high achievement in science and math. Its principal founded the school after realizing that most public institutions neglect their most gifted students, denying them access to materials and opportunities that richer students in private schools and suburbs get. Each student at Camden Hall has a laptop, and many assignments are typed and e-mailed to the teachers. I'm feeling very old—what happened to a good old number two pencil and wide-ruled notebook paper? These kids are so smart, creative, and ambitious. They come from the lowest tax brackets, but their families are committed to breaking those cycles of poverty through education and steadfast involvement in their children's lives. This is definitely a model school and going there all week makes me feel that some good is happening in the educational system, that some people are committed to more than just passing children through the doors with minimal skills and little hope.

Then I get assigned to P.S. 241.

P.S. 241 is an elementary school in my West Harlem neighborhood. It's so close that I am able to stroll the six blocks in a leisurely fashion, my homemade lunch and magazines in hand, excited about facing some adorable third graders and imparting some of my knowledge, arriving fifteen minutes before the eight forty-five morning bell rings, signaling the start of a new day of learning.

When I enter the school I am shocked to find that no one knows where I am supposed to go. When I get to the main office, they have no idea what subjects Ms. Martinez, the woman I'm subbing for, teaches. There are no lesson plans, but the secretary says, "Good luck, honey. You'll need it with that crew." Not a good sign. The kids have Library first period, so I have forty-five minutes to concoct a plan for the day. I'd forgotten that elementary school teachers have the same kids ALL DAY, and I'm praying that these tykes are well-behaved. I enter the classroom and search for clues as to what they've been doing in each subject. No luck. I go next door to Mr. Guzman's room, hoping for help.

"I teach bilingual classes, so I don't know what Ms. Martinez has been doing," he says. "Why don't you read them some stories and make them solve math problems in the workbook? But be careful with these kids, they're a lot to handle, and they will walk all over you. Good luck."

Why does everybody keep wishing me good luck?

When the kids enter at nine-thirty, it becomes apparent. They are a motley crew. Most surprising are their statures. Half of them are as tall as me at five feet four and weigh much more than my 115 pounds. As I call roll, Isabel, age eight, with long acrylic nails, a "baby phat" T-shirt, pleather pants, and a rhinestone-laced bandanna, proceeds to take out her cell phone and place a call to God knows who. I confiscate J Lo Junior's phone and am then confronted by Tyriq, who demands to know how old I am.

"I am an adult, Tyriq. That's all the information you need," I tell him. Good answer, Roxanne. Dignified yet noncondescending, authoritative yet—

"But you ain't got no titties and no bootie," Tyriq responds. Oh Jesus. It's nine forty-five. School ends at three. What am I going to do with these children for five hours and fifteen minutes? Four hours and fifteen minutes when you subtract lunch and recess. Please, God, let them have P.E.—that would mean I really only have three and a half hours of lessons to make up. The good sixth graders at Camden Hall lulled me into complacency. Why did I think that my luck would continue at Future Felons of America Elementary?

Bianca

Inch-High Private Eye

Jordan has invited me over to his apartment for dinner and he's making rack of lamb. He just poured me a glass of surprisingly good rosé. I know what you're thinking. A man who likes rosé? Isn't that just a tad too close to white Zinfandel, otherwise known as a Drink a Gay Man Might Order? It's perfectly fine for a man to enjoy a nice glass of wine, even white wine, but I have to admit that there's something oddly comforting about a man who drinks shit like scotch or cognac. But rosé? I set my gaydar on "High" and accepted the glass with a smile while Jordan returned to the kitchen. The wine was actually very good, so I chose to focus on the other wonderful things about Jordan.

First, and most important, he *adores* me. From what I've been able to gather, he doesn't usually date women like me. Let's put it this way: His last girlfriend was an organic lettuce farmer who bore a disturbing resemblance to Hulk Hogan. Need I say more? Jordan also reads shit like Nietzsche for fun—how fabulous is that? He tells me I'm beautiful with a sort of awed look on his face at least three times a day, and he always calls when he says he will.

Since Jordan was busy in the kitchen, I called out that I was running to the bathroom. As a general rule, when I'm at a guy's house for the first time, regardless of whether or not I have to pee, I ask to use the bathroom so I can conduct the standard Bathroom Check (opening drawers, looking in medicine cabinet, etc.). I do not feel this is inappropriate because according to Taylor, there is no "expectation of privacy" in a room that is open to guests.

When you begin dating a guy, the first visit you make to his living space can be crucial. There are many clues to be found in a man's home that can give you an idea as to whether this relationship has any potential. Here are ten important signs that you need to grab your Kate Spade and get gone.

1. *There are more roommates than there are rooms*: I don't care if he lives in a Man-Shun. If there are too many unmarried men in one house, it just becomes one big frat house/50 Cent video.

2. *Black leather furniture*: Gentlemen, it's the new millennium. Let's move on.

3. *No dining room table*: I will accept an empty dining room space as long as there is a DECENT kitchen table on which to eat. (No, the coffee table doesn't count.) However, using your dining room space for any of the following is unacceptable:

   a. Gym equipment
   b. The weed table (not suitable for eating because there are too many unidentifiable/illegal substances stuck to the surface)
   c. A bedroom (see #1)

4. *Black lacquer bedroom set*: Especially not the ones that have splatter paint "accents."

5. *Poorly hidden/overstocked porn collection*: All men have a porn collection. I accept that. If you think your man doesn't, there's a secret passageway in his house that you don't know about. But if he doesn't at least make an effort to hide it, or there's just

too much to hide, it's time to consider whether you'll be able to fit his Sex Addicts Anonymous meetings into your weekly schedule.

6. *Unsuitable sheets*: Any of the following are unacceptable:
   a. Cartoon sheets
   b. Satin sheets
   c. Soiled sheets
   d. No sheets

7. *Strange items under the bed*: Use your own judgment, but be on the lookout for empty condom wrappers that aren't your brand, not to mention anything that can be called a "device."

8. *High toothbrush count*: Be sure to check your math against the roommate ratio, but generally two is one too many.

9. *Scary mail*: Now, I am in no way advocating opening someone else's mail, but if you happen to see (lying around in plain view) any envelopes marked Final Notice, Past Due, or Notice to Appear, you might want to call your cousin who works down at the County Clerk's Office and do some research on your boy.

10. *Makeup in the bathroom*: As I have so aptly demonstrated, if you find makeup at his house, it either belongs to his OTHER girlfriend or it's his. Either way, it's time to biz-ounce.

Whew. Clean as a whistle. Is Jordan too good to be true? As I came back into the living room, Jordan was setting dinner on the table. Oh my God, he's put out linen napkins. Real linen napkins! I think I'm in love.

• 28 •

Taylor

All by Myself

When my birthday weekend rolled around, I was still pretty messed up over the John episode. Roxanne and Carolyn offered to take me to lunch at Spice Market because they knew how upset I was. Bianca sent me the biggest bouquet of flowers I had EVER seen in my life. So instead of getting ready by drinking a few shots, I'm sitting in front of my vanity on my little tufted stool, flowers shielding my view, and realizing that those little bags under my eyes that I used to be able to claim would go away as soon as I had some sound sleep, were actually becoming permanent. I wasn't at the end of the line by anyone's stretch of the imagination, but the breasts weren't as perky as they used to be (but only a LITTLE less perky, the drop was practically minute); smile lines around my eyes formed and creased when I smiled (they went away when my face was expressionless); my metabolism was slowing (even a hundred extra crunches didn't help that small, and I mean REALLY small, layer of fat covering my abs); and I had a gray hair in the middle of my head (stress-related, of course). I mean no one was going to come and put me out to pasture, but for the first time in my life, I started to take stock of things I'd never noticed before because I never had any wear and tear to measure against.

I've always sarcastically joked that I'm lucky in love, but seriously, everything else in my life runs pretty fucking smoothly; why can't love? Where the fuck is my husband? Clinging to the corner of some mountain in Nepal? Swan-diving off some beautiful cliff in Hawaii? Skiing in the Andes? Crossing a fjord in Finland? Deep-sea diving off the Australian coast? Piloting his way to safety from the Middle East? Hot-air ballooning in the Sudan? Exploring underwater grottos in Mexico? Charting dangerous wasteland in Antarctica?

I don't exactly know where he is, but I know he's not here. I know he's somewhere on this orb we call earth, but which hemisphere, what longitude? I can't even place the time zone, much less pinpoint the spot within a hundred-mile radius, except to say that it's not within the one-hundred-mile radius in which I reside. Well, at least I know that. And that's slightly more than nothing.

I resolved to let the start of a new year in my life be the end of some old ways. The old heartaches, the old baggage, all of that. It was definitely time to move on and it was definitely time to get back in the game. Not only did I miss the obvious physical comfort, I missed the companionship desperately. I wanted to cry, I was so sick of being lonely, and relief was nowhere in sight. Could the magic ever happen again? Well, of course it could, but the nagging question of *when* wouldn't leave my mind. But you can't force chemistry, and you can't make Mr. Right appear, no matter how many parties, museum galas, or Broadway shows you attend. I was out and about and mingling, but each time I opened the door to my apartment, I knew that nobody waited for me on the other side. And unlike some other times in my life, that felt wrong. I craved intimacy and I didn't have it. Curling up under my fur comforter and feeling the warmth of my fireplace only made the empty spot on the other side of my bed feel emptier. My cats, as big as their asses were, just couldn't fill it up. Some days I woke up and half-hoped that Vincent would be there, but he never was. Which is a good thing, because if he'd been able to get through my triple-bolted door, I'd have known he was Satan's spawn indeed.

No, I wasn't ready to walk down the aisle, but I did miss all of the intangible things that having a partner entails. I wanted a playmate who was ready to try out the new restaurant that was opening, who would care that my day was going terribly, who would be there when I came home on a cold night.

Although I'd been closer to marriage than any of the girls, my past experiences taught me that I didn't want a husband yet, but I did want someone to be there for me. On a permanent basis—just not *that* permanent. Not yet, anyway. Sure, the girls were great, but they couldn't replace the testosterone. They were my best friends, but they weren't my other half. I wanted my male complement, someone to be my refuge.

• • •

As we sashayed into Spice Market, I looked at the beautiful surroundings and sighed. *I wasn't getting any birthday dick!!!* How unfair was that? But just when you think you're riding along on fumes, and the Universe couldn't get less fair, it happens. I saw him as soon as I walked into the restaurant. He was tall, with thick, dark hair and piercing brown eyes. He looked up at us, but realizing we weren't the people he was waiting for, he looked back down at his papers, albeit with a slight smirk. He was alone and wearing an Armani suit. He was also White. Now this, I hadn't expected. But shit, I'm grown; I don't need anyone's approval to do a motherfucking thing. And he was fine as *shit*.

"Ladies, I think my birthday present is sitting at that table over there."

"Did you want a martini before you start unwrapping him?" Carolyn asked sarcastically.

"Yes, and he can buy it for me," I threw back over my shoulder as I headed across the floor.

Because he was alone and because I was so horny, I decided not to wait for him to get up the nerve to approach me. I'd seen that smirk, so, taking matters into my own hands, I deposited myself in his booth and looked straight into his eyes.

"So, tell me you're meeting someone here for business. I'd be too disappointed if you were meeting a date," I purred.

"No need to be disappointed. It is business indeed," he smiled as he took me in.

"It's my birthday today. You looked like you wanted to wish me well.

I thought I'd give you an opportunity to take me out to dinner tonight, if you're single."

Now that had to throw him off. Because men always feel so powerful and in control, by taking that control away, they're instantly intrigued. And yet, at the same time, I had offered him a bit of that power back, by suggesting that he would do the taking. See, there's a science to this shit, and I've got a Ph.D.

But before he could answer, three men approached the table, obviously ready to get down to business.

"Well, I'm off," I announced, and before he had a chance to even try to find his next words. It's always best to end the conversation before a man does. That way, he wants to know who the hell you think you are, rather than feeling like he's found out everything he wants to know and is now dismissing you. Score two for Taylor.

So, I wasn't at all surprised when he came over thirty minutes later with his card in hand to request the pleasure of my company at dinner when he returned from Hong Kong, where he was headed the following day. I looked down at the card. Meschach Cohen. An investment banker at GSC Securities. I'd done very well indeed.

• 29 •

Carolyn

Lucy and Schroeder, Sitting in a Tree

"It's two of the other Musketeers," Carter says, holding my phone out, "also known as Bianca and Taylor. Are we still on for lunch?"

"The *breasts*, Carter," I say, taking the phone and pointing at the latest Captain Sabatini mockup, where his most recent creation, a female pirate, again appears to have watermelons under her skimpy peasant blouse. "What are you *thinking* about when you draw these women?"

"I think it's fairly obvious," he says, picking up an eraser and the mockup and disappearing into his office. I spin my chair around so that I am looking out of the huge industrial windows, which give on a row of trendy boutiques. It is a sunny, balmy day and the sidewalk cafes are crammed with heroin addict–thin fashion victims of both sexes sporting the Prada spring line, which appears to consist of varicolored postage stamps, and jabbering into cell phones as they toy with platters of steak frites. I swivel back around and face the chaos of my office.

"Hello?"

" 'Breasts' sounds promising," says Bianca sweetly. "Did you finally get a clue?"

"He sounds finer than ever," adds Taylor, who, judging by the noise, is outside somewhere on her cell phone. "You're fucking him when?"

"It's impossible to tell how someone looks from how he sounds and you know the rule," I say shortly, mindlessly rearranging my Peanuts miniatures into dysfunctional couples—Lucy and Schroeder, Snoopy and Charlie Brown, Peppermint Patty and Marcie. To keep Linus company, I borrow Ronald Ann and her headless rag doll from the Bloom County grouping on the custom teakwood wall unit and create a darling little interracial couple with abnormally large heads and serious emotional issues.

"Which rule would that be?" Bianca is saying. "I have close on a thousand rules, personally, and not one of them says anything even remotely similar to thou shalt not date cute loaded white boys who might give you both sparkly baubles and quality head."

I can hear both fools grinning into their respective handsets. Taylor wasted .75H of billable time doing web research on Cunningham Walker & Holden, which is, as she has taken great pains to inform all of us, one of the oldest and most prestigious corporate law firms in San Francisco, and the Carter Holden who is currently a member of the partnership is the great-great-great-grandson of the Carter Holden who cofounded the firm after making a fortune during the Gold Rush. However, the Carter Holden sitting next door is an intern, my mentee, and I must therefore view him as a eunuch. I am expected to evaluate his work fairly and treat him professionally, and I cannot do either if he has spent the previous evening sipping champagne from the small of my back and the hollow of my throat.

Ahem.

"Carolyn, he is so hot, and he seems like good people!" Taylor said. "You can't make one little exception?!"

"Let it go already. I'm not going to hit on him. Period. End of discussion."

"Bitch, it ain't the end of the discussion until I say so," Taylor says. There is a snicking sound and a hiss as she lights a cigarette. Ronald Ann leaves Linus for Schroeder, who looks a little bit like what Carter might look like if he were eight years old and a cartoon. Babar and Tintin look on passively from the bookshelf.

"What if he hits on *you?*" she says, inhaling. "He didn't seem to be having any trouble hanging out with us the other night, and he bought our drinks, he got your coat, he opened the door for you . . ."

"That was just—" I begin, but Taylor cuts me off.

"Here she goes, Bianca. He just did that because she's his boss and he had to."

"Or because he was just being polite; he'd never ask her out because she's not his type," Bianca adds in a high-pitched singsong.

"He probably only likes blondes," responds Taylor.

"He probably only likes model-thin women."

"He probably only likes heiresses."

"And if he ever *did* ask her out, it's only because he's having a chocolate fantasy."

"Or he's sleeping his way to the top."

"Absolutely, because there is simply no way anybody could ever be attracted to Carolyn, who is very fat, very boring, and very ugly, which is why we three fabulous divas continue to hang out with her fat boring ugly ass," Bianca says.

"Yes, the sharp contrast between us and you adds a certain richness to our lives," Taylor snorts. Carter appears in front of my office, pointing to his watch, then to his stomach. I mouth "two minutes" and he rolls his eyes.

"Honey, you need to give me the money you throw at that therapist every week; I would at least spend it on something constructive, like shoes, whereas this joker is just taking it and you are still so very clueless." Bianca sucks her teeth impatiently.

"Thank you for your professional assessment, Bianca. Now, are we done? Because I'm late for lunch."

"Yes, Miss Stank-n-Snippy, we're done," Bianca says. "For now, anyway."

"Yeah, this issue will be revisited at a later time, Carolyn, because we're not going to stop until you start acting like you have a brain about this boy." I hang up on them and pick up my cardigan. I have not had a single date or prospect of a date since Gil; this much is true. But dipping the pen in the company ink is not the answer, and, again, Carter is not my type. I am in a bit of a funk now, but it is nothing that a massive platter of steak frites cannot cure.

"Let's go," I say to Carter.

• 30 •

Bianca

One of These Things Just Doesn't Belong

It takes money to look good—and I look *real* good today, if I do say so myself. I just had my hair done at THE Black Beverly Hills salon. Matteo is an absolute genius ($100). I'm wearing my favorite necklace, earrings, and bracelet from Tiffany ($400). I have on my Movado watch ($600), a red TSE sweater ($400), my favorite black Trina Turk pants ($150), new Jimmy Choo heels ($425), my Coach tote ($275), and, of course, I have a fresh manicure and pedicure courtesy of Burke Williams, my favorite day spa ($50). I won't even get into makeup; one Chanel lip gloss alone will run you $25. Total cost of this look: over $2,400. Total amount in my bank account: $24. Which brings me to why I'm the best-dressed person in line at Rico's Check Cashing this afternoon. You see, you may not have noticed, but I have a small problem: great taste and no way to pay for it. Somehow my paycheck never quite seems to cover my expenses.

It's not my fault, L.A. is an expensive town. New York was expensive, too, but at least I had my girls around and whoever had money paid, and whoever didn't, didn't. Taylor makes about $200,000 and Carolyn makes somewhere in the neighborhood of $120,000, plus she doesn't pay rent because her folks own her apartment and pay the maintenance, so the two of them always had Roxanne's and my backs when times were tight, knowing that Roxy and I would pay for stuff whenever we could, and the system worked just fine. Here, in L.A., it's every It Girl for herself, and the only thing people do with other people's backs out here is stab them.

This is a town based almost exclusively on appearances, and if you want to be taken seriously here, you have to look successful, even if you aren't. When I first got here and I was still driving the Cabriolet, I went to go pick up Rachel for a party one night. When she saw what I was driving, she quickly offered to drive her car . . . since I was still unfamiliar with the streets, of course. After we climbed into her Lexus truck, I got the message (bitch!). I wish I had the nerve to suggest the fabulous and cheap El Torito happy hour instead of Mr. Chow when I'm meeting my friends, but I don't want them to think I'm an unsuccessful loser. Dinner out at any decent restaurant in L.A. is at least $30 a person, add another $40 for drinks (that's only three drinks), $5 for valet; I spend anywhere from $50 to $100 on a typical night out. I know it sounds ridiculous, and I definitely can't afford it, but I did not move to Hollywood to sit home and watch other people live MY fabulous life on TV.

Look, I like nice shit. I'm not asking anyone else to pay for it (well, maybe Rico—I'll explain that in a second), and eventually I WILL have money, so why suffer in the meantime? I've been working on my screenplay and I KNOW it's better than any of the crap that's out there. It's only a matter of time before my writing career takes off and I can always fix my credit later.

And boy, will it ever need fixing. The reason I'm here at Rico's in the first place is that I've maxed out my Mastercard buying furniture and both my Visas paying for clothes, personal grooming, and dry cleaning. Let's not even discuss the transportation expenses; the Cabriolet was succeeded by a "gently used" late model champagne BMW 3 Series convertible and, "gently used" or not, the payment is killing me. That, combined with the gas, insurance, and weekly car washes (one can't drive a *dirty* BMW), is forcing me to come up with some highly creative accounting practices. You see, Rico is kind enough to loan working people up to $250 until their next paycheck. All you have to do is write Rico a check for $300, postdate it to your next payday, and he gives you the $250 in cash. The only drawback is this dreadful line and all of the downtrodden individuals looking at me like I'm some kind of freak. As if well-dressed people aren't allowed to have money problems. Hello? This outfit is why I have money problems. I'm also secretly afraid I'll see someone I know and be embarrassed, but then again, if they're here, they're just as trifling as I am and they have no room to judge.

Back in Manhattan, I got the designer duds and expensive dinners free, courtesy of the industry. The boyfriend of one of my designers worked at the MAC store on Christopher Street and to thank me for taking such good care of Justin, he hooked me up with almost all of my makeup; the rest I got from one of my boys at Saks or from the fabulous gift bags they gave out at industry events. I got massive discounts at the toniest salons and spas for encouraging the models we represented to patronize them, so my hair and skin were always in the best condition and cared for with gratis top-of-the-line products. The fabulous decor of my apartment? Ninety percent of it was "borrowed" from photo shoots. Regarding everyday basics like dry cleaning, I just sent mine out with my boss's stuff (that cokehead lunatic never noticed). So I'm used to the best of everything, but before now, I had no idea how much that lifestyle really cost. I'm used to Cristal; on my own, all I can afford is Miller Genuine Draft, and it simply won't do. I *cannot* go back to that, back to SuperCuts and ramen noodles. I don't want to stand in lines and hang out with "regular people." I don't want to drive a domestic car, spend vacations in Panama City, shop at Dress Barn, use drugstore shampoo, or eat at Red Lobster or Benihana on special occasions. I'd rather be broke. Or dead.

• • •

Okay, remember when I said I might be in love with Jordan? I was wrong. Very, very wrong. You remember all that adoration for me? Turns out it was just a clever mask to hide his inability to make a decision. About *anything*. All that reading? Because he *doesn't have a TV* (how un-American can you get?!). He didn't even know Donald Trump had his own show! How can I have a conversation with someone who doesn't know that? His love of jazz? I now believe that jazz is the refuge of dorks who don't know what they'd really like to listen to. They've figured out that if they say they like jazz, it makes them sound sophisticated, and if they throw around a couple of statistics about Art Blakey and mention Sun Ra in casual conversation once or twice, everyone goes "Oooooh, he's so learned and cosmopolitan." Bullshit. These guys only listen to jazz when other people are around; the rest of the time they're listening to Beyoncé and Eminem and Coldplay, just like the rest of us unintellectuals, only they think that's "lame" so they don't want to admit it. Now, I have nothing against dorks, Harvard was crawling with them. But Jordan's not just a dork; he's a dork with social anxiety disorder. He can't look people in the eye. He never disagrees with me because he can't stand conflict; if I said the world was flat and orbited the moon, I'd get no argument from him. In short, he's a pussy with the entire Blue Note library and a big vocabulary. Hate to tell you, but nice guys do finish last.

• 31 •

Roxanne

Not Hot for TV

That evening, after another glorious day at P.S. 241, where there were two almost-fights, the real thing, a chalk-throwing episode, and an ass-grabbing (young Tyriq apparently changed his mind and decided I did have "back"), I am calmly filling out a *New York Times* classified ad form offering for sale thirty-six "energetic" preteens from diverse ethnic backgrounds when I get a call on my cell phone from my agent, Maureen.

"Roxanne, you've got a producer's session for the new David Crawford television pilot."

Oh *yeah*, baby. If I get this TV show, my troubles are over. Time to bring out the big guns. What am I going to wear? The part is that of a young, fresh-out-of-Harvard-Law woman who's clerking for a real badass federal district judge in New York. The show shoots in New York, which would be ideal. I can give them smart Ivy League Black girl and I've got Taylor to fill in the legal gaps. The description in the breakdowns was, "beautiful, early twenties, African-American woman with great dramatic chops to play a young lawyer in a new series about the federal courts called '500 Pearl.'" Okay, I will wear black slacks and a brightly colored, fitted, lavender button-down—classic, yet sexy. I'll rehearse with my friend Susan again. This part is mine.

The day after my appointment, Maureen calls and tells me that it's between me and Anitra Stevens, who is yet another model/actress who I've seen on the circuit. I think she's taken one acting class in her life, and she seems like a real moron. Oh, this part is mine for sure.

Another day passes. I should have heard something by now. Maureen calls me with the news. "Well, Roxanne, it was a very tough decision, but they went with Anitra."

"How is that possible?" I say, shocked. "I nailed it and they obviously loved me. They said that I was their first choice."

"Well, Cammie Finnegan just signed on as a new producer, and she wasn't in agreement. It has to be a unanimous decision."

"What was her objection? Did she look at the tape? Why didn't she just meet me in person?"

"Well, this is a very delicate situation, and I shouldn't even be telling you this, but . . ."

"Go ahead, Maureen. I really need to understand what happened. That part was *mine*."

"Cammie feels that, and she got the other producers to agree, that you're not pretty enough."

"What?" I feel as if someone has smacked me in the face.

"They went with Anitra because Cammie didn't ultimately feel that you were pretty enough for the part." Wow. I am stunned. Silence on my end. Maureen quickly adds, "But all of us at the agency think you're gorgeous and wonderful and talented."

"Thanks, Maureen," I say weakly, and I hang up the phone.

I have been highly critical of myself in a lot of areas, but beauty was never one of them. I have always known that I am good-looking. I never dwelt on it because it's just a fact of life. I always took more pride in my intelligence than anything else, because I felt that was more unexpected; it surprises people when they find out how smart I am, not to mention that I'm an acting badass. I forget that the entertainment industry is much more shallow than general society. It's not enough to be smart, funny, and talented; you have to look like a fucking supermodel to get any recognition and appreciation. I've always known that's what it takes to be part of the business, but I never thought it would pertain to me because on the beauty scale I'm closer to Halle Berry than LaWanda Page.

I call my mom to get some love, which was a total mistake, because she and dad both told me that I need to pray on it and get back into church. Thanks. There's no use in talking to them; they understand very little about the daily assaults on my self-esteem. They think church can fix everything. Major self-esteem repair needed; no hymns, please. I call Ram. He tells me that beauty "is within the eye of the beholder." Boys can say the most trite, useless things. Ram's flaws have started to show. He thinks spending two hours in front of a GameCube is a legitimate date. Thank God the sex is still good. I call Sebastian in California and leave him a message. However, I know my girls will come through.

From: TheRealRoxanne@hotmail.com
To: baubles4bianca@yahoo.com; twilliams@mwdc.com;
         carolyn.phillips@gettyassoc.com
Subject: This fucking shallow business

Oh ladies, ladies, ladies, my ego has suffered a tremendous blow today. The producers for the new David Crawford pilot love me and think I'm fabulous, except for one Cammie Finnegan, who is convinced that I'm just not pretty enough and managed to persuade everyone else as well. Maureen thinks I'm very pretty and talented, etc. (she better or I'll be seeking new representation) but that the show was looking for someone a little more glamorous. How awful is this career I've chosen for myself? And when will I get past the bullshit?

From: twilliams@mwdc.com
To: TheRealRoxanne@hotmail.com; baubles4bianca@
         yahoo.com; carolyn.phillips@getyassoc.com
Subject: Re: This fucking shallow business

Uhm, excuse me, what rock did Cammie Finnegan crawl out from under? Has she lost her mind? Fuck that bitch. She is heavily medicated and can't recognize a future star when she sees her. In two years, they'll be begging to pay you millions of dollars. Until then, fuck 'em all. Karma's a bitch, baby. If they don't know that you're the bomb, they can go the way of the jackal—straight to hell.

From: carolyn.phillips@gettyassoc.com
To: TheRealRoxanne@hotmail.com;
baubles4bianca@yahoo.com; twilliams@mwdc.com
Subject: Re: This fucking shallow business

You aren't taking this totally baseless slight seriously, right? Because you realize that these people are clinically insane, right? These people are the same ones who are trying to shove a series of hatchet-faced, emaciated white women with shitty tit jobs down America's throats as The Last Word in Sexy; they are not to be trusted.

From: baubles4bianca@yahoo.com
To: TheRealRoxanne@hotmail.com; twilliams@mwdc.com;
carolyn.phillips@gettyassoc.com
Subject: Re: Re: This fucking shallow business

I guess they weren't aware that you were voted Most Beautiful in high school and that the only reason you didn't accept a modeling contract freshman year in college was that you (a) wanted to finish your education (silly, elitist, Ivy League you); (b) had doubts about the longevity of a petite modeling career; (c) didn't want a nasty heroin habit. Screw them all. And don't believe a word they say. They're threatened by your utter fabulousness. When we rule the world, we won't let them polish our nails, our cars, or our Academy Awards.

Well that's what good girlfriends are for. Even when everything else is falling apart, my girls look out for me without expecting anything in return but my happiness. I hate to get all sappy and sentimental, but I can't think of a single time in my life since I met Carolyn, Bianca, and Taylor at age seventeen that they haven't been there in the critical moments. When I was having a rough time junior year in college because I'd gained a reputation as the weird, artistic, freaky, sex addict chic, these gals were always in my corner defending me. When I was fooling myself into thinking that I should apply to law school and have a "respectable" career, they sat me down to inform me that if I became anything other than an actor, they'd personally beat my ass until I got some sense. My family loves and supports me, but having been away from home for almost a decade, my girls have become my extended family and closer than most siblings. And I suppose we're lucky to have found each other. I know that they have my back no matter what. That if shit went down, Taylor would be there with her knife (we didn't nickname her "Slice" for nothing), Bianca would have her spiky Manolos in hand, ready to stab some asshole in the eye, and Carolyn would reduce them to tears with her razor-sharp tongue. Thank God for them.

Shit list: Cammie Finnegan.

Sebastian left me a voice mail. "Man, it's a bogus situation, but you so can't let those crazy bastards stress you. I'm telling you, my very, very beautiful niece, that you should come out here and catch some waves; it's good for what ails you." There's a pause, and I think he's gone.

"Unless you break your neck," he adds as an afterthought.

I grin. Sebastian is so crazy, and he always makes me smile. Maybe I will; maybe I'll go out there and meditate on the beach, learn to hang ten, play *Blue Crush* for a while. I've never been surfing before, but I guess a part of me has always wanted to learn. Maybe it was *Gidget* or those cheesy Frankie Avalon and Annette Funicello movies that got me started, but *Blue Crush*, as godawful as the acting was, sealed the deal. Seeing women ride those giant waves like the boys made me want to kick some ass in the water. Especially since I'm feeling like I can't kick any ass here on dry ground.

Bianca

I'm Hot for Teacher

AN EXCERPT FROM:

MAN SHOPPING

By Bianca King

FADE IN:

A LARGE, WAREHOUSE-TYPE STORE WHERE THE ONLY CUSTOMERS ARE FEMALE. VERY REALISTIC, LIFE-SIZED MALE FIGURINES ARE PROPPED UP ON PEDESTALS IN A SHOWROOM ARRANGEMENT. SALESWOMEN SIT AT DESKS WITH HIGH-TECH COMPUTERS AND OTHERS WALK AROUND WITH THE CUSTOMERS. SYLVIA, AN ATTRACTIVE, WELL-DRESSED WOMAN IN HER LATE 20S, ENTERS, AND IS GREETED BY ONE OF THE SALESWOMEN, FRANCINE.

> FRANCINE
>
> Welcome to Aunt Kitty's Man Emporium, where our motto is: If we don't have him, he's not good enough for you! My name is Francine. I see

you've found our Premium models, what do you think?

                    SYLVIA

These look great. How much does he go for?
FRANCINE Oh, that's our limited edition European
Royalty model. Very popular. He comes in Italian,
British, and French. He's one of our most
sophisticated models. He has impeccable manners,
knowledge of literature, world events, cinema,
food, and wine and has a three-to-five home
guarantee.

                    SYLVIA

How much?

                    FRANCINE

Depending on his title, this model goes for
anywhere from $675,000 for a granted title like a
knighthood and up to around $2 million for a
landed title, like an earldom.

                    SYLVIA

Hmm . . .

                    FRANCINE

I'm going to be honest with you. These foreign
models may look fancy, but they're not nearly as
durable or as easy to repair as our domestic
models. Let me show you one of our best sellers.

FRANCINE WALKS SYLVIA OVER TO A DIFFERENT DISPLAY.

                    FRANCINE (Cont'd)

This is our Mr. All-American model. Captain of

the football team, great hair, likable
personality, the whole package.

SYLVIA

What about intelligence and sexual performance?

FRANCINE

Well, that varies from unit to unit. As far as
intelligence, he's no rocket scientist, but
everybody sure does love him. This model also
comes with an average- to above-average endowment
guarantee, but we had a recall a few years back
on his staying power chip. This new version comes
with a new and improved stamina chip that has an
85 percent satisfaction rate. It doesn't get much
better than that. However, he has a high failure
rate for remembering special occasions.

SYLVIA

How much are we talking?

FRANCINE

He starts at $96,000 for our blue-collar model
and $225,000 for the white-collar version. The
price difference is to account for earning
potential, of course.

SYLVIA

Well, I like him, but can you show me something
a little sleeker?

FRANCINE

We're all sold out of our millionaire playboys,
male models, and professional athletes, but I
might have a couple of pop stars in the back. I

know I have at least one boy band member in
stock, but approximately one in every three of
those is gay and you can't tell for sure until
you've already taken him home. Since we have a
No Return policy, I wouldn't recommend taking a
chance.

                    SYLVIA
Gosh, I was really hoping to spend in the
neighborhood of $5,000. What can you show me in
that range?

                    FRANCINE
Well, we have our Aspiring Rapper model. Well-
endowed, above-average looks, but his earning
potential is limited. Plus, he only comes with
two outfits: baggy jeans and baggy sweatpants.

THE WOMEN MOVE OVER TO ANOTHER DISPLAY.

                    FRANCINE (Cont'd)
Over here we have our Overlooked Guy model.
Above-average sense of humor, average looks,
average intelligence, but his adoration scores
are off the charts. This one's not fancy, but
extremely durable. His only real drawback is the
Overbearing Mother component, but we're working
on that back at the lab. Other categories . . .
let's see, we're all out of Gorgeous Trailer
Trash, but I can check our other stores for more
Short Men.

                    SYLVIA
Well, I guess I'm just going to have to spend a
little more than I wanted to. I'm looking for a

professional, with average to above-average looks
who's at least five feet ten, well-mannered, has a
healthy relationship with his family and is good
in bed.

FRANCINE

What race? The only reason I ask is that we
only manufacture a limited number of our Mr.
Successful model in Asian, Indian, and
Latino. . . we have to adhere to government
regulations on this. I have several White ones in
stock, but the Black model is on a three- to
five-year back order because of the federal quota.
But, wait, I *do* have lots of Black Mr. Arrogance
models.

SYLVIA

What about a Black, more politically active,
family-oriented version of Mr. Successful?

FRANCINE

Oh, we discontinued the "I Have a Dream" model
about twenty years ago.

SYLVIA

Well, thanks for your time, but I think I'm
going to keep looking.

FRANCINE

Good luck to you. And remember, you get a free
dinner if you buy on your birthday!

I've decided to dust off my screenplay and finish it come hell or high water, plus I need a chunk of money quick because I've got my eye on the
new Louis Vuitton fall line. So I signed up for a screenwriters' workshop

at UCLA that promised to get your screenplay in salable shape in one weekend. Imagine my shock when I showed up to class and the teacher was one of the finest brothers I've ever seen! Professor Nicholas Swift. I got his name from the syllabus because I didn't hear a word he said for the first thirty minutes; I was too busy trying to decide whether his eyes were hazel or just a beautiful shade of green. I heard the student in front of me talking and I was able to gather that he had asked all ten of the workshop participants to introduce themselves just in time for it to be my turn to speak.

"Hi, I'm Bianca King and I'm here to work on my first screenplay. It's called *Man Shopping* and it's about the search for love in the year 2040, when the man shortage has forced women to shop for their partners at a special store. It's sort of a romantic comedy meets sci-fi."

"Interesting," Professor Yummy said with an expectant look on his face, as if to say "And . . ."

"And . . . I'm really excited to be here," I said, feeling stupid, but unable to think of anything better to say.

"So, you feel your greatest strength as a writer is your, ah, excitement?" he asked with a look that was somewhere between curiosity and amusement.

I heard a few giggles behind me and tried to recover before I'd have to flee the room in a shroud of shame. See, that's what happens when the professor looks like a bookish version of The Rock. I'm too busy undressing him with my eyes to listen to the damn assignment.

Taking control of the situation, I continued, "What I meant to say is that my enthusiasm for the writing process is what I consider to be my greatest strength." Wow, that was terrible. I could tell he wanted to explore the ridiculousness of my statement further (for his own amusement), but, mercifully, he let me off the hook and moved on to the next student.

I managed to get through the rest of the morning by keeping my eyes on my notes instead of on Professor Cutie Pie. After lunch, we broke off into groups to discuss our individual projects in depth and I got some good ideas from the other students. It felt great to talk about the creative process with other writers. I had to admit that my screenplay was going to be *far* better after I implemented the suggestions I got in the workshop, and when it was over on Sunday afternoon, I congratulated myself on $400 well spent. As I was leaving the classroom, Professor Scrumptious stopped me.

"Bianca, I would love to read your screenplay when you're finished. Your premise is intriguing," he said with an unmistakable look.

Oh my God. My teacher is flirting with me. Wait, maybe he's just interested in my work, as any concerned educator would be.

"Perhaps we can talk more about it over coffee," he continued.

Now this is just the kind of man I need. Intelligent, well-mannered, *and* cute. You know, I never realized how important the academic process can be.

• 33 •

Taylor

Opening Night Jitters

I called Carolyn, Roxanne, and Bianca for a predate conference call (under the pretext of needing fashion advice) to get me into the right frame of mind. I really wanted them to give me the courage to get out there and try again. I wanted them to tell me that everything would be all right.

"Is this the night you break your 'not on the first date' rule?" Roxanne asked.

"That's *my* rule," Bianca piped up, "it's damn sure not Taylor's."

"Please. Taylor hasn't had sex in so long she wouldn't know where her cootch was if she didn't have to put tampons in it every month. I'm surprised she knows she's a woman," Roxanne replied. "I'm surprised she—"

"You clearly aren't banging him on the first date because you don't know who the hell he is and what he's carrying," Bianca interrupted. "Besides, aren't you the one who's been preaching moaning about sex not being enough to base a relationship on?"

As the girls debated exactly what I wanted from this date, I thought about it, too. After my shenanigans with Michael, I'd resolved to make time to think long and hard about what I was looking for, what I wanted from a man: whether I wanted a relationship, whether it was all even worth it. At first, I hadn't allowed myself to grieve over Vincent because I was too scared to think about the pain. But then I did think about it, and I think I hit upon the answer: I did want a relationship. I did want to be in love. I did want to be married sometime inside of the next ten years. It was that simple. So I was scared as hell, but I had to try again.

I must admit, I was a bit skeptical. A man, in New York City, thirty-five years old, never married, no children, and Head of Market Research at GSC Securities. In other words, too perfect to be true. Why in the hell was he single? I didn't have it in me to deal with one more commitment-phobe, player, closet case, freak, or asshole. Not one more. I felt like I was standing on the edge of a cliff, and the whole thing was driving me crazy.

"Listen, ladies, I just went on this self-induced period of abstinence. I can't give it up every time I see a pretty face," I whined.

"If you're whining, that could only mean one thing: you're scared shit-less." Roxanne had to fuck with me.

"Fuck that. How many times do you run across a rich boy that fine? And tall? And sexy? And aggressive? I'd tell you to ask Carolyn but she's not handling her business with Carter so she wouldn't know," Bianca added.

"Shut up," Carolyn said.

"What am I supposed to do, ladies?" I sighed.

"Well, I know what you *aren't* supposed to do," Carolyn said, "which is to sit at home wondering what to do. Some things you can't control, as I think we may have pointed out before; this is one of them. So stop jack-assing around on the diving board and get in the water."

Well, I guess I might as well. Shit, maybe this was the one who was dropping down from heaven instead of springing up from hell. The problem was, one could never be sure. And while the element of chance used to be part of the thrill of dating, I don't like the mystery and uncertainty anymore. Maybe this wasn't a good idea at all.

"Wish me luck. I guess you never know," I groaned. "But God, I so don't want to do this." But the girls had apparently decided that enough was enough.

"Then fine, don't," Bianca said, exasperated. "Go on and cancel the date if that's where your head is, because you're just wasting his and your time."

"Also ours," Carolyn added unnecessarily.

"Yes, please get yourself together, have a glass of champagne, and try to act like you're going to One If by Land, Two If by Sea to eat a fucking phenomenal meal instead of to the guillotine," Roxanne added.

"For months you've been screaming about no men for miles and now you've got a dinner date with a hot I-banker," Carolyn said. "So stop bitching about the past and trying to predict the fucking future and get dressed, you moron."

Well. They'd cured my trepidation but not my reluctance. With Vincent, things had taken off right from the start. At that time in my life, I hadn't been able to deny myself anything, and so I hadn't. At that time, though, I also wasn't the bearer of a broken heart; when I met Vincent, the thing with John was far enough in the past so that the baggage I was still carrying was small enough to fit in the overhead compartment or under the seat in front of me. Right now was a different story, though: I needed three skycaps to help me cart around my mess. Which is why going slowly was perfect. I hadn't seen, much less spoken to, anyone who made my heart leap. No one had given me butterflies. Until now. Until Meschach. And I was more scared of that than of anything else.

At least I was back in the company of men. Or of one man anyway. When he called me to find out my address, I heard his delight on the phone, and I remembered how good it felt when someone was excited to hear your voice. We spoke for a long time, and his pleasure radiated through the phone in waves. His tone reminded me that I was really missing something. When the conversation ended, he told me how much he looked forward to getting to know me. I was intriguing, he said, and he could tell I was something special. He wanted a spark, some energy in his life, and he hoped I'd provide it. He damn sure wasn't Vincent (thank GOD!), but he certainly wasn't John either. I felt the spark myself, but I was wary of it. With my relationship track record, betting on this possibility was a losing proposition.

• • •

My phone buzzed and my doorman informed me that a Meschach Cohen was waiting for me downstairs. I took one last look in the mirror (perfect!) and headed down.

Meschach looked delighted as he kissed my cheek and handed me a beautiful bouquet of tropical orchids. Bingo!

"You can leave them in the car if you want. I've hired a driver for the evening." Jackpot!

"Well, I guess you can't be too crazy if you're going to all of this trouble. Unless it's because you didn't want to use a cab to haul away my chopped and mangled body." I was mostly joking, but this *is* New York. Having a doorman was non-negotiable for me, for just this reason.

"For our first date, I wanted everything to be perfect." He was good.

"I like you already," I joked. I was beginning to feel a bit more at ease—not for the ostentatious display, but because he wanted to show me what type of woman he thought I was, that I deserved to be treated well. A well-dressed woman walked through the lobby with her schlub of a date and gave me a jealous eye. I gave her my patented "That's right, bitch!" look.

"Let's hope I impress you thoroughly." He was on the right track. "I like to think that dinner at One If by Land, Two If by Sea could melt the coldest heart." How did he know that my heart was frozen?

• • •

During the ride down the West Side Highway, Meschach told me that he'd been so busy working on a series of initial public offerings for the past year that he hadn't had time to socialize. And if I hadn't come up to him, he'd probably be at his office now looking over financial projections for the next IPO until he fell asleep at his desk. We clearly had the same attitude toward work, but that may not be such a good thing.

Meschach and I ordered the tasting menu to allow ourselves plenty of time to compare notes on our lives in the City, life at our respective firms, favorite music, favorite restaurants, favorite movies, favorite everything that makes two people feel like they're destined to be lovers.

When dinner was over, we sailed back up the West Side, and Meschach dropped me off at my door.

"I had a lovely time with you this evening. And I look forward to many more." For a nonlawyer, he sure does have all the right words.

"The pleasure was mine," I replied. "I look forward to seeing you soon."

Before he left, he bent down and kissed me on the cheek softly. I closed my apartment door and leaned up against it to steady myself. I couldn't have imagined a more perfect first date. Particularly with the promise of "many more" to come.

Okay, so I didn't get any sex, but the prospect of getting some in the near future was almost better. One thing was certain, the possibility beats the hell out of the nothing I had before.

SUMMER

Carolyn

Dog Day Afternoon

The air-conditioning has broken and it is approximately eighteen hundred degrees Celsius in this conference room, even with the windows opened as far as they go, which is not very far. I, like most of the other people around this table, am struggling to stay awake.

"Carolyn, I like what you've got going for Diogenes Travel," says Jackson, whose disposition has improved greatly after several months of anger management therapy and Xanax. "The campaign has a real 1930s look to it, and retro is very hot. How many different locations are you going to do?"

"Thanks," I say. "We're doing seven: Paris, London, Tokyo, Munich, New York, Abidjan, and Bombay."

"Interesting. I like that. Estimated completion date?"

"The Art Department's got it now," I reply. "I'll check in with Simone and get back to you."

Speaking of travel, I have no idea what to do about a real vacation this year. At this moment in time, under normal circumstances, Taylor and I would be in on a Hamptons timeshare with Roxanne as our rotating guest, but the rotten economy very neatly shanghaied those plans by causing the "downsizing" of two of the regular house participants and the non-receipt of Christmas bonuses for three others. Since we seem to be in the middle of a "jobless recovery," replacements have been impossible to find, which leaves us at loose ends. Jackson moves down the list to the next campaign and I drift off.

I wonder whether the south of France is the answer. In my mind's eye I see Taylor concentrating on the roulette wheel at the Grand Casino in Nice, ignoring the bevy of tuxedo-clad viscomtes clamoring to fetch her another flute of Moët et Chandon; I see Roxanne gyrating wildly around a bonfire on a moonlit beach, surrounded by half-clad gypsy youths; I see Bianca in a scarf and Jackie O. glasses in the passenger seat of the shopping bag–filled Aston Martin convertible of a Greek shipping magnate, and I see myself . . .

I am not sure what I see myself doing.

A year ago I surely would have seen myself alone, ensconced at a table at the back of a five-star restaurant, with a line of waiters bearing regional delicacies stretching to the front door. Now I seem to see myself posing on the balcony of the gaily-lit Hôtel du Palais at Biarritz, staring pensively at the ocean, fitting very nicely into a dress that I picked up two years ago at Bergdorf's but have yet to fit into, and sipping from a flute of champagne. I hear footsteps behind me, and a cultured male voice is about to speak when I am jerked rudely back to the real world by Jackson braying, "Carolyn, what do you think?"

"Works for me," I say automatically, hoping that I have not just pulled a Beloved Memories, which is the hideous campaign I ended up with the last time I was not paying attention in a meeting. Beloved Memories makes ghastly, saccharine-sweet, semireligious-themed porcelain horseshit that embodies everything that is wrong with Middle America. But no, I appear to have agreed with a concept for a campaign that is not mine, so no damage has been done and I fade out again.

Now I am walking along a black sand beach, clad only in a scanty string bikini and sheer sarong. I note this with some surprise; for years, I have been unable to fantasize about being naked or nearly naked because even in my daydreams, I disgusted myself, and I always imagined my fantasy sexual partners rearing back in horror and disbelief once they had torn my clothes away. But for the past couple of months, I have been rel-atively comfortable with the idea. In fact, it even makes me feel a little sexy.

It is a hot, humid night, and the moon is low and heavy in the sky, and I am walking toward a luxurious bungalow, where someone waits in the doorway. It is a man; it is my lover. As I draw nearer, I can make out his sleek, tanned torso and his dirty blond hair, wet from a midnight dip in the ocean.

"My darling," he says softly. The moonlight shines in his gray eyes as he gathers me to his rock-hard chest and presses his lips to mine. Over his shoulder I can see a table set for two.

"I made dinner," he says softly. "I thought you'd be hungry after that walk. And, my beauty, if you're going to fall asleep in meetings do you think you could do us the courtesy of not snoring?"

"What?!" I say, baffled.

"I mean, Jesus *Christ*," Jackson is saying as I sit bolt upright, wide awake. "You sound like a lumberjack convention."

"Sorry," I say. Carter shoots me a grin and makes a sawing motion. I glare at him and leave the room to go get a Coke.

• 35 •

Bianca

Dream Date

So, finally, Professor Nicholas Kirkland Swift and I have our first "real" date tonight and I can't believe how excited I am. I spent all day shopping for the perfect outfit, something that says I'm a sophisticated woman of the world, but not in a stuck-up, unapproachable way. I finally found this great Diane von Furstenberg wrap top and a pair of dark denim Seven jeans at Bloomingdale's. Unfortunately, the total cost of this outfit was $365. Charging it was out of the question because all of my cards are maxed, including my Bloomie's card. Sadly, I started to put the outfit back, but then my Evil Shopping Voice took over. *Just write a check for it,* it said. *You can always bring it back tomorrow.*

I had just gotten paid and hadn't paid my rent yet, so I had plenty of money in my checking account. If I didn't wear this outfit, that meant I was going to have to go home and try and scrounge up an outfit when I knew good and well that all of my good stuff was being held hostage in the cleaners, which closed thirty minutes ago. So, before my Realistic Broke Bitch Voice had a chance to comment, I double-checked the return policy, wrote a check, and carefully put the receipt in my wallet.

Three hours later when Nicholas arrived to pick me up for our date and his eyes lit up like a Christmas tree when I opened the door, I knew I had made the right decision. He certainly wouldn't have looked at me like that if I'd worn some recycled nonsense from last season.

Nicolas drives a cute vintage Alfa Romeo convertible, but thankfully he kept the top up on the way to the restaurant (it took Matteo three hours to get my hair this straight and he also forced me to get a deep conditioning pack, which was an extra $60; I wanted to protest but I didn't want him to think I couldn't afford it). Nicholas took me to this great little Italian place in Culver City where Carlo, a round little man in a white apron, greeted us warmly as soon as we walked in.

"Ah, Signore Nicolas, you were away too long!" The little man reached up and kissed Nicholas on both his cheeks. "And who is this beauty?"

"Hi, I'm Bianca," I said, reaching out to shake his hand. Well, he was having none of that and wrapped me in a bear hug that was surprisingly tight for such a small man.

Soon we were settled at our table and sipping Chianti. Normally I don't touch anything that cheap but I didn't want to offend Nicholas, plus this place wasn't a "scene," so there was nobody there to see.

"I'm not even drunk yet, and you've already scored major points. Carlo is like something out of a movie," I said with a smile.

"This is my favorite restaurant in L.A. I love that you don't need a reservation and that you don't have to wait two hours at a crowded bar for your table."

"It's very charming," I said. It was no Dolce, obviously, but it was cute and cozy and the spaghetti Bolognese was absolutely delicious; it reminded me of Sevilla, Carolyn's favorite restaurant, a Spanish place in the Village with stereotypically "ethnic" waiters, awful bullfighter paintings, and food so good that it made you forget that you had to fit into a little something for an industry event the next day.

"So are you," he replied, smiling.

"Wow. You're *good.*"

He tried to look sheepish, but he ended up just looking cuter.

Two plates of spaghetti and two bottles of Chianti later, Nicolas suggested that we drive out to the beach for a midnight walk.

"I'm not really dressed for the beach," I pointed out.

"Sure you are," he said, putting one hand on my knee. Sure I was.

Not wanting to spoil what was rapidly becoming my best date in a really long time, I went along, thinking we could park by the water and just put the top down. Nicholas, however, had other plans. When we arrived at the beach, he got out and went to the trunk. I saw him come around the side of the car with a small cooler and a blanket. He set the cooler down and spread the blanket out on the sand. I was a little nervous about sitting outside in my "borrowed" outfit, but my nervousness disappeared when I saw the strawberries and heard the cork pop on a bottle of champagne (Korbel Natural isn't Moët, but it's also not Riunite, and besides, it's the thought that counts), and I decided to take my chances in the sand.

The next morning, I awoke in my bed feeling elated, satisfied, and only slightly hung over. I stayed in bed for another half hour going over the details of last night, savoring every fabulous moment. Admittedly, what happened after the champagne was a little fuzzy, but I distinctly remember Nicholas walking me to my apartment and delivering a kiss and full-body hug that left me swooning in the doorway before he drove off; he didn't even try to talk his way inside. I felt like I was forgetting something important, but it wasn't until I stepped on a very wet, very ruined $365 outfit on the floor of my bedroom that I remembered the midnight swim.

• 36 •

Taylor

Lamb Shanks

"Listen, Mark, all I want to know is when I'm going to be able to see a draft of the scheduling order. That's it," I said in my business voice.

"You'll see it when I send it to you," he snapped. Mark was my least favorite opposing counsel.

"Oh, so it's like that, is it? Let me tell you, Mark, you won't like me when I'm angry," I purred, hanging up the phone. Dealing with assholes all day made me so irritated, I had to do something to perk myself up. I decided to call Meschach, who was in London on business. "Hello, honey," I said. "I've had the ultimate Day From Hell, and it's only five p.m. How was your day? And please tell me that something funny happened, because I need a laugh."

"Taylor! I was, as always, just thinking about you. I've had an incredibly hectic day, but that's long forgotten now." How is it possible that I can hear how sexy he is through the phone?

For the next thirty minutes of our conversation, I forgot all about my job. And then suddenly, my secretary knocked on my door and jarred me back to reality. I had a meeting in thirty minutes. With a very demanding client.

"Sorry to interrupt, Taylor, but David asked me to remind you that he'll need a first draft of the brief as soon as you get back." She gave me an empathetic grimace and closed the door.

I'm tempted to hop on top of my desk (even though it's piled mile high with legal briefs, research, and court papers) and stomp out a little "when it rains it pours" tap dance to show the world I did get the irony of it all and that I didn't need it force-fed constantly down my throat, but instead, I managed to compose myself and head off to my meeting. Yet another emergency at Intertec had popped up.

• • •

"Ladies, you will not believe what just happened to me! I mean seriously, just when I thought that being good at your job was all that mattered, here comes some jackass to drive me crazy," I was probably screaming into my headset at the girls, but I couldn't care less at this moment.

"What in the hell happened?" Carolyn said. "Is it your grandmother? Did something else happen? What is it?!"

"I have never heard you sound so upset or insane," Bianca added in a small "be nice to the crazy lady" voice.

"And for you, Taylor, that's saying a lot." Roxanne knew I was pissy, but she still had to add a little bit of fuel to the fire.

"As you well know, Nana is going into the hospital to have her mastectomy. And as you all also know, I am supposed to be leaving, *today*, to be there for the operation. Well, the fucking associate general counsel of Intertec, the client for whom I have been sleeping under my desk for the past five weeks and living to work for for a good portion of the last two years, said that while he 'understood and appreciated all the hard work I was doing, taking a "vacation" right now just wouldn't be a good idea.' Now that the Federal Trade Commission is investigating their proposed merger, they really need me right now. As you well know, I am not going on a vacation. Of any sort. So now I'm left asking myself, do I need to walk out the door and never come back? I told him that what he was referring to as a 'vacation' was actually a trip to be with my grandmother who has cancer, but I couldn't finish without bursting into tears. You should have heard him backpedal, although he also noted that he was going to call David, the partner assigned to the case, to have the bulk of the Intertec work reassigned to David because the FTC just can't wait. I am fucking *furious*. Two years of hard work, right down the drain."

"Oh, Taylor," Carolyn said, and then there was silence. "Oh, honey, I've never heard of anything more foul and unfair."

"Fuck him. Just fuck him. That's ridiculous." Bianca was furious; I could tell through the phone that her face was probably turning bright red. "Don't you even worry about that bullshit. Nobody can handle that case better than you, and they'll realize it the minute you leave."

"Right now you just need to worry about your grandmother, who is going to be absolutely fine," Roxanne said. "She has more spirit than you do, if that's possible. Cancer may slow her down a bit, but it ain't gonna stop her show."

"I don't guess any of us are too much the praying type, but we're all thinking about both of you and hoping for the best, and you know that," Carolyn said.

"I know Nana is going to beat this thing. That's not even a question. What I want to know is why do these fools think that even trying to fuck with me *now* is a good option?" I yelled.

"It must have been horrific if *you* were crying in front of somebody, because I think I've only seen that happen two other times in the ten years I've known you, and once was because you were being stalked by a mentally disturbed library worker who carved your initials in his hand with a paper clip. I wish you could walk in and piss on all their files before you storm out of that hellhole and set it on fire. I'm sorry your world is full of shitty assholes." Roxanne knew, too, although her experiences were different. I almost think it had to be worse to have a ten-second appraisal by total strangers make the difference between eating and not eating.

"Fuck them. They owe you. All of that hard work you do for them, and this is the thanks you get? What in the hell will it take to make them think twice before they fuck around with you again?" Bianca was screaming louder than I was.

"Oh, I don't know, a resignation?" I was seriously pissed off by now.

"Uh, seeing as *that's* not going to happen anytime soon," Roxanne continued.

"You put on your fucking Dolce & Gabbana and let 'em know you can give as good as you fucking get." Bianca was at fever pitch. This time, unfortunately, fashion was not the answer.

"You need to put this experience away right now and deal with it when things are less hectic," Roxanne said. "And I know you love your job, but I don't know how you work those hours and deal with those fools nonstop, day in and day out."

"Go catch your plane, Taylor," Carolyn added softly. "There's more to life than client billables; your firm seems to forget that a lot, but you shouldn't ever. Let David handle Interdreck; you need to be at JFK."

I didn't need to take up any more of their time screaming about something that wasn't going to change. The obvious answer was to leave. But go where? We, as women, have been told that we can have it all. And usually we believe it. But I know we can't. Perhaps I expect too much from this firm, but to me, only a fool wouldn't expect—and demand—to be treated with respect and consideration. Those are basic fucking *rights*, not privileges. I expect these fools to understand that I will work as hard and as long as is necessary but I demand a certain level of decency in return. I expect them to understand that I didn't sign over my dignity when I accepted this six-figure salary. What in the hell am I supposed to do? Leave this place to go somewhere else where the same problems exist? Check my sanity and self-respect at the door? Is that what it takes to be successful? No one ever told me that I'd have to pay that price. And frankly, it's not a part of the bargain. If I'd been told all this before, while I was growing up, maybe I'd be more amenable to it, but I wasn't told, and I'm not going to stand for this shit. I don't do well with sacrifice, especially when I get served up as the lamb. Fuck these people, and fuck this bullshit. I hadn't planned on taking a vacation before, but I am way overdue for a vacation, and I am taking one.

• 37 •

Roxanne

Cluck, Cluck!

I just had a meeting with the owners of General Lee's Chicken, and after many auditions, they want me to be the star of their new advertising campaign! Tired of being one-upped by KFC and Popeye's (and also of being portrayed as a backward, racist company), General Lee's is stepping up its commercial appeal. They want a classy, upwardly mobile image, and I'll be in all the print and television ads saying: **"General Lee's Chicken—the Rich Flavor of the South, Right in Your Mouth!!!"** It'll be like what Carrot Top did for 1-800-COLLECT; what Catherine Zeta-Jones is doing for T-Mobile; what Jared did for Subway. Yes, it means big bucks. This exclusive fast-food contract pays $150,000 for a year, not including residuals. And I don't actually have to eat any of it, which is great because fried chicken is a heart attack waiting to happen. Oh yes, my time has come. . . .

So I'm on the set, which is a club dressed as a farm, and the director tells me his idea, which is that General Lee's Chicken is so hip and funky that only the coolest people eat it. They're running four hours behind schedule, so I sit and chat with the producers and the crew, getting acquainted with the folks I'll be seeing all year. I spot Patty Andrews, a true hater who has been recklessly eyeballing me since I walked in the door. She's only got one line today, but since she gets a lot of the parts I audition for, she should be happy to share the wealth. Can a sister get some support and camaraderie? Not from this bitch, apparently. I go through hair and makeup, and when I enter wardrobe, the costumer hands me a hideous chicken costume with silver glittery leather feathers and a red boa.

"Excuse me, who is this for?" I ask Jenny, the wardrobe supervisor.

"This is your costume," she replies.

"I'm sure there's been a mistake because I'm the spokesperson. Shouldn't I be in a suit or a dress?"

She looks at me earnestly and says, "Nope, this is what you're wearing. We designed it especially for your measurements. It's a glamorous chicken—look at the glitter and feather boa."

"Well, I'd really love to talk to the director, because this is not what I agreed to," I tell her as sweetly as possible, pressing down the inevitable lump in my throat. Thomas, the director, breezes into the wardrobe area.

"Hey, Roxanne, the client came up with this brilliant idea at the last minute and we had to re-vamp our concept. Don't you love it?" he asks.

"Well it's certainly not what they discussed in the audition or negotiations. I thought I'd be in a pantsuit or something," I say as tactfully as possible.

"Didn't your agent call you last night with the changes?" he questions.

"No, he didn't," I respond, preparing to skin my commercial agent alive.

"I think this new direction is going to be a lot of fun for you, so please give it a shot. I think you're amazing, and this is a great opportunity for you. Everyone in America will recognize your face," he says, dangling the Fame Carrot in my face.

I remind myself, *Remember the $150,000, the residual checks, the national exposure. Put the thing on and shut your mouth.*

I grab my cell phone and furiously dial Alan, my soon-to-be-former-commercial-agent, who after a lengthy pep talk assures me that he knew nothing about this new "concept" and will negotiate more money. A few minutes later, I emerge from my dressing room wearing the chicken garb, red boa, and three-inch orange patent leather stiletto heels. The production designer sees me and exclaims, "Oh, you look perfect! A sexy, hip, funky chicken!"

"You're sure it's not too garish?" I ask.

"No, it's magnificent!" she squeals.

Thomas fills me in on the game plan: "So in this first shot, you'll be at the salon, getting your feathers groomed and nails painted for a night on the town. We'll hear a neo-soul groove in the background and your voice crooning, 'I'm just a funky, funkaay General Lee chick. Other brands of chicken think they're slick.' The next shot will be of you dancing seductively at the farm/club while less impressive chickens from Popeye's, KFC, and Church's vie for the spotlight. You outshine them all."

"I'm dancing?" I ask.

"Yes, doing a cool version of the funky chicken, squawking and shaking your tail feathers to some jamming hip-hop beats. Then we hear your voice chanting, 'Ain't nothing like General Lee, ain't nothing like General Lee!' "

Shaking my tail feathers? *Remember the $150,000, the residual checks, the national exposure. Squawk like a chicken and shut your mouth.*

After my farm/club number is a scene with me and my other General Lee "homiez" reading Shakespeare. "To cluck, or not to cluck? That is the question. We serve the most cultured poultry in our restaurants." When Thomas, the director screams, "Bring out the hicks with the cleavers!" three trailer park rejects in plaid shirts, overalls, and baseball hats with Confederate flags rush to the set.

Thomas informs me, "Now they're going to run after you with the cleavers, but you escape because a General Lee's chicken is too fast, funky, and fresh for the average Joe."

Good ole' boys with cleavers? Remember the $150,000, the residual checks, the national exposure. Run like a chicken and shut your mouth!

The director can't be serious, but, alas, methinks he is. Maybe I can reason with him, and he'll take this scene out. Horrified, I reply, "You know, I'm a little uncomfortable with the Dixie references. Perhaps they could wear regular clothes and not brandish meat cleavers."

"Honey," Thomas says, "this is what the company wants."

I am fuming. "This is the upscale image the company is striving for—Jethro, Cleatus, and Enos hunting a black hen lynch mob–style?"

"Honey, it's just acting."

"It's Roxanne, not Honey, and why don't you put the damn chicken costume on and see how it feels? I did all that other stuff, but this is where I draw the line." I am on the verge of exploding.

"But Roxanne, they don't catch you because you're a finer breed of bird," Thomas says.

"You don't get it, do you? This is demeaning!" I scream. I have to calm down, because I will never get anywhere with this crew if I'm hysterical.

The producer interrupts our conversation and chimes in with, "But, Ms. Newman, you signed a contract."

Is he kidding me? I can always get out of a contract. But I will not allow anyone I know to see me doing this shit. Keep it calm, girl. Keep it professional. I rush to my bag and pull out my contract, searching for the out, because of course, Taylor has gone over every detail of this contract, as all good lawyers should. Where is it, where is it? Okay, I found it. I approach the producer. "If you look in Section seventeen, clause four, you'll see that I have an out if the working conditions are not up to Union standards. My agent says that you never cleared this with him. I'll call the Union Representative as well as my attorney, Taylor Williams at Mills, Waters, Dennis, and Cois, and she will straighten things out immediately."

The producer slows down. "Mills, Waters, Dennis, and Cois? Well, let's not bring lawyers into this. We'll pay you for the day and find someone else." He looks around and spots Patty Andrews (who is my height and weight and will fit my costume perfectly). "Hey, Patty, it looks like this is your lucky day. Any objections to the meat cleaver scene?"

Patty perkily replies, "I'll do whatever it takes to sell more chicken."

"Thank you. Now put on the bird costume so we can stop wasting money."

Being publicly flogged by Jesse Jackson, the NAACP, and Al Sharpton? $150,000. Keeping Your Dignity? Priceless.

· 38 ·

Bianca

It's All About Me

Thanks to Professor Nicholas, I finally feel that things are coming together for me in L.A. Work is excellent—I'm handling three shows now, and there's talk of giving me a fourth, plus I've been tagged to co-organize one of the network's big annual events, which is a *major* coup—but it's still scary to start over in a new town, and it's been especially traumatic for me without my girls. I always put on a brave face when I talk to them, but the truth is, I don't have any real friends out here. My real friends are too far away and I was really beginning to feel totally isolated and lost, and I've found that you can't shop away loneliness. But that's all over now that I have Nicholas (who, incidentally, passed the Bathroom Check and House Check with flying colors). I'm not necessarily saying that I'm in love, but his presence is precisely the stabilizing element my life was missing. It's easy to get caught up in bullshit in L.A. if there's no one around to check you.

It turns out that Nicholas is not only a professor, he's also a writer, so we have that in common. He writes a weekly column in the *Los Angeles Times* that is, in my humble opinion, exactly like him—insightful, witty, provocative, and intelligent. Although he seems a bit uneasy at my

Industry Parties, he still manages to ridicule my more shallow associates without them realizing that he's poking fun at their absurdly inflated senses of self-importance. He's very laid back and easygoing, but superficiality is one thing that drives him crazy. Luckily, I don't have that problem.

It's true that in a lot of ways Nicholas and I are very different, but I think we really balance each other out. At Nicholas's urging, I've even started attending more "cultural" functions, like poetry readings and lectures on the African Diaspora. He's also very politically active, and actually managed to drag me out of bed on three consecutive Saturday mornings to help register Black and Latino voters in Watts and South Central. In turn, I'm introducing Nick to the wonderful world of Barney's and brie. And trying to make him over a tiny little bit—there's not a single designer piece in his closet (a couple of old Polo shirts are as close as it gets), but he's resisting. Pecs like his deserve to be showcased in Armani, not Arrow, and Lord knows he can afford it because he's got plenty saved up and he's super careful about his spending. In fact, he's always pestering me about my financial habits and saying that I need to be more careful and responsible. He's even offered to help me make a budget (I said no because I don't want him to see my credit card balances or find out that I've dipped into my 401(k), which I actually think is not such a bad move—I'm only borrowing from myself, and I pay myself interest, so I'm really *making* money if you think about it). Every time I come home with shopping bags, we have the same discussion, but I've noticed that he's less likely to complain if there's a Victoria's Secret bag sitting next to the Neiman's bag or the Gucci bag. He's a thrifty man, but he's still a man, if you get my drift.

The bottom line is, this man is the yin to my yang, and Lord knows I need someone in my life who (mistakenly) believes that caviar is not one of the basic food groups. Sure, at first, his turning off *Queer Eye for the Straight Guy* in favor of the History Channel was a bit upsetting, but hey, that's what TiVo is for. And did I mention the sex? Who knew professors were so freaky? Wow. If you don't know, now you know.

I think the real reason I like Nicholas so much is the security. I know it sounds clichéd, but he's the only man I've ever dated whom I trusted instantly and completely. If there's a problem, we discuss it like two intelligent adults. I haven't had to get ignorant with him once—and it's been six weeks! That must be some kind of record. I'll put it to you this way: Last week I skipped my weekly massage appointment with Sergei so that I could attend an antique car exhibit at the Peterson Automotive Museum with Nicholas. If that's not love, I don't know what is.

• • •

All the quality time I've been spending with Nicholas has been distracting me from a major problem: the upcoming Harvard trip with the girls. The truth is, I can't really afford to go, but I'll feel like such a loser if I'm the only one who doesn't go. That's the problem with being friends with a bunch of fabulous, smart Ivy League grads. It takes a lot just to keep up, but I refuse to be the weak link. Taylor makes tons of money (even if she never gets a chance to spend it), Carolyn is one of the hottest up-and-coming ad execs in town, and Rox is definitely going to be a huge star, it's just a matter of time. And what am I doing besides paying my Mastercard with a cash advance on my Visa? It's only exciting the *first* time you see your ankle in the background on *Extra.*

I've been so close so many times to telling the girls what a mess I've gotten myself into, but that would be like admitting that my Louis Vuitton carry-on is from a back room in Chinatown (I'll deny that even under pain of death, by the way); it's out of the question. Still, having to show up in Cambridge and mingle with people who actually own their own yachts at twenty-eight is going to take superhuman strength. My only consolation is that at least I look the part. My mother always said, "Fake it 'til you make it." Sometimes I think I misheard her, because I'm clearly working on "Fake it 'til you file for bankruptcy." And all the spin in the world can't make Chapter 11 sound good to your former classmates.

39

Carolyn

Nothing Personal

I am sitting in Taylor's living room preparing to go online and check my love2love.com mailbox. I signed up for this service last Monday by filling out a profile and scanning in a picture, and, for approximately $25 a month, I will purportedly "meet thousands of sensational singles just like [me]!" I have some very attractive, very eligible acquaintances who have ventured onto love2love or similar services, thus debunking the myth that only geeks and losers find love on the Net, so full speed ahead.

"Mail truck!" says the computer. I cross my fingers and hit "Read Mail." A-ha! Nestled amid the spam is a message from love2love! I double click on it and am confronted by the following:

Hi my name is steve, and i saw your profile on love2love, ur a very interesting women and i believe it would be fun owning u. pliz bear with me, i mean i am a lil' wild, uuuuuuuuuuuuuummm!!!!!!!!!!!i found out the hard way that just bcos a woman is pretty on the outside does'nt make her beautiful on the inside. u cant see a persons soul but u sure can feel it. And about relationships, i have a girlfriend but not my soul complement,someone whose eyes can reflect exactly what i feel and well fit like two sides of a broken coin in the garden meant for us where EVEN THE SERPENTS moves with their better half. A place where the stars up in the sky will watch over us like dead lovers eyes,so we can never go wrong! cant wait 2 hear from u."

"Jesus H. *Christ,*" I say, putting my hand to my throat.

Taylor is reading over my shoulder.

"Looks like you've got a live one," she says. "I guess you'll be adding 'being sacrificed to Baal' to your list of hobbies."

"Fuck off," I say, deleting the e-mail and blocking Steve's user profile so that he can never contact me again ever ever ever world without end.

"Some men offer you the moon," Taylor adds. "Steve's offering you broken coins, some snakes, dead people's eyeballs, and a lot of vowels. At least he keeps it real."

I ignore her. This is getting very, very depressing. Just this morning Carter and I were having coffee and making fun of the all-caps pornographic solicitation I received from someone styling himself "tittybomp69" when an e-mail showed up from "profderrick." I opened it and gradually my eyes brightened. Thirty-three, philosophy professor at Rutgers. Profile articulate, witty, indicative of liberal political views and, even better, a clean bill of mental health. Picture very appealing; beautiful eyes and a wonderful smile. In other words, just what the doctor ordered. I crowed triumphantly and read Professor Derrick's profile to Carter, who did not seem particularly enthused.

"Lookit," I insisted, wanting him to be as gleeful as I was. Carter sat down and scrolled dutifully through the profile. Near the bottom he stopped and squinted at the screen. Slowly a huge shit-eating grin spread over his face. He pointed at Professor Derrick's detailed physical profile, which I had not read because I was so entranced by the first three fourths of what he had written and the fact that he probably knew precisely what I meant by "zaftig" and did not run screaming. Eyes gray, hair black, physique athletic, height 5'4".

Five foot Four.

Fuck.

"Let's play a word association game," Carter said. "I'll go first. Elba, Waterloo, Josephine. No? Did you want to buy a vowel? A *short* vowel?"

"Dammit," I said, as the butterflies in my stomach encountered a cloud of DDT.

"You guys could go as Sylvester Stallone and Brigitte Nielsen for Halloween, although if I'm reading this correctly, Mr. Roarke and Tattoo might be a more accurate choice," Carter said, leaning over me and stretching luxuriously and deliberately to accentuate his own personal six feet and three inches. "He'd fit in a carry-on bag. You could rest your drink on his head at cocktail parties. It'd be like having your . . . your own personal Hobbit."

"But I said specifically that I wasn't interested in anyone under six feet," I protested.

"He obviously thought he'd *grow* on you," Carter snarked, picking up the Yoda action figure on my desk and dancing it across the top of the monitor to touch my cheek with a big wet kissing sound.

"Piss off, Carter," I said, a smile tugging at the corner of my mouth despite my distress and my ever-increasing depression over the fact that my love life is God's own personal running gag. "Just because you have supermodels falling at your feet on an hourly basis doesn't mean that everyone's life is that charmed," I added, and, try as I might, there was more than a trace of bitterness in my voice.

"Hey now, hey now," Carter said, sitting down on the drafting table and leaning toward me. "Slow down, Stinger. Where in the world would you get that crazy idea?"

"I mean, I put an ad on the Net, here's my picture, here's what I'm like, please be interested, and the only responses I get are from Bellevue fugitives and people who can't get on the teacup ride at Disneyworld," I said, and this time the bitterness was obvious. "What does that say about me? I've hit absolute bottom, Carter. I've resorted to running a classified Internet ad selling *me*, and nobody decent has made an offer." A tear ran down my cheek and I smeared it away angrily. Carter reared back, startled.

"Holy shit, Chief, don't cry!" he said quickly. "Are you crazy?! You've got it all wrong." I shook my head and reached for a Kleenex. Carter foundered for a minute, then seized Yoda again and thrust him in my face.

"Not to despair," he says in a creaky, froggy little voice. "Man you will find, appreciate you he will. Many things to offer have you. Crazy the man who sees them not." I started to laugh and Carter, inspired, proceeded.

"Midget, porn addict, serial killer—these matter not. Always remember you must—"

Laughing and crying, I waved Yoda away and blew my nose fiercely. Carter, obviously relieved at having averted a waterfall, began to juggle Yoda and two gum erasers.

"And, just for your information," he added, dropping all three of them and picking up the proofs for the bull pancreas drink (slogan: "It's Bad, and That's No Bull"), "it's rough all over. In the last two weeks, I've gone out with a soap actress who was a functional illiterate, a Wall Street lawyer who was so smashed by the time the entrée came that she tried to blow me under the table—"

"Whoa, now," I said.

"—a PA on the *Today* show who talked nonstop for two and a half hours about the time Bryant Gumbel came on to her, and a smokin' grad student who seemed halfway interesting but postponed our date because Mercury was in Astroglide or Everglades or something."

"Retrograde," I said, blowing my nose again.

"Whatever, she was into that yoga drum circle Richard Gere crystal power Dianetics horseshit," he said.

"Ladies and gentlemen," I said, "it appears that we have a winner, perhaps even a world record holder, in the Conflation of Belief Systems category."

"What I'm saying is," Carter said pointedly, "that everybody's out there looking for the right one and nobody's having an easy time. In the past month, you haven't had any dates—"

"Thank you so very very much," I said, blowing my nose again.

"—you haven't had any dates, and I've had five, and we're both still at Square One," he said contemplatively. "It's rough all over. And you're late for your two o'clock," he added.

"I'm going to be even later because I'm canceling my love2love account right this minute," I say.

"Good move, Chief," he said. "You can do better."

"Think so?" I said absentmindedly.

"Know so," he said, and awkwardly patted my shoulder.

"Thanks," I said, looking up at him. He shrugged and headed back to his office.

When I got back from lunch later that day, there was a Frodo figurine on my desk.

40

Taylor

All the Players Came from Far and Wide

The girls knew that my grandmother's surgery was the most traumatic event I'd ever experienced. After the surgery was over and a success, which I knew it would be, they all agreed to join me on my few precious days of vacation. Meschach was back in Asia, and although he'd wanted to take me away, I wasn't quite ready for that. Also, even though the doctors were saying how amazing and complete Nana's recovery had been, and even though she was already back and teaching music at a local community center, I was still shaken by the image of her looking so small and weak and sick when they'd first brought her out of the operating room. I was so worried about her that I didn't feel like having to be on point constantly. That turned out to be the right decision, because the first thing I did when I saw the girls in the airport was lose my shit completely and burst into tears, just stressed about life, exhausted from work, relieved that Nana was okay, glad to see my girls . . . you name it, I felt it, all at the same time. They dragged me into the airport bathroom and Bianca, who had started to cry a little bit herself, fixed my makeup while Carolyn and Roxanne held my hands and told me that everything was going to be okay.

And for the next couple of days, I knew it would be. I was with my friends, and we were young, beautiful, and in Vegas. It was set. It was all good. And it was going to be so, so ugly.

• • •

The moment we arrived on the Strip, we began to notice something strange. Too many men wearing tacky suits. Too many trashy women. At first, we chalked it up to the fact that, hey, it's Vegas. But as we went outside to catch a cab, it was as if *we* were the freaks. Sure, it was ninety degrees outside, but why was every woman we ran into nearly naked? And why did all of the men have on alligator shoes? And in every color of the rainbow. Colors in which God never made an alligator. Neon green. Fuschia. Yellow. It was the burnt orange pair that took the cake, the icing, the cherry on top, and the fucking oven, too.

Still, we ignored it all, and as the air-conditioned cab brought us closer to our new home for three days, the Bellagio, we forgot about the strange scenery. Any hotel with Chanel, Prada, and Hermès boutiques was home. But I'd leave the shopping to Bianca and Carolyn. I wanted to head straight to the hotel gift shop to buy my "beating the odds" books, and then head down to the casino floor to mix it up.

As we waited to check into our double-room suite, we noticed more strangely dressed people, and finally Bianca couldn't restrain herself.

"Just what in the hell is going on here?" she demanded.

"Baby, you don' know?" A man in a jaunty neon green suit responded, slurring his words.

"Umm, none of us knows," Roxanne replied.

"Donch'all know y'all in the presence of a true player?" the scantily clad woman hanging off his arm asked.

"Of course we know that, but we're not talking about me, we're talking about just what in the hell is going on in Vegas. It's packed in here, even for this town," I said.

"Oh, I get it. Y'all joking. Thass funny," Neon Green nodded, winking and flashing his diamond-encrusted teeth. "Doncha know what's goin' down in the get down on tha good foot?" he asked while bringing what looked like a platinum-covered toothpick to his mouth.

"No, I'm sorry, but I did *not* come to Las Vegas to kick it with Cephus and Reesie here," Carolyn said. Roxanne put a hand over her mouth. The rest of us were fascinated: What in the hell was this fool doing here? In the *Bellagio*? I damn sure didn't trek across the country and throw out as much as we were throwing per night to be surrounded by some pimp shit.

Oh, wait, we *are* surrounded by this pimp shit, and I'll be damned if that guy just might be . . . nah. Couldn't be. But that woman did say "player," and they both did sound country as all hell. Could it be? Can I actually believe my luck?

"We're in town for the International Player of the Year Awards! We made it. We finally made it! WE HAVE ARRIVED!" I screamed, truly in awe.

"Yes, in ghetto hell, apparently," Carolyn said, at which point Roxanne turned her around and frogmarched her abruptly in the direction of the Gucci boutique.

"You mean—*he'll* be here? Bishop Don 'Magic' Juan? I'll get to see the golden chalice? I cannot believe my luck." Bianca nearly fainted.

"Whatch'all know 'bout the Bishop?" he asked suspiciously. He didn't understand why we understood what we understood.

"What *don't* we know about the Bishop?" Bianca said, feeling slighted. Of course she knew her Pimpology, what career woman didn't?

After we retrieved Carolyn, we arrived at our fabulous "big spender" suite, upgrade courtesy of the silver-tongued Bianca. I quickly picked up the phone and dialed the concierge to find out where the awards were being held.

"It's like Christmas, Kwanzaa, New Year's Eve, and the Gay Pride Parade, all rolled into one," Bianca sighed, breaking open our complimentary bottle of champagne.

"No gay man I know would be caught dead in that Tommy Illnigger gear those idiots are rocking," Carolyn responded tartly. I wrote down the address on a pad.

"I only wanted to win a couple thousand dollars," I announced. "But it looks like this vacation is going to be priceless."

• • •

I was anxious to call the spa to book some body treatments. The spa in Vegas was truly the best game in town. But as I stepped into my white spa robe and headed toward the wet bar to have a martini as I waited for my ninety-minute facial, I couldn't help but wonder whether my life needed to be more like it was in Vegas. Why is it such a treat for me to get four days away from the office—in a row, with two of them being weekend days that in a normal job would belong to me already—with no worries? While I liked my job conceptually, the long hours and constant need to be perfect in all things and all ways were getting on my nerves. Not that I couldn't be Superwoman, because I'd damn sure give her a run for her money, but I couldn't help but wonder whether it was worth it. I mean, at the end of the day, what was I getting besides money? And the money was good, don't get me wrong, but it wasn't great. I still had to watch my spending. I could go crazy, but not kuh-razy. I could enjoy myself, but I couldn't live it up. Not all of the time anyway. And since I wasn't getting the whole enchilada, I had to think about the price I was paying for three quarters of it.

I had to admit, although I kept trying to push it to the back of my mind, that the incident with the client and my "vacation" had pissed me off. But maybe it was due to a little bit of vacation dementia. Too much of a good thing makes you think that life should always be that way. But while I knew that the idea of a constant vacation was too good to be true, I also knew that constant eighteen-hour days couldn't be good either. Balance is the key to life. Or so I've read.

Feeling completely relaxed after a hot-stone massage, an hour of reflexology, and an oxygen and Vitamin C facial, I returned to the room to change. I called Meschach and we chatted for a while. I felt so good after we hung up that I decided to go down to the casino and kill a couple of hours before our eight P.M. reservation at Smith & Wollensky's.

I had just finished cashing in my chips when I spotted Lime Green and his companion, only this time he was clad in a truly frightening purple ensemble.

"Y'all sho' lookin' fine this evenin'. You know, I never did introduce myself. I'm Pico Pete and this here's my lady, Déjeuner." He gave me a big smile.

It *would* be like ignorant bumpkins to name themselves something exotic-sounding, not knowing what the fuck they were talking about. But in this instance, it seemed like an appropriate name; I'm sure plenty of men had eaten Déjeuner.

"Pico Pete, we were just heading off to the Ball. Shouldn't you be there already? Don't the pimps in the running have to get there earlier than the rest?" I was trying my best to be considerate.

"I wuz last year's winner, li'l mama, so I can't be in the running this year. It's time to pass tha crown on to another pimp. I just thought I'd have one las' stroll down tha strip before my reign is over." He was almost on the verge of tears.

"So, why y'all goin' to the Ball?" he added. "Y'all ain't with nobody. That I seen anyway."

"Oh, we're not in The Life," I said immediately. "We write for magazines, and we were hoping that we would be able to get inside to cover the Player's Ball." Pico Pete nodded and looked impressed.

"Y'all meet me at eleven p.m. sharp in the lobby and y'all can come on with me. Pico Pete gonna take care a y'all."

Carolyn almost had kittens at the thought of the triple play of (1) going to the Players' Ball, (2) in the company of a real pimp, (3) under false pretenses, and Bianca, although she wanted to meet the Bishop, wasn't too hot on it either. Roxanne was thrilled, though, and together we beat them down for two hours over dinner, until at last they agreed to drag along. I know I'm a damn good lawyer because anyone who could convince Carolyn Ware Phillips and Bianca Elise King that it was in their best interests to attend an awards ceremony for pimps and prostitutes is nothing short of a fucking genius.

• • •

Pico Pete's ride was a pimped-out Caddy stretch with 24K gold trim and rounds and a bumper sticker saying "Federation of American Pimps." When the door opened, we saw that there were fifteen other women waiting in there. Ah, so Déjeuner was Pico's "bottom bitch." The tension was ugly and immediate and we all took a step back involuntarily.

"Y'all stupid bitches chill the fuck out," Pico Pete said. "These ain't bitches; they write for a magazine." The atmosphere eased up at once and almost got friendly once Roxanne and Bianca started snapping pictures and Carolyn started asking the women their names and writing them down on a little pad she'd taken from the hotel. Once we got to the Mandalay Bay, Pico Pete got us inside with no trouble and the show really started.

The ballroom was filled with every g-string and thong that Frederick's of Hollywood had ever made. In every color. In every size. We saw male prostitutes. Crack heads. Winos. And then we saw pimp royalty. The Bishop. And with luck still being a lady, we saw seats right behind the Bishop and his entourage.

Bianca maneuvered herself into the seat right behind him. And although she had assured me that The Bishop never let ANYONE drink out of his chalice, EVER, if any woman could pop a pimp's cherry and change his mind, it was Bianca.

Ballin' Bruce walked away with this year's crown, and after the show, the Bishop invited us back to his penthouse suite. He wasn't a pimp anymore, but he still loved being at the center of the action.

"I swear," Carolyn said as Max Julien walked by, "I need to take lessons from these men. That fool over there, Big Daddy Sweet or whatever the fuck his name is, was pitching hoeing in a way that really made it sound appealing, like why the hell would anyone sane ever choose to do anything else? Seriously. I was about to ask him if he had a 401(k) plan."

Bianca strolled by on The Bishop's arm, sipping from the Chalice.

"Oh, yeah, it's time to go," I said.

"Yes, before the entire pimping infrastructure crumbles," Carolyn replies. "I'll go get Roxanne; I think she was pumping Déjeuner for sex tips."

We got back to the room around six A.M. and Bianca popped another bottle of Moët.

"Are you fucking crazy?" I said.

"What the hell?" Bianca shrugged. "You're only young once, right?"

She's right, I thought somberly as she filled four flutes. She's absolutely fucking right.

Everyone raised their glasses.

"To new love—for you three, anyway—and old friends," Carolyn said.

"To cute men and great sex," Roxanne added.

"To the good life and everything that comes with it," Bianca chimed in. Everyone looked at me.

"To us doing this again at Harvard-Yale!" I blurted out. The three of them clapped and we all downed the Champagne at one go, but I was lost in thought. I don't want to grow apart from my friends or sabotage what might be a new love. I want to enjoy a good life, to live well and be happy. But my job makes all of this so hard. What the fuck am I going to do?

· 41 ·

Roxanne

Point Break

Exasperated, I call Carolyn two days after we get back from Vegas and tell her, "I'm done."

"What do you mean, you're done?" she asks, concern growing in her voice.

"The auditions, the callbacks, the waiting to hear, the rejection day after fucking day. Booking the part and then getting fired. I'm moving back home to San Francisco and becoming a teacher . . ."

She immediately interrupts me.

"First of all, you genuinely hate children."

"I do not hate children," I retort.

"Do the words '*rotting, fart-filled corpses*' ring any bells? Allow me to direct your attention to Episode #3 of Your Brief Substitute Teaching Career, working title 'Homeroom,' " she responds.

"Yeah, but that was Harlem. Marin County is different," I counter.

Carolyn ignores me and continues: "A return to suburbia is hardly an escape from bullshit. It'll just be a different kind of bullshit; you'll end up being worried about getting into the Links instead of getting an audition."

This makes me laugh a little. And she has a small point. But she is not nearly finished. Carolyn continues, "Here are some fundamental truths: You should have your own show. You are an excellent actor. You are beautiful. You have to have faith that there is some sort of fundamental order in the cosmos. But the cosmos, being very large, can also be very slow. You have to hang in there and give it a chance to recognize your presence and reorder itself accordingly. Now please hold while I call for backup." She conferences in Taylor and Bianca—the other two founding members of the Roxanne Newman Fan Club. Fuck it, the three of them are the only members.

"What do you bitches want?" Taylor asks in her usual charmingly aggressive manner.

"Bianca, are you on?" Carolyn inquires.

"I'm here, but I'm searching for competitive rates on renting a castle," Bianca states as if it were the most natural thing in the world.

I begin with my dilemma, "I'm thinking about quitting acting, moving back home, and becoming a teacher. I can't take this bullshit business anymore."

"Roxanne, are you crazy? You're fabulous, charming, and beautiful. The world will recognize your talents soon. And when they finally do, they'll have to pay you back for all the gutter scraping, shitty, fucked-up ways they treated you," says Taylor.

Bianca butts in before Taylor can really get going. "Yeah. Move back into your parents' house and wake up every morning to your mother asking you what time you teach your ceramics class at the Color Me Mine store because she wants to bring her bridge club in later to make personalized coffee mugs."

"Very funny," I say, but she's not finished yet either.

"Then your dad'll pat you on the head every morning before handing you your five dollars in lunch money."

"My dad's not that cheap," I say defensively.

"Oh don't worry, you won't have to live there for long because your high school boyfriend Godfrey is back in the picture and he wants to marry you!" Bianca jabs.

"It's unfair to play the wack high school boyfriend card," I sigh.

"Well, he's still only five feet one, but he just got out of the Marines and he's now the Assistant Branch Manager of the Bank of America located conveniently inside Ralph's Grocery Store," Bianca predicts. Carolyn and Taylor are laughing in the background.

"I don't like the Let's Predict Roxanne's Sad Future Game," I tell them.

"Well, if you didn't say such preposterous things, we could play the Let's Predict Roxanne's Fabulous Future Game," Taylor says.

Bianca starts back in. "You and Godfrey will live happily ever after with your three short, mentally unbalanced children, whom you will drive around in your dirty white minivan. You'll get the requisite soccer mom haircut and start shopping at either Talbot's or Sears, depending on how the money is. You'll join a bowling team and even take up knitting."

"You are utterly hateful," I tell them.

"Roxanne's more of a Tog Shop type, don't you think?" Carolyn asks. "With crap knickknacks from Lillian Vernon."

Bianca continues, "Then once a year you'll come with Carolyn, Taylor, and me aboard one of our yachts and get a taste of the 'good life.' Only you'll have to leave early because Godfrey will have gotten drunk again and hit on one of the crew members—Harry—and you'll be too embarrassed to stay aboard with all those rock stars and fashionistas who will look at you with pity every time you come up on deck wearing a sundress you got on sale at Susie's Casuals and looking utterly defeated. Doesn't that sound good?"

"Our job here is done," Carolyn says. "Roxanne, call us when you get some sense."

• • •

Maybe the girls are right, but I am at my wit's end. They can forget me going to Harvard-Yale weekend. I had promised myself that I wouldn't go back to school until I was rich or famous, preferably both. Especially since Finlay will be there, rubbing her new TV show in my face. Saying you're a substitute teacher/struggling actor to a bunch of I-bankers, lawyers, and doctors is humiliating. Ram is still fucking my brains out, which is distracting me from the fact that he's kind of a bullshit artist. I don't think we're particularly compatible when we're not naked, but the multiple orgasms buy this relationship more time.

One more piece of bad news will push me over the edge, so of course it makes no sense to check my mail right now, but something good has to happen soon, doesn't it? The mail usually brings nothing but pain and dreaded bills that I struggle to pay, notices that my loans will soon be in default, angry letters from Blockbuster saying my movies are overdue, jury duty summons. But today is a new day. The girls have given me a tiny bit of hope. I open my mailbox, and staring back at me is a heavy, eggshell-colored formal envelope with the Gray Foundation logo in the upper-left-hand corner. My breathing quickens. I rip the envelope open in the middle of my building's entryway. It reads:

Dear Ms. Newman,

The Gray Foundation regrets to inform you that you have not been selected as a Gray Fellow this year. We can only award a limited number of grants but encourage you to apply again next year. Thank you for your submission.

> *Sincerely,*
> *Ashton Gray*
> *President, the Gray Foundation*

Fuck. I thought that things couldn't get worse, and again, I am wrong. I can't deal anymore. I just can't. I was holding on to that tiny kernel of hope that I could get away for a little while and do something else. Something that would help me recharge, but no. Fucked again.

• 42 •

Bianca

Poverty Doesn't Suit Me

I've come to a very important conclusion: Working is for suckers. So my new plan is that I'm going to marry rich. I mean, fuck being independent; I'll settle for marrying someone who's independently wealthy. I'm fairly certain that feigning interest in my rich husband and picking out emeralds at Cartier is much less painful than trailing behind B-list celebrities on the red carpet, holding THEIR Hermès bags and THEIR Chanel sunglasses—not to mention the pay is MUCH better.

What's come over me, you ask? Where is Nicholas, you say? Well, Nicholas is right here next to me in the bed asleep with his arm around my waist, and I'm sort of mostly bullshitting about marrying someone rich; it's just that I've had it up to here with toadying to disaster celebrities and putting up with their horseshit, which is, unfortunately, a major part of my job description. Last night was ATN's annual fall season launch party, and some of these fools took it to the next level, to the extent that right now I'm so through that I don't ever want to have to work another day in my entire life.

I'd been helping one of the senior publicists plan the event, and two days ago, she came down with the flu. With everyone swamped trying to get coverage on the new season, my boss put me in charge of the event. I was thrilled: finally, I'd get a chance to make an impression and show my boss that I was ready for more responsibility. Lord knows I need the money that comes with it: I saw this beautiful Celine coat with a chinchilla collar that will be perfect for Cambridge, and chinchilla doesn't just pay for itself. Anyway, the party started off great. I had all the talent arrivals timed perfectly and I personally greeted each one as they stepped out of their limos, then escorted them down the press line. To an outsider, the red carpet must seem like a nightmare, with paparazzi screaming and taking a million pictures while reporters from *Access Hollywood* and *E! News Daily* thrust their microphones in people's faces; once you actually get on it in real life, though, you realize that it's actually far worse than that. It's an obstacle course of land mines.

First, before the talent even steps out of the limo, you have to talk to the reporters and make sure they even want to interview your talent. Let's face it, ATN isn't exactly the home of the biggest stars on earth, and the worst thing you can do is escort an actor to a reporter who's not interested in talking to them because they're not fabulous enough. The reporter gets annoyed with you for wasting their time as they ask a couple of stupid questions just to be polite, and the talent is embarrassed about being put in an awkward position. But that's a rookie mistake, and Bianca King is no rookie, so the red carpet parade went off without a hitch. Two and a half hours into the party, the fervor had finally died down outside and I was able to go in and actually enjoy the party that I'd worked so hard to plan. Or rather, make sure the talent was enjoying the party. Unfortunately for me, Mike Madison, the jiveass sidekick on *Craig an' Them*, was having a little too much fun. He was having so much fun that the bartender actually *ran out* of Hennessy.

Sensing an impending disaster, I suggested to Mike that perhaps it was time for him to call it a night. I guess in his Hennessy-induced stupor, he was under the impression that he and I were going to call it a night *together*, because when I walked him out to make sure he made it into his limo without peeing on the red carpet or puking on the senior vice president of programming, he pulled me into the car and proceeded to slide one drunken hand up my skirt. Now, normally, said B-list actor would have drawn back a nub—and if Nicholas had been there, they'd have had to re-name the show *Craig an' One Fewer of Them*—but fearing for my job, I played the whole thing off like a joke and talked my way out of the car ten excruciating minutes later without letting him touch anything more ex-citing than my strategically placed elbow. To my dismay, my boss was standing at the curb, waiting for the valet to bring his car when I finally managed to slip out of Mike's limo. He gave me a puzzled look before I smiled weakly and scurried past him.

Can you believe it? I'm gonna lose my job over a thirty-six-year-old playing a college student whose catch phrase is "Man-o-man, you's about to CATCH IT!" See? This is why I have to marry rich. I have no choice. I can't take this anymore. I know rich men are notoriously difficult and de-manding, but I don't care how much of an asshole the man is, as long as he understands that diamonds purchased at Zales are unacceptable. I can handle it when he tells his second assistant to buy my birthday gift. I don't care if he has affairs. As long as I don't have to answer someone else's phone ever again, he can yell at me all he wants. Gay affairs? I'll be his cover girl. As long as I have a new Mercedes every year, he can . . .

Oh, hell. I can't marry rich. Because I'm in love with Nicholas, and he's not rich, nor is he pressed to be (sure, he's got a pile put away for re-tirement, but it's not a *rich* pile). He always says that as long as he has a roof over his head, food on his table, books in his bookshelves, and his *bella flora* in his arms (that's what he calls me; God, he's *so* fantastic), he's satisfied. So I guess I'm not marrying a rich man, which means I guess I'd better tear up my resignation letter.

• • •

Luckily, my boss was well aware that Mike Madison is a skeevy, drunken pervert and thought I handled the whole situation beautifully. He con-gratulated me on running the party so smoothly and even hinted at a pos-sible promotion. Unfortunately, I had no time to celebrate because my finances have continued to slip further out of control. I'll put it this way: Rico is now my best friend. Along with "Today Is Payday," "Advances R Us," and "Quickie Cash." I have four cash advances out right now, all due on my next payday, which is tomorrow. Total amount of the checks I've written: $1200. My paycheck: $1073. I'm sitting at my desk pretending to work, but I'm officially panicking now. I can't afford to bounce any more checks at my bank. If I do, they're going to cancel both my checking account and my savings account. Oh wait, they've already closed my savings account due to the fact that there hasn't been any money in it since I got out here.

I blame all of this on L.A. and this job, which is going really well but which doesn't have the perks my old job did. I'm making contacts and meeting people, some of them pretty important, but instead of being up to my ears in complimentary gift bags filled with designer goodies, I'm up to my ears in debt. Instead of figuring out how I'm going to get the $150 I need to cover my checks by tomorrow, I decided to go downstairs and get some lunch, thinking that I'd be able to think more clearly after a sashimi salad and a Jamba Juice. It wasn't until I placed my order at Udon Palace that I realized that I didn't have any cash. I could have given her a credit card, but why waste this nice woman's time? Embarrassed, I canceled my order and slinked out the door and back to my cubicle. Hungry and desperate, I rummaged around in my desk and came up with half a box of stale melba toast and a can of split pea soup. I'd never been that excited about soup and crackers in my life. While my soup heated up in the microwave, I helped myself to one of the free sodas in the office kitchen.

After lunch, I gave in and made the call every twenty-something dreads: asking my parents for money. My parents aren't wealthy people, but they did teach me to appreciate the finer things in life in a sensible manner. My father taught me that you should always save 10 percent of your paycheck for a rainy day and my mother taught me that EVERY-THING eventually goes on sale. I have consistently ignored both of these sage pieces of advice. So I was relieved in a perverse sort of way when Dad's secretary reminded me that my parents were on a cruise in the Bahamas and wouldn't be back until next week.

Closing my eyes, I shoved my hands through my hair, an old habit that surfaces when I'm really stressed. As I lowered my hands, my tennis bracelet got tangled in my hair and in my frustration I ripped out some of Matteo's best work. Then it hit me: I was wearing the answer to my problems! Feigning a headache, I left work early and headed straight to Beverly

Hills Pawn. Did you know that you have *three months* to claim pawned merchandise? Jesse, the pleasant young man behind the steel cage, gave me $200 for the diamond tennis bracelet my parents gave me for my twenty-first birthday. I will definitely be able to pay back the money (plus interest) by November. I don't know why I was ever worried. I'm a very resourceful girl. I always think of something.

· 43 ·

Carolyn

That's the Way I Like It

"How are you feeling about Harvard-Yale?" Dr. Guisewite says. The answer is, not particularly good. I cannot wait to see Bianca again, I will enjoy visiting some of my former professors, and it will be great fun to wreak havoc in the streets of Cambridge, but there will be Other People at the reunion, people whom I have managed to avoid for the past seven years by attending no alumni events of any kind. There will be old flames and old rivals, old enemies, and very few old friends outside of our foursome.

"I don't want to go," I say.

"Why not?"

"I don't want everyone to see how fat I've gotten," I say in a very small voice.

"Is that the only thing that you think they'll see when they look at you?"

"It's the only thing I would see," I reply. "Nobody is going to notice or care that I'm doing really well at a great job or that I'm slightly less crazy than I was then."

"Nobody else is going to care, or *you* don't care? I think you may be assuming that your appearance is the only thing that will make an impression on others because, in a certain sense, it's the only thing that makes an impression—a negative impression—on you. In your mind, the self-loathing based on your body image has completely overshadowed and blotted out all of your personal and professional accomplishments over the last eight years. And I think you may be projecting that onto your former classmates."

"Maybe," I say. "But be realistic. Most people aren't going to be asking me what's going on at my job; they'll just see how fat I am and snicker to their friends."

"Why would you care what people like that think of you?"

"I don't know," I say. "I just don't want people laughing at me and talking about me the way they did when I came back from crazy leave," I add, and reach for a tissue. Dr. Guisewite waits for me to stop crying.

"You've come a very long way since then, Carolyn," she says softly. "And if these other people haven't progressed similarly, their opinions shouldn't matter to you, because they're beneath you. I firmly believe that you should attend. And I think you'll find that if you just be—"

"Are you about to tell me to be myself?" I say suspiciously. "Because that is the dumbest advice ever. It's like telling someone to 'do the right thing.' What the hell does that even mean, 'be yourself'?"

Dr. Guisewite smiles.

"I was indeed going to tell you to be yourself, and I agree that it is a deceptively simple suggestion," she says, "but it is, at the end of the day, solid advice, and I think that it gives us a platform for an exercise that you might find useful. Our time is up, but I want you, over the course of this next week, to make a list of things you like and bring it with you next time. Not ideals or ideas, not people, just things."

I look at her out of the corner of my eye.

"And Carolyn," she adds, "don't do it in the cab on the way over here next Wednesday," she says.

She knows me a little too well.

"I want you to spend some time on this and really think about it."

So on Saturday I sit down with pen and paper and start my list. It flows easily, but when I look back over it, I realize that at least a couple of things on it are not quite right.

For example, the third item on my list is "Gangsta Rap." Now that I think about it, I do not like gangsta rap. In fact, I believe that I hate it. With a passion. But Darrell, whom I dated for a year and a half in college, absolutely loved it, and it was all he ever listened to. I would put on anything from Tribe Called Quest to Coltrane or Handel over dinner and the minute he put the last bite of food in his mouth he would jump up and go to the CD player, and shortly someone would be bellowing about bitches on they nutz and niggaz this and gatts that for the rest of the evening. Rather than shove his CDs up his ass sideways and risk losing him, I convinced myself that I liked it.

"Environmental awareness." These days, I recycle only when someone is watching, but because of Mark, I was in the front line of every Earth Day rally and sporting a rat's nest on top of my head for eight months because hair spray is bad for the ozone layer, blow dryers guzzle electricity, and the chemicals in relaxers are toxic.

"Verdi." He was Giuseppe's favorite composer because Verdi was his namesake; I stifled yawns as he, enraptured, conducted imaginary orchestra after imaginary orchestra, waiting patiently until the last strains died away and he turned to me, dark eyes blazing, and said in broken English, "Now it is the time that we make the love, *cara mia.*"

Huh. Verdi stays on the list.

The madness did not stop after graduation; far from it. I Brazilian bikini-waxed for Joseph and stopped shaving my legs for Kwame; I stopped wearing heels for Dennis and wore nothing but black for Jim; I became an opera buff for Bilal and a vegetarian for Matt; a football junkie for Damon and an earth mother for Tommy; a rabid Afrocentrist for Alec and a bourgeois princess for Malik.

In short, I became insane.

And this list is completely wrong.

Three hours and a pile of crumpled paper later, my list looks like this:

reading	crabmeat
neo-soul	stiletto heels
old school funk/soul	cartoons
doing nothing	drawing

jewelry	comedy
massages	champagne
interior design magazines	violins
action movies	dresses
sleeping	trip-hop
mashed potatoes	candles
wine	my job
KFC	the beach
jazz	
perfume	

This is more like it. I read the list again. Even if Bilal, Damon, Matt, Tommy, Brian, Dennis, Kwame, Giuseppe, Willie, Andy, Chinua, Jerome, Mark, Gil, Ray, Darrell, and Jack would find fault with the girl on this piece of paper, she seems like someone I would want to hang out with.

And because I will be hanging out with her twenty-four hours a day for the rest of my life, I think that perhaps mine is the only opinion that matters.

I just wish she were thinner.

· 44 ·

Taylor

The Dirty Deed

I was just turning the key in my lock when I heard the phone ringing through the door. I looked down at my watch and nearly pissed on myself—Meschach was finally back in town, and we had a date tonight.

We'd had a great time on the three or four dates we'd managed between his travel and my Wells submissions, and there had been some high-quality necking, but we hadn't done the deed. Although we'd been thousands of miles apart almost from the minute we met, we'd grown very tight. Through our phone calls (each and every day, count 'em, baby!), we'd managed to find a closeness that I don't think we would have found if we'd had sex in the meantime. We'd probably have ended up spending more time fucking than talking. But finally, with no further ado, it was time to go for it. He actually seemed like he could be a keeper, for real, so I decided to show him my softer side.

The gong of my doorbell snapped me back to reality. I looked through the peephole and smiled. It was Meschach and, to nobody's surprise, he looked fabulous. There really was nothing like a good-looking man to make a woman feel incredible. The night suddenly seemed full of possibilities. My stomach was cramped in knots. I opened the door to a whiff of his cologne. Burberry's. My sense of smell was hardwired to my sexuality, and a good-smelling man was my weakness. The caterpillars were turning into butterflies. Meschach bent down, enveloped me in his arms, and gently grazed his lips against my cheek. The butterflies took flight. All of the meditations, all of the soul-searching, and it all came down to this? Burberry's?

"You look wonderful," he whispered while handing me two white orchids. I melted.

"Thank you," I said shyly. "Black looks very good on you." He knew what I meant, but fortunately, he didn't run with it. His eyes simply gleamed. So maybe it's more than Burberry's, it's definitely those dark, warm eyes, too.

"Would you like champagne or a cocktail?" I asked, my heart racing.

"Whatever you're having," he grinned. Okay, it's not just the Burberry's or those dark, warm eyes, it's that beautiful, inviting smile as well.

"Moët it is." If I can just make it to the wet bar.

As we passed the time with predinner conversation, I couldn't help but notice how good it felt to be in the company of a man again. Someone I wanted to listen to. Someone who didn't make me want to roll my eyes into the back of my head. Someone who wasn't so suave that you knew it had to be an act. Someone who was gentle and respectful, but still masculine. I was determined to savor the feeling.

As we walked out of my apartment, I looked back over my shoulder to catch him making sure my door was pulled tightly against the frame. Protective. A good sign. I stepped in front of him, bolted the locks, and smiled to myself. My hands trembled. Not just the Burberry's, not just those dark, warm eyes, not just that beautiful, inviting smile, but his presence, period. He gently placed his hand on the back of my head and stroked the back of my neck. He looked at me and smiled. I smiled back, finally feeling calm. As we waited for the elevator, I leaned against him. He placed his chin on the top of my head. I smelled his cologne again. This was what I'd been missing. I'd almost forgotten what this felt like. And I resolved never to let myself go long enough to forget all the way.

After dinner, we headed over to Meschach's place—it was fabulous. Delightful. He lived at 80th and Amsterdam, in a fabulous prewar building that he had completely renovated with the newest amenities. Although we'd been dating a while, I had refused to come back to his place. I needed a bulletproof no-booty insurance policy. I excused myself to go to the bathroom and ran a Bianca Bathroom Check. Nothing incriminating.

He brought out a cold bottle of champagne and lit the wall sconces—a nice touch. Thinking of poor Carolyn, I waited to hear the phone ring with a call from the fiancée who was halfway across the country, but after half a bottle of champagne, and no call from anyone, I started to relax. Now it was time to enter Bitch Mode. I wanted to set up some ground rules and boundaries. Most women don't have enough sense to take that route.

"Meschach, I don't have time for bullshit, and neither do you. I think you're charming, handsome, and sexy. We've been getting closer over the past two months, and before we take this any further, particularly in this sketchy day and age, I need to know whether I can count on you to be with me and me only." Hardly the way a man wants to start off a romantic evening, but shit, I had more to be concerned about than his ego; I also had to worry about my health and my fucking heart.

"I was just thinking," he said, "how glad I am, in retrospect, that we were separated all of that time. I've wanted to tear off your clothes from the moment I met you, but if I'd been able to do that, we probably wouldn't have gotten to know each other the way we have."

Shit, is he in my head or what?!

"And I firmly believe that you are a woman that I want to continue to get to know." He bent and kissed my hand, then slid his tongue across my knuckles.

"In several different ways," he added, winking up at me slyly. I damn near died.

"That's not an answer," I managed to say. Horny or not, I need to know what the fuck is going on.

"I respect your boundaries and I respect you for delineating them so clearly. I respect that, and you're not asking me for anything I wouldn't ask of you. I have not been with another woman since we started getting to know one another, and I don't plan to do so as long as you and I are involved in this manner. Does that satisfy you?"

I nodded, weak with relief. I'd needed to hear him say that so badly; I needed to have at least the token assurance that I wasn't going to put myself out there and get fucked over for my pains.

"Now," he said, coming toward me and sweeping me up into his arms, "there are some other things that need to be satisfied, aren't there?" He pulled my head back and attacked my throat with his mouth, right there on the balcony.

"I'm going to eat your pussy until you cum all over my face, and I won't stop until you're absolutely exhausted, until the thought of having your body shake from one more orgasm makes you want to beg for mercy." His tongue snaked in and around my ear and I shook, knowing that if he could make my *ear* feel like that, I was in some seriously deep shit.

"All night, at dinner, I wanted to throw you face first on the table. I'd planned on reaching my hand in the ice bucket to pull out some cold water to cool off your hot pussy. But I knew you wouldn't be satisfied until I'd put my mouth on you. And that is precisely what I plan to do."

He was supposed to be coming undone, not me, but he didn't have a hair out of place. I had never met a man this intensely sexual or heard anyone talk to me like that. He bent down and lifted up my skirt, moved my panties over and began to give me the night of my young life. I was mesmerized. Dick-whipped. Tongue-lashed. It was so good, I was almost in love.

Almost.

The next morning, I barely managed to escape his apartment with my clit intact. But escape I did. On the cab ride home, I didn't even care about being late for work.

• 45 •

Roxanne

Lifeline

I have been in a funk for almost two weeks. I can barely talk to the girls, and when I do, I'm so snappy they want to shoot me. I'm hiding from Ram. I told my parents that I'm going to move home, which actually upset them. Then I realized that I can't move home or the monotony will kill me. I can barely get out of bed. I'm so tired of this emotional roller coaster and I'm particularly tired of feeling like my life is one big series of bad choices. This blows. I can't get an acting job, the Gray Foundation won't let me escape to Brazil, I have to look at Finlay's ugly mug on my TV screen and in my magazines, and the streets of Harlem seem paved with chicken bones and urine. The phone rings and instead of ignoring it, I check the caller ID. It's Sebastian. I'm really not in the mood for him right now, but I answer anyway. I'm desperate for some joy.

"So I hear you're bummed out," he says, all mellowed out.

"Yeah. Shit's terrible right now," I halfheartedly respond.

"Well, now's the time to come to California," he coos in an annoyingly upbeat tone.

"The last thing I can afford right now is a plane ticket, unless I'm packing up my shit and going home to Mom and Dad."

"Sounds to me like somebody's a quitter."

"Hell, yeah. I'm a quitter."

"Go to JFK Airport tomorrow at seven p.m. To the American Airlines terminal. If you swipe your credit card, I'm pretty sure you'll find an e-ticket with your name on it."

"What are you talking about?" I ask incredulously. "I don't have any credit cards with enough room on them for a plane ticket, so I think you're mistaken."

"I bought you a ticket. You obviously need some time out of the rat race, and you'll spend it with me. Talented, gorgeous chicks in my family can't have breakdowns and give up on themselves. It's just not cool. Come for a month, then make a decision about what you're going to do." *Wow.* I can't believe this.

"Thank you. You don't know how much this means to me, Uncle S."

"Uh huh. That's why I'm doing it. You need a lifeline, and if I don't throw it to you, who will?"

I call Carolyn and tell her the good news. She's relieved. "I was convinced that we were going to have a replay of sophomore year, only we were going to be calling your parents, not mine, so I'm *so* glad to hear that. Sebastian's living proof that there are good Black men in the world."

"Yeah, yeah."

"I'm just saying that sometimes men come through for you when you least expect it. Have a great time, soak up some California sun, and come back as the Roxy we know and love."

I call Ram and he comes over to give me a proper send-off. Then the questions start. "What does this mean for our relationship?" he probes.

"There's no other man in my life but you, and I'm taking the B.O.B. bullet with me for those lonely California nights." I accompany this information with a kiss and he seems satisfied.

"Yeah, but what if you find some sketchy surfer dude to fuck?"

"Listen. I either leave or I get put in a straitjacket."

"You're so melodramatic."

"Yes, I am. Get over it." The glowing sheen of new love has faded fast, and Ram's officially on my nerves.

But the bright side is that I'm leaving all this behind tomorrow. All I need to take are some bathing suits, some shorts, and some sunscreen. I desperately need something in my life to change.

· 46 ·

Bianca

Saint Nick

Shit. I am so late. Nick really hates it when I'm late, but they lie when they say you can get anywhere in L.A. in twenty minutes. I was supposed to meet him fifteen minutes ago, but I'm coming from the set of *Craig an' Them*, which tapes in godforsaken Sun Valley, and the 405 is an absolute nightmare. A normal person would just call him and tell him they're running late, but a broke bitch like me had her cell phone cut off last week for nonpayment. I know I shouldn't complain, but I am not looking forward to a lecture when I show up. That's the thing about professors, they're always lecturing. Even when people would rather not hear about the wonders of punctuality for the millionth time. It's funny that the things I like most about Nicholas (his realness and honesty) are also the things that irritate me the most. In all other ways, he's great. He's got a twisted sense of humor like me, he's a gentlemen, and he never lies. Although I'm beginning to wonder where one draws the line between honesty and tactlessness.

I had planned to leave the set much earlier, but one of the senior publicists got an emergency phone call (probably from his coke dealer) and had to leave, so he asked me to wrap up things on the set with a visiting reporter from *TV Guide*. Rule number one in publicity: Never leave a reporter unattended on the set, not even for Nicholas. And thank God I didn't; China Barry, a notorious PCB who's playing the female lead, threw yet another tantrum because the craft services table didn't have hot sauce, so while she was turning the air blue with "motherfuckers" on one end of the set, I was deftly steering the reporter toward the other to introduce him to the rapper who plays the male lead, Malik Walker, a.k.a. "Groove," who is every publicist's dream: witty, charming, and polite. That interview went beautifully and by the time it was done, someone had gotten China's ass into her trailer. I avert at least one major crisis every day; I am so good at this job that it kills me sometimes.

But speaking of killing me, when I finally got to the Louisiana Shrimp Company forty-five minutes late, Nicholas was Cajun hot.

"Sorry I'm late, sweetie. I got stuck on the set," I said breathlessly, sliding into the booth.

"A call would have been nice," he said a little tightly.

"I gave up my cell phone last week. I'm trying to save money." Gave up, cut off, what's the difference?

He started to smile a little, like I knew he would.

"That's great, Bianca. I'm glad you're taking control of your finances. Don't you feel better now? Oh, and have you looked at those mutual funds we talked about last week?" he asked hopefully. It was sweet that Nicholas was always encouraging me to be more responsible with my spending, but did he have to hound me about it? I was doing the best I could.

"Not yet, but I'll do it first thing tomorrow, I promise," I said, picking up a menu. "So, what looks good?" I added, trying to change the subject.

"I think I'm having the fried oyster po' boy. What about you?"

"Amazing," I said, scanning the sticky, laminated menu decorated with little shrimp dressed as cowboys, "nothing on here costs more than ten dollars, including the steaks." Shit, would it kill him to take me somewhere where a celebrity sighting other than Gary Coleman wasn't an utter impossibility? If only he would just agree to eat at normal places like Balboa or Ago, but no, he always wants to go somewhere "cozy." I'm beginning to think "cozy" means "cheap and fattening" in Italian. Last week he dragged me all the way to Pasadena for macaroni and cheese at a place called Bubba's. I left Texas for a reason.

"Don't be such a snob, Bianca. Just because it doesn't cost a lot doesn't mean it's not good."

"Right, and just because it's cheap doesn't mean it's not bad," I snapped.

I saw Nicholas starting to get angry again, and right then the horrors of the L.A. dating scene passed before my eyes in a sickening blur.

"I'm so sorry," I sighed, reaching across the green picnic table to take his hand. "I'm just tired. This place is great. It reminds me of home, actually." Yeah. Yee-fucking-haw. Round 'em up, boys.

Calmed, Nicholas smiled back at me and I remembered why I was with him. That smile. Not many men can turn you on with just a smile. And later, as I lay sated in his arms, I reminded myself that no man is perfect, and, like a cashmere sweater, sometimes the most beautiful things in life make you itch a little.

• 47 •

Carolyn

Blind Date, Blind Rage

"Carolyn Phillips. I've found the perfect man for you," Jackie Wickham trills into the phone. I am instantly wary; Taylor and I showed up to the Harper-Wickham nuptials thirty minutes late and three sheets to the wind, and while nobody appears to have drawn any inferences from the facts that (1) there was a great uproar in the kitchen of Grace House, where the wedding was held, about five minutes before Taylor and I appeared in the back of the room where the ceremony was being held; (2) a significant number of the crystallized sugar roses were missing from the crème brulée desserts, and (3) both Taylor and I displayed indelibly bright red tongues for the remainder of the evening, it is impossible to be sure.

"No, thanks," I say, "I'm actually not looking right now. You see, I've decided that being single is actually—"

"He's a filthy rich doctor," she continues, "and he enjoys rowing, scuba diving, travel—"

"I don't want—"

"—opera, the Sunday *Times* crossword, and racing his sailboat and his Harley. He drives a Range Rover, keeps a Mercedes Maybach, and lives—"

"Does he own a space shuttle? Those other phallic symbols are fine and dandy but they're far too subtle and I'm looking for a man who just takes it to that next level, really, and I don't think—"

"—on the Upper East Side. He's thirty-eight, and I'll e-mail you his picture right now. Carolyn, you'll *love* him; he's so polite and he's really together. I've told him about you and he's dying to meet you, so I told him you could do drinks on Saturday because I knew you probably wouldn't have plans. You don't, do you?"

I am coldly resentful of her presumptuousness and equally aware that, no, I do not have any plans for this Saturday, have not had any plans for the last six Saturdays, and am unlikely to have any plans for the rest of my Saturdays. To illustrate, I spent last Saturday night with a literary work from the remainder bin at the Strand, an AATN (African-American Television Network) romance by the name of *Black Satin Sheets, Black Satin Skin* that was penned by one Charleathia Arquetta Wilkerson. I had just reached the part where the heroine, Dashielle "Diamond" Chateaubriande di Lammermoor, an aspiring singer/actress/ model/dancer and nail technician, goes out with the hero, Captain Rashad "Injun" Wilson-Kensington, for the very first time. When I left them, Diamond was staring

. . . into Rashad's piercing jade eyes. Her skin was the color of over-brewed Starbucks-brand Arabica ground coffee with two large dollops of nonfat milk and two heaping teaspoons of Cremora, or, if that is too much to remember, butterscotch. Her hair was long and shiny and Indian straight, and her Indian features were startlingly Indian-like in their Indianness. The look on the caramel skin of Rashad's face touched her as it confused her. Was this love?

"Girl, I want to put my sting in you," he murmured huskily. Dashielle blushed up to the roots of her long, straight, shiny, straight, silky, straight, Indian, straight hair. This was all so confusing, yet so touching at the same time.

"Oh, Rashad," she murmured.

Rashad remembered the first time he had seen her. His skin, the color of the varnish used on IKEA's "Götterdämmerung" line of bedroom furniture, had flushed red. He had brushed his hand huskily over his Indian-straight nose and clutched at the arm of his friend, Walter "Fat-Ass" Hopkins. Walter was the color of a 1962 Chevette with a missing distributor cap, and his kinky naps stood out from his head like a halo. At the time, both men were completing their fourth year at Princeton Law School.

"I just want to put my Tootsie Roll in your Good & Plenty and make you Yodel until you're Chock Full-o-Nuts," he murmured.

Given the choice between (1) a Saturday night spent discovering whether Diamond and Rashad, armed with nothing but their love and their Indian-like features, can survive the wiles of the treacherous "Fat-Ass" Hopkins, who is determined to prevent Rashad from putting his sting in Diamond, and (2) a Saturday night spent in the company of a doctor with a wee penis, I choose the latter.

As I hang up the phone, I hear the chimes indicating that I have new e-mail. It is a photo attachment from jwickham@aol.com, and when I open it, I see a decent-looking man posted up in the middle of the plaza in front of the Eiffel Tower. It is obviously winter, and a muffler is concealing the bottom half of his face, and he has on sunglasses, but he seems decently tall, with a respectable build. I shrug and pick up the phone to call Jackie and ask her to make the necessary arrangements.

I show up at Cafe Fez at eight p.m., the designated hour. By eight-fifteen he still has not appeared. My phone rings at eight-thirty—it is Taylor and Roxanne with the Blind Date Loophole Call, where, under normal circumstances, I would have the alternative of telling them that I am busy and will call them later, or letting my eyes grow wide with shock and alarm and clapping my hand to my mouth, then informing my date regretfully that I was oh so sorry, but something truly horrible has happened, and I must fly. However, none of this is required at this time because he still has not shown up.

"What kind of person shows up this late for a first date and doesn't call?!" Taylor snaps. "This is not a good sign. You should just leave."

"I can't," I say. "Right now I'm in the right; if I ditch, I'll be in the wrong and I'll have to hear about it from Jackie, and, besides, this is actually a good thing, because once I let her know how badly her date turned out, she'll stop playing Cupid forever."

"Okay," Roxanne says, "but seriously, you should leave."

"Duly noted," I say, slugging down another glass of wine. "I'll call you guys later."

They click off and just as I am beckoning to the waiter, I see him. He waves and makes his way over to the table.

Oh, my God. I now see why he was wearing the muffler up to his nose. He has a plump little pink sweetheart of a mouth, a full, simpering Cupid's bow that descends into a short, receding, completely smooth, shadow-free chin. He is a Marlboro Man from the nose up and a Madame Alexander doll from the nose down, and I am fascinated by the notion that somewhere there is a dewy junior high cheerleader with a jutting, stubble-ridden jaw, and that one day the World Chin Foundation will bring the two of them together and perform a daring, cutting-edge medical operation that will give this world-traveling, suture-stitching, Harley-riding, yacht-racing forty-year-old the face he was always meant to have.

"Carolyn?" he says. "I'm sorry I'm so late; I couldn't find a space for the Maybach and I forgot to charge up the Vertu."

I do not hear what he says the first time because I am still staring, mesmerized and repelled, at the lower half of his face. However, when I ask him to repeat himself, he does, verbatim, and from that point on I am unable to hear anything else he says because the internal alarm on my Jackass Detector is going absolutely berserkers. What kind of cretin drives from the Upper East Side to the Village on a Saturday night and expects to find parking?! Number two, innumerable points lost for unnatural and conspicuous brand-name references in the first sentence out of his mouth when the generic terms *car* and *cell phone* would have done equally well. And, of course, the lateness. Oh, fuckin' Jackie, you are so in for it.

"No big deal," I say, offering my hand and waving frantically at the waiter.

"Did you want to eat here?" he says, looking around.

"I don't mind it," I answer.

"I don't like Moroccan food," he says shortly. "Let's go somewhere else. I know a little spot over in NoHo." When the waiter comes, I ask for the check, and then Dr. Bitchlips squints at me and says, "Do you want me to pay for all the drinks you had?" He clearly feels that he should not have to pay for expenses incurred while he was trying to park The Maybach and having trouble with The Vertu, and he also resents my ability to run up a three-drink tab in forty-eight minutes. I just stare at him until he looks away.

"I'll get it," I say sharply. The polite portion of this date is now officially over. I slap down a couple of bills while he checks his reflection in the window behind me, and we leave. I expect us to drive over—why else would he have brought The Maybach down here?—but instead we start walking. By the time we get to Houston and West Broadway, my feet, clad in pretty but impractical Manolo Blahniks, are complaining.

"Aren't we going to drive?" I say. He looks at me incredulously.

"Are you kidding? After all the time I spent finding that space?" Then he looks down at my feet for the first time and there is a pause while he considers the situation.

"Do you want to catch a cab or something?" he says at length, with no small degree of reluctance. It is then that I realize that he is just plain cheap, and that he drove not because he is stupid but because he wished to save cab fare. And now he would walk me almost a mile in the footwear equivalent of an Iron Maiden to do the same.

"Yes," I say through clenched teeth. He hails a cab and we ride in uncomfortable silence through the crowds on Houston Street until we make a left and pull up in front of the NoHo Globe. He tells the driver to stop. I am underwhelmed. The phrase "little spot" conjures up visions of an unnamed grotto in the sub basement of a lower East Side tenement, glowing with dripping candles and fairy lights, where singing waiters serve incredible and unidentifiable meals. The NoHo Globe is none of these things, and while it is not T.G.I. Friday's, it is nowhere near fabulous and obscure enough to merit that moniker. Fucking jackass.

We get inside and he asks me what I do for a living. I give him the short version, the one that neither answers nor invites any questions, whereupon he begins to drone on about his excursions to foreign lands and the wonders of other cultures. It is when he is halfway through his steak frites (he made a unilateral decision that there would be no appetizers) that I realize that he is looking at me, obviously waiting for an answer to a question he has asked.

"I don't guess so," I say, taking a wild stab in the dark and hoping that I have not just agreed to a second date, although I am not sensing that he is any more impressed with me than I am with him. Yet, strangely, I am not bothered by this, although there was a time not very long ago when I would have been trying desperately to make this date work just because I wanted so badly for someone, anyone, to be interested. That same Carolyn also would have blushed, cringed, and apologized for occupying herself most pleasantly with a more-than-decent pinot grigio while Date took forty minutes to park The Maybach, then would have ruined her shoes and her feet with a mile-long trek rather than risk offending Date by suggesting that something he had chosen to do was anything other than wise and correct. Huh.

There is a lull in the conversation. Terrified that he will expect me to entertain him, I ask him in my best Stupid Coed voice whether being an ER doctor is "just like that TV show *ER.*" Bingo. I am rewarded with a condescending smile and a twenty-minute exposition on the Trials and Tribulations of Being an Emergency Room Care Provider. I go away again mentally as he speaks, and I only return to the conversation long enough to stifle a gag as he says, in a voice thick with emotion, "I love working with tots; it really reminds me what is important, and what isn't. Sometimes we get so caught up in all this," he says, making an elaborate gesture around the restaurant as if everything about the fifties diner interior of the NoHo Globe smacks of self-indulgence and debauchery, "that we forget what really matters."

He sighs and shakes his head, frowning concernedly. In addition to the fact that some might see The Maybach and The Vertu as prime indicators that Dr. Womanface has bought into "all this" with a vengeance, the smarmy, wholesome aura hanging about the word *tots* makes my skin crawl.

"Are you talking about Tater Tots?" I say. "I'm not a big fan of children, but I like potatoes very much." He glares at me, and the lips purse, which makes them even more unacceptable. There is a long, awkward pause.

"Right," I say, looking into the debris of my crabmeat omelette. "Well, then."

He waves for the check. When it arrives, he has the nerve to look at me expectantly. However, after his ungracious behavior earlier in the evening, I feel in no way obligated to put a single penny on the table, and, smiling sweetly, stare defiantly right back at him, daring him to ask me to put in. Finally he huffs and reaches for his wallet.

"Whatever happened to women's lib?" he says nastily.

"Same thing that happened to chivalry and gallantry, I guess," I say, rising and picking up my bag. "It's been an experience unlike any other," I say, "and for that I thank you most sincerely."

· 48 ·

Taylor

Why, God, Why?

"Taylor, can we walk out of here and go to lunch some time this calendar year?" Roxanne said, spinning idly around in my desk chair.

We were supposed to go to lunch thirty minutes ago, but I'd had to take two client calls, fax a pleading over to co-counsel, and do some research on LegalWorld, a very expensive legal search engine that gives me access to millions of domestic and international court opinions, statutes, rules and regulations, and news.

"Even Clarence Darrow ate lunch, they say," Carolyn added.

"I've got an arbitration tomorrow, and I've got to be on top of the top of my game. Plus, it costs five bucks a minute to run a search on LegalWorld, and I've prepaid for the next ten minutes. Of course, that's on top of the four-hundred-dollar rate the clients have to pay for me to formulate the search, think about whether the cases the computer spits out are even good for my position, and then printing what I find, which costs two-fifty per item."

"I couldn't afford you for more than five minutes," Roxanne said, spinning around again.

Just then my secretary buzzed me to let me know that Meschach was calling from Germany. I picked up and purred, "Honey, the girls are visiting me and they're trying to steal me away for lunch. Let me call you when these ungrateful creatures have left."

"So this really is what you do all day in here, talk to jerks on the phone and make piles of paper everywhere? When do you make closing arguments? When do you defend truth, justice, and the American way? Where's the action?" Roxanne questioned.

"On television; I recommend *Boston Legal*," I said shortly. She didn't seem to realize that in real life, you didn't just waltz into court and give eloquent speeches about why your client should win, and in the world of major corporate and commercial litigation, you often never waltzed into court at all.

"Jerks and paper aside, this is my life. It's what keeps me going every day. I don't define myself by this shit, but it damn sure is a major part of who I am. But anyway, let me lay it down for you. I'll give you an example from a public case. This guy decides to sue Intertec Corporation, one of my biggest clients, for firing him because he screwed up on the job. He can't very well walk into court, throw down his pay stubs and say, 'I used to work there. They fired me. PAY ME NOW!' "

Before I could explain further, my phone rang again. It was a partner: one of our clients had just gotten indicted and there was a helicopter waiting to take us to Jersey; I had five minutes to get downstairs.

"Ladies," I said, hanging up the phone, "I am so, so sorry, but I literally have to go to New Jersey right this minute. Can we try this again next week?"

"We can try, but succeeding is another thing entirely," Carolyn said wryly as she picked up her bag.

"I know; I'm sorry. That's just the way it goes." I'd really wanted to go to lunch; I hadn't seen either of them in almost two weeks and I hadn't had a complete phone conversation with Bianca in almost three.

"Call when you get back," Roxanne said over her shoulder as they walked out.

As they left my office, I began to wonder whether I was honestly and truly meant to work from sunup to sundown this far after the issuance of the Emancipation Proclamation. And still, something within me wouldn't let me quit.

If I'm being realistic and honest, I have to admit that I'm still paying my dues, and I can't be mad at anybody for that, can I? I've learned so much during my years here that part of me knows that I wouldn't trade the long hours or seven-days-in-the-office weeks for anything in the world. I can politely cuss anyone out in a letter and still not make them think I'm being a smart-ass. I can manage my cases without missing a beat. I get along with anyone I need to to get the job done. I thrive on the fast pace, and I love seeing older, more experienced lawyers plan straight-up legal warfare. I loved the fact that, in a way, it's all a game, let the best side win.

It's not that I feel like people are trying to work me into the ground for no reason. I know that I'll never get to the top of my game by going home at five-thirty P.M. But some nagging doubts are creeping in. I have fabulous friends, a great new boyfriend, a wonderful apartment, and a wardrobe even Bianca can find no fault with, but somehow the job overshadows and absorbs all of that and has managed to seep into every nook and cranny of my life. I see Roxanne and Carolyn once in a blue moon, and half the time I have to leave whatever we're doing to go back to work. And if it weren't for the Jubilee, I wouldn't see Bianca again until we're both grandmothers. As for Meschach, God help us. His job is insane, too, so he understands, but how are we going to make a relationship work with schedules like these?

• 49 •

Roxanne

California Dreaming

October in California is quite different from October in New York. It never rains, the sun is always out, and people are friendly. La Jolla is gorgeous and my uncle has an amazing community of friends who welcome me at the airport. As I'm getting settled in Sebastian's tiny, but cozy beach house, there's a knock on the door. Haggard and a little bit jet-lagged, I open it to reveal a six-foot-three, blond, chiseled god whose hair is wet, skin is sun-kissed, and chest is glistening from either beads of sweat or the ocean water coating his body. He's got a broken surfboard in his left arm. I am speechless, so he starts in, "Dude, you must be Roxanne."

"Must I?" Words are hard for me to utter because I am facing the most beautiful man I have ever seen other than Ram. California is going to be better than I imagined. I finally pull myself together. "Sebastian's not here right now. He's at Lily's house. He should be back in a few hours." Lily is my uncle's girlfriend who was a champion surfer in her day, but quit to become a massage therapist. They are the perfect hippie couple.

"That sucks," he says, "because I broke my board on some pretty gnarly rocks out there and I need it fixed."

"Sebastian can fix that?" I ask, astonished.

"Of course. Your uncle designed and built this for me. He's like a genius."

The board is beautiful, and it's funny, because this is my first glimpse into my uncle's world. I always knew him as the wacky guy who didn't quite fit in my black bourgeois world, but he's apparently a legend in La Jolla.

"I hear you want to learn to surf," he says nonchalantly. This golden god clearly knows his way around Sebastian's house and he wastes no time making himself at home. He goes into the kitchen, gets some juice, and pours me a glass.

"Who are you, by the way?" I say. "I mean you could be some ax murderer slinking in, knowing that I'm home alone, wanting to chop my body into little pieces and toss it into the ocean."

"You New York babes are funny. I'm Quincy. Come on, let's go surfing."

Quincy turns out to be a twenty-three-year-old student at UCSD who doesn't quite know what he wants to do. He just wants to be happy, apparently. That seems simple enough.

I quickly put on my bathing suit, and now it's Quincy who is speechless. "Your body is amazing," he says, staring at me lustfully. "The water's pretty warm today, so you don't need a wet suit." He searches around the living room and hands me a rash guard, which is a short-sleeved top that protects your body from the friction with the board. He finds me a pair of board shorts and we leave the house.

Then I see the waves, and I am terrified. Why do I always do this? Why do I always rush into something that sounds cool and exciting in theory only to face the reality and be scared shitless?

"All right," Quincy says, totally oblivious to the fact that I'm paralyzed with fear. "Before we hit the water, we need to go over a few things. The first thing you have to do is watch the ocean. You need to observe how the waves are breaking, how quickly they're coming in, if they veer to the left or the right, because it changes every day, every hour."

"There's actually a science to surfing?" I ask, slightly distracted from my terror.

"Of course. The ocean is like a woman. She lets you know how she's feeling and it's your job to be aware. You cannot change her. Because she will humble you." Huh. Quincy is actually smart, too.

While we are on the beach, he explains how to do "pop ups." That's the way you jump up on the board to assume your balanced stand. He talks about how to paddle out and how to catch waves. By now, I've calmed down and am ready to hit the water. I carry my surfboard on my head, the way Carmen Miranda wore her hat of fruit. It's surprisingly heavy. I get in and put my "leash" on. That's the length of cord that fastens around my ankle with Velcro, connecting me with the board so that it doesn't escape me when I fall off. Luckily, the water temperature is warm enough once I submerge myself. Quincy tells me to walk the board out pretty far into the white water—the area of water close to the shore that has small waves after the big ones have broken. We're going to paddle out, turn the boards around, and he'll tell me when it's time. We wait about a minute, watching the waves break, and then it's my moment. "Hop on!" he exclaims. I climb on the board and lie down horizontally, with my face toward the shore. "Paddle!" he instructs. I stroke with my arms, him holding on to the back of my board when I get the order. "Pop up!" I jump up on the board in a perfectly balanced stance as he pushes me forward. I ride for several seconds before getting wobbly and falling into the water. I tug on my leash, pulling the board toward me, and wade back to Quincy, who is in deeper water. He has a huge smile on his face.

"*Dude.* You just rode your first wave."

Wow. I really did.

We spend about two more hours in the water, him coaching me on when to pop up, me having better luck with standing. Quincy says that all my yoga training has given me better balance than most first-time surfers. I am pleased with myself. All of my problems were left on shore. I seriously can't remember the last time I had this much fun without liquor or sex. California's all right.

Actually, it's way better than all right. Lily, Sebastian's girlfriend, has generously agreed to give me a free massage every week. Lily is quite a woman. Her quick-witted sense of humor is perfectly matched with Sebastian's. She works in a fancy, high-priced spa, Oceana, where rich La Jolla ladies pay about one hundred and fifty dollars an hour for the healing properties of Lily's magical hands. I really like her energy; it's very earth-mother. She does my massages at her house on the beach. It is tiny but gorgeous and really reflects Lily's eclectic style. Her hardwood floors are sporadically covered with lush area rugs that cuddle your bare feet when you sink into them. Her massage table is in the living room, next to a huge floor-to-ceiling window that faces the ocean. It's funny that I've known Lily for almost ten years, but I've never spent this much time with her, particularly in such an intimate way.

I lie facedown on the massage table, and Lily starts with the knots in my shoulders. "Roxanne, you need to breathe more or these balls of stress will never go away."

"I have been breathing," I groan as she digs in deeper. This really hurts.

"You seem to store all of your tension here. Let it go," she says in a very soothing voice.

"Ouch!" I yelp as she hits a bad patch.

"But on the bright side, I can see that you are a lot more relaxed than you were your first day here," she says, optimistically.

"Thank you. See, I'm making progress," I say defiantly. "So, are you and Sebastian ever getting married?"

"I don't think so."

"Are you going to move in together?" I probe.

"Why should we? I love him, but I also love solitude. Your uncle's a great man, but he's a man, and they have certain sides that I don't want to experience all day, every day." Lily makes a valid point.

"Well, what made you fall in love with him?"

"His sense of humor, his generosity, his adoration for me." Her hands suddenly feel warmer. These are all admirable qualities.

"How did you know he was The One?"

Lily stops massaging for a beat before she speaks. "I don't believe in that 'one soul mate per person' thing. He came around at a time in my life when I was tired of being treated like shit. I liked the super-pretty surfer boys with the super-hot bodies and super-gigantic egos. It's fine to date that when you're twenty-one, but when you're older, you need more than just good looks. You need to be with a man who respects you and your intelligence, who doesn't want to change, control, or belittle you. I was fed up with the bullshit and along came Sebastian."

I smile before responding, "Yeah, pretty boys are always more trouble than they're worth, but they look so damn good."

"True, but everyone else thinks they look good, too, and they start to believe the hype, start fucking around, and leave you feeling like a fool. It's important to love a man who feels like he's the luckiest guy in the world to be with you," Lily says as she starts back in on my shoulders.

"I guess you're right." I do tend to fall for egomaniacs.

"I am, but we should stop talking so you can focus on releasing the bad energy you've been storing in your shoulders and neck." Lily gets back to her work, and I try to breathe and think about releasing tension and not about Ram, who is still angry at me for coming out here, and whether it's time to release him, too.

· 50 ·

Bianca

Losing It

This is like a bad dream. It was hideous enough having to go back to Houston for my cousin Lisa's wedding, or as I like to call it, the Bridesmaid's Walk of Death, made all the worse by the fact that in Houston, you're an old maid if you're not married by twenty-six. Luckily for me, I don't live there anymore. Unfortunately, most of my relatives still do, and the one thing about them is that no matter how much additional money they manage to accumulate, they never seem to acquire any additional class, and this wedding was the Univer-Soul Circus meets *The Best Man*, to put it bluntly. I was all set to come up with an excuse not to go since I couldn't afford a bus ticket to Houston, much less airfare. Well, my dad took care of that by offering to charge my ticket on his airline miles reward credit card. I promised to pay him back, but I hope he didn't actually believe me. It was hideous enough that Nicholas had to lecture in San Francisco, so he couldn't come with me (although, thank God, to make it up to me, he paid for the Tiffany flutes we got them, because at this point I can't even afford Dixie cups), *and* hideous enough that I had to wear a hundred-dollar ill-fitting homemade "dress" that looked like what happened the time my cousin Brandon vomited up a dish of orange sherbet, *and* that both of the seamstress's sons managed to walk in on me while I was trying it on, *and* that, contrary to all known etiquette, the bride didn't pay for the hair and makeup for the bridesmaids (which forced me to borrow fifty dollars from my brother), *and* that the hair and makeup people were apparently hired away from Tammy Faye Bakker, *and* that there was a *cash bar* at the wedding reception, *and* that I ran into an endless string of horrible ex-boyfriends and horrible smug recently married ex-friends from high school who snarked at my apparent single status. You would think that that's more than any woman could handle, right? It is, and it was, which is why I had four minibottles of Chardonnay on the plane back to L.A. and had a furious headache when I tumbled off the plane and slouched off toward the baggage claim. Imagine my surprise when the last of my fellow passengers walked away from the mostly empty carousel and I had yet to see one piece of my Louis Vuitton come sliding down the little chute. More angry than buzzed at this point, I flounced over to the little office where you go complain about lost luggage. A bored looking young woman in an airline uniform glanced at me and gave me an unsympathetic look before she stopped what she was doing to address me.

"Can I help you?" she asked, managing to sound altogether UNhelpful. Hey, it's not my fault you have to wear polyester, sister, I thought.

"The airline seems to have misplaced my luggage," I said, trying to sound sweet instead of stank.

"What flight were you on?"

"Flight 302 from Houston."

"How many bags did you check?"

"Two," I replied, barely concealing my annoyance.

"Can you describe the bags?"

"They're both brown with the Louis Vuitton logo on them. One is a soft-sided suitcase and the other is a hanging bag."

She gave me another "poor little rich girl" look and started typing something into her computer. She studied the screen for what seemed like an eternity before I caught her smiling evilly, but she covered it up quickly before she spoke.

"It seems there was a problem with your bags."

"Problem? What kind of problem?" I asked as I really began to panic. Shit! Did my suitcase still smell like weed as a result of sitting in my brother's closet for three days? Did the zipper break? I double locked it. Or did I? The walls of the little office were beginning to close in on me.

"The bags are here in the airport, miss. Just let me go and check with the baggage department," she said a little too happily. She disappeared behind a door that didn't seem to lead anywhere.

I was fairly certain that there wasn't anything illegal in my luggage, but just in case, I started looking around nervously for any sign of the airport police.

The luggage girl emerged from the back room carrying two large plastic bags. Then, in a haze of terror, I saw that the plastic bags contained what was left of my luggage. As she placed the mangled remains of my wardrobe on the counter, I felt the bottom drop out from under me.

"Miss, it seems the clasp on your suitcase was broken en route, as well as the zipper on your hanging bag," she said.

Choking back tears, I gently peeled away the plastic covering my suitcase. I pawed through the contents, taking a quick mental inventory.

"All my good stuff is missing!" I yelled hysterically at the woman. "My Tiffany bracelets, my shoes . . ."

"Miss, calm down," she interrupted.

"Calm down? Someone has just stolen thousands of dollars worth of MY STUFF! Things I can't afford to replace!"

"Fill out this form and please list all the missing items. The airline will compensate you for the value of the items, provided you can produce receipts and very detailed descriptions. Up to five hundred dollars, that is."

Five hundred dollars wouldn't begin to cover it! Nevertheless, I grabbed the paper from her and I had just filled in my name. With horror, I realized I hadn't checked my hanging bag yet. As I parted the now zipperless brown leather, I saw that the only garment that remained was the orange bridesmaid's "dress."

• • •

By the time I left the luggage office with my designer plastic bags, all I could think about was that somewhere in the valley, there was a very well-dressed baggage handler's wife. Trying desperately not to completely fall apart, I concentrated on getting home so I could take a nice long bubble bath. Digging around in my purse for my keys, I walked the endless walk to the long-term parking garage. Luckily, I had found a place on the first floor, so at least I didn't have to climb any stairs.

Ten minutes later, I found myself standing in the empty spot where I could have SWORN I parked my car. I must be losing my mind. Chalking up my confusion to the stress of losing my favorite Gucci shoes, I was about to check the next row when I realized that the red Mustang that I remembered parking next to was still there. I know it was the same Mustang because at the time I recalled thinking the license plate, which said GIDDYUP, was stupid.

Exhausted, I collapsed on the dirty, greasy pavement and cried my little eyes out (flagrant violation of the Public Decorum Act of 1994 but who gives a shit?). I might have stayed there in that spot in the LAX long-term parking garage forever if the airport police hadn't driven by and stopped to question the obviously mentally ill woman crying on the ground with two plastic bags in her lap. At some point the real police were summoned and I told them my sad story. Robbed twice in one day. What in the world had I done to deserve this? All the officers stood apart from me, talking among themselves. They probably didn't want to stand too close to the red-faced girl who someone had obviously put a curse on.

Finally, one of the LAPD officers emerged from his squad car.

"Ma'am, I have some news about your vehicle," the officer said solemnly.

"They found it?" I asked hopefully.

"It seems your car has been repossessed for nonpayment."

Even after they put me in the back of the squad car, drove me home, and I was finally sitting in my long-awaited bubble bath, the reality that I was in serious financial trouble still hadn't sunk in. I think it became real right after I dropped my money into the little box at the front of the bus the next morning on my way to work.

• • •

With my world falling down around my ears, I clung to the knowledge that at least I had Nicholas. So, I invited him over in search of a sympa-

thetic ear and some horizontal distraction. Imagine my surprise at the first
words out of his mouth: "Well, Bianca, I can't say I'm shocked."

Huh? Could someone pass this boy a manual? Where was the support?
Where was the sympathy? Where was the generous offer to loan me
money? Incredibly, it got worse. He yammered on for nearly twenty minutes about financial irresponsibility, outrageous spending habits, etcetera,
etcetera. Unfortunately, I tuned back just in time to hear him say, "I don't
think this is working, Bianca. I need to be with someone who takes life seriously and has the same interests and priorities that I do. I need a woman
who understands that value and price are not the same thing."

"What?" I said incredulously. "Excuse me, but are you actually breaking up with me because . . ." My voice started to crack and tears were
welling up in my eyes. ". . . because I'm broke?" Talk about kicking a girl
when she's down!

"You're not listening to me, baby," he said softly. "That couldn't be
further from what I'm saying. I'd never leave you because you were broke,
or because you wore secondhand clothes, or didn't shop on Rodeo, because none of that matters to me." He reached for my hand, but I snatched
it away.

"I think you're absolutely incredible," he continued. "You're beautiful,
you're smart, you're witty, you're sexy, you're warm. And how much you
make, or what you wear, or where you eat, or who does your hair is irrele-
vant. But the whole problem is that you can't seem to understand that,
Bianca, about yourself or about anyone else, and your entire life revolves
around superficialities to the point that you've destroyed yourself financially. I can't be with a woman like that, a woman who can't see past the
material things to the things that really matter, like love, and communi-
cation, and friendship, and trust."

"But I *do* trust you," I squeak. "You're the only man I've ever trusted
like this."

"But *I* can't trust *you*," he said sadly. "Instead of telling me the truth
about your finances, you shut me out and lied to me. We always said we'd be
honest with each other, but now I'm finding out that you kept secrets from
me, and when you needed help, you refused to level with me and talk to me
about it. That's not how adult relationships are supposed to work, Bianca."

Nicholas put his hands on my shoulders.

"I love you," he said in a low voice. "I care for you more than any woman I've ever met, but this just won't work. I can't tell you how much I'd hoped that it would, but I don't think it can."

I stood there, stunned. Nicholas touched me gently on the cheek and I turned my head away.

"Just leave," I said stiffly, turning away from him and willing myself to wait until he left before I let the tears start to fall.

"Bianca, please don't be like this," Nicholas said gently. "You need help, and I can't be with you, but that doesn't mean I'm not going to do anything and everything I can for you. What do you need from me? What can I do?" he said.

"Actually, now that you mention it," I said through clenched teeth, "you can go fuck yourself, you self-righteous prick." Why, it turns out that he's right; saying that didn't cost me a thing but it made me feel so much better!

• 51 •

Taylor

Cruel Fate

Fall was here, and I couldn't wait to spend those crisp, chilly autumn evenings by the fire with Meschach; things were going so beautifully. He was coming home from London the next night, straight from the airport to my apartment, right into my waiting arms. My phone rang; it was Meschach, but before I could say two words, my secretary knocked and then poked her head in the door.

"You need to come out here," she said. A deliveryman. With flowers. Blood red roses. Black orchids. White lilies. Attached to the front was a card that read, "Sleep sweetly tonight, my beauty, my love, for tomorrow there will be no rest." Men weren't perfect, lots of times they made you feel wonderful, made you want to scream, and they almost always made you cry, but sometimes they make you feel wonderful by doing something little at just the right time. God, please let me remember, if I ever want to scratch his eyes out, that there was at least one time he was not only charming, but he reminded me that I deserved nothing less than a prince.

• • •

When Meschach stepped over the threshold we couldn't (as clichéd as it sounds) even wait to close the front door. After a quick and powerful round, we headed to the bedroom for quieter action. You know when having sex transforms into making love? You know when you can feel it in the moves he makes, and in the responses he gives? When you both ache to say something so badly, but can't, that you have to let your bodies do the talking? I almost cried.

Right after we finished making love for the final time that evening (my lips—both sets—were too swollen to go any further), Meschach dropped a fucking hydrogen bomb on me. He told me that he'd been asked to spend the next year in GSC's London office. It was an opportunity he couldn't refuse, we both knew that. He said he told them yes on the spot.

It was then that I realized how much anger I'd been harboring at men. I'm furious with them. Here was my prince, and there was the sunset. Only it looked like I was going to be riding off into it alone. Again.

He told me that he wanted us to try to maintain our relationship. He reasoned that a year wasn't so long—and he could easily afford to fly me to London once a month. If we'd made it work for two months during his trip to South America, we could definitely do this.

I'll admit, it all sounded good, but I just couldn't rationalize devoting myself to a long-distance relationship at my age. I'd be setting myself up. What if he came back wanting nothing, and I had turned down other opportunities because I was waiting for him? Where would that leave me? At square one, that's where, but a year older. No, I had to be smarter than that. I couldn't play around anymore. He sounded serious all right, but I'll believe serious when I see a ring on my finger. I'll believe serious when our bank accounts intermingle. And at this stage in our relationship, that was definitely not an option. Well, at least I'd learned another fundamental lesson: if something is too good to be true, it's probably a man.

• • •

I'd been tossing and turning and unhappily mulling over every aspect of my life ever since I'd asked Meschach to leave several hours ago. Time to get out of this funk and wake up the rest of these lazy hoes to solve the problem. As I dialed the girls, I made myself a Bloody Mary, which is the true breakfast of champions.

"Ladies, there is trouble in Paradise," I said softly.

"What is it? What's wrong?" Carolyn said, sounding sleepy but anxious. She didn't even give me shit for the fact that it was four a.m. and a weeknight; I guess my voice said it all.

"Meschach is going to work in London for the next year. While that makes perfect sense as far his career is concerned, that doesn't help my heart. I told you all I couldn't take one more failed relationship. I have given up, completely, utterly, totally, and for the last time, on love."

There was a silence.

"Are you saying that he broke up with you?" said Roxanne. "I don't understand."

"No, he wants to try to make it work long-distance."

"So the problem is what?" Carolyn said. "So you won't have sex as often; what's the big deal?"

"The big deal is that I'm leaving the motherfucker, clearly," I said angrily. "Are you fucking kidding me? I should stay with him so he can come back and let me know he's changed his mind about us, and in the meantime I've lost a year of my life behind him?"

"Yes, hel-*lo*," said Bianca. "Is he crazy? Long distance, especially a distance *that* long, is an automatic hell no. And it's not like he's just going to D.C.; he's leaving the *country*. No *way*. Not that I'm mentioning names, but certain professors were right here in the fucking city and we had a tough enough time without the extra bullshit that comes with distance."

Roxanne cleared her throat. "Taylor, you're going to hate me, but, no pain, no gain."

"Roxanne, do you just like to dig the knife into my spine and then turn it for effect? Do you have anything of worth to say?" These fucking clichés are ruining my life.

"I just wanted to wake *you* up, since you woke all of us up. Listen, if what you're afraid of is Meschach getting crazy on you and leaving you, Vincent *lived* with you, and that didn't stop him."

"What the fuck are you trying to say, Roxanne?" I shouted.

"She's saying, Snappy McNastybitch, that the possibility of a man looning out on you and walking out at the drop of a hat one day is not made any more or less likely by his location on the globe in relation to yours," Carolyn said, "so if that's the only concern raised by the London move, it's not a very good reason to let Meschach go."

"Oh, you're on his side, too, huh?" I snapped, angry and hurt.

"God, grow *up*, Taylor," Roxanne said, yawning. "This isn't about *sides*. It's about trying to figure out where you go from here."

"You two are crazy," Bianca said. "Not that it's a secret, but seriously, you are. She can't keep tabs on him all the way over there. How is she going to know if he's cheating?"

"How do you *ever* know?" Roxanne said, disgusted. "Thomas lived less than a mile from me and I didn't know about his boyfriend. Gil lived two subway stops away from Carolyn and she didn't know he was engaged. If a man wants to cheat, he will, and it won't matter if he lives with you or in Timbuktu."

"It's not like he's just being trifling and skipping town," Carolyn added, "this is something he has to do for his career, and Taylor, you'd do the same thing in his shoes. The difference is that I don't think Meschach would cut you off for doing it because he obviously wants to be with you, even long-distance. I mean, look, instead of using the relocation as an excuse to cut himself loose, he's trying to suggest arrangements for making it work until he gets back. Doesn't that count for anything at all?"

"Plus, you guys already practically did this for two months and it worked out fine," Roxanne added.

"I. Am. Twenty-eight," I said very slowly. "I. Cannot. Afford. To. Waste. A. Year. On. A. High-risk. Proposition. Like. This."

"Preach," said Bianca.

"Who's wasting a year?" Roxanne asked. "You'll be with Meschach that year."

"You're the gambler, babe; having Meschach in London is like a nineteen blackjack hand; you're a lot more likely to lose if you don't hold your cards," Carolyn said.

"And you've seen what New York has to offer," Roxanne chimed in. "What the fuck makes you think you can do better with what's here?"

"What makes you think she can't?!" Bianca snapped.

"We *live* here, stupid," Carolyn murmured.

"Even if you could," Roxanne persisted, "what makes you think that this hypothetical better deal won't go insane, too? Men go insane at all stages of the game—they break engagements, they leave their wives . . . you're never safe from their insanity. *Never.* You just have to make an educated guess as to whether it's worth the risk, and here you have too many factors indicating that Meschach is worth it."

I gathered my thoughts.

"I know I care about this man, and I could fall in love with him. He could be the love of my life, easy. And that makes me vulnerable. And I don't want to be vulnerable, because vulnerable means you can get hurt, and I'm so fucking tired of getting hurt." I didn't realize that I was crying until the first tear plopped into my Bloody Mary. "I just don't want to take any more chances."

"You want a sure bet, and there's no such thing," Carolyn said softly. "You know I hate clichés, Taylor, but every relationship is a gamble, every single time, no matter what the circumstances are, because as long as another human being is involved, you've got an unpredictable X variable."

"That's a sididdy way of saying that men are crazy, and I'll agree with you on that point only," Bianca said grudgingly. "I think Taylor's more likely to get hurt if she does the long-distance thing, and I stand by that. It's a young relationship, and the distance will put too much strain on it. And, sure, maybe he'll go crazy no matter where he is, but what good is he to her a billion miles away? She'll still be coming home to an empty house every night."

"Please. There's a big difference between coming home to a truly empty house and coming home to a house where your man just doesn't happen to be at the time," Carolyn said shortly.

"And you haven't been around the two of them, but this boy makes her eyes light up, Bianca. He makes her glow, and I don't mean afterglow, but happy glow," Roxanne said. "And he breaks her back in the bedroom. And if that's not worth gambling on I don't know what is."

I fucking hate Roxanne and Carolyn because this fucking decision was totally simple a few hours ago but now it doesn't seem so cut and dried, which means I'm going to have to continue torturing myself to get it worked out.

• 52 •

Roxanne

Reunited and It Feels So . . . Ugh

I am so excited that Bianca is driving down from L.A. to visit for the weekend. Sebastian has agreed to give us his place so we can have some quality girl time. She's coming straight from work, so we'll make some dinner, maybe watch a movie, just catch up. I haven't seen her in what feels like forever.

She knocks on the door and I open it to reveal her decked out in head-to-toe designer wear, carrying her stuff in a Coach duffel, Prada sunglasses perched atop her head.

"Bianca, you look great!"

"Roxanne, you look so surfer chic." She gives me the two air kisses on the cheek before we hug.

"Let me get your bag," I offer.

"There's a Gucci train case and another Coach duffel in the trunk."

"But Bianca, you're only staying two days."

She looks at me with disbelief. "What if we get invited to a cocktail party? I have to be prepared!"

"Um, okay," I say, looking down at my ensemble of sweatpants, a wife beater, and flip-flops.

"Where's the Beemer?" I ask.

"Oh, it's in the shop, so I rented a car for the weekend. Foreign cars require so much maintenance. So," Bianca says, "I heard about this amazing restaurant called Brioche that we have to go to."

I'm hesitant. "I've heard of it, too, but it's really pricey."

"You only live once; eat well."

"Girl, you are so Hollywood."

"If by Hollywood you mean fabulous, I'll take it as a compliment. So how is life as a beach bum?" Bianca asks, skeptically. I tell her that it's better than I ever imagined, how wonderful Sebastian is, how I feel surrounded by unconditional love, but I get the feeling she isn't really paying attention.

"But enough about me," I say, "what's going on with you?" I put her bags near the couch and I cross to the kitchen to make some cocktails.

"You know, living the life, trying not to get caught up, beating the men off with a stick," she says flippantly.

"Those are sound bites. How are you really doing?" I'm trying to have a real conversation.

Bianca pauses for a beat, as if she's trying to decide whether to be honest or not. "L.A. is harder than I thought it would be, especially now that I'm single again. Everybody cares what kind of car you drive, where you get your hair done, what you do. Well, I don't really care, but I'm expected to. Everyone in the industry is." I stare at her blankly.

"Maybe it's time to stop being who you think everybody else wants you to be and start being who you are. Why do you think I had to escape out here? I was caring way too much. Because being an actor means your whole worth is based on how others perceive you. It's a fucking head trip, but I'm slowly trying to turn the tide." There was a long, awkward silence, and then Bianca asked about Ram and changed the subject completely.

The rest of the weekend with Bianca was okay, but the truth is that her energy was really weird and she didn't really feel like Bianca; she felt like some name-dropping, label-dropping, credit-card-flashing pod person who looked like Bianca, had Bianca's voice, and knew all the old inside jokes that Bianca knew from school, but otherwise was a total stranger. It made me uncomfortable, but I didn't want the whole weekend to be ruined by a fight, so I tried to keep things light. The point of being friends is that you don't have to pretend. You don't have to act like you're Wonder Woman or that you can do everything. Every time I tried to probe a little deeper, she kept brushing me off, insisting that everything was "fabulous." But of the four of us, I can see how Bianca might be the most likely to change to please people. It's that whole Southern woman thing of wanting people to like you, even if you must sacrifice who you are. In my artistic mind, the point of life is to be your most authentic self. I want to be a person who is always honest, even when the truth is painful, because that's the only way to evolve. When Bianca leaves, I think about calling Carolyn and Taylor, but decide not to. I'm going to try to talk to Bianca again about this at the Jubilee; maybe she'll be in a better place, mentally.

• • •

I've spent three cool, relaxing weeks with Sebastian. I feel mellow, I'm tan, I'm becoming a decent surfer, and I haven't stressed about my lack of fame. One Sunday evening, Sebastian, Quincy, Lily, and I are in the kitchen, making Sebastian's famous tortilla soup.

"So Roxy, when do you think you'll go back to New York?" he asks. I stiffen. I've been avoiding this topic. I've been having so much fun being a surfer girl that I was pretending my life back in NYC didn't exist. But it does, and I have to deal with it.

"Never. I'm going to hide out in paradise with you forever," I joke.

"Is that what you really want?" he questions, more serious than usual.

"Of course not. I love it here, the freedom, the ocean, the people, but I do still have this dream, and I'd regret it forever if I didn't find a way to make it happen."

"I've been seeing you writing a lot," he says, chopping garlic. "Anything good?" he probes.

"I started something that I call *Surf Girls Are Easy*. Who knows?" I reveal.

"You're welcome to stay here as long as you want," Quincy offers, oblivious to the fact that this is not, technically, his house, even though he's always over here. We surf every day; I've gotten pretty damned good.

"I know." He means it, but I have to go soon.

Taylor calls me that night. "What's up, bitch?" she barks. Some things never change.

"You know, hanging, being good to myself and shit."

Her voice lightens. "Hey, you sound happier."

"I am. I was just taking shit personally, and it's really not that deep." I can tell she wants dirt. "And how's Quincy?"

"Riding big waves, adorable as ever. But I'm being faithful to Ram. He sent me a care package that consisted of a clipping of his hair, the television section of *TimeOut New York*, and a leaf that had fallen off a tree in Central Park."

"Damn, he's good."

"Okay? I'm horny as hell, but I've got my vibrator and phone sex." We hang up. I miss my friends.

• • •

Now I am sitting on Sebastian's couch, staring at my packed bags and plane ticket, knowing that I only have one more night in California. I've spent a lot of time over the past weeks thinking about how I want my life to be when I get back to New York, because yes, it's nice to chill in paradise where the sun always shines brightly, but I have to do something that will enable me to live a more meaningful and balanced life while existing in the thick of Midtown rush-hour traffic.

Part of that must entail controlling my creative destiny. I finally realized that I am solely responsible for the artistic direction my life takes. Sure, there's no road map, no guidebook, and while initially daunting, it is incredibly liberating. So I've come up with some compelling characters for a one-woman show. The trick with this format is figuring out what I want to say without being heavy-handed and alienating the audience, and I'm glad to be thinking more like a creative artist than an unemployed actor. What I'm envisioning is Tracey Ullman meets Whoopi Goldberg meets Diana Ross meets Monty Python. Sure, every yahoo with a pulse has a "story to tell," but developing interesting characters with a fresh perspective on the world is a heady task. Laura Briggs, a college friend of mine, has started her own theater company and is looking for new plays to produce, so she and I have talked about collaborating on this project; I really think this could be something amazing, and Laura agrees.

I also have to do something about my self-image and self-esteem, something that will enable me to brush off the constant criticism and sniping that, as unpleasant as it may be, is simply part and parcel of the career that I have chosen. I realize that I can't afford to take it to heart every time some assface says my nose is too big, or my breasts are too small. Being here *has* helped; I have benefited to no end from seeing women of all sizes in bikinis and short shorts. I can't believe that I was holding myself to such an absurd and impossible standard of beauty before, and the funny thing is that I've gotten in the best shape of my life here once I stopped restricting my food intake and beating myself up; all the surfing and swimming and walking have made me more muscular and more in possession of myself. For the first time in my life, I am fully aware of my beauty. I remember my suburban childhood, being the only Black girl in all my classes, feeling a need to apologize for my brown skin, being ashamed of my nappy hair, and I am finally letting that baggage go, because I see now how amazing I am.

And I don't only love myself; I love food again! I eat fried fish, I eat meat, I eat like a normal person. Everything tastes better here, and when I get back, I'm going to remember that food is a good thing, a blessing, not something to be avoided.

In fact, this whole trip was a blessing, and it has truly changed my life. Being an actor is fun because you can be so many other people, but while I was here I had to look at exactly who Roxanne is. I've been running from her because I was afraid that the Real Roxanne was crazy, unstable, unlovable, but I found that quite the opposite is true. I sometimes allow other people's problems to become my own, but there is nothing wrong with me. I am smart. I crave love and acceptance. I enjoy sex. And that is just fine.

I have also come to realize that I must stop defining my success in terms of other people's perceptions of what that is, or of what my parents think, or whatever warped residual Ivy League shit I've got going. And I have to stop judging myself so harshly, because I've put too much pressure on myself to be perfect and ignored the basic truth that shit ain't never gonna be perfect. Who cares if I don't book a mouthwash commercial or if I don't get that part playing Will Smith's girlfriend in a movie/TV show/whatever? I must be accountable to myself alone, and my only responsibility is to do my best with what I've got. So dude, no stress.

• • •

Ram is waiting at home for me with flowers and a very serious expression on his face and greets me with a long, warm hug.

"You smell like the ocean," he says.

"I'll take that as a compliment."

"We need to talk." Oh God, I hope this fool doesn't ask me to marry him. I know he missed me, but it's only been a month.

"Sure, honey. What do you want to talk about?" I ask.

"Let me give you a little massage," he says as he begins rubbing those smooth hands on my shoulders. Isn't it funny how that high school trick of massage leading to sex still works? I guess it helps that I never play hard to get anymore. As his hands dig into me, I get more and more excited and decide that I really need to give him a blow job.

Just as I unzip his pants he pushes my hand away and says, "No. This is what we have to talk about."

"I don't give good head?" I say flirtatiously.

"Of course you do, it's just that I'm trying to attain this new level of spirituality, and I really want to abstain from sex so that I can reach a more enlightened state. Sex clouds your judgment, and I want to see how I can navigate in the world without penetration. Your time away showed me that abstinence is possible and quite invigorating." Huh? Who is this android, and what have you done with my boyfriend?

"Are you kidding me? We've been apart for a month, I've got sexual energy oozing from my pores, and you don't want to do it?" I ask, knowing that he *has* to be joking.

"Well, I feel like our relationship could go to a higher level if we remove the sexual pressures," he explains.

"You feel I'm pressing you to have sex?" I say, my eyes narrowing.

"Well, you are very sexually charged." No, really. This has to be a fucking joke.

"I thought that was something you liked about me. But if you wanna get with a nineteen-year-old virgin who'll just lay there like a log and not want you to eat her pussy, or tie her up, or stick your tongue up her ass, be my guest."

"That's just it," he says. "I want to be with you, but I want us to be celibate."

"You have lost your damn mind. It took us forever and a half to have sex in the first place. My pussy has been dripping wet for weeks upon weeks and you want to be celibate?"

"Roxanne, you're being a little dramatic. Besides, you haven't cornered the market on spiritual epiphanies this month," Ram says. He is certifiably insane.

"I'm gonna go and let you think about this. I need to calm down, and I'm obviously gonna have to let my vibrator welcome me home. You're crazy. I mean, California had me horny as shit; so many sexy people, so much heat and sweat, all those pheromones. I kept thinking 'When I get back home, I am going to fuck Ram's brains out.' And now this? Oh, no."

I leave him at my place and practically sprint the forty blocks to Taylor's apartment, where the ranting spree begins. "I mean, what's the point of being with a man if he's not going to fuck me? If I wanted to talk I could call you or Bianca or Carolyn. The only point of putting up with these jackasses is so we can have mind-blowing orgasms."

"Basically," she responds, handing me a flute of Moët.

"I mean, this fool fucked the shit out of me at least five times a week and now wants to quit, cold turkey. The sex we had before I left town was so good I thought I was going to die, and even if I did die, I couldn't think of a better way to go," I complain.

"I know. It seems like you can't give away good pussy these days," Taylor sighs.

"Yeah, I'm a sexy chick with a hot, wet, tight pussy, and I can't get anybody to fuck me."

"There's something very wrong with that. You're twenty-eight, not seventy-eight. You deserve good dick, and there's none to be found," Taylor agrees.

"But I'll be damned if this fool expects me to hang around with him and not come. I felt like a horny teenage slut when I was trying to persuade him to let me suck his dick," I shout. "What world do we live in where men don't want blow jobs from fine, horny women?"

"A very unjust, horrible world that wants to torture us," Taylor responds, refreshing my glass.

"Well, I'll give him a few days to come to his senses, and if he doesn't, he's getting the boot! What kind of welcome home is that? I'm sorry, but while I'm still young, a fabulous evening should conclude with me naked with jiz on my breasts!" I snap sulkily.

The thing is that throughout my life, boyfriends have made me feel like an oversexed nymphomaniac, and I've always wondered what's wrong with a woman having a healthy sexual appetite? Men say they want women who love sex, and as soon as they get one, me specifically, they head for the hills because I won't just lay there. I love sex, and I find that as I get closer to thirty and become more comfortable in my own skin, my sexual desire increases. I should go find a horny eighteen-year-old, because even if he came quickly, he'd want to do it all night like I do. Never again will I apologize for my libido; shit, I'm going to celebrate it. Bring it *on*.

• 53 •

Carolyn

Party People in the House Say Hmmph

"Where in the shit are your costumes, bitches?!" Roxanne snaps. People are staring, perhaps because they recognize her from one of her plays, perhaps because she is holding a foot-long dildo covered in glitter and wearing a chain of vibrators interspersed with bottles of K-Y over her sparkly white spandex bodysuit.

"You're looking at it," I say. "I've come as a Black Republican. All evening I'll be kissing the ass of the white conservative establishment and endorsing policies that stab my less fortunate black brethren in the back."

"I'm a recovering alcoholic who's fallen off the wagon just this afternoon," Taylor says, "and to prove it, I'm going to get absolutely fucked up. Starting now."

"I'm a devastatingly attractive former child star who has fallen on hard times but still owns several pieces of very fine jewelry," says Bianca, who has flown in from the West Coast on a publicity junket.

"You three really fucking suck," Roxanne hisses, her wings quivering with rage.

"Never mind us, Glinda," Taylor says, "you think anyone's going to be looking at us once they get a look at you?"

"Yes, which sort of fairy might you be?" I say curiously.

"I am not a fairy," Roxanne says haughtily. "I am the Multiple Female Orgasm, an elusive spectre that haunts every bedroom encounter despite my rare occurrence."

There is a short silence.

"Well, points for creativity, anyway," Bianca says as we spot Roxanne's friend Laura waving to us over by the bar. "Shall we?"

Roxanne's costume is relatively mild compared to the rest of what we see that evening; this is New York, and the Bon Vivant Costume Gala is an HIV/AIDS fund-raiser sponsored by several actors' and dancers' associations, so we are treated to an assortment of creatures straight out of central casting. The Multiple Female Orgasm vanishes into the ether and the three of us decide to escape to a back table and put a bottle of champagne through its paces. Taylor goes to the bar to get it and Bianca and I stake out a booth in the back of the lounge.

"Carolyn," Taylor says, slamming a bottle and three flutes onto the table and squinting into the distance, "isn't that Carter?"

Bianca's ears pop up and she whirls around in her seat.

"Ooh. Ooh. Ooh. Where?"

I turn around, too. It certainly is. And he is not wearing a costume; he is instead wearing an exquisite brunette draped gracefully over his arm. This woman stands about five feet eight inches tall and has the ideal bust, waist, and hips to go along with her olive skin, long, wavy dark hair, doe eyes, and perfect mouth. She is, of course, dressed as Scheherazade or Salome or something in that line, meaning that she is barely clad, with jewels dripping everywhere. I turn back to the table. My stomach hurts suddenly, and I am not sure why. Bianca takes one look at my face and slops so much champagne into my flute that she soaks the tablecloth.

"Yep, that would be Carter," I say dully.

"Shut your cakehole," Taylor says without moving her lips, "they're coming over here."

"Carolyn? Taylor? Is that you?" He leans down, smiling widely, and hugs me, then Taylor.

"Well, hello there, Carter," Taylor says. "And I know you know Bianca, even if you've never seen her."

"Ah, the infamous third Musketeer," Carter says. "The pleasure is mine."

"No, it's mine," Bianca says, shaking his hand. "It's about time; I've heard so much about you."

"Nothing good, I'm sure," Carter grins, and turns to his date. "Carolyn Phillips, Taylor Williams, and Bianca King," he says to Scheherazade. She nods, barely acknowleding the introduction. "Carolyn, Taylor, Bianca, this is Melina de Gonsalves y Rodriguez. She's a guest artist with the ABT."

But of course she is.

"Hi," I say, feeling like Blaboonda of the Whale People from the Sixth Moon of the Planet Inferior.

"Melina is my brother's fiancée," Carter adds, "I'm showing her around until he gets back into the country."

"That's nice," I manage to say, before I am overcome by the strong feeling of relief that washes over me at the phrase "brother's fiancée." Almost immediately, the relief is replaced by a very different kind of dismay as I realize why I am relieved and why my stomach jumped into my throat when I first saw him across the room and then plummeted into my shoes when I saw Melina.

Shit.

I cannot believe that I have managed to let this situation develop, unnoticed, to a level of severity where I experience digestive turmoil at Carter's unexpected appearance. This position is all the more untenable because Scheherazade's presence is an omen—while she personally is not His Girl, there is some other *Harper's Bazaar* model out there who is, and eventually she will make her presence known.

"Carter," the dancer says suddenly, in a heavily accented alto, "I want a drink, and also to dance." She disappears into the crowd. Carter looks after her and then turns back to the table.

"That's a pretty poor excuse for a costume, Carolyn," he grins. "I expected something better from Getty's resident creative genius." I smile wanly and say nothing. Bianca, sensing the weirdness, jumps in and expertly picks up the conversational slack. Finally her emergency resuscitation effort fails, and, in the midst of an awkward silence, Carter looks at me very strangely, then says hesitantly, "I guess I'll see you guys." I wave.

"See you at work," I say tonelessly. He frowns. Bianca and Taylor compensate with too-effusive farewells, and he takes his leave.

"I don't know who that Ali Baba bitch thought she was, but I have news for her," Taylor says. "You look me in the eye when you're being introduced to me; don't stare every which way but at me."

"You are beneath her," Bianca says in a perfect imitation of Scheherazade's accent. "You are common, while the blood of the *conquistadores* runs in her veins; her forefathers gazed upon the Incas with the exact same contempt with which she gazes at you."

I realize that, like a jackass, I am staring pensively at the place in the crowd where Carter disappeared.

"Earth to Carolyn," Bianca says. "Honey, what's going on?"

"I told you the bitch did protesteth too much," Taylor says, pouring out more champagne, but her voice is gentler than usual. I shrug. As best friends always do, they immediately divine that I am not interested in talking about anything that happened in the past ten minutes and change the subject.

• 54 •

Taylor

No Pain, No Gain

Meschach was leaving for London soon, and I still hadn't told him how I felt. He had told me, his eyes sparkling, that he'd never imagined that love could feel this good. When he did, I smiled weakly and bleated out something similar in return. He looked happy, but somewhat disappointed. He had probably wanted me to bound gleefully into his arms (shit, who wouldn't), but I just couldn't bring myself to do it. I'm sure he was thinking, damn, either don't say it back and be a total bitch or say it and put some fucking enthusiasm in it. But no matter how much I wanted to be happy, I couldn't. I kept trying to be more enthusiastic about it, because I didn't want to lose Meschach by seeming lukewarm on love; then I'd have no one to blame but myself.

When Carolyn found out how I'd responded, she read me so bad that for a second I thought *I* was yelling at me, and I finally decided to break down and take the leap. So, last night while we were at dinner, I finally broke down. Under the guise of trying to fix things, I asked Meschach how a man as fabulous as I thought he was, could possibly be so wonderful, not crazy, and still single. He told me that he didn't consider himself still single, and I smiled. I poured out my heart. The past wounds, the fact that I was so scared to love him that I got nauseous, all of the things I'd told the girls, when Meschach, not them, was the one who needed to hear it. I was tired of telling everyone but the one I loved how I truly felt.

And then, as if the floodgates were opening on both sides, his story came out. Meschach had been engaged before, at twenty-five. He had planned to marry his college sweetheart. I couldn't quite believe that some people still did that. More important, I couldn't believe he hadn't brought this up before. But then again, what could I say? I hadn't mentioned John either—after our last encounter, I hadn't wanted to think about him ever again.

Far from being a runaway groom, he told me that his fiancée had died in a car accident six months before their planned wedding. At that point, he was a junior research analyst at GCS, and rather than deal with his pain, much like me, he threw himself into his work. He admitted that while he hadn't exactly behaved like a eunuch since then, he'd tried to keep things "light" (how I hate that phrase!) because he didn't have the emotional energy to go through the same utter despair he felt after Cynthia's death. It wasn't until the morning of his thirty-third birthday that he realized his life was slipping by him, and that there wasn't much to life without someone special at home, someone who gave a damn about him and wanted the best for him, someone about whom he felt the same way. So while he hadn't set out looking for a "Ms. Right," he was no longer averse to finding her.

But why he hadn't brought Cynthia up before? It wasn't until I saw his eyes mist over that I realized that, even ten years later, he still felt a great deal of pain, and that drove me to confess everything about John. Meschach took it all in and then gave me a hug that squeezed all the breath out of my lungs. Having shared the experience of thinking you'd found the "one," only to have that dream evaporate definitely brought us closer. As we got up to leave the restaurant, Meschach noted that "we couldn't spend the rest of our lives wondering how the future would have been if the past had been different."

Looking at Meschach and thinking of just how compatible we were made me happy that I had let John go. He hadn't been the "one," given the way things ended, and living in some fantasy world about how things could have been different if only John had not done this, not said that, was silly, and a waste of time.

I realized then that I can't expect a man to promise me that he won't change, that things will always stay wonderful, that we'd always be together, forever. My problem with men is that I only ever asked that they *try*, but they never ever did. But maybe, just maybe, Meschach is different, and I'm determined to at least give him a chance to prove me wrong. This was the one time, probably since I'd been born, that I didn't want to be right.

• 55 •

Bianca

Slumming It

The nasty scene with Nicholas was quite a wake up call for me (that and riding the bus). The trip to New York—even the trip to La Jolla to see Roxanne, which was weird because she kept nagging me about how things were going and acting like I was acting strange, which I know was just her projecting her own insecurities but still creeped me out—practically bankrupted me the rest of the way, and I'm now doing my best to lead what they call a "simple life," although there's nothing simple about maintaining a weekly food budget of fifty dollars when one McDonald's combo costs six dollars. I cut up all my credit cards, which was a purely symbolic gesture since they've all been cut off anyway. I bring my lunch to work every day now and have rediscovered the joys of peanut butter and jelly. My digital cable has been canceled, so now there's nothing distracting me from my screenplay when I get home. I'm even reading a new book in my spare time called *Debt Free by 30*. Fuck Nicholas. I know I could just ask Taylor for a loan, but the only way I'm going to get out of this hole is by taking control of my finances and my life by myself. These little sacrifices I'm making now will just seem like a distant memory when I'm in the south of France next summer. Or maybe, to be honest, the summer after that. Or after that.

My schedule has changed a lot. I told Rachel and the rest of my acquaintances out here that I'm really busy these days and that I totaled the Beemer. That seemed to work, and on the few occasions that I've gone out since the repossession, Rachel picked me up like she used to. But now that I can no longer afford to pay twelve dollars for a chocolate martini (I told them I'd quit drinking, too), there's no point in going out because I've noticed that these people are so boring that the only way to get through an evening with them is to be butt-ass drunk. Plus, now they're all sporting the latest Dior bags and I'm ashamed of my two-seasons-old Louis.

I've actually started hanging out with my neighbor Selma more; she finally gave Marc the for-real boot and she's really good at finding fun stuff to do that doesn't cost much, like street fairs and film festivals. Also, she wouldn't know Michael Kors from Michael Jackson, so it doesn't matter what I wear to hang out with her.

It's funny; I'm not really sure when I started to become a Trend Monster. In college, if you had told me that there'd come a time when I wouldn't think twice about dumping four hundred dollars on a pair of shoes that would be out of fashion in two months, I'd have looked down at my trusty three-year-old black Steve Madden platform boots and told you you were out of your mind. I guess it started once I got into the fashion industry, but then it was part of my job. You can't rep up-and-coming avant-garde designers in a three-year-old Gap cardigan (unless it's in immaculate condition and you're wearing it semi-ironically over an Azzedine Alaia slip dress with a pair of Jimmy Choos). And once we all started working, Taylor and Carolyn got into clothes and shoes, too; they could afford designer pieces, and they bought them, but they weren't insane about it, and they only bought designer if they couldn't find the look anywhere else for less. Roxanne, on the other hand, never shopped anywhere but consignment stores and vintage thrift shops, and sometimes she even made her own clothes, but she always looked fabulous and had a very funky Cynthia Rowley thing going. It strikes me now that some of my "friends" out here would make fun of her because of the way she dresses, and I wonder if, had I met her as a stranger out here, I wouldn't have done the same. I hope I wouldn't have, but I don't know.

I still haven't told the girls back East about my financial (and emotional) breakdown and I haven't told my parents either. I can still call everyone I need to from work, and I can get calls at home, even if I can't make them because my long-distance service is long gone. I just wouldn't know how to explain how I'd gotten into such a hole, and I frankly don't want to bother. I'm still not sure myself.

Other changes: No more Starbucks because I need the four dollars I would spend on a Chai Latte *venti* for bus tokens. I'm doing my own hair and nails, which takes up most of my Saturday morning and afternoon, and I'm avoiding my hairdresser Matteo's calls. I don't go window-shopping on Rodeo anymore, mostly because I don't want anyone to see that I ride the bus, but also because I don't need the temptation. I threw out the Neiman Marcus and Nordstrom books when they came, and I've discovered Old Navy, which isn't so bad if you have a good eye and a nose for fabulous, which I, of course, still do. I've started cooking again, which is something I used to do all the time at home and in undergrad. I am proud to say that there's still nothing I can't do with a chicken. It's actually more convenient to cook on Sundays and Wednesdays and have leftovers ready and waiting the other five days than it is to get stuck in traffic trying to get to a drive-through or wait ten thousand years for delivery.

However, they turned off my gas on Monday and my enthusiasm for "roughing it" is beginning to wane after an extremely cold shower this morning. I've been over an hour late to work twice, which I've never done before in my life, because I missed my bus and didn't have the forty-five dollars to take a cab. Nicholas was home and I know he would have driven me but I'd rather shave off my hair and set my scalp on fire than ask that bastard for shit. Maybe he was right about some things, but he sure could have handled it differently. Jackal. I don't even think about him at all that much anymore.

I was in a particularly low mood that day because I realized that I have absolutely no idea how I'm going to cover my expenses at the reunion; I bought the plane tickets before my cards were cut off but the card holding my reservation at the Charles Hotel is no good, so I'm going to be humiliated the second I try to check in. I won't even be able to cover my friends for a round of drinks. I'm the only one of us who technically was doing better eight years ago than I am today, and that's so fucking embarrassing that it's making me want to cry. Then I discovered a hole in my Versace leather skirt after I got on the bus and the tears really did come.

Trying artfully to cover the hole with a TSE cardigan that smells of cigarettes and bus fumes (I was up to seventy-five dollars a week in dry-cleaning expenses and that was one of the first things that had to go) wasn't working. So there I was, red-eyed, sitting at my desk, looking up "Chapter 11" on the Internet, and trying to figure out whether I had enough money for a tiny box of Godiva (it had been so long and I've been really good) when my boss called me into his office.

"Bianca, got a minute?"

I got up and went in. I like Larry; he's the one who gave me this job in the first place. He drives an old Volvo, he's got pictures of his family all over his office, and he's one of the few people I know out here (excepting certain jackass screenwriter/columnist/professors who shall remain nameless) who don't seem to have gotten caught up in the whole Hollywood bullshit.

"You may or may not have heard this, but Janet Wallace is leaving to go to the WB."

I nodded. Jan's a couple of steps up from me in the department. I'd heard rumors about her departure but I hadn't really been paying attention because I don't have time for much of anything these days that doesn't involve my job or my brokeness.

"We're looking for a replacement, and I put your name up for the job because you handle yourself well, you're great with people, and you're able to get results in situations where a lot of other people, many of them more experienced, have been unable to. To make a long story short, the rest of the committee agreed that we couldn't think of a more qualified or dedicated candidate, so we'd like to offer you the position, and we'd like to ask you to start immediately."

"Oh, my God," I said. Larry grinned and continued.

"You probably won't mind knowing that you'd get a raise, which I think," he stopped to flip through some papers on his desk, "yeah, it's about twenty thousand dollars. You'll also get a corporate American Express for business expenses, and—"

I didn't hear anything he said after that because I was too busy doing the math in my head and freaking out. Twenty thousand dollars? Twenty. Thousand. Dollars. TWENTY THOUSAND DOLLARS. I could get my gas turned back on. Pay off my credit cards. Take my student loans out of deferment. Get my cable, cell phone, and long distance turned back on. Get my clothes cleaned. And an AmEx! My very own American Express corporate card! When I tuned back in, Larry was staring at me expectantly.

"I'll take it," I practically shouted. "Oh, this is great. I'll absolutely take it. Thank you so much. This is great!" I stood up and shook his hand, then bounced out of the office.

Oh my God, my problems were solved. Thank you thank you thank you God, thank you Larry, thank you Jan! I'm saved! I sat down at my desk and closed the Chapter 11 Web page—no need for that now! Bianca King is back on top, and I'm going to lead a financially prudent lifestyle! I'm going to save! I'm going to invest! I'm going to hunt for bargains! I'm going to clip coupons! Now I know that I can do just fine without all of the extra crap that I used to think I couldn't live without, and I'm ready to do it. I can still cook and do my own facials. This is going to be *great*.

· 56 ·

Carolyn

Sing Hey, Sing Ho,
for the Big Girl at the Sto'

Nothing distracts one from a possible incipient crush on a completely in-appropriate object—who, again, is not one's type to begin with—like shopping. As I stroll down Madison, balancing two armfuls of shopping bags, the top catches my eye from across the street. It is a wee piece of a shirt in gas blue, my favorite color, and it is very simple and looks very good on the mannequin in the window, who is wearing it with a pair of faded low-rider jeans. I hesitate at the door of the boutique; I have lost a little weight, but it is not enough yet to get me into this top. I think of Dr. Guisewite's latest advice, which is to try celebrating every little bit of progress instead of brooding over the obstacles yet to come, and I decide that I will buy the shirt and put it away for when I can wear it, which will probably not be before the Jubilee, but will eventually happen.

A chime sounds as I open the door and step across the threshold. A slender salesgirl looks up, her face alight and expectant; when she sees who her customer is, the bright smile dims and she returns to her phone call without so much as a nod. Undaunted, I scan the store, spot the shirt on the far wall, and walk over to it. It is made of rayon and is gossamer thin, almost as thin as stockings; the neck and the short sleeves are unfinished, and a faint sprinkling of glitter dusts the chest. It is very pretty, and I can see myself wearing it and a pair of faded low-rider jeans, glittering and laughing gaily in the dim light of Space or VII as I flirt with some bedazzled swain. I pick through the hangers but cannot find a Large. I walk over to the salesgirl, holding a Medium, and wait patiently as she interrupts her phone call to deliver a polite greeting to a redhead walking in the front, then returns to the phone call.

When she finally turns with an exasperated "What do you want?" expression on her face, I hold up the shirt. I have barely gotten "Do you have" out of my mouth when she snaps "We don't carry that in your size," and turns back to the phone. Two girls standing near the register titter.

My face goes bright red. I am completely humiliated. I plod back to the rack and replace the shirt, feeling that everyone is looking at me and giggling at the idea that I, a disgusting ball of lard with feet, aspired to the ownership of such a beautiful shirt, which is clearly only meant for beautiful people. I feel tears welling up in my eyes and I can feel a lump in my throat. I turn to go and pass by the cash register, where the salesgirl is wrapping the purchase of a wafer-thin blonde with a Swedish accent. Now butter would not melt in her mouth. An almost electric jolt passes through me and I stop short, realizing that the lump in my throat is not tears so much as it is an absolutely foreign feeling.

It is rage.

And what a rage it is.

Ever since moving to the city, I, like many professional Black women, have been treated as something less than human by shopgirls and shopboys up and down Fifth Avenue and in the trendy boutiques of Soho and Midtown. Sometimes I am shadowed by salespersons who do not seem to realize that my handbag cost more than what they take home every week; sometimes, like today, salespersons act as if I am taxing them beyond the limits of their duties when I request assistance; sometimes I am asked for additional identification when I make a credit card purchase, while the White woman in front of me, whose card is not even signed, passes on, unhindered. Intermingled with this general lack of respect for Black customers is the unbridled scorn that this sort of person seems to feel obliged to exhibit toward overweight people, and I have had enough of both. I am shaking with anger; I want to knock over the displays, smash the counters, and kick this girl's front teeth out. Instead I confine myself to stepping back up to the counter and tapping my fingers on the glass loudly.

Both the Swedish customer and the salesgirl notice me at the same time and their pleasant banter dwindles to a halt. The salesgirl, obviously annoyed, opens her mouth to speak, but I hold up my hand and cut her off.

"Where is your manager?" I say shortly.

"She's in the back," the girl replies eventually.

"Get her," I say. The salesgirl huffs exasperatedly and rolls her eyes knowingly at the customer, who merely looks bewildered.

"Get her *now*," I say, and while I have not raised my voice at all, there is something imperious and steely running underneath it that I have never heard before in my own voice. Whatever it is, it works; the girl flounces off into the back of the store. Five minutes later, she comes back alone.

"She'll be with you in a second," she says grudgingly.

"You're far too kind," I say shortly. The manager appears shortly, wiping her mouth.

"I'm Deena, the senior manager," she says. "You wanted to see me?" She is guarded but not necessarily unfriendly.

"I'm sorry to disturb your lunch," I say amicably enough, "but I just could not leave your store without letting you know how your sales staff treated me. I thought it was only fair to give you a heads-up before I put it out on the street."

The manager's eyebrows go up.

"When I came in here, the salesperson on duty registered my presence but did not greet me, probably because she was too busy on her personal phone call. She did not come over to ask me how I was doing or if I needed help. When I approached her with a T-shirt that I'd found, before I could even finish my sentence, she snapped 'We don't have that in your size,' then turned her back on me and went back to her personal phone call." The manager's face is very difficult to read at this point. Undaunted, I proceed.

"She had no idea what I was going to ask her. I am going to pass over how insolent it was for her to tell me what I can or can't wear, or how stupid she was to assume that I was shopping for myself and not for one of my friends and just ask you whether your salespersons are instructed to treat some customers differently from others, as I note that her attitude toward me was markedly different from her attitude toward your other, Whiter customers."

The manager shakes her head.

"It's not our policy at all, and I'm terribly sorry that you were given the impression that—"

"That's good to know," I say, cutting her off, "because I work in the advertising business myself, and I have a lot of friends, thin friends, friends with a lot of disposable income, some of whom do publicity and who work with and for various celebrities—many of whom have been known to spend large amounts of money at this store. I'd hate to have to tell them that this store is not a place that deserves their business because the salespeople have been told that personal phone calls are more important than being polite to customers, or that African-American customers don't deserve the same level of solicitude and assistance as other customers," here the manager flinches, "or that people over a certain weight are not welcome here, and I'd hate for them to spread the word and for your store to get a . . . well, a reputation."

There is a long silence as the manager sizes me up, and then I see her make a decision.

"I'm sure that won't be necessary, Miss . . ."

"Phillips. Carolyn Phillips," I say. The manager extends her hand and shakes mine.

"I'd like to offer you my personal apology for any unpleasant experiences you had here," she says. "Can I offer you a cup of coffee in my office?" she says. "Perhaps we could discuss this further."

I shake my head.

"I have to be going," I say, "I've already spent far more time here than I had planned to."

"Oh, well . . ." she says, and is somewhat at a loss. Then her face brightens. "Perhaps I could help you with the shirt you were looking at?"

I shake my head.

"Deena, I'm sure you understand why I would have some reservations about spending any money here after having been treated so shabbily by your sales staff."

I see her mind working, and suddenly she nods.

"It's on the house," she says. "We'd very much appreciate it if you'd let us comp the shirt for you."

I point out the shirt.

"And I need it in a Large," I say, glaring pointedly at the offending salesgirl.

"Amy, go in the back and get it," the manager says, gesturing brusquely at the salesgirl and not taking her eyes from me. Amy moves remarkably fast and is back with my Large.

"Gift-wrap it," the manager says shortly. She smiles at me. "Our gift to you. And we hope that you will favor us with your business again, and if you are made to feel unwelcome for any reason," she also glares at Amy, who shrinks, "please ask for me immediately." She reaches into her back pocket and hands me a business card. There is a question in her eyes.

"Thank you. I appreciate the way you handled this; I'm sure my friends will be pleased to know that the manager, if not the general staff," and I pause to glare again at Amy myself, "of this establishment is courteous and professional." Deena nods, relieved, and I walk out.

Once out in the street, I whoop and wave my shopping bags delightedly at the sky. Today I discovered that I just might have a backbone instead of a wishbone, and while I will not be able to wear the spoils of this victory for some months, I can pin it on my wall and gaze at it triumphantly until then.

• 57 •

Roxanne

He Will Be the Flame

Well, now I'm back in full Roxanne mode, and I am not going to let Ram's celibate nonsense get me down. I'm already on the hunt for replacement dick. I'm all for spiritual connections, but I can't understand why Ram thinks we'd have a better one if we stopped having sex; I talk a lot of shit about sex, but I honestly see it as being just as spiritual as it is physical, and I can't see the point of shutting that down. In any case, for shits and giggles, Carolyn, Taylor, and I have decided to hit this bar called Cockfight because they have the best apple martinis in town and because they have a wonderful little competition offering a hundred dollars to whomever does the most creative thing onstage. Since there are no cameras allowed inside, I know that it will be safe to do anything outrageous and not be held accountable for it. With my new attitude, I've got a thing planned out involving my "pop ups," elaborate yoga moves, pasties, and half-full martini glasses. I've been practicing all day, and I am in rare form tonight. It's my welcome home performance, and the shaking of my ass should help me forget about Ram and his withholding ways. Right before I head to the bathroom to prepare my costume and put on my bikini bottoms and character, I see onstage the man I know I'm going to marry, or at least have a meaningful conversation with.

He is tall, dark, and glistening—just the way I like 'em—and performing an exotic dance that looks like a cross between Alvin Ailey and Capoeira, with a little Chippendales thrown in. We are all mesmerized by the fluidity and strength of his hips, and I think that if he can do that onstage, offstage he will break my fucking back. I'll be "cumming [back] to New York" in no time!! Taylor and Carolyn see the lust in my eyes.

"You do know that any man doing an oiled-up striptease in a bar called Cockfight can't possibly be straight, right?" Taylor asks in that condescending tone of hers. She isn't really asking me, she's telling me.

"You've clearly got seawater in your gaydar," Carolyn adds.

"I'm inviting him over for a drink, and I'm going to have that dick tonight. My gaydar is on full alert, and he is playing on our team, chicas. If he's straight, you have to get me a massage at Bliss, and if he's gay, I'll cook your favorite meal," I say with total confidence.

"It's a bet," Taylor and Carolyn say in unison, giggling loudly. I grab him at the bar and drag him over to our table.

"Ladies, this is Roger, and he wants to have a drink with us," I say, pulling a chair up for him.

"I really enjoyed your performance, Roger. Have you studied dance professionally?" Carolyn inquires.

"Naw, that was just some shit I made up to win the hundred dollars." *Not a professional dancer—point for me.*

Then Taylor pipes up with the inevitable bitchy question, "So, how does your boyfriend feel about you performing half-naked onstage?"

Roger chuckles and says, "I'm single, so I don't have to answer to anyone." *Not quite sure what that means. Neutral.*

"So how did you find out about this place?" Carolyn asks innocently.

"My friends Tony and Gabe are the bartenders." *Damn. He knows two employees, and if Tony and Gabe are the guys behind the bar now, they're flaming. That's two for them; it's not looking good for me.*

I'm hoping to get a few more points for my side, so I just cut to the chase and ask him, "Would you like to eat my pussy tonight, Roger?"

There is silence. A huge grin emerges on Roger's perfect face, followed by hysterically high-pitched laughter.

"Girl, I like dick," he says, his voice now quite shrill. My face cracks. "You should know better than to look for a man at a bar called Cockfight!" Roger, Taylor, and Carolyn are cracking up. I've been out of town far too long.

"All that sun melted your brain, girl. But that's all right, because I'm sure as fuck going to enjoy the surf and turf you'll be preparing for me this weekend," Taylor cackles.

"I want grilled salmon with Roxy's Infamous Garlic Mashed and creamed spinach," Carolyn adds. "Your gaydar may be smashed all to hell but I assume your food processor still works."

Okay, maybe I shouldn't be trolling bars for dick. We live near the Atlantic Ocean; maybe She will see my need and wash him ashore.

58

Taylor

No Way, No How

Meschach dropped a huge *good* surprise on me this morning at breakfast. When I opened my napkin, a cascade of little pink seashells fell out of it, and he announced that he was taking us (capital *U*, capital *S*, capital *US*) on a four-day vacation to Martinique for some quality alone time before he left for London. Harvard-Yale is the weekend immediately after I return from Martinique, so I've been going nuts clearing my desk, practically putting myself in the loony bin to make sure everything is current and everything that isn't is being handled by someone else. It's nine p.m., and I'm about to leave to make sure I can get some beauty sleep before showing up at the airport at the crack of dawn; Meschach is literally jumping onto our flight from the LAX red-eye, so this is the only night in the next five that I expect to get any kind of sleep at all.

Then my phone rings. It's David, the pain-in-the-ass senior associate. He is so high-strung he makes Carolyn look catatonic, and he's well known for being shit to work for, between his shit-ass temper and his tendency to blame his mistakes on the junior associates under him. If it were six p.m., okay, but it's nine p.m., and I'm not answering the phone, especially not for this kuh-razy asshole. I continue e-mailing my caseroom, letting my head legal assistant know where I'll be. Then my door bursts open, no knocking.

"Taylor, if you're here, why didn't you answer your phone?" David asks, although it's clearly a rhetorical question. "We need you upstairs right now! It's another Wells submission, and you've only got three days to get it done! Rob said you wouldn't mind helping."

"I told Rob several times over the past two weeks that I'm going on vacation tomorrow," I say, "and I really can't help you. I'm very sorry."

"This is an *emergency*," he says in the tone you use with retarded children.

"I understand that, and I'm sorry," I say smoothly, "but I can't just change plans like that."

"Well, let's just see what Rob has to say about that," he snarls, nostrils flaring. "It's a client emergency, and you know that takes precedence over everything else, vacation or not. Didn't some issue come up with you about this very same subject a few months ago?"

No. He. Didn't. "You know what?" I say. "I'll just go see Rob with you and we can find out what he has to say together." I am absolutely furious, but my demeanor is calm. David is at a loss, since he's used to throwing that bullshit on junior associates and watching them cower, but it's not working on me; he's got the wrong bitch this time. We walk through the halls to Rob's office, where I see Rob and two other partners. A third partner is on the speakerphone; this is obviously a war council.

"Taylor!" Rob says, obviously relieved. "Thank God; we need a draft of this by Thursday morning. Here's the SEC letter. Call David if you—"

"Rob," I interrupt. "I can't take this assignment. I'm going on vacation starting tomorrow. I told you."

"We'll pay for your canceled plane ticket," snaps one of the other partners without looking up, "just give it to my secretary."

"Taylor, Intertec needs you," Rob says pompously.

"Oh, they *need* me?" I say, my eyes narrowing. "They didn't want me when I had to take time off for my grandmother's operation but *now* they *need* me?" The blood floods up into my face and the vein in my neck begins to throb. Rob realizes that he's fucked up and starts to backtrack.

"No," I spit. "I can't change these plans. I can't cancel this. I've lived here for weeks on end. I've slept in this office almost as much as I've slept in my apartment. I have done what you asked, I did it well, and I never complained. But this is not an emergency. This is a routine matter that anyone here can handle."

"But we don't want 'anyone here' to handle it, we want *you* to handle it. David is only going to be here for one more day before he leaves for his vaca—" He stops himself as he hears what he is saying. David's vacation takes priority over mine. David can dump his work on me even though he sent his vacation notice out two weeks after I sent mine. They've chosen him over me.

"My vacation takes priority over David's."

"Not today it doesn't," they both say in unison. Now, I'd expect that from David, but not from Rob. I'd thought he was better than that. Clearly, I was wrong. But so are they. And I've finally had enough. To get where you want to go in life, sometimes you've got to put one foot in front of the other and get to steppin'.

"Wrong, counselors. Today it *does.* Because I quit. You can send the severance paperwork to my house; consider this the exit interview."

It's like I'm looking at four cartoons, four portraits of Oh My Lord What Is This Black Girl Saying? I turn on my heel and march out the door. Fuck this bullshit; I should have done this months ago. I've got money in the bank to cover me easily for six months, probably more, and the headhunters are blowing up my phone, so another job is not going to be a problem. Working hard is one thing, but being disrespected is not in the cards.

I go back to my office and jam my purse, my blanket (for when I have to sleep on the floor), my three changes of clothes and four pairs of shoes (for when I have to shower and change in the gym downstairs), my pictures of me and the girls, me and Meschach, me and my parents, my plant, all of the crazy little cartoons Carolyn has sent me over the years, and I bounce. The whole time my phone rings off the hook, and I see that the call is coming from Rob's office, but I don't answer. I storm out to the elevator bank, where a red-faced David is just stepping out of the elevator.

"Taylor, you're going too far—" he begins, but I walk right past him and throw him a death stare.

"No, I'm just going. Now get. Out. Of my motherfucking face."

He looks at me, too shocked (or scared) to speak.

"That's right, back the fuck up off of me," I whisper as I step two inches away from his face. I smile. Then I turn and I drop my passkey at the security desk.

Stepping out of Mills, Waters, Denis, & Cois for the last time. Stepping into the cool night air. Stepping toward my apartment, my vacation, my girls, my man. I don't even stop to look back, because there's nothing to see; my life, the life I want, the life I deserve, is in front of me.

59

Bianca

Back from the Dead

"Oh, my God, does she think that looks *good?*" Rachel says, wrinkling her nose. "What is that, four, five years old? Nobody's carrying the graffiti Louis anymore, nobody. What does she think this is, *Croatia?!* Ugh, that is so tired!" I throw back the rest of my chocolate martini and giggle. Rachel is a total bitch, but the purse does look completely crazy. I look down at my new Marc Jacobs bag in satisfaction; nobody can say that *I* look crazy.

This looks bad, I know, but it's just temporary. After all, I didn't have any fun for so long that I think I deserve a little now, as long as I keep it under control. Plus, I think we all know that I can't show up in Cambridge wearing Old Navy jeans and Payless flip-flops, especially not with my new fabulous job title. The Marc Jacobs bag ($750), the Jimmy Choo boots ($800), and the new TSE sweater set ($575) are just little gifts I bought to reward myself for the promotion. Same thing for the half-day at Burke Williams ($425), the two-hour session with Sergei, my masseur ($230), and the wash, mudpack, deep conditioner, trim, and set from Matteo ($240), who refused to see me until I practically burst into tears on the phone (and it's still going to take me months to get back into his good graces). And, okay, I did put all the charges on my corporate AmEx, but they're practically business expenses (I do have to look good to get the job done) and, besides, they're barely a drop in the bucket compared to the endless, bottomless balance on that card. Who's going to notice two or three thousand extra dollars at the end of the day? The network probably drops that much on a weekly basis for weave maintenance for the Monday night lineup. In the meantime, I am proud to say, I have paid something—not as much as I'd like, but something—on my Visas and MasterCard, and my gas, long distance, and cell phone have been restored fully. I haven't gotten into that saving thing yet, but I will start as soon as I pay down the rest of my credit cards.

Speaking of saving, I ran into Nicholas the other day in Westwood. I was coming out of a cafe with Selma and he was coming out of the vintage bookstore next door. I almost dropped my iced latte; he looked better than ever in his old jeans and corduroy jacket. Then I remembered the last thing I'd said to him and my stomach flipped over. I tried to duck into the next store but it was too late; he'd seen me.

"Hello, Bianca," he said evenly. "How are you?"

Redfaced, I came back down the steps.

"I'm fine, Nicholas," I said, offering my hand. He took it, and when he touched me, I'm ashamed to admit, I had ten thousand sex flashbacks.

"I'm glad to hear that," he said. "Our last meeting was—"

"I'm sorry I called you what I called you," I interrupted him. "I was really upset. You didn't deserve that."

"Don't apologize," Nicholas said, still holding my hand. I didn't yank it back; it felt too good. "I'm just glad to see that you're okay. I was really worried about you, and I wanted to come back and try to talk to you again, but I didn't think that was such a great idea after the way we—you—left things."

"It probably wasn't," I said. "But that's all a closed book now; life is too short." He nodded, and there was an awkward silence. I looked around for Selma so I could break the tension by introducing her but she had disappeared into the next store over. Damn!

"How's the screenplay?" he said. I nodded.

"I got a lot of work done on it during the salad days," I said, "and I think it's ready to shop." He smiled, and that smile made my heart melt, the way it always had. And for that split second, I wished I could have "do-overs" on the last six months. Nicholas is a wonderful man, and I lost him, and there was nobody to blame for that but me.

Well, me and Jimmy Choo, Michael Kors, Donna Karan, Stella McCartney . . . you get the idea.

"I'm glad to hear that," he said. "If you need someone to take a look at it, or if you need to run it by someone, I—"

"All taken care of," I said hastily. "Thanks, though." He looked at me for a long time.

"Well, then," he said, "I won't keep you. You look like you're busy," he added. "Good-bye, Miss Bianca King. You take care of yourself."

"You know I will," I said.

He laughed.

"Yes, I do know that," he said. He gave me one last look and then he was gone. I was barely able to stop myself from turning to look after him, but I managed not to; that would have been in violation of the Dignified Yet Still Desirable Ex-Girlfriend Act of 1997, and one *must* stick to the rules.

Okay, fine, if you must know, I turned around, but it was okay, because Nick had stopped about twenty yards down and was looking back at me, too. So, technically, it doesn't count. And besides, some rules are only made to be broken, right?

· 60 ·

Roxanne

Artistic Tendencies

Even if I don't make it as an actress, I have a full life with friends and family who love and support me, and a strong sense of who I am and what I can contribute to the world. Still, thank God that four days after I returned from California, I got a call from my friend Laura, the theater producer, who found the money to do my one-woman show; enlightenment is great, but it doesn't pay the bills.

• • •

We've had three weeks of rehearsal for *Surf Girls Are Easy*, and tonight is opening night. Watching this process unfold has been unbelievable. I'm performing it at this tiny theater near Times Square called Primary Stages, and it's been so much fun exploring the full range of my talent. I've done a lot of rewriting, trying to delineate between what sounds good on paper and what translates on the stage as a riveting performance.

The scariest thing about being a writer/performer is that it takes away any pretense of a safety net. As an actor, I can always blame the failure of a show on the writer, the director, anybody. But with me doing the writing, I have no one but myself to blame if it tanks. The pressure is great, but the added responsibility is empowering. I got to pick the director, the costume, sound, set, and lighting designers; and I'm even throwing in a D.J. for a more festive atmosphere. My philosophy is that going to the theater should be like going to a party—you want someone to get you hyped up and leave feeling super happy. Not only should it be fun, but the audience should be changed in some way. It should be a shared experience between the performers and the audience—no elitist hierarchies here. A bit ambitious, I know, but I hate feeling alienated when I enter the theater because I'm not rich and White. I really hope my folks will come check me out. This play is the first step on my road to greatness!

There is no blueprint for an actor's career. Being at the mercy of an industry that values neither talent nor ethnicity is ridiculous; I can't believe I wasted so much time hoping that someday, someone in this business that doesn't care about Black girls would choose me and make me a star. Now I don't care what those people think about me. Sure, there are those people who want to be liked and adored, to have fans, but I just can't be bothered with that. Most people are driven by fear of what everyone else will think of them, and they don't realize that everyone else is just as scared and insecure as they are. I realize that now, and I'm not getting caught up again.

I have a brain, a sense of humor, fierce ambition, and a very unique worldview. I am a thinking, feeling woman. This sounds so cheesy, but for the first time ever, I feel one hundred percent in charge of me. I feel free. Every woman must explore what she really wants and who she really is. I'm in the initial stages of that journey, and from what I've seen thus far, it's going to make my wonderful, fabulous trip to California look like a walk across the street.

But, fuck, I'm nervous, and this new attitude hasn't erased the fact that my stomach keeps flip-flopping like last summer's glitter platform thongs. A very cute, but expensive fashion mistake.

The backstage drama: I'm running around like a madwoman, trying to put all of the pieces in place. I feel so completely responsible, like I'm giving birth, and no matter how many people on the crew have said that the show's great, I, of course, don't believe them. I did my yoga an hour ago. I just finished my vocal warm-ups, and my makeup looks pretty good. It's just gonna be me, a chair, and the stage. I've never had this kind of anxiety before, but it's going to be fine. My stomach is going crazy, and maybe I should take some Imodium, but then that would dehydrate me. All right, Roxanne, calm down, breathe. It's going to be okay.

LIGHTS UP ON A YOUNG WOMAN, STANDING ON A CHAIR, LOOKING OUT LIKE SHE'S GOING TO JUMP INTO SOMETHING.

GIRL:
I learned to swim when I was four. My parents signed me up for lessons at the local YMCA. I stood on the edge of the pool in my yellow two-piece Cookie Monster bathing suit, teeth chattering, terrified. I cried and cried. I told my parents I didn't want to do this, but my father said in his deep, husky voice, "We paid for these damn lessons, and she's gonna learn to swim!" The teacher told us to jump in, I held my breath and did it, and that's when my love affair with water began.

Ninety minutes and six characters later, I am taking my final bow. The audience is giving me a standing ovation. I see Carolyn and Taylor in the front row, clapping so hard their hands should be bleeding. Someone hands me flowers. I am stunned. An audience of New Yorkers actually liked the play that I wrote and performed in. This is crazy. I actually did it. I am an actor/writer/ass kicker!

· 61 ·

Carolyn

The Reunion

As the cab passes through Harvard Square, Taylor looks around contemplatively.

"It's changed a lot since graduation," she says. "But then, I guess I have, too; law student to practicing lawyer to unemployed, engaged to unengaged to who knows—"

"Okay, so this weekend is dedicated to drunken debauchery," Roxanne whoops, interrupting Taylor's reverie.

"Our *favorite!*" Bianca proclaims.

I look out of the window. I am dreading the moment that I see someone I know, and the only person in the cab currently less enthused than myself is the driver, who is probably wishing that he had left our already tipsy selves and all seventeen pieces of our luggage at the taxi stand at Logan Airport. Carter was on the same flight as Taylor, Roxanne, and me—he is a Yale man, poor slob—but Taylor and I had checked bags and he had not, so I told him that it was silly to wait and he went on without us. I look out at the passing cabs and the snarl of rush-hour traffic and wonder idly which cab is his and, then, less pleasantly, whether he is currently stepping out of a cab and into the waiting arms of some blond,

green-eyed dryad who broke his heart in New Haven and recently has decided to win back what she let slip through her fingers.

"What's up, sport, doesn't it feel good to be back?" Taylor asks, knocking me gently with her purse.

"No," I say softly, but Bianca is already calculating aloud how much
damage she can do this weekend.

"We actually have the money to do all the things we couldn't afford
to do before, like raid Newbury Street and Copley Square. What more
could I want? Well, actually, a lot, but I'll start with everything Boston has
to offer."

"Now that someone's gotten a promotion and raise, I'm sure she'll do
everything she can to contribute to Boston's tourist economy," Roxanne
said wryly.

"It feels strange," I say, looking out the window. "I wonder what everyone looks like now, what our old professors will think about us, whether
our old boyfrie—" I stop myself and look over at Taylor.

"No worries," Taylor says, grinning, and she looks like she means it.
"We'll get through it all. Besides, I don't even know if John's coming. But
if he is, I look incredible and I have a fabulous tan from Martinique, so it's
all good."

"You have a triple chance of seeing him tonight because there are
three cocktail events we have to go to," Bianca says, poring over her
PDA, in which she has plotted every hour of this weekend with meticu-
lous care, "so we'd better get moving if we plan to get anything done before then."

"Let's drop all of this shit off at the hotel and get started, then, fools,"
Roxanne replies, throwing her arm affectionately around my neck in an
attempt to get me into the groove. "Thar's drinks to be had and men to be
chased."

What Happened to Bianca

"I can't believe they closed the Tasty," Taylor says glumly. "I was really
looking forward to some old school grease." We all stand around, staring

at the scaffolding surrounding the place where King Atherosclerosis had ruled supreme for so many years.

"I wanted bacon on mine," I mutter to nobody in particular.

"Cheer up, ladies," Bianca says gaily, "you didn't want any of those nasty old burgers anyway, not when there are all of these darling little cafes dying to be sampled and all of these fabulous little shops that require our urgent attention." She grabs me and Taylor by the arms and pulls us toward Brattle Street. Roxanne trails behind us, stopping occasionally to look back at the Tasty and sigh. But Bianca is incorrigible, and before we know it, we are all staring into one of the shop windows.

"That," she says with conviction, "is a gorgeous bracelet, and I need to own it."

"You don't have any room left on your arm," Taylor says. "You're Gucci'd down to the socks already."

"You can never have too many baubles," Bianca responds, pushing open the door of the shop. The three of us troop inside after her. Bianca goes straight for the salesgirl and is soon modeling the bracelet on her arm, holding it up to the light, and admiring the way the metal flashes and catches the light. Taylor checks her BlackBerry, Roxanne sifts through the rings in a shallow stone dish standing on a white stone pillar in the center of the room, and I trail my fingers absentmindedly over the glass tops of the display cases.

"Won't this be gorgeous with that green TSE turtleneck I brought to wear tonight?" she says. All of us nod enthusiastically; it is a very beautiful piece of work. "I'll take it," she says to the salesgirl.

I turn away and focus on a garnet bracelet inside the display case. I concentrate on one of the blood-red cabochons and try to clear my head of the vision of Carter surrounded by gorgeous, giggling coeds at tomorrow's game. I am having some minor success when I hear Bianca's raised voice.

"That can't be right," she is saying. "Try it again."

"Ma'am, I already tried it twice, and it was declined both times. If you have another card, I'd be happy to try it, but this one won't go through."

"Fine," Bianca says huffily. She opens her Louis Vuitton wallet and pulls out another credit card, which she thrusts at the saleswoman. "Here."

The woman swipes the card and there is a tense silence. Finally she shakes her head.

"Declined," she says.

"Try it again," Bianca says. Her cheeks are beginning to turn red. The saleswoman swipes it again, pursing her lips.

"Declined again," she says, handing the card back to Bianca. Bianca pulls a third card from her wallet and practically throws it down on the counter.

"Ma'am, I honestly don't think—"

"Run it through," Bianca says through clenched teeth. "Please." At this point, Taylor has put her BlackBerry away and Roxanne has stopped looking at jewelry. The three of us are standing in an uneven half-circle watching what is happening at the counter.

"Ma'am, this card isn't any good either," the saleswoman says. Bianca's neck and face have flushed dark pink, and she does not bother to ask the saleswoman to run the card again. She gathers the three cards with shaking hands, her nails clicking on the counter, and jams them back into her wallet, which she then jams into her purse. She turns on her heel and storms out of the store without waiting for any of us.

"*Bitch*," I hear her mutter as the door swings closed behind her.

Taylor and Roxanne and I glance at one another, then outside, where Bianca is sitting on a low brick wall and rummaging furiously in her purse.

"Do we ask?" I say.

"I think yes," Taylor replies.

"I *told* you something wasn't right when I saw her," Roxanne says. "And she's not going to want to talk about it any more now than she did then; you know that."

"Yeah, but something is clearly quite wrong," Taylor responds, "and I'd rather piss her off now than let it ride and find out after the fact that she was in deep shit and needed help."

"Let's go," I say, and we go back out into the cold. All of us sit down next to Bianca on the wall. There is a long, awkward silence, which is eventually broken by Bianca herself.

"Well, go on," Bianca says harshly, wiping her nose. "What are you guys waiting for? Taylor, tell me I'm a stupid bitch. Roxanne, ask what's wrong with me. Carolyn, say something sarcastic." It is clear from Roxanne's and Taylor's faces that they are as taken aback as I am by the vehemence of her tone.

"I don't—" Taylor begins.

"Clearly, I'm completely broke," Bianca blurts out, interrupting her. "I'm in a huge financial shithole, I don't really know how I got here, and I'm not sure how to get out. I thought I was out when I got the raise, but somehow I'm not; in fact, somehow I have less money now than I did before. My credit card bills are ridiculous; I paid about five hundred on each card last week but I guess I was maybe already maxed out on them or something, I don't know. And I know how stupid this is, but I put my hotel reservation and a lot of other personal stuff on my corporate card, and I ran up a $7,500 balance on it, so it's suspended right now." Tears are rolling down her face. The three of us continue to stare at the sidewalk. Out of the corner of my eye, I see Roxanne take Bianca's hand.

"I knew something was wrong with you when I saw you in Cali," she said softly. "Why wouldn't you talk to me about it? Why did you keep sidestepping it?"

"Why didn't you tell us?" Taylor echoes. "We could have helped you."

"Because I'm almost thirty years old, and I guess I didn't want you guys to know that I was still handling money the same way I did in undergrad, when I had a huge allowance and *still* had to call home every two weeks because I needed money for a dress for a formal or a weekend ski trip or Spring Break or my phone bill. I promised myself I wasn't going to do that once I got 'in the real world,' but the 'real world' in New York was full of free stuff, stuff that would have cost thousands of dollars otherwise, and by the time I got to the *real* real world and realized that I had no idea what money meant or how to handle it, it was too late. I had no idea what I was doing; it just seemed like there was so much stuff I had to have to live the way I wanted to, and all of it cost so much . . . thanks."

She pauses to take the tissue I have offered, smiles bitterly, and dabs at her eyes.

"It sounds so stupid now, but I just never grasped the concept of simply not being able to afford something. I would never look at something and think 'That's too expensive and I just can't have it'; I'd think, 'There's a way for me to get that; I just have to figure it out.' So I came up with all of these sketch ways to buy what I wanted and make it from month to month, like getting advances on my paychecks and juggling bills so that I could go as long as possible between payments, floating bad checks between two different bank accounts, switching back and forth between cell phone providers, everything. And the stupidest part of all is that I thought that by doing all of that, and by not asking my parents or anyone else for help, I was being mature and solving my financial problems creatively when I was really just making everything ten thousand times worse.

"I even pawned stuff; do you believe that? I pawned my Elsa Peretti earrings and necklace set because I needed cash for a night out with some random industry people I don't give a shit about beyond the fact that I didn't want them to know I was broke. I didn't want them to think that I hadn't 'made it' out there, that I wasn't a success." She stops and looks at the three of us in turn.

"And I guess on some level that's why I didn't tell you guys either," she says quietly. "I didn't want you to know that the Fabulous Bianca King wasn't drinking Cristal and living out of Prada bags; I didn't want you to know that she was eating beans for dinner and worrying about how many past-due notices she could get before her lights got cut off. I wanted you guys to think I was a success, like all of you." She bursts into full-fledged tears. I put my arm around her and Taylor takes her other hand. We wait until she finishes crying.

"I didn't want to be the only one in the group who wasn't doing well," she says, hiccoughing. "I didn't want you guys to think I was a loser."

"We do set a very high standard," Taylor says, "seeing as I'm currently unemployed." Bianca smiles a very small smile.

"It seems to me," I say, "that it's not that you're not doing well, because that's not true. Look at you: Your job obviously loves you because you got a raise and a promotion, and you've written an absolutely hilarious screenplay. It's just that, at the same time that you're doing really well professionally, you're also doing really badly with managing your money."

"Yeah, and that doesn't mean that you're not a success, dopey," Roxanne says, "it just means you need help learning how to make and stay on a budget. And you know that's my specialty; having made ten dollars last an entire week in New York City, I feel comfortable saying that I'm a budgeting guru. So if you need a hand with that, I can definitely give you one. And this part you won't want to hear," Roxanne adds, much more seriously, "but I tried to say this before and I'll say it again; you need to stop giving a shit about what those fools out there think of you."

"And is it even about them, Bianca?" I say. "Or is it about you? Are you the one who thinks you're a loser if you're not all Prada'd up?"

"Because if that's where your head is, you need to check yourself," Taylor says. She gestures at Bianca's Louis Vuitton tote. "That's a *bag*, baby. It's not even leather, mostly. It's a piece of coated cotton canvas covered with the initials of some old French nigga you've never even met."

Bianca laughs despite herself.

"You can say that, though," she says, the laughter fading. "You've got ten thousand of them stashed away."

"That's exactly why I *can* say it," Taylor said sharply. "I was busting my ass night and day, getting paid out the ass, but I saw you guys maybe once a month, I saw my other friends maybe once a year, I hardly ever even talked to my parents, and, if I'd stayed, it probably would have come between me and Meschach. And I realized it wasn't worth it, because eventually I would have died completely alone, in a totally empty, silent apartment, surrounded by a pile of money and minks and jewelry and empty Louis Vuitton totes. They're just *things*," she reiterates. "Why would you give a fuck about someone who doesn't give a fuck about you just because you don't own a lot of designer bullshit?"

Bianca is silent.

"You think about that shit for a minute," Taylor says, seeing that her point has hit home. "And if you need immediate help, which it looks like you might," she adds, "I'll write you a check before we leave. I know you're good for it. And I also know where you live."

"I can write you one, too," I say, "*but* you have to promise all of us that if you get in a tight space again, you'll say something. I have to admit, I'm a little pissed that you thought we would consider you a loser just because you were broke."

Bianca hangs her head.

"Now the next time you get in trouble, you *will* tell us. You *will* get shit from us, but it'll only be because you need it, and what the hell else do you think we're here for, decoration?" Roxanne hugs Bianca's neck and stands up.

"Now bring your broke ass on," she says, grinning, "this conversation isn't over by a long shot, chickadee, but my buttcheeks are frozen and it's time to take it indoors and add liquor."

What Happened to Taylor

And, God help us, we did exactly that. Yet despite the fact that the four of us partied like freshmen until early Saturday morning, as Bianca and I stagger next door to wake the other two for breakfast, a glowing, perfectly coiffed Taylor swings their door wide open. She is fully dressed and wearing a bright crimson handknit sweater with cream trim at the cuffs and collar and a massive "H" in the center. We walk into their room and see on the carpet a sports bra, tennis shoes, and sweats, obviously recently used.

"You jogged this morning," Bianca says, awed. "You got up, put on sneakers, walked out of the hotel, and put your feet one in front of the other, gradually moving faster and faster, until you hit a target heart rate and began burning calories."

"I try not to miss a day," Taylor says. "Mostly because I'm trying not to let myself go to hell, since I don't have the firm gym membership anymore. It's my 'me' time; it gives me a chance to clear my head and do something good for myself, endorphins, better body, all of that. Plus, I need to look alive this morning at the game; if I meet the right alums at the tailgate or the alumni dinner tonight, I just might have a new and better job before I get back to the City on Monday. Are you ready, ladies? Because it's time to *tailgate*."

"It's eight forty-five a.m. and my head feels like a frat house after Hell Week. So you can take all of that spunk and that energy and that get-up-and-go and shove it straight up your ass," I say.

"Have some of this, you'll feel much better," Taylor says, handing me a thermos of hot chocolate laced liberally with peppermint schnapps. I sniff it, grimace, and hand it back to her.

"Okay, I've got this all worked out. We have to start out at our respective houses, head over to the Afro-Am House, then hit the alum and fraternity tailgates, then go to the game," Bianca announces, consulting her Palm Pilot, "even though I personally hate football and feel that the only part of the game worth watching is the Saybrook Strip, and that's only if there are any cute boys living there this year."

"I have no interest in seeing those morons get naked and rush the field," I say. "It always looks like Waltz of the Tiny Cocks anyway because of the cold."

The lump in the far bed stirs.

"All of you either get the fuck out of here or shut the fuck up," it groans. "I'm dying."

"Do it while you're taking a shower, then," says Taylor, whacking the lump repeatedly with a pillow until it sits up, flips everyone the bird, then stumbles into the bathroom, dragging all of the bedsheets with it.

• • •

"Damn, can I just say how much I love fall?" Taylor says as she and I wander out toward Memorial Drive, having left Bianca back at the hotel to herd Roxanne out of the shower, into some clothes, and through some breakfast. I am feeling slightly better after pancakes, sausages, three scrambled eggs, home fries, and three different kinds of juice—I eat more when I'm nervous—although I still wish that I had stopped five beer bongs earlier than I did last night.

"And I love watching the river, too," Taylor is saying. "Will you look at them go?" she adds as a crew team glides by on their way back to one of the boathouses. We hear the cox's faint cry of "Pull!" and watch a flock of startled birds rise into the sky before we turn around just in time to be mown down by a jogger completely engrossed in his run.

I am still brushing myself off when I hear Taylor gasp, "Shit!"

"I figured you might be here," John mumbled, getting to his feet and taking his iPod plugs out of his ears.

"I thought you might be here, too, but I didn't figure on running into you, literally, out here." Taylor picks at a small stone that has apparently embedded itself in her knee. They look at one another strangely, and I recognize the look—they are trying to figure out whether this is going to be pleasant or belligerent.

"How have you been?" John says, adding "Hi, Carolyn" as he notices me standing at the side of the path.

I nod curtly and step back enough to give them a little more privacy but not so much that Taylor thinks I am deserting her.

"Good. I quit my job," Taylor says.

"You quit your job?!" John exclaims, his face contorting. "After all that, all of the 'my career' this, 'my career' that, you quit?!"

"Yes. And, listen, it's too early in the morning for bullshit and I'm not in the mood, so if you feel like going there, think twice," Taylor shoots back, bristling.

"Look, I'm sorry, Tay. I know how much you loved that job. More than anything else, it seemed sometimes."

"You've got one more chance to come out of your mouth with something like that and I'm out. I came up here to see my friends and have a good time; I don't want or need any drama, and if drama is what you have to offer, we can cut this off right now." John takes a deep breath, then nods.

"You're right. No drama. The weekend won't last that long, and after that I'm off to Hawaii anyway, so, yeah, let's not fight."

"Finally taking some time for yourself? That's good."

"Well, it's a little more than that. I'm coming back to the States fulltime. I've got a job at Harvard Medical Center." He looks at Taylor expectantly.

"You're what?!" Taylor exclaims. "I thought you were staying in Nairobi for at least another few years?!"

"Do you want to just head back to the Square?" John says. "We can talk about this over coffee."

"You didn't answer my question: What made you decide to come back?"

"They gave me an offer I couldn't—"

"Refuse. That happens to you a lot, huh? So you would have had me come to Nairobi for a few months just to uproot my life again?"

"It's not like that. I just . . . look, things are moving very quickly for me now, and I need someone in my life who can appreciate that, and who's willing to roll with the punches."

"Roll with the punches sounds more like roll over and play dead."

"That's exactly why things didn't work out between us, Taylor: your fucking attitude."

"My fucking attitude?" Taylor asks, her voice going up two octaves. I groan. So much for peace and quiet by the water. "My *fucking attitude?* You know how hard I've worked to do the things in my life that I've wanted to do? How hard it is to have to eat nails for breakfast to make it through every day? And you're telling me I've got attitude? Let me tell you something, motherfu—"

"Taylor, wait, wait, I don't want to do this at all, but if we have to do this, let's not do it out here. Where are you staying?" John says, taking her hands to calm her.

"At the Charles," Taylor says sullenly, yanking her hands away.

"Me too. Can we go back there and just try to work this out?" The two of them set off across the grass and I trail behind them, catching bits and pieces of their conversation.

"—no one wanted this to work out more than me—"

"—someone has to be willing to give—"

"—as stubborn as you are—"

"—don't want a man who wouldn't stand up to you—"

"—demand that I give up everything—"

We pass through the lobby and into the elevators. Taylor and John both press eleven. Obviously I am staying on the eleventh floor also, but I press nine because it is time for me to exit stage right.

"I didn't say that," Taylor is saying, "and I hate to admit it, but I needed you to be able to let me go first."

"Is that what it took? Why couldn't we press forward *together?*"

The elevator stops on the ninth floor and I move toward the door.

"Where the hell are you going?" Taylor says, turning to me.

"I'll be in the room if you need me," I say, squeezing her hand quickly, "but I think you two need some real privacy." Before the doors close behind me, I hear Taylor say, "Let's just finish this once and for all."

• • •

I locate Roxanne and Bianca having breakfast on the second floor in Henrietta's Table and brief them on the morning's events.

"God," Bianca says, looking at her watch, "it's not even ten a.m. and the drama's already started. Where are they now?"

"I think they went back to his room or hers," I say. "And, no, I don't think passionate makeup sex was on the schedule."

"I can't believe that asshole's coming back after showing up at her place with all of that 'Come to the jungle with me' nonsense," Roxanne grumbles around a mouthful of toast. "That wasn't even six months ago, was it? Asshole. What was he—" Roxanne's voice trails off and her mouth drops open, revealing half-masticated toast. Bianca and I turn slowly and follow her gaze, and our jaws drop as well.

Taylor, John, and a woman we have never seen before are coming toward our table. Taylor's face is a mask, John looks sheepish, and the woman looks uncomfortable; it is impossible to tell what has happened.

"Ladies, I'd like you to meet Ashanti, John's new wife," Taylor says stiffly, taking the woman's left hand and holding it up so that we can see the sparkling two-carat stone and the wide platinum band below it. As if on cue, the three of us look at John's hand and see a matching band on the third finger of his left hand.

"John's new *what?*" Bianca says, startled.

"Been busy in the bush, Johnny?" Roxanne mutters.

"This is a little awkward, but John had hoped to reach Taylor before we came to the Jubilee," a clearly embarrassed Ashanti says, by way of explanation. Taylor bites her lip. It is clear that she harbors no animosity toward Ashanti, who obviously has no idea what happened only a few short months before she and John married, but it is equally clear that she would like to rip John's balls off for putting her in this situation to begin with. The look on John's face is more difficult to decipher. Part of it is sorrow, but part of it—although it is very difficult to tell—appears to be some sort of twisted triumph. I guess he feels that he has put one over on Taylor by showing her that her rejection of his marriage proposal failed to slow him down.

"Yes, but I recently left my old job," Taylor responds, "so since you only married him a couple of months ago, it might have been difficult for him to reach me to tell me the good news. Although I think he still had my home phone number," she adds pointedly. "In any case, I wish you all the best."

"No hard feelings?" says Ashanti hopefully.

"None," Taylor says, shaking the other woman's hand. I want to hug Taylor right then and there, because I know full well how much it cost her to do that. "John and I have been over for a long time," she adds, looking John directly in the eye. "He's entitled to do what he wants with his own life. I wish you luck, Ashanti."

"And you *will* need it," Roxanne adds softly. Ashanti has already begun walking away, so she does not hear it, but John does, and his dark skin flushes as he turns on his heel and follows his new wife.

"I need to make a call," Taylor says. "I'll meet you guys downstairs in half an hour."

• • •

To our collective surprise, when Taylor returns to the lobby, she looks perfectly composed and happy.

"You're okay?" Bianca says.

"Yep. John and I really were over; I wasn't kidding. He basically admitted that he wanted my career to be second to his career; if you'd been there when he said that, you would've applauded my restraint. He's coming back from Nairobi to Harvard Medical; he can't keep his ass in one place, and he basically wants a woman who's willing to follow his ass all over the damn world. Ashanti's only twenty-three and she just got out of the Peace Corps, so she can be that for him; I can't. I just talked to Meschach about it, and he told me how much he loved me and how glad he was that John had been self-centered and stupid enough to lose me," Taylor says, at which point she gets slightly dewy-eyed.

"Awwww," I say in spite of myself. "Awwwww, *shucks.*"

"I told Meschach that if he ever tried to make me choose between him and my dreams, I'd break his neck."

"Not so awwwwwww," I say.

"What did I tell you? I always have the last laugh," Taylor says, sipping from Bianca's mimosa. "I won't lie, it threw me, but give me a few hours and a few drinks and I'll be back to my old self."

"You're sure?" Bianca says, uncertain whether this is bravery or bravado.

"She's sure," Roxanne says. "She's the one who called it off with John."

"I'm serious. I'm not putting on a game face. It's over. Even if I didn't have Meschach, it would still be over." She does mean it.

"Well, there's nothing like a man to help you forget a boy," Roxanne says, downing her grapefruit juice and champagne.

"Hey, if I've learned one thing this year," Taylor says, "it's that I can't live in the past. Now that doesn't mean I haven't learned anything from it. But shit, I can't *stay* there. If that damn job taught me one thing, it's that I've got to live for today, every day. And today, the four of us are here together, I have a wonderful new relationship, and the headhunters are ringing my phone off the wall. So it seems to me that, as we stand here to-day, I don't need anything more than what I've already got. Now, who's up for some football?"

What Happened to Roxanne

"I can't believe I'm back here after all these years," Roxanne says. "By the way, are you sure you want to go to this play? There's no way it's going to be anything but a piece of shit, but I promised the old theater crew I'd meet them here." I shrug. Bianca and Taylor are meeting friends for drinks, and I would rather catch a quiet nap here in the dark of the Leverett Old Library Theater, which is home to the Industrial Theatre company but is being used on this Saturday evening by an undergraduate group calling itself Bard's Rule Theater Company, which, inspired either by an avant-garde vision or incredibly bad taste, has chosen to put on a musical version of *Titus Andronicus*.

"I'm anxious to see the musical mayhem that erupts when Lavinia gets her tongue cut out and gets mutilated," Roxanne says.

"How is she supposed to sing after that?" I say.

Roxanne shrugs. "I don't know, and she's going to have trouble doing jazz hands, too."

We giggle.

"You have to admire college kids, though," Roxanne says. "They're willing to take a lot of risks. And this is definitely a risky production."

We meet Roxanne's friends in front of Wigglesworth Hall in Harvard Yard: Juliette, who is married but has left her artistically uninclined husband at home, and Aaron Hubbs, the flamboyantly gay member of Roxanne's undergraduate crew of artistic misfits.

"Fanfare, please; the king has arrived." We turn to see Aaron strolling over to us dressed in a purple velvet smoking jacket, ascot, jodhpurs, and riding boots, dragging luxuriantly on a Gauloise.

"Don't you mean the queen?" Roxanne says. "Look at you; some things never change."

"Roxanne, my love, you look flawless!" Aaron exclaims as he clutches her to his breast. "And . . . and Carolyn!" I can see the shock in his eyes and my face turns red. I suspect that "flawless" is not a word I will hear from his lips in reference to me.

"Aaron, my darling, you are divine!" Roxanne says, and they kiss. As Aaron hugs me, I look over and see Roxanne frown and swipe at her cheek, then look closely at her hand. Lip gloss.

"Darling, I read all about your one-woman show," Aaron says to Roxanne. "I wanted to fly up from North Carolina, but I couldn't make it happen. Training to be a real estate mogul is a full-time commitment."

Aaron looks exactly the same, just a little more settled in his fabulousness. I laugh as I think back to freshman year, when he attempted to date Bianca. We were all various degrees of stunned by the intensity with which he pursued her. When he told us that he was interested in her, Roxanne had blurted out, "Interested in dating her, or interested in being her?" The result of which being that he did not speak to her for the next two months. He finally came out senior year and seemed shocked that nobody was surprised by the news.

Juliette crosses the square and joins us. I hardly recognize this lightly tanned woman with light brown hair and blue eyes; the Juliette I remember was an Agonized and Misunderstood Goth with a pitch black bob and yellow cat's-eye contacts who was always clad in shapeless black frocks, torn fishnets, and Doc Martens. Roxanne yelps with joy and hugs her.

"Juliette, baby, it's *great* to see you again. You look fantastic, and you look so much happier than you did when I saw you in Minneapolis," Roxanne says as Aaron puts his arms around both of them and they jump up and down in a group hug.

"I *feel* fantastic! And I *am* happier; I left Sam!" she enthusiastically informs us. Roxanne looks shocked. I am curious; she has not left her husband at home; she has left him, period.

I see Roxanne thinking about the best way to approach the subject. "What happened?" she says carefully.

"Our time was over. The marriage was suffocating me. And he didn't ever want to have sex," she tells us. Roxanne's face twists in a pout of disgust.

"Well then he needed to be kicked the fuck out. No sex is a deal breaker," Aaron weighs in. Roxanne nods heartily, then blurts out, "There's no point in being with someone who can't or won't fuck you." I wonder if she is thinking about Ram; none of us have mentioned him since he declared his intent to be celibate and got pink-slipped for his pains.

"Amen. Well, to celebrate your freedom and all three of us not gaining a pound since graduation—" Roxanne quickly steps on Aaron's foot; he realizes what he has said and looks at me, an apology forming on his lips; before he can say anything, I shrug. "It's okay," I say, wishing that I could fade into the pavement.

"I'd . . . I'd like to toast us with this," Aaron says, recovering, and reaches into his perfectly aged English leather schoolboy satchel to pull out a bottle of Patron Reposado.

"Ooh, the good stuff," Juliette exclaims. "You always did fly first-class, Aaron."

"You know the motto: Life's too short to drink cheap liquor," Aaron replies, delighted with himself.

"Oh, God, it's gonna be one of those nights," Roxanne says. "Let's put it on hold, though, because the show is about to start."

The show is, as promised, a travesty. Aaron the Moor is played by a White guy, the kid who plays Saturninus obviously saw the film *Titus* and is doing a terrible impression of Alan Cumming; something goes wrong with the hydraulics used for Lavinia's mutilation and the entire first row of the audience is drenched with red dye, and last, but hardly least, the set designer had the bright idea of having actual severed body parts visible in the meat pies that Titus makes out of Tamora's sons, so that halfway through a dramatic climax, a penis flops out of one of the pies and rolls off the table. Roxanne, Juliette, Aaron, and I are trying so hard not to laugh that Juliette blows snot out of her nose. The only thing keeping us in check is the knowledge of how hard the cast and crew have worked on this, and the knowledge of how much it takes in the way of courage to get up on stage, even if what you do once you get there is awful. Finally the house lights come up and we applaud heartily even as we trip over the seats and other attendees in an attempt to get out of the theater as fast as we can.

"I need to go to the bathroom," I announce.

"You weren't pissing on yourself the whole play?" Aaron says. "I know I was."

"Only figuratively," I say, and head for the ladies'. As I do, I hear a voice behind me call my name.

"Carolyn? Carolyn Phillips?" Oh, *God*. I consider not stopping, then turn around, resigned.

It is my senior thesis adviser and favorite professor, Dr. van der Meer. My face lights up.

"Carolyn! I thought that was you! Well, don't just stand there, child, come give an old woman a hug!" I do, and even though she seems even more gaunt now than she did then, she still practically squeezes the life out of me. I am so glad to see her; I arrived too late on Friday to drop in on her classes but I was planning on calling her tomorrow to see if she could do lunch.

"So tell me what it is that you're doing now!" she says. "Have you written the Great American Novel yet?"

"No," I say excitedly. "I'm working at Getty & Getty; I'm a team leader in the Food, Beverage, and Clothing unit, and . . ." My voice trails off as I see the look of mingled contempt and sorrow on her face.

"Carolyn, you're in *advertising*? All of that talent, and you're *writing copy*?"

"I—"

"Carolyn, I have been teaching for more than fifty years, and I have always thought that if any of my former pupils were going to go on to greatness, it was you. And now you tell me that you have taken all of your skills and funneled them into thinking of new ways to get people to buy tampons and fried chicken?" Her lip curls.

"I like what I do," I say faintly. Then, less faintly, "I love what I do, Dr. van der Meer. It's a way for me to work with both writing and visual art."

"Ad copy is hardly *writing*, Carolyn," she replies.

"It is," I argue. "It's still conveying ideas via the written word. They may not always be dignified messages," I say, thinking of some of my campaigns, "and they aren't necessarily noble and filled with higher meaning, but that doesn't make it bad."

"But Carolyn," Dr. van der Meer says, "Carolyn, you are wasting a God-given gift. Think of what you could be doing instead." There is a silence.

"Any number of things," I say slowly. "But this is the only one I want to be doing. And I'm sorry you don't approve, because your opinion has always meant a great deal to me, but I don't agree with you. In any case, I have to go, Dr. van der Meer; my friends are waiting for me."

I leave her shaking her head in the corridor and shove open the door to the ladies' room, where I run cold water on my face and wait for my heart to stop racing. Then I use the toilet, wash my hands, fix my face, and step back out into the corridor, then out into the cold night air. Thankfully, Dr. van der Meer has left.

"I thought you were going to use the bathroom, not build a new one," Roxanne says. The bottle is out again and the atmosphere is merry. "Guess who I saw? Dr. van der Queer, leaving the—"

"I saw her, too," I say shortly. "Come on, let's go get shitfa—"

I stop dead as I spot Finlay Burrows coming out of the theater. Roxanne sees her at the same time and stiffens.

"I'm not talking to her. Let's keep it moving," Roxanne says quietly, and we start to walk, but Finlay has spotted us (which was inevitable, as Aaron's getup could have stopped a train) and starts to call to Roxanne, Aaron, and Juliette across the lobby. Roxanne's face is completely expressionless as she watches Finlay scurry across the plaza. Aaron puts his hand on Roxanne's back and hands his flask to her.

"I will not let this no-talent rich bitch get under my skin," she says, swigging it and handing it back to Aaron.

"Hey, you guys! It's so good to see you! Do you guys have anything else to drink?" she says, looking at the flask. "My buzz is starting to wear off," she explains. Roxanne stiffens even more; I can see that Finlay's super-friendly tone is grating on her.

"No," Roxanne snaps. "We don't have anything," she adds. Finlay draws back, looking hurt, but tries again.

"Oh, come on, Roxy, you guys. You have to share. For old time's sake," she insists. Roxanne grimaces, but Aaron pulls out the Patron and offers it to Finlay. He will never hear the end of that, judging from the look on Roxanne's face. As we stand there, passing the bottle around, Finlay starts talking about life in L.A. and how hard it is to find authentic people, and how she got so caught up in her own hype, which is something none of us expected to hear.

"Congrats on your one-woman show, Roxanne. I hear it was all the rage in New York. You're shaking things up, but I always knew you would," Finlay says quite sincerely. Roxanne softens a little.

"Thanks," she says.

"I'm going to be in New York next week," Finlay continues, "and I'd love to come see it." The group continues walking and Roxanne, Finlay, Aaron, and Juliette reminisce about all of the sleepless nights spent rehearsing crazy plays and building sets.

"Well, if you're ever in L.A.," Finlay is saying to Roxanne, "you should come stay with me. It's a tough town, and it's easier when you already have friends there," Finlay adds. Roxanne looks at Finlay as if she cannot believe what she is hearing, and I have to agree; apparently Finlay thinks Roxanne is her friend.

"I'm serious," Finlay said. "Look, here's my cell phone and home phone," she says, pulling out her ticket to the play and jotting something down. Roxanne takes the ticket.

"I'd love to have you come to my show," Roxanne says as her face lights up with a brilliant smile. "Here are my numbers; call me next week and I'll make sure you get a comp ticket."

"Thanks, Roxy!" Finlay says. "I can't wait; we'll have to go out afterwards." They talk for a few more minutes about their respective careers, and then Finlay bids us all good-bye and heads off toward the Square.

"Well," I say to Roxanne. "Well."

"Finlay has changed," Roxanne says. "She's not the bitch I remember, the one I've been hating all these years. Or maybe she never was a bitch, and I just resented her for having handed to her on a silver platter everything I've had to bust my ass for. Or maybe it's the fact that I've changed, and that I'm learning to accept people for who they are, without attaching all the baggage from their pasts to our current relationship."

"Maybe it's all three," Aaron says, adding, "go on with your bad self, Zen Master Roxanne."

"Anything that gets your mind off the past and focused on the future is a good thing," Juliette says.

"Exactly," Roxanne says. "And my future has some Grendel's appetizers and a Scorpion Bowl from the Hong Kong in it. Don't yours?"

"Not mine," I say, excusing myself. "Scientists around the world remain befuddled by the contents of that drink, and I need to go for a walk; I'm just going to head over to the Charles and chill for a minute."

"We'll wait for you at Grendel's," Roxanne says. "Taylor called while you were in the bathroom and she and Bianca are already there anyway, so catch up with us." I say my good-byes to Aaron and Juliette and head off into the night.

What Happened to Me

"Where the fuck are you?!" Taylor slurs into the phone an hour later. "We've been at Grendel's for ten thousand years; are you coming or not?"

"I went for a walk," I say. "I'm at the river."

"Are you okay?"

"Yeah," I say.

"No, I mean, are you *okay?*" she says, and this time her voice is crystal clear and tense. What she really means is "Are you about to do something stupid and do we need to come get you and/or call Campus Police?"

"Yeah," I say again. "Yeah, I'm really okay. I'm going to stay out here for a while, though, and I'll find you guys later."

"Okay. We're going to stay here for a minute and then we're going down to the Kong," she says, reassured. She moves away from the phone to exclaim, "Oh my goodness, what is *up*, girl?" and conduct a brief exchange before coming back on long enough to announce, "I'm freezing my ass off, so bye," and hang up.

I look around and realize that I am standing at approximately the same spot where I threw my burning books into the river so many years ago and where, shortly before that, I'd considered throwing myself in as well. I sit down on the bank and look across the river at the glittering towers of Boston. I did the same almost every day in undergrad after I got back from "vacation." Sometimes Roxanne would come with me if she was trying to learn lines, but I usually came alone, and I usually brought a book, which sat, unopened, in the grass next to me, while I stared for hours at the water rushing by and tried to make some sense out of what I had done to myself and what was wrong with me. I used to sit and look at the water and try to understand why I could not take the world by the throat like Taylor and make things happen my way or no way at all; why I did not possess the focused ambition of Roxanne, who had known since the age of six that she was going to be an actor and had been in single-minded pursuit of that goal from then on; why I could not take the spills and thumps of everyday life with a laugh and a shrug like Bianca, who never let anything from a breakup to a broken heel stop her for more than a millisecond. And I would pull up little tufts of grass and hate myself for not being more like my friends. I hated myself for being Carolyn, the "emotionally fragile" one (a.k.a. the one who was referred to, behind closed doors and cupped hands, as That Girl Who Lost Her Shit), the loser who tried so hard to fit in everywhere that she fit in nowhere, the coward who was afraid to say what she thought in case other people would think it was stupid, the slacker with no ambition or direction, the spaz who was incapable of flirting and excruciatingly uncomfortable around everyone except for three people on the entire campus. Loser. Coward. Slacker. Spaz.

But now that I am a little older, I can see that I am, for the most part, none of the above. Not any more than most people, in any case, and a little less than some. No, I do not weigh what I want to weigh, and sometimes I hate what I see when I look in the mirror so much that it makes me cry. But I have some good things going. I am funny. I make my friends laugh all the time and always with me, never at me. I look down at the perfect late-fall football-game-into-night-out outfit I am wearing and congratulate myself on having a great sense of style, which is a godsend because being overweight and resembling a yard sale with feet is more than any one person should have to bear. I am talented and creative and *very* good at what I do, regardless of what certain professors think about it, and I am like a magician; in my hands, under my care, a soda containing a postslaughter bovine castoff becomes a tonic that will make you stronger and more alert; slips of polyester that reposition the top of one's asscrack at the nape of one's neck become tools of seduction; unnaturally colored chunks of oats and wheat that contain slightly less sugar per serving than a bowl full of sugar become part of this complete breakfast and a shitload (literally) of fun in the bargain.

So why do I automatically move to the back when the four of us run into a gaggle of guys? Why do I always look down when I talk to people because I am afraid that if I look directly at them they will see my whole face and think that it is ugly? Why am I afraid to start a conversation with someone because I am afraid that they will find me dull or annoying and walk away? Why can I see on the grass the faint shadow of someone walking up behind me on the left?

"Want a drink?"

I shriek, then attempt to leap to my feet while simultaneously going into Hop-Ki-Do-On-Your-Rapist-Ass Mode, which nearly results in a broken ankle before I land smack on my own ass in the grass.

"And lo! the graceful swan alights," Carter says, settling himself on the ground next to me and opening the bottle of Glenfiddich Twenty-One-Year-Old that he is carrying. He takes a giant swig from the bottle before holding the bottle out to me.

"Have you got a cup?" I say. He looks at me, disgusted.

"Damme my sainted codpiece, but I *am* sorry," he says in a snooty, shitty British accent, "Forsooth, I had forgotten that at fair Hahvahd one doth not engageth in such plebeian vulgarities as drinking straight from the bottle. Rest here, milady, and I will getteth for you a goblet of the finest—"

"Shut up and give it here, ass," I say, yanking it from his hand and turning it up. I fell in love with Glenfiddich back during the Macho Sexy Girl phase of the late 1990s, when no female celebrity could be photographed without a Macanudo poking out of the corner of her mouth, but that was a while ago; I manage not to drop the bottle but cannot stifle the subsequent gasp and cough.

"So why aren't you off across the river getting tanked with your Skull & Bones buddies and tearing up Newbury Street?" I ask.

"Not every White man who went to Yale was in Skull & Bones," he replies, adding, "any other assumptions you'd like to throw out there?" He takes another drink and settles back on his elbows.

"No, I'm done for tonight," I say. I turn and look behind me at the lights of campus. It seems to me that I can hear the muffled roar of the Square, hear the *ching!* of the cash registers in the Coop, which is keeping late hours tonight, and smell the stuffed mushrooms from Grendel's even at this distance. But out here on the river it is just Carter and me, the better part of a bottle of whiskey, and relative silence.

I hold out my hand for the bottle and Carter passes it. This time it goes down easily.

"What are you doing out here?" I ask.

"Ran into Winkin, Blinkin, and Nod at that place in the Square, that basement place," he replies. "They said you might be out here."

"Did you already have the bottle?" I say snidely.

"No, ma'am, I did not," he replies. "I purchased it with legal tender on my way out here. They were out of Thirty-Year-Old," he adds. I consider the fact that he has bought a bottle of very good whiskey just to drink with me, and that he would have liked to buy an even older vintage for us, then put both that thought and the word *us* aside, right next to the costume gala incident, because together the three of them are turning a formerly black-and-white situation a murky shade of charcoal. With tentacled things lurking in it.

"Why Glenfiddich?" I say curiously.

He turns and looks at me briefly, then turns back to the river and shrugs.

"I don't know," he says. "You didn't strike me as much of a beer drinker, and you don't like juice or soda, so no mixed drinks, not that I was planning on doing any mixing out here in the dark—"

"And with no cups," I remind him. Carter ignores me and looks up at the sky thoughtfully.

"Women who like frozen umbrella drinks tend to be hicks or whiny pains in the ass, so that wasn't right. Women who like Jagermeister and Goldschlager and shit like that tend to be on the sunny side of twenty-five—"

"Danger, Will Robinson," I say dryly.

"—and skanks," he adds hastily.

"Nice save."

"I live to serve," he replies, then continues. "I think you might be a white wine or champagne person sometimes, but it's already cold enough out here." He sits up. I pass the bottle back to him and he looks at it thoughtfully.

"It's just something I thought you wouldn't mind," he says finally. I nod. We sit quietly, passing the bottle back and forth.

"I saw one of my old professors today," I blurt out suddenly, and I am startled because I had not intended to talk about this. I have not mentioned it to my girls; I have not allowed myself to think about it, but despite all that, I think it is why I came out to the river in the first place. "She told me I could have been a serious writer, a 'real' writer, if I'd continued to work at it instead of selling out." Carter passes me the bottle again and I hit it hard.

"She was my favorite teacher," I add.

"So what'd you say?"

"I told her I loved my job, and that I was sorry that she didn't think that it was serious just because it didn't involve starving in a garret and did involve the occasional ape in a cowboy hat."

Carter laughs, and while he does, it dawns on me that today I refused to accept someone else's opinion of what I was supposed to want. Something good to report to Dr. Guisewite this coming Wednesday.

"My dad says shit like that sometimes," Carter says, knocking back two shots. "He's still pissed that there won't be a fourth Carter Elliott Holden at the firm."

"Why won't there be?"

"I've got a thing for monkeys in millinery."

"Seriously, oaf."

He turns to look directly into my eyes.

"Because it wasn't what I wanted, and I knew what I did want, and so that's what I'm doing." There is something different about the way he is looking at me, and I think he may be moving imperceptibly closer to me, and I think I may be moving imperceptibly closer to him, and I think I may be doing it because I want to kiss him. And suddenly I am paralyzed with terror because it occurs to me that I am seeing him through Glenfiddich Goggles and that if I kiss him he will laugh at me, or, worse, pull away in disgust. It occurs to me that I may be about to make a fool of myself in a way that will make me cringe at the memory until the day I drop dead, and I pull away and sit up straight.

"Tell me the truth," I say sharply. "Did they ask you to come out here? Did they send you to hang out with me? Because I'm fine, and I don't need—"

Carter jerks back as if I hit him. The look on his face is so strange that my voice trails off.

"What in the hell are you talking about?" he says.

"I'm asking you," I say, "whether Roxanne, Taylor, and Bianca sent you here to sit with me because they didn't want me out here by myself."

Carter continues to stare at me for what feels like forty minutes, then turns back to the river and shakes his head.

"You know, Carolyn," he says, chuckling incredulously, "you are an asshole."

Huh. I am drunk indeed, but not drunk enough to fail to register that (a) Carter is upset, and (b) he is upset with me.

"I'm not out here because anyone sent me; what am I, some fucking babysitting bike messenger?! I came out here because your friends said you were out here, and I wanted to hang out with you. I don't know what's going on in your head, but that's all it was. That's it."

Whoops.

"Carter, I'm—"

"You're a total head case is what you are, do you know that?" he splutters, getting to his feet and striding back toward Memorial Drive. Then he stops, turns on a dime, comes back toward me, and squats down two inches away from me. "*That's* why you're single, Carolyn. It's not because you're not a size two, or because you've got a Harvard degree, or because you're too smart or too assertive, or because the guys you insist on dating are douchebags, or because of any of the ten thousand reasons you've come up with; it's because you're so busy believing that you're worthless that any time some guy comes along who thinks you're amazing, you can't get your head out of your ass long enough to notice!"

If Carter had slapped me across the face, I would not have been more shocked. He is close enough for me to see that there is perspiration forming at his hairline despite the cold, and that his gray eyes are angry, his brow is furrowed, and his cheeks are blotchy.

"Your self-esteem is in the toilet and you're completely neurotic," he continues in a low, strained voice, "which should be more than enough to cancel out the fact that you're an artistic and creative genius, you've got this wild sense of humor, you're a blast to hang out with, whatever perfume you wear makes me crazy, and, sorry, excuse me for being sexist and un-PC and disrespectful, I don't give a shit, blame it on the fucking booze and have me fired when we get back to the city, but I modeled the racks on the Captain Sabatini girls after yours because yours is fucking *perfect*."

There is never a therapist or girlfriend around when you need one. I briefly consider asking Carter to hold on just a sec while I conference in the crew, then asking him to repeat into the phone what he has just said so that we can do a hasty postmortem, but he is not finished.

"And, for those reasons, despite the fact that you are a certifiable lunatic," he continues, "I cannot get you out of my head." He smacks his forehead with his open palm in a gesture of absolute frustration. "In fact, I'm so gone on you that I find your neuroses *endearing*. Your fetish for the MSG-laden carbohydrate-fest marketed under the brand name of Taco Bell is *captivating*. The way you go shoe-shopping in the wake of emotional disaster is *entrancing*. Your floor-based filing system is *magical*. Your inability to show up for anything even remotely on time is fucking *seductive*."

I remain speechless, expecting either Rod Serling or Allen Funt to pop out of the river at any minute.

"Now, if I were talking to a rational woman, I would ask her what she thought of the fact that I've just spilled my guts to her," he continues in the same bitter tone, "but I'm talking to *you*, and you probably think this is a big sick joke, or that I'm so drunk I have no idea what I'm saying and I don't mean any of it, or that I'm trying to climb the career ladder or, my personal all-time favorite, that I'm trying to work out a chocolate fantasy."

I have the grace to blush at this point and Carter laughs mirthlessly, plunking back down on the grass next to me.

"I know you, Carolyn," he says, looking out at the river. "I've spent ten hours a day with you day in and day out for nine months and I know who you are. I know what's great about you and I know what's not so great. And I really, really, really like you," he says, his voice softening, pleading. "Why don't *you*?"

A ghost of a smile flits across my face as I consider the irony inherent in the fact that Carter is asking me the same question I have been asking myself for almost a decade.

"The thing is," I say slowly, "I like myself a lot better than I used to." I stop and think about what I have said, and nod. That is correct. "I'm working on that. I'm working on a lot of things. I try all the time to tell myself that I'm an okay person, you know, that I'm good and smart and nice and pretty, but I don't believe it just yet. I believe it more than I did before, but I still have a long way to go." I pause. "That doesn't make any sense at all, does it?"

There is a long silence.

"No, it's okay," he says gruffly, and I cannot read the expression on his face.

Suddenly I realize that it is very cold and I am very tired, and I wearily heave myself to my feet in preparation for the walk back to the hotel. I have ruined his evening and mine as well, half a bottle of whiskey is roiling around in my mostly empty stomach, and the only thing I want to do now is go to bed, or puke, or both. Carter gently taps my shoe.

"Hang on," he says. "I'll walk you back. Just give me a minute." He gets up, stoops back down momentarily, straightens, and walks toward the river. I watch him intently as he goes, shell-shocked, unable to make any sense of what has just happened because my brain is hopscotching from what he said to how he looked when he said it to what I should have said and what I should be saying now. At the river's edge, he stops, at which point I realize that he is not being romantically moody and pensive in a Merchant/Ivory sort of way but is in fact taking a whiz, and I turn, red-faced, and stare intently at Eliot House until he reappears at my elbow.

"I'll walk you back to your hotel," he says, his face and voice composed and neutral. "It's almost one o'clock and there are robbers and rapists and performance artists all over the place." I nod awkwardly. We walk back to JFK Drive in silence. Once we hit the center of the Square, which is still full of lights and noise and revelers, I turn to Carter.

"I've got it from here," I say, pointing back over my shoulder. "My hotel's just right around there."

"You sure, Chief?" he says.

"I'm sure," I say. "Listen," I add in a low voice, "listen, I . . . I had a really good time, Carter, and thank you very much for the drinks and for hanging out."

"It was, whether you want to believe it or not, my pleasure," he says, and there is the slightest hint of a grin on his face. I am so relieved to see that glimmer of a smile that I feel my shoulders sink three inches.

"Guess I'll see you Monday afternoon," I say.

"In all likelihood," he replies, adding, "see you." He shoves his hands in his coat pockets, turns, and disappears into the crowd. I watch him walk away. Part of me wants to call out to him, but I cannot; if I were to do so, and if he were to come back across the Square and stand in front of me and look quizzically at me with those cool gray eyes, I would fumble around with little bits and pieces of sentences until I finally strung enough of them together to say precisely the wrong thing. So I stand mute and stupid in the middle of the sidewalk until a passing drunk stumbles clumsily against me and gets as far as the "Boo—" in "Boola-boola!" before doubling over and belching vomit into the gutter.

"Well, I think that just about does it for me," I say to nobody in particular, and, stepping around him, trudge back to the hotel, where I stare out of the window until I fall asleep. I do not wake up until someone begins shaking me. It is Bianca, flushed with cold and champagne.

"God, we thought you were dead," she says. "Why didn't you come to Grendel's or the Kong? What happened? Did you see Carter? We saw him at—"

"Don't," I say, cutting her off and rolling over to face the wall. "Don't go there. Please. I blew it, and I don't want to talk about it. What time is it?"

"Four something," she says, sitting down on the bed. "Roxanne and Taylor are upstairs at Aaron's party; he rented the entire hospitality suite and hotel security's already had to come up there three times. I told them I'd go check on you, since you weren't answering your phone, and . . . oh, well, no wonder." There is the sound of paper tearing.

"What are you doing?" I say.

"Oh, you had a package at the front desk," Bianca says, nonchalantly continuing to open it as I roll back over. "And what I'm saying is, no, you couldn't answer your phone if you didn't have it with you." She holds up my BlackBerry, cocking one eyebrow quizzically at me.

"I guess not," I say, sitting up.

"Wait, there's a note in here." She reads it, then grins.

"Give it," I say, snatching it from her.

" 'C,' " I read aloud, " 'you left this at the river. Forgot to give it to you in the Square.' It's signed 'C,' " I say, looking up at Bianca.

"Well, his name does start with that letter," Bianca says, "so I think he's within his rights to sign it to a note he wrote. Your light is blinking," she adds, examining the BlackBerry. "It's probably the two thousand voice mails and e-mails from us. And you've got an appointment pop-up, too," she says. "Oh, Carolyn, *please* tell me you didn't set up something with some old asshole flame. New or none, okay?"

"No, I scraped enough dignity off the grass to keep from calling any-one. It's probably some stupid alumni brunch that I have no intention of attending; you can just erase it," I say, flopping back down on the bed. There is a silence.

"Actually, Carolyn, this appointment I think you should keep," Bianca says in a strange voice. I shove my hair out of my eyes.

"Bee," I say, annoyed, "I'm tired. I'm nauseated. I don't want to get out of bed until our flights leave on Monday morning and I'm not going to."

"Suit yourself, but at least look at it first." She tosses me the BlackBerry, her eyes twinkling. The calendar screen is up, and I see "8:00 P.M. First date with the handsome and capable Carter Holden at Sandrine's, 1 Shepherd St." In the "Notes" section, I see "Note to self: he is doing this of his own volition, not because your friends paid him just over $200."

I look up at Bianca, blinking.

"Did you—" I start. Bianca shakes her head and puts her hand over my mouth.

"I don't know whether you're about to ask whether I put that in there or whether we really paid him two hundred dollars, and I don't know which question is stupider or sorrier, but the answer to both is 'no.' You've got a date, dummy. Carter asked you out. And there's only one thing you need to ask yourself now."

"Whether I'm going to go?" I say slowly.

"What you're going to wear, you jackass." She leaps onto the opposite bed and starts screaming, "Carolyn's got a date with Caaaaaaaaaaaar-ter!" until it finally dawns on me what has happened and we grab hands and jump up and down on the bed, screeching, until hotel security makes a de-tour on their way back from their fourth trip to the hospitality suite to convey to us a rather curt message from the rest of our floor and the rooms directly above and below us.

• • •

Due to being sent back to the room repeatedly for failure to show enough cleavage and being so distracted and nervous that I get halfway to Porter Square before realizing that the stupid cabdriver is going the wrong way, it is eight thirty-four P.M. by the time I reach Sandrine's, and I do not see Carter anywhere. I panic until I finally catch sight of his back up the street from the restaurant, and his back appears to be in a state of high dudgeon. I cross the street and tap him on one pissed-off shoulder.

"Uh, hi," I say breathlessly, thanking God that it is far too cold to sweat. "I'm so sorry I'm late, but you did say that you found that seductive, and I guess I took that to mean that you liked it." He turns around. He is frowning, but there is a grin right behind the frown, and finally the grin wins.

"I didn't think you'd show," he says. "I really didn't think you would." And before I can say anything he bends down and kisses me gently, barely more than a peck, on the mouth. He straightens and I am not sure what he sees on my face, but I see a question on his. I do not know how to answer it, so I smile, and that seems to be good enough for him. He takes my hand.

"Ready to eat?" he says. "I'm starving because for some reason we're running a bit behind schedule," he adds wryly.

"Well, you're in luck," I say, "because the food here is pretty much perfect. I mean, although it's not you-know-where," I add.

"Got you covered, Chief," he replies. "Rented a talking Chihuahua, hired a surly teenage waitstaff, plastic chairs and tables, the whole nine."

And then, for no reason at all, he stops me in the middle of the street, wraps his arms around me tightly, and kisses me, a real kiss this time, and oh my Christ if this is an accurate indicator of his other abilities in this realm, I will be more than happy to add my name to the list of women who were unable to make it out of Carter's Den of Love with virtue intact, because dear *God*. Cars swerve around us, honking angrily, and a pack of teenage hooligans whizzing by on bikes whistles and offers words of advice and encouragement.

Right now I do not want to be anybody in the world but me, and I do not want to be anywhere in the world but here.

And that is a good thing.

ACKNOWLEDGMENTS

The authors of FAB would like to thank: our agents Manie Barron, Marc Provissiero, Jonathan Pecarksy, and the William Morris Agency; our editor, Janet Hill, for her brilliant restructuring and creative voice; Tracy Jacobs for the footwork; Doubleday for believing in four unknown Black girls; Alice, Phyllis, Connie, Evelyn, and Zoë for their inspiration; and everyone who has supported this project along the way.

Kieran Batts Morrow:

I would like to thank my parents, John and Diane Morrow, for being infinite sources of encouragement, support, and love, and for providing a fantastic and long-lived example of that increasingly rare animal, a healthy, happy, and functional marriage. Thanks to my brother, Sgt. Evan Morrow (U.S.A.), for being both a wonderful younger brother and a good man. Eternal love and gratitude to the late John H. Morrow, the late James A. Batts, the late Rowena A. Morrow, Ruth V. Batts, and all members of the Batts and Morrow/Granger families, as well as to Marian, Shelli, Alex, Jennean, my Duke crew, Ella, Brenda, Karen, Amy, Francis, Aaron, Justin, and Willie (and, of course, my incredible co-authors). Thanks also to Madaleine Berley, Drs. Sharon Curtis and Suzanne Canning, the Powell Family, Sebastian at Edge Hill Salon, and Mrs. Margaret Leary, the first English teacher I ever had who demanded better than good.

Tiffany Anderson:

I would like to thank my family and friends for all their love and support. My father, James Anderson, my sister Jamie, and my brother James. A special thank you to my grandmother Helen Burdette. Thanks to my aunt, Sylvia King, and the rest of the King family. Thanks to Alé, Traci, and Chandler, and the rest of my L.A. crew. Thanks to everyone in Houston;

Sarah, Ambrose, and The Gyrlz: Nickie, Anika, Dee, Tiki, and Sharee. Thanks to everyone at *Eve* and the William Morris Agency. And to my fellow co-authors, Adrienne, Kieran, and Tracy, thanks for hanging in there with me. Finally, I would like to acknowledge my mother, my idol and my mentor, the late Claudia Anderson, who will always be with me and without whom I wouldn't be the woman I am today.

Adrienne Carter:

I want to thank God for making my life so imperfectly perfect; my tirelessly supportive parents, Kathleen and Andrew Carter, who have always believed in me; my brother and sister-in-law Drew Carter and Lisa Stephenson, who came to every show; my nephew Ellis Jeremiah Carter for showing me that I can love someone unconditionally; and the rest of the Carter/Williams clan. My girls: Sarah, Scyatta, Monica, Traci, Amy, Esther; my boys: Ed, Damon, and Sam; Chris G., for making me smile; my beauty brigade: Jenae, Andrea, and everyone at Millennium; the staff of *Eve* for keeping me laughing all day; the Center for Yoga and Surf Diva for keeping me spiritually balanced; my co-authors for being so damned smart; my colleagues and classmates at Yale College and the Yale School of Drama, specifically Wesley Fata, who taught me that "Champions Adjust" and "The Body Never Lies."

Tracy Richelle High:

To God first, and my family second. Brenda and Melvin High, my parents, who gave me everything, both tangible and intangible. On my mother's side: Granny, Papa, Aunt Sissy, Uncle Mitchell, James, Uncle Ed, Aunt Gertrude, Gardea, and Grandad Christian and Uncle Michael, no longer here, but with us always. On my father's side: Drue, Dola, Opal, Quincy, Darrell, Sandy, Janelle and little one, Bob, Angela, and Grandma and Grandad, who are never forgotten. To my friends, through laughter and tears (with the oldest first): Damali, Scyatta, Aaron, Monica, Charles, Cameron, Jane Ann, Kuhn, Lancz, Alex, Brenda and Quentin, Anastasia/Curly, and Kathleen, Maurice. To my firm—I truly do love my job! To my work colleagues, you know who you are; if I put down some and not others, then I'm in a whole world of trouble, and I'm too smart for that. To my hair crew, Carla, Susan, Tai, Ronald, Sebastian, and Twana. Last but not least, much love to my old man Carlos, you know what you mean to me.

To the Jackals, without all of you, this book simply wouldn't be possible. Ha!

To my co-authors: WD, we cannot accept any less.

ABOUT THE AUTHORS

KIERAN BATTS MORROW got her B.A. from Duke University and her J.D. from Harvard Law Scool. She is currently a sixth-year litigation associate at the New York City office of a large California law firm and lives in New York City.

TIFFANY ANDERSON is full-time writer for the UPN show *Eve* and previously has been published in the magazine *Honey*. A graduate of the University of Texas at Austin, she currently lives in Los Angeles.

ADRIENNE CARTER is an actor/writer who has appeared in multiple television and off-Broadway roles, and is currently a writer for the UPN show *Eve*. She got her B.A. from Yale College and her M.F.A. in acting from the Yale School of Drama, and lives in Los Angeles.

TRACY RICHELLE HIGH is a sixth-year litigation associate at a white-shoe Wall Street law firm. She got her B.A. from Yale College and her J.D. from Harvard Law School, and currently resides in New York City with her two cats, Marley and P.J., who, just like her ex(es), refuse to be trained.